RIBBON DANCE

RIBBON DANCE

A New
Liaden Universe®
Novel

SHARON LEE &
STEVE MILLER

A Baen Books Original

Baen Publishing Enterprises
P.O. Box 1403
Riverdale, NY 10471
www.baen.com

ISBN: 978-1-9821-9344-7

Cover art by David Mattingly

First printing, June 2024

Distributed by Simon & Schuster
1230 Avenue of the Americas
New York, NY 10020

Library of Congress Cataloging-in-Publication Data

Names: Lee, Sharon, 1952– author. | Miller, Steve, 1950 July 31– author.
Title: Ribbon dance / Sharon Lee and Steve Miller.
Description: Riverdale, NY : Baen Publishing Enterprises, 2024. | Series: Liaden Universe ; 26
Identifiers: LCCN 2023055234 (print) | LCCN 2023055235 (ebook) | ISBN 9781982193447 (hardcover) | ISBN 9781625799654 (e-book)
Subjects: LCGFT: Science fiction. | Novels.
Classification: LCC PS3562.E3629 R53 2024 (print) | LCC PS3562.E3629 (ebook) | DDC 813/.54—dc23/eng/20231208
LC record available at https://lccn.loc.gov/2023055234
LC ebook record available at https://lccn.loc.gov/2023055235

Printed in the United States of America

10 9 8 7 6 5 4 3 2 1

Dedicated to
Benjamin Franklin, Richard Carrington, James van Allen,
and all who celebrate the magic of an aurora

With thanks to The Crystals for
"Then He Kissed Me"

ACKNOWLEDGMENTS

My thanks to crack tyop hunters
Art Hodges, Bex O, Marni Rachmiel, Kate Reynolds.
Your eagle eyes, patience, and good humor
are greatly appreciated.

For Steve, who gave us the stars.

Prologue

· · · · · · · · · ·

GODS WILLING, SHE HAD NOT LEFT IT TOO LATE.

She was done pretending they could ever be safe here; too many had fallen, proving otherwise.

Indeed, she had been on the edge of flight two years ago, but she had let Pel dissuade her. Pel, with his strength and his brilliance, and his close ties to the Council and the Warden himself.

It had seemed—*truly* it had seemed there was nothing that Pel could not bring right.

But even his light had been extinguished by the curse that pursued her bloodline.

If it were only herself, after Pel, she might not have cared enough—to run.

But there were others—innocents—and it fell to her, and her alone, to protect them.

There was no one else she could turn to. No one who would believe her. No one who cared what happened to them.

So she stood up again, after Pel's death. Stood up to fight for her children.

She had already proven that she would do anything—commit any atrocity—to preserve their lives. If—when—doom found her, they would have only themselves—an indignant protest flickered past her Inner Eyes, of a small plump shape, fur grey-striped and plush. In spite of—everything—Zatorvia felt her lips twitch.

The children would, she amended her thought contritely, have each other, and Eet. As she had Eet, then and now.

There was a sense of mollification. Zatorvia continued to the safe, traced the unlock pattern against the aether, and caught up the bag inside when the door sprang open.

It was by no means all her fortune. She had not dared to

1

access accounts that were doubtless being watched. But nor had she ever been foolish enough to put all of her money into accounts.

They were funded. She had skills. What they needed was to leave this place where every card fell to their enemy's hand.

They would go tonight. The bargain was made with the trader, their passage secured. The car—the safe car sent from the escort agency—was due in moments. The children were in their room with the small travel cases they had packed, overseen by Eet, who would protect them with his last breath.

She closed the safe, slipped the bag away into an inner pocket of her coat, took a breath.

Something moved in the side of her eye. She turned, crying out as the figure took shape from a swirl of mist and smoke.

The weapon made no sound; the assassin's aim was true.

She was dead before she began to fall, and the room was empty by the time her body hit the floor.

...not *quite* empty.

On a shelf by the door, barely distinguishable from the assembled bric-a-brac, was a furry, grey-striped shape. Bright eyes gleamed in the shadow, then vanished.

The doorbell chimed.

And chimed again.

On-Grid
The Sakuriji
Council Chambers

. . . .

A TRADE MISSION HAD ARRIVED AT COLEMENO!

This was, in Majel ziaGorn's opinion, the single most significant thing that had happened to the planet—to the entire Redlands System!—since the arrival of the Dust itself.

Not that Colemeno had lacked for trade—the Iverson Loop was regular, as were the Evrits; the Mikancy less so—traveling from worlds likewise caught inside the cloud. Colemeno had been the terminus of their routes.

But now the Dust was—not gone, not yet. But it had thinned enough that the Redlands were once again visible to the universe. The proof of that was the arrival of the Tree-and-Dragon Trade Mission.

The Council of the Civilized had not been best pleased by this sudden arrival. History had taught Colemeno to be timid, and it had seemed that the majority of councilors might have called the Dust back, had that been possible.

However, confronted with the reality of an orbiting ship proposing to deliver a master trader and his team to the port, their purpose to explore mutual opportunity, the Council had risen to meet duty. They had allowed the trade mission to arrive, and had produced a reception in their honor.

Subsequently, Portmaster krogerSlyte had assigned the trade mission offices on Colemenoport, and the penthouse suite in the Wayfarer, the port's best residence, meant to house important visitors.

The Tree-and-Dragon Trade Mission being greatly important to the future of Colemeno, in Majel's opinion, this was only proper

courtesy. However, Council Chair gorminAstir had seemed . . .
surprised . . . when the portmaster revealed this during her report
to Council.

Still, the thing was done, and Portmaster krogerSlyte continued
speaking with scarcely a pause, relating that the master trader
had inquired after his opposite number on-port.

"We have no master traders on Colemeno," Councilor tryaBent
said tartly. "Shall we elevate someone so that the Liaden master
trader may converse on his own level?"

Portmaster krogerSlyte frowned slightly at the councilor, and
professed herself saddened to have so poorly conveyed the master
trader's intent.

"He wondered if he ought to interface with my office, or with
the market master, or if perhaps there was in place a liaison committee. He wishes to keep us current with his work, and also seeks
a—source, should he—" She smiled briefly. "Actually, he had phrased
it—*when* he comes athwart law or custom—to advise him."

She looked back to tryaBent.

"He was everything that was polite and forthcoming, Councilor. Merely, he wishes to proceed in an orderly, efficient manner, while avoiding law-breaking or offenses against custom." She
paused, half-smiling, and added, "He said that local custom trips
even master traders and that at his point in life, he needed to
be wary of falls."

A slight ripple of amusement passed through the council
chamber as Portmaster krogerSlyte resumed her seat.

Council Chair gorminAstir drank from her glass. Other
councilors likewise refreshed themselves, or shifted in their chairs,
leaned over to talk to their neighbor, or glanced at their notepads.

Majel looked at the agenda projected on the wall above the
council chair's head.

New business was next.

A shiver wracked him. This was it, he thought. This was
opportunity, and it was his to seize.

Majel took a sip of water and a deep breath.

Council Chair gorminAstir put her glass down, glanced around
the table, and nodded. A clear tone sounded.

The babble of voices died as the councilors looked toward
the head of the table.

Council Chair gorminAstir folded her hands before her.

"Who," she asked, "has new business?"

Majel raised his hand so quickly the foot of his chair squeaked against the floor.

Council Chair gorminAstir inclined her head.

"The Chair sees Majel ziaGorn of the Citizens Coalition."

Majel came to his feet and bowed to the honor of the Council Chair.

"Chair gorminAstir. Colleagues." His voice was firm; that was good. He had practiced long hours to perfect a firm, reasonable address. "I propose the creation of an official trade liaison, to stand between the Tree-and-Dragon Trade Mission and the Council, in order to facilitate understanding and the open sharing of information."

"Do you?" Council Chair gorminAstir said softly. "Do you, indeed?"

"Ridiculous!" said Councilor tryaBent, somewhat more loudly. "Who would take on so much additional work?"

"I would," Majel said. Out of the corner of his eye, he saw Portmaster krogerSlyte smile, even as Councilor seelyFaire leapt to her feet.

"Absolutely not! It's too dangerous."

Majel gritted his teeth. Councilor seelyFaire was one of those who saw him, and his constituency, as little better than clumsy children, whom it was the primary duty of the Council of the Civilized to protect.

"Colemenoport is hardly dangerous," he said now, and glanced aside. "Am I correct, Portmaster?"

"Councilor, you are. Colemenoport is not as a rule dangerous. In addition, it has its own guard house, with a full complement of proctors, and Truthseers. There are holding cells, which Chief bennaFalm assures me are seldom in use."

"That is not what I meant!" Councilor seelyFaire snapped. "Plainly put, the trade mission is dangerous!" She glared 'round the table. "You who were present on Ribbon Dance Hill, you saw what the master trader and the ship's captain managed there! Will we put one of our most fragile in their way?"

Majel ground down on the flare of anger. Useless—even counterproductive—to be angry at someone who wished only to protect the vulnerable.

"I was at Ribbon Dance Hill," said the council chair, "in

company with the Warden, Councilor targElmina, and Councilor azieEm. What we witnessed was, indeed, extraordinary. Master Trader yos'Galan and Captain Mendoza were god-ridden. This had been foreseen by our own Oracle, and reported to this Council by the Warden of Civilization some time ago. The intent of the gods was to reunite themselves with the universe. They accomplished their intent, whereupon the master trader and the captain were returned to themselves. Attending councilors and the Warden made this report to the Council."

She glanced around the table, her eyes lingering on Majel.

"It is true that the Trade Mission's principals are Talents—"

"Which is where the danger lurks," Councilor seelyFaire interrupted. "Ma'am, Councilor ziaGorn is Deaf. He cannot defend himself from an attack."

"Which is why," said Councilor azieEm, in her soft voice that was nonetheless perfectly intelligible to the entire table, "we routinely send the Deaf to deal with the Haosa."

Councilor seelyFaire blinked.

"I can vouch," Portmaster krogerSlyte said into the small breach created by seelyFaire's astonishment, "that the trade mission is composed of civilized persons. I do not foresee an attack of any kind—what would be the purpose? Master Trader yos'Galan wishes to evaluate Colemeno's value to ongoing trade, and to perhaps establish a Tree-and-Dragon office at the port. Attacking citizens is inconsistent with those goals."

"And yet it *is* Tree-and-Dragon," tryaBent said. "Clan Korval was well known for precipitating violence."

"For precipitating *unlooked-for events*," Councilor ivenAlyatta, their archivist, corrected sharply. "I can provide you with cites, Councilor. Also, I believe the Council is aware of the debt the citizens—*all* of the citizens—of Colemeno owe to Clan Korval and Clan Ixin. Had they not defied the Council of Liad, our ancestors would have been purged, rather than removed from harm's way."

"And placed into the way of harm of another type and disposition," growled tryaBent.

Council Chair gorminAstir raised her eyebrows.

"Surely not even you, Coracta, can blame Clan Korval for conditions peculiar to Colemeno."

tryaBent pressed her lips together, and glanced down at her notepad.

Portmaster krogerSlyte raised her hand.

"Speak," said the council chair.

"Thank you, ma'am. As I believe you were about to say, the principals of the trade mission are Talents, but their security team are not. Surely that tells us something about the trade mission and Tree-and-Dragon?" She glanced around the table. "I think that Councilor ziaGorn's proposal has merit, and I second it."

"Thank you," Council Chair gorminAstir said. She looked around the table once more. "Councilor seelyFaire, you have been heard. Is there further discussion?"

Councilor seelyFaire sat down. No one else spoke.

Council Chair gorminAstir inclined her head.

"Those in favor of establishing the adjunct position of trade liaison, to be filled by Councilor ziaGorn, in the particular case of interfacing with the Tree-and-Dragon Trade Mission, effective immediately, raise your hands now."

Two abstained—seelyFaire and tryaBent. Majel took a deep breath.

A bell rang, the sound silvery in the silence.

Council Chair gorminAstir inclined her head.

"The motion passes. Councilor ziaGorn, if the liaison's office requires anything in order to facilitate its work, please let the Council know. We will expect reports at every meeting of the Council of the Whole. In between, your contact will be Portmaster krogerSlyte, unless she objects."

"No, ma'am," said the portmaster, "no objection at all."

What did you just do? Majel asked himself, feeling panic starting in his chest. He breathed it down, rose again and bowed to those assembled.

"Councilors, I thank you," he said. "I will do my best for the citizens—all of the citizens"—he smiled at Archivist ivenAlyatta—"of Colemeno."

He sat down.

"Very good," said Council Chair gorminAstir briskly. "Is there other new business?"

Colemenoport
Offices of
Tree-and-Dragon Trade Mission

. . . .

IT WAS TWO WEARY TRADERS WHO APPROACHED THE OFFICES OF the trade mission in the early evening hours.

"So, Padi yos'Galan, are you still excited by the glamour of opening a new port, or are you regretting Trader Veshtin and *Maribel*'s interesting route?"

Padi eyed the master trader—no, surely, it was her father who asked the question; there was that certain tilt to the eyebrow, just there. Still, his *melant'i* was necessarily fluid, given the subject, and it did her no harm, she thought wryly, to practice diplomacy.

"Certainly, I must regret Trader Veshtin, who is by all reports a skilled trader, and an exemplary teacher," she said evenly. "I believe that I could have learned much from her. But you know, sir, that one cannot be in two places at once."

"Very true," Father said, gravely. "One did wonder *particularly* after the glamour."

"Well, the glamour—" Padi gave him a tired smile. "The glamour has perhaps been replaced by exhilaration, trepidation—and exhaustion."

Father laughed.

"Yes, let us by no means forget exhaustion! I wonder at myself, if you will have it, Trader Padi, that I darted off with only the two of us—formidable as we are!—on this venture. The guild, as I am sure you know, recommends a master and three traders, with at least two *qe'andra*, for a trade team set to open a port."

"We mustn't discount Dyoli," Padi said, "who was trained to trade. Nor Mar Tyn, who is as quick with his figures as any port clerk I've encountered."

8

Mar Tyn pai'Fortana of their team, Dyoli ven'Deelin's partner, had grown to adulthood in Liad's Low Port, where the chiefest draw on one's time was merely staying alive. In Mar Tyn's case, his life had been further complicated by the fact that he was a Luck, the most inconvenient Talent that Padi—no expert—had yet heard of. If Mar Tyn had lived a more regular life, with a clan to support his ambitions, and leave to study, he might well have been an accountant.

"You approach a topic that I have been considering," Father said, putting his hand against the plate. The door opened; he waved Padi in before him.

Sighing, she put her case on the conference table. They were just come from a reception hosted by the market manager, so that they might be introduced to the principal vendors on-port. They had stayed somewhat after to finalize the details of tomorrow morning's facilities tour, while the rest of their party had returned to the apartment assigned to their use.

The message-waiting light was blinking on the comm, which had been the case very nearly since the portmaster had opened the office to them.

Father put his case next to hers, and touched her hand.

"I would like to have your advice regarding a notion of mine, if you will. Your comment just then brought it forward."

"My comment?" Padi blinked. "Regarding what?"

"Regarding Master pai'Fortana's skill with numbers, and 'counts. The ship's library does have the complete educational module published by the Accountant's Guild. Do you think Master pai'Fortana would view the arrival of that module as a gift? As a demand? Or—there was something else—ah! Or a subtle message reinforcing his certainty that his only service to the mission is that he somewhat softens Dyoli ven'Deelin's demeanor?"

He paused with a half-smile, and added, "You understand that I do not wish to do further violence to Master pai'Fortana's self-esteem."

"I do understand, yes," Padi said, wrinkling her nose as she stared down at the table.

It was a difficult case. One quite liked Mar Tyn, who, aside his facility with numbers, was quick-witted, observant, and genuinely kind.

"I think..." she said, looking up to meet Father's eyes, "if the module were accompanied by a note from the master trader, stating that his skill deployed on behalf of the mission is noted, and valued—he would believe that from you. Following, you might say that you thought he would find the attached of interest."

She sighed sharply, and looked up to meet a quizzical silver gaze.

"That's a very light touch. Is it better to baffle than offend?"

"In the case, I think so," Padi said. "If he is baffled"—which, she owned, he likely would be—"he will bring it to Dyoli."

Father raised an eyebrow.

"So he will. And we may, I believe, depend upon a child of Ixin to explain the matter in a way that will see profit come to her hand. Yes. Thank you, Padi. I believe that the master trader will follow your suggestion."

He patted her hand, and looked over his shoulder at the implacable glow of the message-waiting light.

"I propose that I check the comm," he said. "Absent emergencies, we may then go home."

Padi glanced up.

"I am promised to Tekelia this evening," she said, and there was a warmth in eyes and pattern that could only give a father pause.

"Of course," he murmured, and went to the comm.

There were two messages in-queue. The first revealed that Trader Isfelm wished to meet with Trader yos'Galan at her convenience to finalize the purchase of six adapter kits, which would let the older pod mounts on *Ember* accommodate the pods carried by *Dutiful Passage.*

Shan glanced over his shoulder. Padi nodded and made a note on her pad.

The second call was from Portmaster krogerSlyte, received only moments before he and Padi had entered the office, referencing the matter of a trade liaison, and asking for a call back. She left the code for her private line, which she had previously given him.

Shan did hesitate. Surely, the matter of the liaison was not an emergency, it was late in the day, and it took a great deal to wring an admission of exhaustion from Padi. But the portmaster was the trade mission's staunchest ally so far among the so-called Councilors of the Civilized. It did not do to offend allies, nor to put them off when they were laboring on your behalf.

He entered the code into the comm.

"krogerSlyte," the portmaster answered briskly.

"Portmaster, it is Master Trader yos'Galan. I have only just returned to our office, and found your message waiting. How may I serve you?"

"I have here in my office Councilor Majel ziaGorn, who has been appointed by the Council to stand as liaison to the trade mission. I wonder if I might bring him to you for an introduction."

"Of course!" Shan said, and glanced over his shoulder at Padi. She inclined her head, bold heart. He smiled and went back to the comm.

"Would now be convenient to you?" he asked.

"Very much so," the portmaster said, relief in her voice. "Expect us inside the quarter hour."

She ended the call, and Shan stood up, stifling a sigh of his own.

Padi was at the buffet, pot in hand.

"I'll make some tea, shall I?" she said.

"An excellent idea! I will set out some of those pretty iced cakes, in case our guests are peckish."

"I hope they are," Padi said frankly. "There are entirely too many pretty iced cakes in this undertaking."

"A hazard of the trade," Shan replied solemnly. "There's nothing for it, save to recruit one's fortitude."

Padi laughed, her face lighting; her pattern flaring with such fey energy that—old and experienced Healer that he was—he was momentarily caught in thrall.

She disappeared behind the wall that hid a small, efficient kitchenette. Released from thrall, Shan took a breath and went to the buffet for the tea things.

She was a bright light, his daughter—intelligent, Talented, and fierce. That they did not precisely know what her Talent happened to be, was, he suspected, of more concern to her elders than to Padi herself. She had little interest in Talents, despite being the daughter of a Healer who was lifemated to a Witch. No, Padi's whole desire was to trade.

That she would someday wear the amethyst ring that marked out a master trader was not in doubt, though she had only recently achieved the trader's garnet.

He put the tea tray in the center of the table, with the cups;

dealt out the napkins and little plates, and returned to the buffet for the cake tin.

Even before Colemeno, Padi's Gift had been—strange. Now, with Colemeno's field acting upon it, she was almost too bright to behold.

He had weighed—doubtless overweighed!—the wisdom of bringing his unSorted, brilliant child to Colemeno, with its invigorating atmosphere. Thus the offer of an apprenticeship with one of Tree-and-Dragon's most gifted traders. Padi, however, her eye on trade, had seen that participating in the opening of a port, and the possible design of a hub, would stand her in better stead than a merely *interesting* trade route.

Padi returned, bearing the teapot, and set it among the cups at the center of the table.

"A festive arrangement," Shan said approvingly. "The only thing lacking is guests."

A tone sounded, and the blue light over the hall doorway flashed twice.

Padi grinned.

"On cue. How *do* you manage that?"

"You won't get my secrets that easily, Trader," he answered.

He tapped the release button set into the table, and stood next to Padi as the door opened, admitting Portmaster krogerSlyte, followed by quite a young man with short red curls clinging to his skull like a cap, square face dominated by a pair of very dark brown eyes. He was wearing a simple tunic over flowing long pants. His face was composed, but his emotive pattern was a jumble of excitement, trepidation, and wariness.

"Master Trader yos'Galan." Portmaster krogerSlyte stopped before the table and made one of the shapeless bows that served as courtesy on Colemeno. "I thank you for agreeing to see me so quickly. My purpose this evening is to make you known to Majel ziaGorn, Councilor and Chair of the Citizens Coalition. Councilor ziaGorn will be the liaison between the trade mission and the Council of the Civilized."

"Councilor ziaGorn, we are well met."

Shan bowed as to an honored colleague, having not yet mastered the Colemeno style. He moved a hand, directing attention to Padi.

"Allow me to make you known to my second, Trader Padi yos'Galan."

"Councilor." Padi's bow was nearer to that offered by the portmaster. Shan owned himself impressed.

Majel ziaGorn attempted to reproduce Shan's bow, which was bold of him, and not badly done, for a first effort.

"Master Trader. Trader. I am honored. I look forward to working with you and the rest of the trade mission." His voice was calm and firm, despite his inner turmoil. *A person of discipline, then*, Shan thought. *Excellent.*

"Our colleagues are elsewhere at the moment," he said. "However, let us see if we cannot contrive to allow you to meet them soon." He moved his hands, showing them the table and the tea things waiting. "Please, sit and refresh yourselves while we establish some beginning protocols."

Portmaster krogerSlyte lifted a regretful hand.

"My purpose is accomplished," she said, "and duty will have me elsewhere. Please, traders, do not hesitate to call on me if I can be of service to you or to the trade mission. Councilor ziaGorn has my pledge of assistance as well."

"Thank you, Portmaster," the councilor said. "For your support."

"Councilor, it is my pleasure," she assured him, which Shan Heard as pure truth. She produced another bow in the direction of the table, and Shan came around to walk the short distance to the door with her.

"You have been everything that is helpful to strangers on your port," he murmured, touching the plate.

Portmaster krogerSlyte bent a humorous look on him as the door opened.

"I foresee a time when you will not be strangers on my port," she said calmly.

"May your Seeing be true," Shan said, politely.

"Oh, I think it is," she said. "All that's required is to do the work. Until soon, sir."

She stepped out into the hall, the door closed, and Shan returned to the table.

Padi was pouring tea. Councilor ziaGorn sat calmly, face and emotions still at odds.

"I find it noteworthy," Shan said, taking his seat next to Padi, "how often simply doing the work will accomplish wonders. Do you find it so, Councilor?"

There was a flicker of *some*thing as the man lifted his dark gaze to Shan's face.

"Master Trader, my life has been built on the belief that work is the foundation of success. Thank you, Trader."

The last was directed to Padi, as he accepted a cup of tea from her.

"Please," Shan said, "make free of the cake. We have both just come from a reception at the port market."

"And you are therefore replete, with tea and with cake," Councilor ziaGorn said, humor lifting a corner of his straight mouth.

Shan received his teacup from Padi with a smile, and looked at the guest with approval.

"Exactly. Trader yos'Galan was only just now remarking on how very *much* cake is on offer, everywhere we go."

"Well, but it must be, mustn't it? No one wants an incident. And cake is a very simple thing."

"Very true," Padi said. "And so we follow the path laid out for us, and offer tea and cake."

She raised her cup and sipped, Shan and Councilor ziaGorn following suit.

"I appreciate your hospitality," Councilor ziaGorn said seriously, when he had put his cup down.

"And we are pleased to offer it," Padi said. "Please don't imagine that I am going to force you to eat cake; it is merely there, should you desire it. I don't wish to give the wrong impression."

That won an actual laugh and a further settling of the councilor's unruly emotions.

Shan hid his smile behind his teacup.

Well done, Padi, he thought.

He put his cup down and leaned forward somewhat, to meet the councilor's eyes.

"What I propose, sir, is that we share contact information, and find a mutually agreeable time to introduce you to the rest of the team. Is this satisfactory to you? I assure you that I intend to do the work. Trader yos'Galan oversees me sternly in that regard."

"I believe we all intend to do the work," Councilor ziaGorn said. "I know that I've come to you, unexpected, at the end of a long day. Truthfully, I hadn't hoped for an introduction so soon. I was only appointed by the Council this afternoon. Portmaster krogerSlyte has given me copies of her notes, but I haven't had the chance to review them as yet."

"Then we are agreed."

Padi rose and went to the desk, returning with their general information packet, and the local card.

She put those items at the councilor's elbow and resumed her seat.

"Those will give you some background on Tree-and-Dragon, on Clan Korval, and on the members of the trade mission," Shan said. "Our local addresses and comm codes are on that card. Ah—"

He produced his case, extracted a card and handed it across to their liaison, who received it with wide eyes, and a return of some emotional tumult.

"Those codes are linked to *Dutiful Passage*. If you cannot find me locally, do not hesitate to use them."

"I thank you," Councilor ziaGorn whispered, and cleared his throat. "I am honored. I do know that master traders are not free with their cards, sir."

Shan raised an eyebrow.

"You are our liaison, and we have all quite agreed that we are committed to getting the work done. You may never need it, but I would rather you had too much information, than too little."

"Yes." Councilor ziaGorn slipped the card into the tunic's sleeve pocket. "I have nothing so organized to offer. I can give my codes and my address, if—"

Padi pulled out her notepad.

"Please," she said. "They will be most helpful."

"Majel ziaGorn," he said, and recited his personal code and the one that would reach the offices of the Citizens Coalition. "You might also find me at my business, though it is somewhat out from the port. Cardfall Casino, on Riverview Street, in the Citizens Sector." He recited that code, as well.

Padi inscribed it all while Shan fetched the screen from the desk, and brought up the team's common schedule.

"The entire team is promised to the market manager for a tour of the facilities, first thing tomorrow. We are told that this will consume the better part of three hours. How are you fixed for the midday meal tomorrow?" he asked. "A working nuncheon is already on the schedule, and we may easily accommodate one—or even two!—more, should you have a second that you wish brought current. We will provide the meal, proper introductions will be made, and a list of topics and protocols drafted."

"I believe we may also promise," Padi murmured, "that there will be no cake."

"Surely not!" Shan eyed her. "The cake must at least be *present*, Trader Padi."

She raised her eyebrows.

"Of course it must. What was I thinking?"

It was a fair imitation of him at his most vacuous. He gave her a nod and looked back to their new liaison, who had gone so far as to look—amused.

"Tomorrow, here, for the midday meal, introductions, and preliminary planning," he said. "I anticipate it with pleasure."

"Excellent," said Shan, making a note in the calendar before he looked up and met the other man's eyes. "Is there anything else that we ought to address immediately?"

"I believe we have made a good beginning," said Councilor ziaGorn. He rose, bringing the information packet with him, and bowed, this time in the common Colemeno fashion.

"I leave you now to your rest."

Shan rose and saw him to the door with another bow and murmured well-wishes.

When he returned Padi had already carried the tray into the kitchenette.

He put the cake tin away, and tidied the table.

Home, he thought, or at least the suite they had been granted, and some time in the company of his lifemate. A glass of wine would also be a comfort. Then, he had work to do.

"I'll confirm our order with the caterer before I leave," Padi said, recalling him to the present. "Shall I meet you here tomorrow, or at the market?"

Ah, yes, he thought; the facilities tour. And Padi was promised to her friend Tekelia this evening.

Shan took a breath and smiled.

"I think that we risk nothing with a separate arrival," he said. "They will need to become accustomed to seeing us solitary at our work."

"And it is not too soon to begin," Padi said with a smile. "I will meet you at the market."

She stepped to his side and rose up on her toes to kiss his cheek.

"I wish the master trader will allow my father some rest this evening," she murmured, and Shan laughed.

"I'll tell him you said so."

"Yes, that is correct," Padi told Catering Manager jakValin, at Skywise Provianto. "And that is against the Tree-and-Dragon draw account."

"Yes, Trader. Will you wish servers?"

"We will serve ourselves."

"Very good, Trader. The order will come to the Tree-and-Dragon office suite at the midday meal hour, tomorrow. Is there anything else?"

"Not at present, I thank you."

"We are pleased to serve. Good evening to you, Trader."

"Good evening," Padi answered, and closed the connection.

She rose, and crossed the room, to be certain the door was locked, then returned to the table, where her case awaited her. She did have work to do this night, but Tekelia was an easy companion, and apt to have work of their own, after the evening meal was done. It would seem that the universe did not lack for work to be done.

She smiled slightly, picked up her case and murmured, "Tekelia."

Mist swirled, or smoke, and Tekelia stood before her, in sweater, tough pants, and boots, dark hair caught back with what had been the extra hair ring Padi carried in her belt in case of need. There was a smile on the round, tan face, and the eyes at the moment were one amber, and one green.

"The meal is prepped and the wine is breathing. Will you join me?"

"With the greatest pleasure—yes," Padi said, and stepped forward to take the arm offered to her.

Mist swirled, glittering briefly.

The office was empty.

Colemenoport
Wayfarer

. . . .

"GOOD EVENING, PRISCILLA."

Smiling, she looked up from the desk in the window. He felt her regard sweep over him even as she pushed back her chair and rose.

"Sit down," she said. "I'll pour the wine."

Shan raised his eyebrows.

"As dire as that?"

She moved across the room to the refreshment stand.

"Only half as dire," she said. "Sit down, love."

"Since you ask so nicely."

He put his case on the chair near the door, slipped off his jacket and hung it on the back before crossing to the U-shaped half-sofa that had become their preferred meeting spot.

He sat with a sigh.

"Truly, Priscilla, I don't mean to disturb your work."

"It's scarcely work, and well worth interrupting. Portmaster krogerSlyte sent me a list of lectures on the topic of the mosaic depicting the Landing at Colemeno that we had all admired on our arrival, and professes herself at my service as an escort to any I might care to attend."

She came to the sofa, handed him a glass of the red, keeping a glass of mint tea for herself, and sank down next to him.

"Ought the portmaster's attention concern me?" Shan inquired.

"I'll try not to break her heart," she answered dryly.

"You are always so nice in these affairs, Priscilla," he said earnestly, and raised his glass.

"To work worth interrupting."

Priscilla tipped her head, though she raised her glass and touched it to his just hard enough to waken a ring.

"Hardly the most auspicious of toasts," she murmured.

"Well. I fear I may be instructed by my daughter, who expressed her wish that the master trader would allow her father some rest this evening."

"Not so ill a wish. Do you think the master trader will grant it?"

"In some measure, I believe he may. There are documents to review, but I believe most may wait upon tomorrow." He sipped his wine and sighed. "Indeed, *ought* to wait until we have toured the facilities, and know for ourselves what is in hand and in what condition. This whole venture being sky-pie, there's surely no need to make more."

"Not entirely pie in the sky," Priscilla said. "Unless the Dust hasn't actually receded?"

"Oh, no, that seems to be a certainty. Whether Colemeno wants to open itself and boldly rejoin the rest of the universe— *that* remains at question."

He sipped his wine, and leaned forward to put the glass on the table.

"On that topic, you may be gratified to learn that the Council has assigned one of its number as the liaison to the trade mission."

"That is news. When will we meet her?"

"Padi and I met him briefly this evening. The entire team will meet him at nuncheon tomorrow, after the tour."

He moved his shoulders.

"His name is Majel ziaGorn, and his honor is Chair of the Citizens Coalition. Portmaster krogerSlyte places great confidence in him, and brought him herself to make his bow. We have exchanged contact information, by which I find that he also owns a casino."

Priscilla lifted her eyebrows.

"A casino?"

"You don't approve of casinos?"

She did not dignify that with an answer, and nor, Shan thought, reaching again for his glass, should she have.

"It only seems very odd that there would be casinos in a place where everyone is Talented."

"Yes, but do you know? Majel ziaGorn *isn't* Talented. He is quite refreshingly normal."

Priscilla's brows knit; she sipped her tea, and put the glass aside.

"And the Council of the Civilized assigned him to us," she said. "That's interesting."

"Isn't it? And a casino argues that he is not alone in lacking a Talent."

"So it does. I'll be pleased to meet him tomorrow."

"Excellent. Speaking of tomorrow, Padi will be meeting us at the market. She is tonight promised to Tekelia."

Priscilla tipped her head.

"And that distresses you?"

He half-laughed.

"I would put it no higher than concern, but that would merely be a quibble," he said.

"Yet Tekelia stood as a staunch ally, and assisted you, and Padi, when there was need."

"And in addition seems a person of honor, if quite appallingly strong for even a *dramliza*." Shan moved his hand. "Forgive me, Priscilla; I fear I am coming the parent."

She laughed gently.

"As a parent, my love, you must trust your work. You have raised a strong, sensible woman, who is both generous and fierce."

He sighed.

"She is all of that," he allowed.

"So," Priscilla said, after a moment. "Padi will not be joining us for the meal. Dyoli and Mar Tyn have already said that they will dine in their rooms. Grad, Karna, and Tima are reviewing a new training module that came down from the ship today. Tima told me that they would order some cold trays and *browse*."

"Which leaves us alone for the meal," Shan said.

"So it would appear."

"Then I have a proposition for you, Priscilla. Allow the master trader an hour to read the documents necessary to tomorrow's tour. We may then follow the excellent examples before us, and retire to our room to dine tête-à-tête and take whatever recreation may seem good to us."

"I accept your proposition, sir, and note that the captain still needs to read that same documentation."

"We might read it together, then," Shan said.

"So we might. Let me refresh our glasses while you get your case."

On-Grid
Cardfall Casino

. . . .

MAJEL HAD GONE THROUGH THE TRADE MISSION'S INFO-PACKET once, and left the pages spread over his desk while he got up to go to the window.

His apartment on the casino's third floor gave him the view promised by the address. At this hour, the river was dark silk, the reflections of the lumenberry trees twinkling in its depths.

Normally, it was a view he found soothing and renewing.

This evening, however, his thoughts were occupied with the information in the packet, seeking to rectify it with the traders he had met.

The traders—in a word, the traders had been charming. The master trader was not an elder, despite the white hair. His manner had been easy; his whole aspect open and frank. The younger trader—the master's daughter, according to the info-packet—had been at pains to put him at ease, which argued that she had been privy to his initial dismay at the speed with which everything had happened, from the moment he had brought his new business before the Council. That was not a surprise; he had been fairly warned that the mission's principals were Talents. They were ethical persons, so Portmaster krogerSlyte had been at pains to assure him—and certainly they had seemed so, to him.

Portmaster krogerSlyte...In Majel's experience, the portmaster had been a stolid sort of councilor. She voted with the majority more often than not, and introduced nothing more than the quarterly port budget into the Council's business.

Her partiality for the trade mission might be seen as worrisome, Majel thought, until one recalled that the portmaster's concern had *always* been the port. If Colemeno became a hub, or merely expanded

21

to accommodate a permanent Tree-and-Dragon trade office—then Portmaster krogerSlyte's worth to the Redlands increased.

Looked at from that angle, her eagerness to have the mission succeed made a great deal of sense.

Nor was the portmaster the only one who stood to benefit from the success of the master trader's work, he thought wryly.

Why, only see that upstart, Majel ziaGorn, newest councilor at the table, who had been vinsEbin's aide for a scant six Standard Years before being seated in her chair—practically leaping out of that same chair in order to grasp a position of influence.

Majel half-laughed. Yes, well. Durella had warned him that ambition would be his downfall.

And to be perfectly fair, he had not fallen. He had placed himself into a position of trust, the like of which had never before been held by the Chair of the Citizens Coalition. If he were careful, and honest in his duty, he stood to gain much, not only for himself, but for those he represented. If the Council— if *the Civilized* could be brought to see that being Deaf meant nothing more than an inability to interact with the ambient, and did not also carry a meaning of vulnerable, half-witted, or frail— that would be success. For the Deaf to become accepted fully as citizens into Civilization—*that* was where his ambition led him.

So. The traders were charming, mannered, and Civilized. The info-packet had outlined some difficult times for Tree-and-Dragon Trade family and Clan Korval, directly preceding their arrival at Colemeno, including banishment from Liad. In that trouble, at least, they held solidarity with the Redlands, the ancestors having been likewise banished from the homeworld.

He was minded, here, of tryaBent's assertion that Clan Korval was known to promote violence, and the archivist's counterproposal of "unlooked-for events," backed by cites. That was information that might also be of value to the liaison to the trade mission.

He turned from the window toward the desk, intending to make a note to ask ivenAlyatta for the cites regarding Tree-and-Dragon's propensity for—trouble.

The on-floor comm buzzed, and Majel slapped the button, stylus forgotten.

"ziaGorn."

"Sir, we've got a chizler down here at the security station. Do you want to talk to her, or should we just call the proctors?"

Majel sighed. This was the fifth chizler in the last twelve days. They'd turned the previous four over to the proctors and pursued full penalties. Word of that *must* have gotten to the siblinghood of rascals by now. Truly, after the fourth, he had expected to see no more.

Twelve days, five chizlers.

The situation had graduated from annoying to worrisome.

"I'll come down," Majel said. "Do you have the vid?"

"Yes, sir, all queued up and ready to show."

"Fine. On my way."

The chizler had watched the vid of herself manipulating the cards at the Sixes table with an air of cool, professional interest. She had made no plea of innocence, nor protested the arrival of the proctors. Merely, she rose, and bowed to Majel, thanked him gravely for an evening of interesting play, and allowed herself to be taken away to the station house.

"That," said Seylin, who was head of in-house security, "was almost more worrisome than the act itself. As if she intended to be caught, and the evening has proceeded exactly to her expectations."

Majel looked up from the vid, which was replaying on loop.

"*Intended*," he said. "She meant to be caught."

Seylin blinked at him. "What are you thinking?"

"I'm thinking of five chizlers in twelve days. This last had the coolest head, but none of the others displayed any outrage at having their honor impugned. Did even one of them say, 'Sir, I do not cheat at cards'?"

"I don't recall that any did, but we have the tapes. You think they're—probing? Looking for the weak point in our security?"

"Something like that."

"But we caught them," Seylin said. "The only thing they've learned is that our security is tight."

Majel bit his lip, not liking where his thoughts were tending, but one looked for *reasons* to explain anomalies. Five chizlers in twelve days. Oh, he *didn't* want to go any further down that road. Only—

He met Seylin's eyes.

"Did we?" he asked. "Did we catch *all* of them? Or worse, are the ones we caught only a diversion?"

Seylin took a breath.

"The vids—"

"The vids require time to review," Majel interrupted. "Assuming each chizler was cover for something else, we have twelve days to review." He paused, eyes narrowed. "Even if the *first* chizler was a probe..."

Seylin looked sour.

"Close tomorrow?" she asked.

That was prudent, Majel thought. One didn't wish to tip one's hand.

But—five chizlers in twelve days. Ample time to have altered machines. And if the manipulation had been done by Talents, it might *not* show up on vid. Which would mean calling in specialists, and a longer delay before reopening.

"Close tonight," he said. "Tell the floor crew and the bouncers. We don't want a rush, just a general feeling among the patrons that going elsewhere would be...pleasant."

"Yes, sir," Seylin said, clearly unhappy, which made two of them.

Majel stood up.

"I'll be in the bar, if you need me."

Colemenoport
Wayfarer

. . . .

THE SUITE OF ROOMS THAT THE COLEMENO PORTMASTER HAD made available to the master trader's team was spacious, and, by Mar Tyn's standards, at least, elegant. He and Dyoli had adjoining rooms, each with its own bed, desk, drawers, and freshening facilities. By mutual agreement, they left the connecting door open, and more often than not would work together in what the roster listed as "Dyoli ven'Deelin's quarters."

"Mar Tyn pai'Fortana's quarters" was their sleeping room. Mar Tyn had never lived in such spaciousness, where he might rise and pace four dozen steps before returning to the place where he had begun.

More, they had direct access to the building's kitchen—a call at any hour would see a meal or beverage arriving in their room via an ingenious lift system built into the wall.

Truly, it was a place of such comfort that he found himself repeating the mantra, "This is temporary," several times a day, in the hope that he would mourn it less when it was reft from him, as it surely would be.

Most of the circumstances of Mar Tyn's life had been temporary, the partnership with Dyoli bidding fair to become his longest, and most stable association...ever. He did *try* not to tell himself that it, too, was temporary, though in his secret heart, he feared it.

Dyoli had no doubts that their partnership would endure. Nor did she have any patience with arguments that would set the daughter of a High Liaden House properly well above the touch of a ragged Luck out of Low Port.

Dyoli would have it that they two *would be* the managers of a joint Tree-and-Dragon and Ixin trade office, located on

25

Colemenoport. Indeed, she was more certain of the establishment of this office than was the master trader himself. There were, so Mar Tyn understood from the master trader's explanations of the mission's work, procedures mandated by nothing less than the Trade Guild, and to stint them was to court disaster.

In Mar Tyn's opinion, having observed him now for some time, the master trader avoided disaster. Unquestionably, he was bold. Was not *Dutiful Passage*, the master trader's own ship, the first to arrive at a port only recently released from the depths of a hazard to navigation that had held it aside for two hundred Standards? Bold, but not *careless*.

The master trader's ultimate success in opening Colemeno to the wide universe aside, the question that very much occupied Mar Tyn's interest was his role in the future.

Dyoli might be certain of their partnership, and he himself unwilling to break it, still one wished to be...

...of use.

It was a strange desire, to be sure—whenever was a Luck *of use*, save for what his Gift might bring?

Well. He shook himself. At the moment, he thought, he might be *of use* by reading the information given by the market manager to prepare them for tomorrow morning's tour. Mar Tyn could have no opinion of whether the facilities were suitable for the master trader's scheme, or what upgrades might be reasonably made to bring it current. Still, he ought to read the document, and talk it over with Dyoli, so that he might be as informed as possible.

He glanced across the room, where Dyoli sat, reading from her screen—doubtless the information he had yet to access.

Extending a hand, he tapped his screen on, tapped again for his work queue—and sat blinking.

There was a letter *to him*—*only* to him, not as part of a group memo—from the master trader.

Such a thing had never happened before, and it unsettled him, until his native humor reasserted itself.

Were you not only a moment ago wishing to be of use, Mar Tyn Luck? He asked himself. *Perhaps the master trader has a task for you.*

This seemed unlikely in the extreme; still, to sit gaping was scarcely informative.

Mar Tyn tapped the letter open, noting that he was greeted by name, and with gentle words of appreciation, before—

He read the letter again—and again, his breath coming short.

"Mar Tyn?" Dyoli said from across the room, for of course her own Gift would have allowed her to feel his distress. "Is something amiss?"

"I—scarcely know," he said. "Have you a moment to—look at this with me?"

"Certainly."

She came to stand beside him, her hand on his shoulder. Her fingers tightened slightly as she leaned forward to tap the screen, and made a small sound of satisfaction when the attachment opened.

"The complete accounting course, with tests, accredited by the masters of the Liaden Guild of Accountants," she murmured, and looked down to smile into his eyes.

"The master trader makes you a splendid gift, my Mar Tyn."

He stared at her.

"But, I am not an accountant!"

"Exactly so! He has seen that you have the potential to *become* an accountant."

His breath was short, and there was a particular tingling that felt ... *akin* to his Gift, which—

"Dyoli," he gasped. "What do you See?"

"See?"

She stepped 'round the chair, and turned to face him, her hip propped against the desk, and her eyes serious.

"I see that the master trader has made an assessment." She cocked a whimsical brow. "It is what master traders do, my Mar Tyn; he can scarcely help himself, and you must not be cross. Instead, read what he has sent to you—*Your unfailing attention to detail, and aptitude for plain figuring has been noted. These are qualities that a master trader values.*"

She paused, and leaned slightly forward to meet his eyes.

"Do you think that the master trader is making sport?"

No, Mar Tyn thought; no, he did not think that, at all. The master trader was sportive, but he did not *make sport*. He *did* make assessments, and he was frank when he discussed them. More, he had no possible reason to play a prank on the least important member of his team. Such a thing would be—cruel. And the master trader was *not* cruel.

"I do not think that this is ... like the master trader's humor," he said to Dyoli, who was still waiting for an answer. "It is only—Dyoli, I have no education, nor any accomplishments!"

"I will dispute that at another time," she said. "For the moment, however, you are being given the opportunity to add to your accomplishments. And you know, my love, that we will be even more valuable in terms of managing a trade office, if one of us is a Guild-certified accountant."

"Who will certify me?" he wondered, eyeing the screen, and the page displayed there.

"There are self-tests included in the module," Dyoli told him. "And as for certification—the ship's *qe'andra* is certainly qualified."

"The ship's *qe'andra*?"

"Yes—you recall her. She sat with us and went over the inventory sheets for consistency and competitive pricing."

Mar Tyn frowned. Yes, he thought suddenly, he did remember her. A woman of middle years, very solemn, with eyes only for her screens, and a clear, well-modulated voice.

"*Qe'andra* dea'Tolin," he murmured.

Dyoli smiled. "You do recall. Trained in the dea'Gauss firm, so she told me. She is new to the post on *Dutiful Passage*, but has been on Korval tradeships for some years. She is a very experienced person, and will be a good resource for you in your studies."

"My studies."

He closed his eyes, feeling his breath go short again, but no tingle from his Gift. It would appear that he had a *choice* to make, based on his own preferences.

Would you like to be an accountant? he asked himself gently.

Truly, he had no idea.

"What if I—fail?" he said, suddenly certain that it would be so. He opened his eyes to look at Dyoli. "All honor to the master trader, but what if his assessment is—inaccurate?"

"What if it is?" Dyoli answered carelessly. "We do not all succeed at everything to which we turn our hand. You may sample, and find that the dish is not to your taste, or that you have no aptitude. There is no dishonor there. Where there is *disrespect* is to ignore the offer altogether. The master trader thought of you with kindness. For that, you may wish to read the first chapter." She moved her shoulders. "Or not. That is entirely your judgment to make, my Mar Tyn."

Entirely his judgment to make. How very strange, to be sure.
"Thank you," he said to Dyoli.

"You are welcome. I am pleased that you asked for my input."
She smiled and straightened, holding her hand down to him.
"Since we are interrupted, shall we eat now?"

"I haven't done the reading," Mar Tyn confessed.

Dyoli grinned.

"Then we will have to talk of something other than business,"
she said. "Come, help me choose the meal."

On-Grid
Cardfall Casino

. . . .

"PRINCIPAL ZIAGORN."

Mardek was on the bar—Mardek had been on the bar since his father had opened the casino, before Majel was born. He was a Sensitive, as all bartenders were Sensitives, and the fact that he looked worried was—telling.

"Old friend," Majel murmured, coming to the bar and putting his foot on the rail. "Is something amiss?"

"You'll know that better than I," Mardek said, pulling a glass from the overhead rack, and placing it on the bar. He reached beneath—sent a bright glance into Majel's face—and brought out the cut crystal bottle, from which he poured liberally.

Well, Majel thought. There was nothing to protest, there. It had been an unsettling evening, following a stressful day. A glass of the Andram would be—welcome.

"Surda vinsEbin is in the booth. She is waiting for you, and she has been waiting for some time."

The day wasn't done with him yet, Majel thought, resignedly. He glanced at the glass Mardek had poured for him and thought of asking for the bottle. Which—

"How many has she had?" he asked.

"The second bottle was opened a few minutes ago."

That was restrained, indeed. Durella must really want to speak to him.

"Thank you," Majel said to the old barkeep. "I'll go to Surda vinsEbin. If any call comes from the floor, do interrupt me."

"Yes, sir."

Majel picked up his glass, and went down the room to the privacy booth.

✳   ✳   ✳

Possibly, Durella had begun drinking before she had gotten to the casino. Her face was flushed, and her eyes red. A single bottle of wine would not have produced such effects in so experienced a drinker. Also, he saw as he took the seat across from her, her hand was unsteady as she raised her glass.

"You're early," she remarked, and then pointedly looked at his glass. "Have you come to a sense of what you've done, Councilor? I must say that I'm surprised."

Majel sighed, and raised his glass, allowing himself a sip. He closed his eyes to savor the smooth heat before he set the glass aside and opened his eyes to Durella's angry face.

"It has been a long day, fraught with stress, not the least of which is an apparent attempt on the casino. Be brief, Durella."

"Brief?" Her eyes narrowed. "Very well. You're an ambitious idiot who will be the cause of the Deaf losing everything they have gained over the last twenty Standards."

This was a familiar theme—Durella had always decried his ambition. However, there was a new pleat—that his fall would raze the Deaf. The usual tale of his downfall ended with Durella coming out of retirement to resume her painfully careful game of advancing the Citizens into Civilization.

Not that she had accomplished nothing during her years of service, Majel told himself. In the early years, she had made significant gains toward equality. For the last decade, however, she had confined herself to preventing the likes of seelyFaire from passing laws that took those gains away, or infantilized the Deaf in some other way.

Though that had, as Majel also acknowledged, taken a good deal of political maneuvering and social engineering.

"What's changed?" he wondered now, as Durella knocked back her half-glass of wine.

She paused in the act of reaching for the bottle.

"Did you or did you not put yourself forward as the liaison between the Council and the Tree-and-Dragon Trade Mission?"

"I did. It was just the sort of opportunity I've been looking for. Ambitious or not, I am qualified to stand as liaison. I am in business; I understand and can navigate particular levels of bureaucracy that might frustrate a stranger to Colemeno; I have been appointed by the Council, and therefore have its ear. I have an opportunity to match useful people from my constituency with the aims of the trade mission. Deaf might even gain positions on the ships that will be arriving. Not only will the Council and the Civilized see that we are neither frail nor foolish, but it is an opportunity to advance twenty years in one step. I would be a fool *not* to seize it!"

There. He had perhaps been too warm, even given that Durella could strike temper from a paving stone. But it was said, and said truly. He did not regret that.

He allowed himself another sip of Andram. Across from him, Durella refreshed her glass.

"I ask you, Councilor, to imagine that this bold plan for success and acceptance—goes awry. I do not ask you to imagine *how* this happens. We have both seen enough to know that *any* plan may go awry, for any reason, or none."

Majel tamped down on the flare of irritation. This was an old game. His father had taught him the first level: *Every bright thing casts a shadow, my child. Remember to look into the shadows.*

And Durella herself had taught him the political form.

Imagine that the plan goes wrong—it doesn't matter why, only that it has. What is the worst that can happen? Is it acceptable? No, never mind the original plan—that's gone. You must now decide what you can salvage, and if it is enough to fight for.

"If I fail," he said now, "then we return to the square we now occupy. If I fail spectacularly enough, I may have to resign in favor of another. I will do what I can to be certain that whoever is chosen as my replacement will be ambitious on behalf of our constituents."

Durella sighed.

"I had thought you had learned better. Is seelyFaire no longer a Councilor?"

"You know that she is."

"Yes. And I know that what she will see in a failure is proof that the Deaf are in fact—what was it you said, Councilor? Frail and foolish. In need of protection. We will see what few rights we have stripped away, and caretakers again set up to oversee us, and shield us from harm."

He opened his mouth—

"Hear me, Dreamer ziaGorn! *That* is what I held against. It had been brought to the table more than once during my time. Once, it came far, far too close to being implemented. We fought it to a standstill—I and tryaBent and krogerSlyte. Then we fought the compromise. We *held*. But seelyFaire is only biding her time. Give her *anything* to build into a case for another Citizens Protection Act, and she will do her utmost. Which is not inconsiderable. And she learns from her mistakes."

"If it should happen that I fail," Majel said, evenly, "then I will fight. And if I fail there, too, then perhaps it is time to implement that other plan, which was always deemed too bold: to form our own council in truth, and declare ourselves separate from Civilization."

Durella stared at him.

"Because that has worked out so well for the Haosa."

"The Haosa are few, as we are. It comes to me that we are natural allies, and might usefully band together."

"The Deaf band with the Wild? You had used to have wits, Majel, but—"

There came a knock at the door.

Majel touched the button for the comm.

"ziaGorn."

"Principal, it is Seylin. The last patrons have left us, and the floor supervisors have gathered in the meeting room, as you requested."

"Thank you. I will come at once."

Majel looked across the table at Durella.

"I'll send someone to escort you home," he said, expecting her to deride the suggestion that she might need such an escort.

She sighed; looked at the bottle, the empty glass—and met his eyes.

"That is a gentle courtesy. I will await them here."

Off-Grid
The Tree House

. . . .

RIBBON-LIGHT WASHED THE ROOM, DANCING PASTELS PIERCED with blades of darkness. It was scarcely an hour for calling, even calling on kin, and Bentamin had considered waiting until he might bring breakfast and therefore at least seem convenable.

Only the matter nagged at him until finally he accepted the hour with the necessity and thought himself into the main room of his cousin's house.

It was a comfortable room, with large windows overlooking the wild wood, through which the Ribbon-light now danced. There had been some rearrangement of the furniture since the last time he had visited: the desk had been brought out of its alcove, and set with a better view of the window for it and the second desk that now faced it. This relegated the dining table to the alcove, which he found a pity, until he saw a smaller table out on the porch, last evening's wineglasses reflecting the dancing pastels.

The lights were out, which of course they should be at this hour, when only the guilty were awake. Bentamin opened his shields the tiniest bit, seeking. He touched one pattern—or was it two?

He sighed sharply. The ambient in this location was always turbulent, and he had known he was going to wake Tekelia. Only one had not expected Tekelia to have a guest, if indeed that second pattern was anything more than a Ribbon-born reflection.

He turned back to the larger room, thinking that he must of course go, when he felt a definite and distinctive flutter against his senses, and his cousin came into the room, tying the belt of an extremely colorful robe and shaking dark hair back from an irritated face.

"Good morning, Tekelia," he said politely, keeping his voice low against the possibility of that second pattern.

"Bentamin," came the response, with scant courtesy. "Have you a clock?"

"Several," he replied. "I was minded to take their counsel and seek my bed, save a certain matter did not allow of sleep."

Fierce eyes, equally black in the Ribbon-light, considered him.

"That sounds dire," Tekelia said at last. "I suppose you had better tell me. Tea? Cake?"

"I would not...disturb the house," Bentamin said delicately, and his cousin grinned.

"We'll take to the porch, then, and see how far your good intentions carry us."

Settled comfortably in the chair, Bentamin looked out over the wood, letting the turbulence swirl around him. His shields were barely open; he was Civilized and the full force of the ambient was not for him. Tekelia, however, was entirely open to the chaotic dance, so that Bentamin could scarcely see where his cousin ended and the ambient began.

Or, he thought, perhaps there *were* no boundaries. Tekelia was what the Haosa—the unCivilized, who lived off the Grid in the shadow of Ribbon Dance Hill—dignified as a Child of Chaos, which might be more literal than was comfortable for a Civilized man—though he be the very Warden—to dwell upon.

"Ah," Tekelia said, "*now* you are able to find your rest. Shall I bring you a blanket?"

"Your pardon, Cousin; I was reflecting on the nature of comfort. Which brings us to my topic." Bentamin took a breath, releasing the name on a sigh.

"kezlBlythe."

There was a sharp creak, as if Tekelia had shifted in the chair, though the reply was perfectly calm.

"I understand why sleep refused you. Tell me, Cousin, what *will* you do about the kezlBlythe?"

Bentamin raised his hands, showing empty palms to the dancing Ribbons.

"That had always depended on how and where they made their mistake," he answered. "My concern is that they *have* made it, and if so, lives are in it."

Another creak as Tekelia leaned forward.

"Lives are *always* in it with the kezlBlythe; death is the only seasoning they can taste. The twins are safe with us—"

"Are they?" Bentamin interrupted, sharply, and waited until Tekelia murmured.

"Yes, as of this heartbeat. They are asleep, healthy, and well guarded. Now, *tell me*, Bentamin."

"Yes, of course. Yesterday, Avryal kezlBlythe filed a petition with Haven City Council that xinRood's fortune be transferred to the kezlBlythe holdings and xinRood be listed as a Failed Line."

"That seems precipitate. What was her reasoning?"

"That the children now living off-Grid is in practical terms no different from the children being dead. Real property must therefore pass according to the law, and the kezlBlythe have long been the heirs of everything xinRood owned."

He paused.

"The suit to have xinRood entered as a Failed Line was separate. In my opinion, it is merely spite."

"Others have put forth these gambits," Tekelia remarked. "The Councilors have precedent to guide them."

"It's not the precedent that bothers me," Bentamin said. "It's the timing."

"You think—no. Tell me what you think, Bentamin."

"I think that the kezlBlythe sent Civilized children off-Grid, and are confident that they will succumb."

"Then they have fallen into the error of overconfidence," Tekelia said. "Vaiza—the boy—is a Wild Talent."

Bentamin blinked, recalling the twins' patterns as he had last seen them. Surely, they had been Civilized—*then*. Yet Tekelia—like him—was rarely wrong in such matters. "You're sure?"

"Yes." Absolute certainty rang against the ambient.

"And the girl?"

"Torin is a difficult case. She burns not so brightly as her brother, but she does burn. If her Talent is Wild, it is very modest. If she is Civilized, you will shortly have competition for your honors."

"I'd welcome a 'prentice gladly. But how is it that you don't *know*, Cousin?"

"Well." Tekelia sounded amused. "For one thing, they are siblings, for another, they are twins, for a third, they have been in close proximity to a norbear for the entirety of their lives, and for a fourth, they have seen all of their kin fall to kezlBlythe's malice, and therefore trust no one but themselves." Tekelia paused, and added, "Geritsi has made some progress there, and I believe Dosent is becoming intimate. In addition—"

Tekelia flung an arm up toward the sky where the Ribbon-dance was paler now, ceding pride of place to the rising of the star.

"In addition, it is rather noisy in this locality. Perhaps you have noticed."

"If the girl is Civilized, she ought to be showing distress by now," Bentamin said.

"Not," Tekelia countered, "if her brother is shielding her."

"They're very young."

"They are. I submit that necessity is a stern teacher. Nor ought we to discount the norbear. As for surety..."

Tekelia lifted a shoulder.

"We have been reluctant to probe too deeply, given their history. And, to be honest, I had thought we would have some time to allow them to become accustomed to us. However, you tell me that the kezlBlythe are on the move. I will therefore make it my business tomorrow to discover the twins' specific condition. When I have done so, I will inform you."

Tekelia paused, hand raised. Bentamin waited.

"You ought to know that there is a village meeting tomorrow evening, and that the twins' future is on the agenda. Shall I reveal the kezlBlythe's new actions?"

"Not all, I think. Merely make it known that the kezlBlythe have not forgotten their cousins. As for the twins, their lives and their futures..."

Bentamin looked into his cousin's eyes, revealed under the lightening sky to be one blue and one brown.

"I would rather the twins stay at Ribbon Dance Village, than being sent further out from the Grid."

Tekelia laughed. "If you think the village will not vote to keep them, here and safe, Cousin, you very much mistake your Haosa."

"No, I don't think I've mistaken my Haosa at all," Bentamin said earnestly. "Only have a care. kezlBlythe does not merely think that the children *will* fail; they think that they *have* failed. Given that the kezlBlythe never wager save when a win is assured, it concerns me that they have...done something to ensure the children do not disappoint them."

Tekelia sighed and seemed about to say something when the door opened, and a firm voice said, "There you are. I've started the kettle warming."

A slender woman stepped out onto the porch, pale hair loose along her shoulders, wearing a robe only slightly less colorful than Tekelia's. Bentamin shifted, and she raised her eyes to find him.

"Warden," she said calmly, inclining her head.

"Trader," he answered, matching her tone.

"Padi," Tekelia said, rising to place light hands on her shoulders. "Did we wake you?"

"Not at all—I've an early meeting at the port."

"I remember," Tekelia said. "I'll make the meal while you get ready. Bentamin, are you staying?"

"I think not, thank you, Cousin. I have meetings as well."

He rose and bowed more fully. "Trader yos'Galan, it is good to see you again," he said composedly, while his mind raced. Were they lovers? But how could that be? He supposed he would have to ask eventually. But now was not the time. Now was the time to take his leave.

Padi yos'Galan returned his bow with precision.

"It is good to see you again, also, Warden," she murmured, and went back inside.

Bentamin turned to his cousin, who spoke before him.

"Will you at least take one of Entilly's cookies?"

"That's kind, but I am not in need," Bentamin said. "Tekelia, find what you can. I fear—"

"As I do," Tekelia interrupted. "I'll look, Bentamin. In the meanwhile, trust the Haosa to keep them safe."

"I do," Bentamin said with more honesty than the Warden was often permitted. "Only—the kezlBlythe."

Tekelia grinned, feral. "Despite their chosen mode, the kezl-Blythe are Civilized. *Let* them try us in our home."

"Let it not go so far as that," Bentamin countered, and thought himself back to Civilization.

On-Grid
Cardfall Casino

. . . .

THE VIDS HAD REVEALED NO QUESTIONABLE ACTIVITY AROUND the machines nearest the Sixes table last night or on the two previous occasions.

Majel rubbed his face and gave the order for the technicians to strip out, clean and reset all of the floor devices.

Seylin sighed.

"It could be," she said tentatively, "that it's nothing more than five chizlers in twelve days—an, an *initiation rite* or some such—and not meant to divert our attention from something serious."

"It could," Majel said tiredly. "But that's not the way the smart money bets." He sighed.

"I need to get some rest. I have an appointment tomorrow—today—for luncheon with the Tree-and-Dragon Trade Mission, and I'll need my wits hard by me. Send the vids out to the surveillance company, and have them deep-scanned from three days prior to our first chizler through this evening. Concentrate the technicians' work in the two main rooms. That will be enough to let us open tomor—*tonight*. Offer a bonus if the Yellow Room is likewise cleared and ready to open. Close the Sixes table."

"Close the Sixes!" Seylin repeated. "But it's our most popular—"

"So it is," Majel interrupted. "And we are working on a new configuration which will put Sixes, Ante, and Snakes in their own parlor, with refreshments on offer, and dedicated staff."

"Oh," said Seylin. "And dedicated cameras, too. I suppose we'd better, considering."

She sighed and stood up.

"What's the trade mission to do with us?"

"I'm the liaison between the mission and the Council," Majel said, though it sounded surreal.

39

"That's new, is it?"

"Since yesterday's meeting," Majel admitted. "If you need me, I'll—"

"We won't need you," Seylin interrupted. "Go on upstairs and sharpen your wits. I'll take care of things here."

Off-Grid
The Tree House

. . . .

THE RIBBONS HAD FADED TO MERE PASTEL STREAKS AGAINST A
pale celadon sky. Colemeno's star had not yet cleared the top of the
trees. Padi yos'Galan stood on the porch overlooking those trees,
sipping what the Haosa styled the "morning wake up," delighting
in the cool, fragrant breeze against her cheek, and—thinking.

They were not pleasant thoughts, despite an evening of exploration with a delightful and attentive partner. That they were
both inexperienced brought an aspect of levity to the enterprise,
which surprisingly increased pleasure.

Truly, she thought, if her preferences were to rule the day—

But, there was the crux, wasn't it? Her preferences were divided.

The lure of opening a new port, of becoming more skilled
as a trader, and learning the fine points of negotiation—those
struck at the core of who she was, who she aimed to become.

She had not anticipated finding something else that struck
her so nearly. Surely, it was too soon to have formed a lasting
tie, yet she could not deny that Tekelia had become dear to her,
and this place, the house overlooking the untamed trees, the wind
that carried the sweet scent of greenery on its back, the Ribbons
that danced across the night sky, obscuring even the stars, had
become—a haven.

That might be no more than inconvenient, since her work,
and her necessities, were at the port, but the person who had
also become a haven, and at the least a friend, was Speaker for
the Haosa, who took calls from the very Warden of Civilization in the small hours of the morning, to discuss matters of
importance to both.

Padi yos'Galan, she told herself, closing her eyes and sipping
her wake-up, *you have made an error.*

41

"Padi?"

Tekelia's voice was in her very ear. She opened her eyes and smiled.

"I am, I swear to you, awake. Only, this is so pleasant a prospect."

"It is, isn't it?" Tekelia turned to follow her gaze, and lifted an arm, pointing.

"Just down there—you see the glint?—is the river, and a wide, shady bank. We might visit one day, for a swim and a cold luncheon."

Padi laughed softly.

"When we both have time."

"Well—yes. But that's bound to happen, eventually. Or do traders never stop working?"

"There are gaps, now and then. Understand, I have until lately been a 'prentice, and this concept of *not working* is very little encouraged by diligent masters."

Tekelia laughed. "Naturally. Still, let us keep ourselves open to opportunity. An afternoon free of labor may come our way."

It sounded—so delightful. Padi drank the rest of the wake-up, and turned toward the door.

"Allow me," said Tekelia, taking the cup from her hand. In the next moment, it vanished, and would, Padi knew from experience, manifest in the sink, ready to be washed.

"I believe it is time for me to go, if I'm not to be late for the tour," Padi said, unwillingly. "I'll get my case."

Tekelia went with her back into the house, and stood by while she made sure of the contents and order of her case.

"Will you be coming this evening?" Tekelia asked. "There is a village meeting, which will occupy me for a few hours, but you are very welcome to use the desk, or the porch, while I'm gone."

Now is the time to rectify your error, she told herself sternly, and turned to face Tekelia.

"Time with you here is everything that is pleasant," she said slowly. "But I fear we must call an end, my friend."

Tekelia blinked.

"Must we?"

"I believe so. My work is at the port; my team is at the port. To make this house my base, as much as it calls to me—it is not supportable."

"Because of the distance? But you know that all you have to do is call me. I will be pleased to take you anywhere you need to be."

"Yes, but, Tekelia, that is a misuse of your *melant'i*. I should have seen it, but—" She hesitated.

An affair of pleasure must bow to the necessities of work, she told herself. She supposed this would not be the last time she would be obliged to explain this reality, but she very much wished that it were not necessary to do so now.

"I did not take proper care of you," she managed. "Indeed, I did not see, until this morning, that of course I cannot make the very Speaker of the Haosa my taxicab. That is not seemly; and it makes your *melant'i* less than mine, when the case is far otherwise."

"Ah, *melant'i*," Tekelia said softly. "Can we not be equals?"

"We might," she said slowly, "but not while one of us is commanded by the other."

At the moment, one of Tekelia's eyes was green, the other black, and the force of that mismatched gaze was not inconsiderable.

"If you do not wish to visit, then there's nothing else to say," Tekelia said, voice strained.

Padi drew a hard breath.

"If the universe were ordered to my wishes, I would come here, to this place, to see you, whenever my work allowed."

"Hah. May I ask leave, then, to think on this? Or must we quit each other this moment?"

That, Padi thought, was a strike to the heart.

"Certainly, think on it," she said, feeling a little breathless.

"I will."

Tekelia extended a hand, and Padi met it, feeling strong fingers close warmly around hers.

"Come, I will bring you to the market square. Is that well for you?"

"Very well, I thank you."

There came the now-familiar frisson, a smear of grey—and they stood, hand-in-hand next to the walled garden and its profusion of blossoms that was the centerpiece of the Port Market Square.

"Thank you," Padi said.

Tekelia raised her hand, and she felt the pressure of warm lips against her knuckles.

"It is my pleasure to assist you."

Her hand was released, and Tekelia stepped back.

"I will be thinking. In the meanwhile—profit on your day, Trader."

There was a faint swirl, as of mist; the very slightest displacement of air.

Tekelia was gone.

You might have handled that better, Padi told herself, though she hadn't any clear idea how.

She heard a familiar voice from beyond the garden.

Yes, well.

It was time to be about business.

On-Grid
Cardfall Casino

. . . .

MAJEL WOKE AT HIS USUAL HOUR, BROKE HIS FAST WITH BREAD and jam, and carried his second cup of tea with him to his desk.

Sipping, he went over the Tree-and-Dragon info-packet again, then Portmaster krogerSlyte's notes, paying special attention to the Talents held by the team members.

Master Trader yos'Galan was a Healer; Captain Mendoza a multi-Talent; Dyoli ven'Deelin was also a Healer, and Mar Tyn pai'Fortana, a Serendipitist. Security personnel—Grad Elbin, Karna Tivit, Tima Fagen—were Deaf. Trader yos'Galan was—"Very bright," krogerSlyte had said. "Too bright for me to read."

Which meant nothing, really. As Majel understood the case, the portmaster was a very modest Truthseer, and not anything like a Sorter.

Majel carried his cup over to the window, and looked down at the morning sky reflected in the river below.

It was interesting—even disturbing—that no mention was made of the team's various Talents in their info-packet. There was a bio for each member, but that confined itself to experience at trade, fields of specialty, professional affiliations, and the like.

The résumés and info-packets Majel most usually handled listed Talent directly after the name, excepting those like him, who had no Talent to list. One immediately understood that résumés listing no Talent were those of Deaf applicants.

Had the members of the trade team expected to pass as Deaf? He frowned down at the blameless river.

It made no sense. The reason for subterfuge was to gain an advantage. There was no advantage in being Deaf. And how could they have hoped to carry off such a deception, when nearly

45

everyone they met would be able to read them, if only a very little, and know them for Talents?

Perhaps, in the wide universe, it was *not done* to...boast of one's Talents? Perhaps it was seen as a challenge? Surely, a master trader had better things to do with his time than to have his Talent evaluated at every port.

Majel sighed, and drank off what was left of his tea.

Truly, the wide universe must be very strange. He would have to mention the point of etiquette at luncheon today. The trade team surely would not wish to falsely convey to the whole of Colemeno that they were Deaf.

The comm buzzed. He went to the desk and tapped the button. "ziaGorn."

"I'd hoped you would be awake," Seylin said, sounding not so weary as he felt, though he was willing to wager that she had yet to seek her bed. "We have something that you might want to look at."

"Where?" Majel asked.

"The Yellow Room," said Seylin, and Majel sighed. Of course.

"I'll be right down," he said.

Colemenoport
Port Market

. . . .

IT WAS A PROMPT TRADER YOS'GALAN WHO JOINED THE REST OF them at the Market Master's office, her manner so perfectly placid that Shan knew a qualm. He did not, however, succumb to the urge to scan her, merely inclining his head.

"Trader Padi, a good morn to you," he murmured as she joined them at the table.

"Master Trader," she replied calmly.

Market Manager banIngi had laid out a small sampling of foodstuffs—cheese, nuts, cake *and* cookies, tea, a carafe of pale liquid that might have been wine, and juice—and had taken up the role of host with enthusiasm.

"Trader yos'Galan, welcome!" he beamed.

"Thank you, sir," she said, stepping closer. "This is very festive."

"Please sample what you will. The dawn-wine is a specialty of the Vintners Collective, and the cheese was aged in the Caverns at Rochshile. The cake and cookies are from our own Market Bakery."

"Of course," Padi murmured, skewering a piece of cheese with one of the gaily colored picks provided, and choosing a cup of juice.

She moved down-table, where she was met by Assistant Manager Saru bernRoanti, with whom she had established a rapport, and Shan heard her ask after the origins of the juice.

He sipped the last of his dawn-wine, put the glass on the tray, and glanced 'round the room.

Dyoli and Mar Tyn were speaking with an intense person who had been presented as Chief Expediter rooBios, while Priscilla gave serious attention to Financial Officer graeLi. Their security personnel—all three—were in earnest conversation with their opposite numbers in Market security.

He turned at the sound of an approaching step and smiled at Market Manager banIngi.

"A very pleasant beginning, sir," he said.

"Thank you, Master Trader. It is my pleasure to showcase our local goods, and to introduce them to those who have not yet had the felicity."

He, too, gazed around the room.

"I think we may begin the tour now, do you agree, sir?"

"I agree," Shan told him. "Will you be leading us yourself?"

"I have an hour before I am wanted elsewhere. Assistant Manager bernRoanti will take over from there. She is every bit as knowledgeable as I am."

"Excellent. Let us begin."

On-Grid
Cardfall Casino

. . . .

SEYLIN WAS WAITING FOR HIM BY THE DOOR TO THE YELLOW ROOM.

"Will it get out?" Majel asked.

"It might try," she said seriously, "though I think it's too timid. The reason I called you down—one of our Sensitives caught an Intent when we were sweeping the room just now." She sighed. "It's an unfortunate meeting of our least robust Sensitive and a rather explicit Intent. Quite gave him the headache, poor love. He ought to be lying down, but I thought you should hear it from the source."

Their least robust Sensitive was Ander makEnontre. His Talent was, according to Seylin, erratic in the extreme, so that sometimes it seemed as if he were Deaf, yet at others, he received every Intention, hope and desire within three meters. It was the erratic nature of his Talent that had made him timid, in Seylin's judgment, as he was never certain when he would be bombarded.

Majel sighed. Of course, it *would* be Ander. He might have predicted it.

"I will see him at once then," he said to Seylin. "Then he may go and get some relief."

"Yes."

She stepped aside, and Majel advanced, the door opening before him.

The play lights were off, and the Yellow Room comfortably dim. Head down, arms wrapped tight around himself, Ander leaned against the wall to the right of the door, as distant from the premium machines as he could be while remaining in the room.

"Sir!"

Ander straightened away from the wall, lifting a face that was set in pain.

49

"Ander, forgive me for putting you in harm's way," Majel said.

The boy moved his shoulders uncomfortably.

"Not your fault, sir. You didn't Intend mayhem so hard and so long the machine caught it and kept it."

"No," Majel said, without irony, "that I did not. But tell me now"—he spun on a heel so that he faced the rows of machines—"which has acquired an echo of this Intention?"

"The room master, sir."

Majel blinked. He had expected one of the floor machines. The room master was not in play. Its purpose was purely administrative. The Yellow Room was member-only; the room master kept track of key codes, account balances, losses, payouts. It kept its own accounting and deposited directly to the bank.

Majel looked at Seylin.

Seylin looked grave.

Right.

He turned back to the Sensitive.

"Is there anything else you can tell me about this mayhem, Ander? Perhaps there was a signature, or—"

There were tears in Ander's eyes.

"I wish I could, sir, but I don't have that kind of control. I—the only other thing I can say is that it feels—worn in, if you understand me, sir?"

"As if this Intention had been expressed to the room master many times?" Majel said, feeling his stomach tighten.

"Yessir, exactly that."

"I see. Thank you, Ander. Please get yourself looked after, and when you are able, go home and rest. Do you need someone to help you get to the medic?"

"No, sir. It's only a headache, and it's pretty much passed off now."

Majel frowned.

"Nonetheless," he said sternly, "you will present yourself to the medic for an examination and whatever treatment she feels will benefit you."

"Yessir." Ander took a breath and straightened to his meager height.

"You will also," Majel told him, "take your next shift off. I expect you to rest, and in light of that expectation, you will be paid for the shift."

Ander swallowed. For an instant Majel thought he would produce an argument, but after a moment, he merely inclined his head.

"Yessir. Thank you."

Seylin walked the boy out the door just as one of the casino's
courtesy jitneys pulled up. She must have sent a thought ahead,
Majel realized. That was well done.

The jitney executed a U-turn in the hallway, and Seylin came
back into the room, the door closing behind her.

"This," she said, "is not good."

"I agree. Clearly the Yellow Room cannot reopen tonight.
What progress on the main gaming rooms?"

"There were no Intentions found in either room," Seylin said,
leaning her shoulder against the wall with a sigh. "The technicians did the purge and resets, as you directed. The two main
rooms will open on time tonight."

"Good." Most of Cardfall's income came from the low- and
mid-tier machines housed in the two main rooms. But, with the
card tables *and* the Yellow Room shut to play—

Mayhem, Ander had said.

"We'll need a technician to interface with the room master,
to be certain that it's not actively causing mischief. I will call
the security firm and the bank. Seal the room, except for those
who are necessary to the room master situation."

"Yes," Seylin said, and Majel gave her a hard look.

"Take a sleep shift—this *is* an order, Seylin."

She gave him a tired smile.

"Yes, Principal ziaGorn. Nester's due back from *her* off-shift
in the next quarter. I'll bring her up to date and get some rest.
You still for that working nuncheon?"

"That—yes," he said absently, looking around the room. He
sighed.

"Does it occur to you, old friend," he said to Seylin, "that
our two problems may—*not* be related?"

"It does seem like two different hands of work," Seylin agreed.
"Maybe the chizlers are—just chizlers, after all."

"Perhaps," said Majel. "That Intention—tell me, is it possible
that it is a thing of long-standing?"

Seylin frowned.

"I see what you mean. It's normally pretty noisy in here during play. Even loud Intentions aren't *that* loud."

She sighed.

"Could be the only reason Ander heard it is because the room's empty and all the machines are asleep."

Majel closed his eyes.

Certainly, the Cardfall had been targeted in the past, by this one, or those two or three, working together. But two independent efforts against the house at the same time?

Improbably, it made him want to laugh.

He suspected that might be a panic reaction.

"Majel?" Seylin said softly.

He opened his eyes.

"Merely—speculating," he said. "I'll make those calls."

Off-Grid
The Rose Cottage

. . . .

"TEKELIA!" VAIZA SHOUTED GLEEFULLY, LEAPING TO HIS FEET AND rushing down the path. His gladness was as sincere as it was startling. Tekelia paused on the path to allow the child to continue at his own pace, alert for a misstep. When the twins had first met the Haosa, Vaiza had tried to hug Tekelia—a disaster smoothly averted by Geritsi.

They had not erred since. Still, a child might forget—most especially a lonely child in strange circumstances, his mother dead, might forget—and Tekelia held ready.

But Vaiza did not fly into an embrace. Rather, he stopped eight of his short paces back, and threw his arms wide.

"Tekelia!" he cried. "I hug you!"

There came a moment of crystal calmness, as sometimes occurred in the flow of the ambient. In that moment, Tekelia distinctly felt arms laid about their neck, the pressure of cheek against cheek, holding—and withdrawn.

Tekelia took a careful breath, allowing pleasure and pride to be seen.

"Now that was a welcome, indeed! Who taught you?"

"I taught myself," the boy asserted, glancing over his shoulder to where Geritsi and his sister were still at work among the plants. "Geritsi let me practice on her." He turned back.

"It wasn't too tight?" he asked, lowering his voice. "My first was too tight."

"It was well modulated and well placed. May I hug you in return?"

The eager eyes told the story, but Tekelia waited until the boy said, "Yes, please," before whispering to the ambient.

Vaiza closed his eyes, his arms lifting—and then falling. Carefully, Tekelia ended the embrace, and waited with some concern.

Vaiza opened his eyes—bright with unshed tears—and smiled. "Thank you. It's good to hug a friend."

"So it is," Tekelia said, thinking of Padi. "I am pleased that you're my friend."

Another smile, this without a hint of tears, before Vaiza bit his lip, apparently recalled to duty.

"Are you here to see Geritsi?"

"In fact, I am here to see you and Torin. I have some questions that I hope you will be able to help me answer. Are you at liberty?"

Vaiza glanced over his shoulder. "We're helping Geritsi with the garden."

"Then let us find if she can spare you," Tekelia said, moving slowly down the path. Vaiza stepped aside to allow clear passage, then walked along behind.

Geritsi showed them to her bookroom, and left them alone, Dosent padding silently at her heels.

The twins sat together in the wide upholstered chair near the hearth. Tekelia spun the chair out from beneath the desk and sat facing them.

Torin was solemn, her usual expression; and Vaiza half-smiling, which was his. He reached out and took his sister's hand, where it rested on her knee, and looked at Tekelia.

"What questions can we help answer?"

"The first, and most important, is—How are you faring under our care?" Tekelia said. "Do you want for anything that we can provide to you?"

Torin's mouth tightened, and she took a breath.

"Geritsi and Dosent have been everything that is kind," she said, with a steadfast formality that made her seem Vaiza's elder by years, rather than minutes.

"It would be good to go to school," Vaiza added, looking wistful. His sister bent a look of surprise on him.

"You never used to like school," she said.

"I didn't used to like the lessons, or the tests," Vaiza corrected. "But I did like the teachers and our schoolmates." He paused, nose wrinkled, and amended, "Some of our schoolmates."

He looked to Tekelia.

"Do the Haosa have a school?"

That...was something of a problem, Tekelia thought. The four children Ribbon Dance had under their care were now at The Vinery, learning what that Haosa settlement could teach them. In the usual way of things, The Vinery's children would have at the same time come to Ribbon Dance Village, only—currently The Vinery had no one to send.

Which meant that Torin and Vaiza were the only children in their keeping. The village could teach them, well enough, but the camaraderie of their agemates—that they could not provide.

There *was* a school in Pacazahno, the village hard by Peck's Market, and a number of children, too. The residents of Pacazahno were largely Deaf, leavened with a few Haosa. If the kezlBlythe were not in the equation, the twins might be sent to school there—similar arrangements had been made in the past.

The kezlBlythe, however, spoiled that easy solution.

Truly, Tekelia thought angrily, it would seem that the kezlBlythe's sole function was to spoil and lay waste.

"As you have seen, we are a very small village," Tekelia said to the twins. "In the past, when we have had only one or two students, they were tutored by the village in whole. This means that students learned skills from each household in turn."

Vaiza's face fell. Torin maintained her mask of solemn politeness.

Tekelia sighed.

"Is there any other comfort that you lack?"

"Truly, we are well cared for," Torin said, as one might have known she would.

Vaiza sighed.

"We're getting along well," he said. "And it will be fun, I think, to go among everyone in the village, and meet them, and learn from them."

It was a brave face, Tekelia thought, and smiled for the pair of them.

"I found it so, when I first came. Also, the village will be meeting this evening. Be sure that I will bring up the subject of school. Many heads together may solve what mine alone cannot."

Vaiza grinned. Torin looked polite.

Tekelia leaned slightly forward.

"We come now to my necessity. I wish to examine your patterns, your strengths and your weaknesses. Perhaps you've had others perform such examinations previously."

Torin said seriously that they had been examined, many times, at school.

"We need to be very quiet and just breathe," Vaiza amplified. "No making up stories in our heads, or thinking about the next class, or what's for tea."

"Exactly the thing," Tekelia said. "You might feel a little tickle, but nothing more, and perhaps not that. If you feel pain, or you want me to stop for any reason, say, 'Tekelia, stop,' and I will, at once."

Tekelia looked from one face to the other, evaluating serious eyes and patterns. The ambient glittered with their desire to do well.

"Any questions?" Tekelia asked.

There were none.

"Very well. Close your eyes. Let go of your thoughts, and listen to your breath, just that."

"I see colors," Vaiza said, sounding startled, "behind my eyes."

Of course he did.

"That's the ambient," Tekelia said. "Wait a moment and I'll ask it to make a quiet space for us."

The room was quiet, and the twins, too, seeming half-asleep to Tekelia's senses, their patterns laid open and vulnerable.

Tekelia spun a connection between them, and Looked.

The first thing that came clear was that Torin was, indeed, Civilized, and to a very fine degree. Small wonder that she was unhappy with her current situation, and all gods be praised that she was nothing more. Had Vaiza not been shielding her—

Looking more deeply, Tekelia found Vaiza's pattern—Haosa, indeed, and as strong as his sister—then cast about for the shield.

But, there was no shield.

No, there was something far else. A—tying together of the patterns, very subtly done—here, a thread from one tied to a corresponding thread in the other; there, a deft weaving together of Intent and Talent; there, a few gossamer threads twisted together to form one.

Tekelia's mouth dried.

Fine work—very fine work it was.

And very wrong.

Patterns were not meant to be combined in such a way. Even in the case of lifemates, the patterns together produced new threads, and new weavings, which reinforced both partners.

This had been done with great deliberation, greater skill, and an understanding of patterning that surpassed Tekelia's own.

And if it wasn't undone, the twins would eventually die of it.

Tekelia withdrew very gently, careful not to disturb a single strand of that beautiful, doomed weaving. One had gone deeper than one had intended, tracing the intricacies, assessing the strengths, searching for a single loose thread, for any sense of a release, or a key to unravel what had been done.

The ambient had shielded them so that there were no distractions for the examiner, as much as the examined, who were now asleep in fact, Vaiza's head on Torin's shoulder, and their fingers woven together.

Wholly withdrawn, Tekelia thanked the ambient, and dismissed the quiet bubble, at the same time partaking, just a little, of Chaos as it flowed back into the room.

"You did well, both!" Tekelia said brightly. "You may now ignore your breath, and make up all the stories you care to, inside of your head."

Vaiza laughed, opened his eyes and stretched. Torin did not laugh, but she did incline her head.

"Thank you," she said, "you are deft."

High praise, Tekelia thought, and meant sincerely.

"I had willing helpers."

"Do you want to hug Tekelia?" Vaiza asked his sister. She turned serious blue eyes on him.

"People who touch Tekelia get unraveled into the ambient," she said, which was precisely what she had been told.

"But I showed you how to make the air hug," Vaiza persisted.

His sister looked to Tekelia.

"I would like to hug you," she said softly, and more, so Tekelia thought, to keep the peace with her brother than from any desire of her own.

Still, good manners ought to be rewarded. Tekelia smiled. "And I would like to hug you, if you'll permit."

"Yes, please," she said, still dutiful, and Vaiza ordered, "Torin first."

It came, the feeling of arms about the neck, the faint pressure of a cheek. It was nothing so bold as her brother's salute, and Tekelia Watched Torin through the ether, trying to learn if she was only shy or—

The embrace was withdrawn.

"Now Tekelia," Vaiza commanded.

Tekelia engaged with the ambient, and hugged Torin very gently, whispering for her alone, "You're safe with us, child."

She gasped, and Tekelia felt her anger strike the ambient.

So *much* anger.

"Pel said that," Torin said, starkly—"that we were *safe*, and then Pel died, and Mother, too! Cousin Jorey killed them."

There was no mistaking the absolute certainty of that accusation.

Tekelia touched Geritsi with a thought, before asking the terrible question.

"Did you see this thing happen?"

Torin closed her eyes.

"Eet..."

Vaiza moved, wrapping his arms around his sister.

"Eet made us stay in our room," he said, looking over Torin's head to Tekelia. "He—he *growled* at Cousin Avryal when she tried to come in to us."

"After," Torin said, her face pushed against Vaiza's shoulder, "there was a—a person. To test us. And then Cousin Avryal said we were *abominations* and had to go away from Civilization and never come back."

"Eet was pleased with that," Vaiza added. "I think he was right. Cousin Avryal will never come near us here."

"Only it's so strange," Torin whispered. "I—Vaiza, remember how I used to help you with your lessons?"

"Yes. Now it's my turn to help you with yours," Vaiza said sturdily. "We'll take care of each other, like Mother said."

Geritsi arrived just then, Dosent at her side, and paused, head tilted.

Apologies, Tekelia sent her. *I asked the wrong question.*

Too easy to do, Geritsi answered.

Aloud, she said brightly, "I'm going to have some tea and cookies. Who wants to join me?"

Vaiza's response was boisterous, Torin's less so, but still eager.

"Tekelia?"

"Sadly, I'm wanted at Maradel's."

"Another time, then," said Geritsi, "when you can stay longer."

"Come back soon," said Vaiza.

"Yes," Torin echoed, moving out of her brother's embrace. "Come back soon, Tekelia."

Maradel, the village medic and Healer, opened the door, blinked, and stepped back, to allow Tekelia to enter her kitchen.

"You've Seen it, then?"

Tekelia paused, head tipped.

"Have you?"

"I have," Maradel said, moving to the counter and putting her hand against the teapot. "And I've researched it. I was going to talk to you this evening, after the meeting. Sit, Cousin, and have some tea."

Tekelia sat. Maradel brought the pot and cups to the table. Tekelia poured for them both while she went back to the cupboard.

Returning, she put a tin of jelly squares on the table between them.

She sat down, pushing the tin toward Tekelia.

"You eat, I'll talk, then we'll do roundabout."

Tekelia chose a jelly square and bit into it.

Satisfied, Maradel leaned back in her chair and picked up her cup.

"Those children have been deliberately tied together with a sure and knowing hand," she said. "I'm not telling you anything you haven't Seen for yourself. I've never Seen anything like it—not as an artifact, you understand me?"

She paused.

"I understand you, Cousin," Tekelia assured her, having dispatched the sweet and swallowed some tea.

"It's served them well so far, in terms of both being able to tolerate what one might not, but so far as I can see it, they're at the tipping point. Careful as those ties are, they're still *ties*, and they're starting to stretch both patterns."

She gulped tea.

"It's my professional opinion that the children need to be untied, sooner rather than later. And I'll tell you right now, Cousin, I'm not the one to do it."

Tekelia paused in the act of choosing another cookie, and shot Maradel a quick glance.

"No?"

"No," she said firmly, pointing a jelly square at Tekelia's nose. "And I'll tell you why that is. We, Cousin, are blunt instruments. Heavy lifting and gross manipulation are our strengths. Fine work and precision are what the Civilized train for." She took a bite out of her sweet, shaking her head as she chewed.

"I could no more have crafted that binding than I can undo it. In plain truth, the thought of touching it terrifies me." She sipped tea. "My best advice would be that we have the one who did the work undo it." She sighed. "But I suppose that's not possible."

"My guess is that the binding is their mother's work. There's an intensity—"

"Yes," Maradel said. "I felt it, too."

Tekelia drank tea.

"We are fortunate that the Warden takes an interest in these children. He will be able to find a Civilized Healer of sufficient skill to do the needful."

"Well." Maradel sat back, her relief a cool wash in the ambient. "They're in good hands, then. The Warden's a clever one, Civilized though he is."

"Yes," Tekelia said, pushing the chair back, and rising.

"Thank you, Cousin, for the gift of your expertise and advice. There is someone else I must speak to before I make that report to the Warden, and I don't want to be late for tonight's meeting."

"I understand," Maradel said, rising to open the door.

"Until soon, Cousin," she said.

"Until soon."

It had been difficult to find the last person Tekelia wished to interview—so difficult, in fact, one might have concluded that the prospective interviewee was... hiding.

Perseverance won out, however, and the culprit run to ground— or rather, to tree—in the orchard, where a wide branch offered a pleasant location to lie on the back and sun the belly, after it had been filled with fruit.

"Young Eet," Tekelia said, leaning a shoulder against the tree and smiling down into a startled furry face. "Let us dream together."

Colemenoport
Offices of
Tree-and-Dragon Trade Mission

. . . .

THE LUNCHEON TRAYS HAD COME, NOT FROM THE PORT MARKET caterer, as Majel had assumed they would, but from Skywise Provianto, on Schoodic Street in the port.

That was notable for two reasons. It was Majel's own favorite eating establishment on Colemenoport, not only because it was Deaf-owned and operated, but because the food was superior to the Port Market's offerings, and at half the cost.

The trays presented very well, with various breads, cheeses, and other food appropriate to a working meal. The cake, he saw with amusement, was indeed on offer.

He had been caught up by the master trader on arrival, and made known to "Priscilla Delacroix y Mendoza, captain of *Dutiful Passage*. Dyoli ven'Deelin, adjunct trader, representing Clan Ixin, our partner in this survey. Mar Tyn pai'Fortana, assisting Trader ven'Deelin. Our security team—Grad Elbin, Karna Tivit, and Tima Fagen. And Trader Padi yos'Galan, whom you have previously met."

The younger trader gave him a smile and a nod.

"Councilor ziaGorn, it's good to see you again."

"Excellent!" the master trader declared. "The first order of business for this working nuncheon is—assembling nuncheon. Councilor ziaGorn, will you lead us?"

"Chief Expediter rooBios has asked me to give a presentation to his section regarding just-in-time delivery, deep inventory, and typical turnaround times," Dyoli ven'Deelin said, in answer to the master trader's query. She was plump and red-haired, her eyes blue and slightly dreamy, as if, Majel thought, the opportunity to give a presentation on delivery protocols was a rare and special treat.

The master trader nodded, and glanced down at the notepad by his plate.

"I will open the appropriate files, so that you may review them and get a feel for how we managed in the past," he said. "We cannot deal in specifics, given that we are so new on-port."

"Understood. I did have the feeling that Expediter rooBios wishes to have a general lesson laid for his section. He said to me that they had been operating in the same way for so long, he feared that they had come to think that there was only one way to go on, and that they have refined their methods to—" She paused, lips twitching.

"Perfection?" guessed the master trader.

"I was going to say *near* perfection, as the expediter did, himself."

"That's a hopeful sign," said Captain Mendoza, who was possibly the most beautiful woman Majel had ever seen, despite being outlandishly tall. "If they know that their system can be improved, they may be helped to see that there are other systems."

"My goal will be to show them exactly that," Trader ven'Deelin said. "Since I will be limited to generalities, I may introduce several systems, to—"

She frowned, as if groping after a phrase.

"To shake up their certainties?" Trader yos'Galan murmured.

"That, yes. And also to—my brother had used to say, quick-start their thinking."

"*Gently* quick-start their thinking," the master trader said. "We have time for several discussions, and will obviously need to be more thoroughly informed regarding the near-perfect systems already in place."

"Yes, sir. I anticipate at least one follow-up meeting with the section, once they have had a chance to think."

"Excellent." The master trader smiled at her. "Those files are open to you, now."

He glanced down the table.

"Priscilla?"

"I've been invited by Yard Master tineMena to the next meeting of the Port Authority Readiness Committee," she said. "Their facilities haven't been upgraded since before the Dust arrived, and they'd like a *modern eye* on them."

That visit, Majel thought, from his place at the master trader's right hand, could snare the trade mission a customer, for surely the traders would have catalogs and contacts and be pleased to assist with the purchase of new equipment.

Indeed, the info-packet had not held shy of stating that the mission was firstly interested in establishing trade. One expected that trade ships were expensive to operate, and even with the Dust's departure, the Redlands were inconveniently located. That had been part of the charm for the original settlers, and had certainly attracted Clans Korval and Ixin, racing against time to bring Liad's Small Talents well out of peril.

No one had thought that the Council would send eliminators after those who had decided to leave the homeworld. But no one wanted to make it easier for them, should eliminators suddenly come into play.

"Trader Padi?" the master trader said. "What gay roistering is in your future?"

The young trader smiled, and used her chin to point at the notepad by her hand.

"I have letters from at least half a dozen people of those we met at yesterday's reception. I am invited to call, to either bring or receive catalogs—on several instances to do both. Also, I have a meeting with Trader Isfelm at her office in just a few minutes, and I ought to leave now." She inclined her head gracefully.

"Forgive me, master trader. I had not thought the tour would go quite so long."

"Neither did I," the master trader said. "What, beyond Trader Isfelm?"

"Back to the market. Saru—Assistant Manager bernRoanti—asked that I call this afternoon. She has a point she would like clarified. Is there any errand I might accomplish for you while I am out on port?"

"None that springs to mind. Come to me here, when you are done with your obligations, and let us go through our lists of invitations, for I do not hide from you, Trader Padi, that I have been getting similar letters."

"Yes, sir."

She stood, Security Officer Tima Fagen rising with her, and bowed to the table.

"Until soon," she said, and left them, her security trailing after.

The master trader looked around the table.

"Grad? I saw you talking with market security. Did you gain any insights?"

"Yes, sir, we did," said Security Officer Grad with enthusiasm. "They'd noticed we didn't have a Talent on our team, and had—questions. Good questions, and a couple of tips. We'd like to sit down together and"—he grinned—"talk security shop, get some idea of how the port operates, what we might be up against, in terms of safety measures."

"This sounds worthwhile," the master trader said. "Do set up a meeting to share information and techniques. Understand that I do not wish to say that we can do very well without you, but for a few hours—"

"No, sir," Grad said, shaking his head. "We'll keep you covered. After—" He closed his mouth abruptly, and looked down at his plate; looked up again.

"We'll keep you covered, sir."

The master trader considered him for a moment before inclining his head.

"Thank you, Grad. We appreciate your care."

"Thank *you*, sir," Security Officer Grad murmured and picked up his cup, more, so Majel thought, to stop himself from saying anything else than because he craved fruit juice just then.

"Councilor ziaGorn," the master trader murmured, then, and Majel lifted his gaze to meet those calm silver eyes.

"Now that you have seen us in action, sir, and know the awful whole, have you any advice to give us, or observations to make?"

Majel smiled.

"The awful whole is scarcely awful, sir. I believe that Colemeno is fortunate in its first new trader after-Dust. However, there is a matter of—local custom, as I believe you dignify it, sir—that I feel I must discuss."

"By all means," the master trader said, leaning back in his chair. "We do not wish to err against custom."

He inclined his head.

"Show me our error."

"Yes, sir. It is in your information packet."

He paused to look around the table. Captain Mendoza gave him a small, encouraging smile. Trader ven'Deelin gazed at him with blue eyes abruptly sharp. Mar Tyn pai'Fortana sat quietly, as he had throughout the nuncheon, watching and listening with every evidence of interest. The two remaining of the security detail were politely waiting for his revelation.

Majel drew a deep breath.

"Specifically, the biographies in the information packet," he said, looking back to Master Trader yos'Galan.

"On Colemeno, it is done to list one's Talent directly after one's name, in order to give the Civilized all of the information they must have in order to treat with one appropriately."

The master trader's eyebrows rose. He glanced at Captain Mendoza, then to Dyoli ven'Deelin and Mar Tyn pai'Fortana.

"That is a very interesting custom," he said, returning his gaze to Majel's face. "Unique, in my experience."

"On Sintia," Captain Mendoza murmured, "the Talented are brought into the Temple and trained as priestesses."

The master trader nodded.

"Very true. And the priesthood have distinctive clothing, which must be thought to give sufficient notice to all."

Another glance to the captain.

"Your pardon, Priscilla."

"None needed; it's perfectly true."

"Trader ven'Deelin, do you have any objection to having your Talent listed in your biography in the mission literature?"

"I do not," Dyoli ven'Deelin said, crisply. "I am, in fact, a Healer, and if called, I will serve."

"And I," said Captain Mendoza calmly, "have no objection, but I wonder what we might call me."

Majel shifted, and her ebony gaze was immediately on him.

"Please, Councilor ziaGorn. I welcome your advice."

He took a breath.

"As I understand from Portmaster krogerSlyte's notes, Captain, you are a strong multi-Talent."

"Am I?" She turned her smile to the master trader. "I have no objection."

"Excellent."

"Master pai'Fortana? Have you any objections to having your Talent listed as part of the trade mission's info-packet?"

Majel relaxed, expecting another agreement. Mar Tyn pai'Fortana was insignificant in comparison to the rest of the team. Surely, he would follow where stronger Talents did not hesitate.

However—

"Yes, I do have objections," he said firmly, and looked, not to the master trader, but to Trader ven'Deelin. The tight line of his mouth eased somewhat, and he looked then to Majel.

"At least—I have questions," he amended.

"I will be pleased to answer your questions to the best of my ability," Majel assured him. "If my answers are not adequate, then I will bring Portmaster krogerSlyte into the discussion, so that you may be satisfied."

In addition to being the least of the team, Mar Tyn pai'Fortana was insignificant in his person—the smallest in the room, by height and girth, with neither beauty nor, so Majel had supposed from his reticence, wit. Still, the man had questions, and if Majel read this correctly, some distrust of the Civilized.

Well. He could certainly sympathize with that.

"Thank you," said Mar Tyn pai'Fortana. "I offer information which you may not have. I am a Luck, born on Liad. I came of age in Solcintra Low Port, which is a dumping ground for those of whom the... civilized... do not approve. Lucks are distrusted, reviled, abused, used, and thrown away. We die young, as a rule. I am an anomaly, having survived my thirty-sixth Standard." He reached for his cup, but merely turned it this way and that, until he raised his eyes again to Majel.

"Perhaps I was lucky. Understand that I mean to say that it was not—it was *never*—in my own best interest to declare my Gift, even when my Gift was my means of survival."

He took a breath. Majel held his tongue, hearing the anger in the soft voice.

"I would not expose myself to more abuse. And now I ask: What is the policy of the *Civilized*, regarding Lucks?"

Majel did not look away from that angry gaze.

"Civilization understands you as a Serendipitist, Master pai'Fortana. There *are* certain constraints placed upon Serendipitists. For example, I own a casino. You may not enter my business, and you may be asked to distance yourself from a very short list of events, which are codified in Civilization's charter. I will look up the relevant section and send it to you this evening, so that you may be informed."

He took thought, and added, "There is no Low Port here,

Master pai'Fortana. You have a particular, recognized Gift. You are, according to Civilization's laws and charter, a Talent. Civilized."

Mar Tyn pai'Fortana frowned.

"But you—are you *not* Civilized?"

Majel drew a breath, a little sharper than he had intended. Surely, everyone in the room, absent Security, was aware of his handicap.

Mar Tyn pai'Fortana raised a hand, showing empty palm and widespread fingers.

"Forgive me. I did not mean to distress you, after you have given me such a fine and honest answer. But I have lived beyond the limits of civilization. I think that I see certain...kindred signs."

His distress was on display, Majel understood, with chagrin. That was poorly done. He produced an official smile.

"I am what Civilization is pleased to term Deaf. This means that I have no Talent for working with the ambient. Indeed, the ambient is invisible to me."

He paused, then added, "According to Civilization's charter, the Deaf are a vulnerable population, deserving of protection."

It might have been sympathy he saw on Mar Tyn pai'Fortana's face before the other man inclined his head.

"Thank you for that information. I look forward to receiving the sections from Civilization's charter."

"We all thank you for your forthrightness and care, Councilor ziaGorn," the master trader said gently. "Have you anything else for us? Is there any way in which we may serve you?"

Majel shook himself.

"I think not, Master Trader. I thank you for the opportunity to participate in a working nuncheon, and hope to enjoy another, soon."

The master trader smiled.

"You will be most welcome," he said.

On-Grid
The Wardian

. . . .

HIS MORNING MEETINGS FINISHED, AND, FOR A WONDER, NOTHING
scheduled for the afternoon, Bentamin sat in his office with a cup
of tea, a plate of Entilly's cookies, and his mail.

According to *The Record*, the Council of the Civilized had
named an official liaison to the Tree-and-Dragon Trade Mission—
and an interesting choice it was.

Not only was Majel ziaGorn a very new member of the
Council, but his presence was due to his position as the Chair
of the Citizens Coalition, which was rather new, itself—formed
a mere thirty Standards ago, to "ensure that the Citizens of
Civilization, referred to casually as 'the Deaf,' had their proper
voice in governance."

The first Citizens Chair had lived only a few years after her
hard-won success, succeeded by Durella vinsEbin, who had managed to put forth legislation that allowed Citizens to hold their
own businesses without being required to have a Civilized mentor
review and approve every decision, as well as making it legal for
Deaf and Civilized to marry.

Those had not been inconsiderable gains. Unfortunately, the
strain of the continuing push for Citizen equality had taken
its toll on vinsEbin's soul, and she had—wisely, in Bentamin's
opinion—retired from her post in favor of Majel ziaGorn, owner
of a casino, employer of both Civilized and Deaf, whose father had
been among the first to take advantage of the new law allowing
him to dismiss his Civilized mentor.

Majel ziaGorn was shrewd, ambitious, well-educated, and
occasionally naive. vinsEbin had never modified her aggressive
approach to her fellow Councilors. On the other hand, ziaGorn

proceeded as if he were equal, as the law allowed, and that there was no question he would provide valuable insight into any debate.

He had not yet put forth any legislation, but Bentamin had a hunch that he was biding his time.

And now, he had apparently proposed himself as the Council's liaison to the trade mission, with the support of krogerSlyte. *That* was interesting, too. If there was anything in life that Urta krogerSlyte loved more than Colemenoport, Bentamin had not heard of it. That she was willing to have ziaGorn, both ambitious and Deaf, in a position that might equally do great good, or grievous harm to—

"Your pardon, Warden," his assistant said through the intercom. "Tekelia vesterGranz, Speaker for the Haosa, is here to see you regarding *ongoing business.*"

Tekelia *here*?

Bentamin blinked—then snorted. Turnabout was fair play, after all, and even more so, were one Haosa.

"I will see Speaker vesterGranz," he said, rising and moving to the front of his desk.

The door opened, and Tekelia stepped through, looking every bit the Civilized merchant, hair neatly braided; long vest over silky shirt and soft trousers.

"Warden." Very grave, with a slight inclination from the waist.

"Speaker," Bentamin replied, with matching gravity. He looked beyond Tekelia, where his assistant hovered in the door. "Speaker vesterGranz and I will want an hour, Luzant macNamara."

"Yes, Warden."

She retreated and closed the door. Bentamin turned his hands palm up.

"Good afternoon, Cousin. May I offer you tea and cookies?"

"I have examined the children," Tekelia said, after they had settled into the soft chairs, tea and cookies on the table between them. "I confirm that Vaiza's Talent interacts directly with the ambient. I confirm that Torin is Civilized."

Bentamin shifted forward in his chair.

"You did not bring her with you? Is she at risk?"

Tekelia moved a hand.

"She is not in immediate danger. There is somewhat more—will you hear it?"

"I will. Forgive me, Cousin. My entire family is abrupt and graceless."

Tekelia laughed.

"Well, that's so, isn't it? To continue, after I completed my examination, I spoke with Medic arnFaelir. She supports my reading that the children are entwined a-purpose, likely by their mother, as protection. While they lived Civilized, Torin led them, and compensated for her brother's lacks. Off-Grid, it is Vaiza who leads, and protects his sister from the effects of the ambient."

Bentamin stared.

"Entwined," he repeated.

"In fact. Their patterns have been tied, and in some cases woven together, producing, if you will, a single system, which serves both sets of needs. This is why Torin is in no danger while she remains tied to her brother. However."

Tekelia paused to eat a cookie and sip tea. Bentamin did the same.

"It is Medic arnFaelir's professional opinion," Tekelia said, "that the twins ought to be separated—sooner, rather than later—to prevent long-term damage to both."

"See it done," Bentamin said, slowly, "and deliver Torin to me. The Wardian will keep her."

"And her brother?" Tekelia asked dryly.

Bentamin frowned.

"Her brother is a Wild Talent. He will naturally remain with you—the Haosa, I mean to say."

"I daresay." Tekelia's tone was even drier.

Bentamin glared.

"I am being obtuse, I gather."

"Yet another family marker," Tekelia murmured.

Bentamin waited, and eventually Tekelia met his eyes.

"Torin and Vaiza are twins. They have been together since before birth. They are even closer than simply twins, due to this entanglement that has been provided to them. Their mother is dead, and their mother's consort."

Bentamin moved a hand.

"Yes," Tekelia said. "In a word, they will miss each other. Separating them immediately will wound both. Periodic visits will not be enough. They are not only used to seeing each other daily; they are used to seeing each other *hourly*. Eventually, given the resolution of the entanglement, they will grow more able to be apart and to live their separate lives. But that may not be for some years."

Bentamin stared.

"Torin cannot stay off-Grid," he said. "Once she is disentangled, and no longer partaking of her brother's Talent, she will break. Even if she were helped to build the sort of shield that might protect her, to live without accessing her Talent—it would be cruel."

"Indeed, it would. Whereas Haosa may thrive, on-Grid or off. A child who has not yet come into the fullness of his Talent might not even find the constraints imposed by the Grid... too irritating."

Bentamin reached for his teacup.

"I could have them both here... for a time, I suppose. But you know as well I do, Cousin, that in the end Vaiza must go to the Haosa."

"I may know that now," Tekelia said. "It might be that I will know something different, years from now. But, Bentamin, rough ground remains before us."

"Which is?"

"Medic arnFaelir professes herself a blunt instrument, and as such unequal to the task of disentangling the children. The thing was done with such precision, such care—truly, Bentamin, you ought to visit and see for yourself. That aside, our medic advises that the needful work be done by a Civilized Healer, who will have been rigorously trained in such fine work."

"Ah." Bentamin put his cup down. "I will engage to find a Healer of sufficient skill. It may take some little while, but I understand that the danger is not acute."

"That is correct. The Haosa will—your pardon. I *imagine* that the Haosa will keep Torin and Vaiza safe from the attentions of their kin. The question is on the agenda of tonight's meeting. If my imaginings are proved wrong, then you will fall guardian."

"I can take them now," Bentamin said slowly. "And lessen the danger to the Haosa. The Wardian is formidable."

"As is the ambient. And the kezlBlythe *are* Civilized. We are twice protected."

"Fair enough. I will contact you when an appropriate Healer

has been located." He began to rise—and settled again as Tekelia remained seated.

"I wonder, Bentamin—are you very eager to deal with the kezlBlythe as they deserve?"

"Cousin, that is fast becoming my ruling desire."

"In that case, you might be interested to learn that there was an eyewitness to Zatorvia xinRood's murder."

Colemenoport
Offices of
The Iverson Loop

. . . .

"I'LL BE TAKING AN EVEN DOZEN OF THOSE ADAPTERS," TRADER Isfelm said, looking down at her notepad. "You can deliver 'em to Trans-Three." She looked up to meet Padi's eye, her own slightly humorous.

"That is, *can* you deliver 'em to Trans-Three?"

Padi considered her. Trader Isfelm was an example of what Vanz had let her know was a device found in popular romances along the Edges—a Dust Cousin, long cut off, and raised in alien circumstances, suddenly reunited with the main family. According to the romances, Dust Cousins were as common as port dust. In real life, Vanz supposed there might be as many as one or two.

And of course Trader Isfelm, a Clan Korval offshoot via Line yos'Phelium, *would be* the exception that proved the rule.

"I will not myself be making the delivery," she said to those faintly mischievous eyes. "However, I repose every confidence that Cargo Master ira'Barti will accomplish the thing with aplomb."

One corner of the straight mouth lifted, and Trader Isfelm glanced back to her notepad.

"Always good to be confident of your team," she said. "I can make that transfer now, if you like, Trader."

"Half up, to seal the deal, Trader," Padi returned firmly. "I have an account at Colemenoport Merchant Trust."

"Solid choice," Trader Isfelm murmured. Her fingers moved on the keypad, light and quick, the room lights glittering across the many facets of the big, gaudy ring she wore. Many might find such a ring in poor taste. Padi, daughter of a clan of pilots, and a pilot herself, knew it for the treasure it was: a Jump-pilot's cluster, old and precious beyond the worth of the gems that adorned it.

The trader finished her input, and put the notepad on the table before Padi.

"Your thumbprint, please, Trader."

She obliged. Trader Isfelm took the notepad back, applied her thumb to the screen, and sat gazing downward, but not, Padi thought, at the screen.

She was looking at her ring.

"Is there some other matter in which I may assist you?" Padi murmured.

Trader Isfelm looked up.

"You know, there just might be." She paused, brows pulled, as if considering how best to proceed.

"It's clear Redlands-talk is close enough to what you're used to or we'd be having this conversation in Old Trade, but I'll lay odds it scrapes against your ear." Trader Isfelm raised a considering eyebrow. "And that's not to mention the bows."

Padi tipped her head. "As traders, we of course have a great deal of forbearance," she murmured.

"Oh, that goes without saying," Trader Isfelm assured her. "I'm only meaning to ask that, if—let's take a personal example. If I was to walk off a ship in Solcintraport, talking Redlands like I am to you, would I be understood?"

Ah. Not an unworthy question. Trader Isfelm had been not at all shy regarding her desire to go, as she expressed it, *Out*, which proved her Line even more than her possession of the ring. Padi had not understood that the trader's ambition had included raising the homeworld, itself.

She leaned back in her chair.

"Understood—yes. Open to spite and protests of *not* being understood—that, too."

"So, I'd be laughed at? Treated like a barbarian?"

Padi frowned.

"That might be the best case, yes."

"Hah. Then I do wonder if you can help me, Trader. I require a complete set of Liaden language tapes. For these, I will give language tapes for Redlands-speak, and also for the other three dialects spoken along the Iverson Loop."

"I have an interest," Padi said promptly. "Also, I offer additional information pertinent to your side of the bargain."

"I am buying," Trader Isfelm told her.

"There is no price for the information I now share: First and most importantly, Clan Korval has been banished from the homeworld, and forbidden to return, in whole or in part."

"Read that in the mission's information packet," Trader Isfelm said, with great unconcern. "Shouldn't be an issue, unless you're thinking to adopt."

Padi inclined her head.

"I wish to be certain that you have adequate and up-to-date information."

"'Preciate that."

"If you do wish to raise Liad, and want neither to be laughed at nor challenged to a duel, you will want to study the most recent edition of the *Liaden Code of Proper Conduct*, and review *A Child's Guide to Melant'i*."

She paused. Trader Isfelm waited.

"The second work was written by Scholar Jen Sar Kiladi, a Liaden, for Terran consumption. It is quite the best work on the topic, according to a number of scholarly reviewers. I offer a file of the reviews as part of the additional information shared freely."

"I accept your gift of information. In return, I offer a list of the most untrustworthy trade banks, cargo agents, and bars along the Iverson Loop."

"I accept," Padi said, adding truthfully, "A handsome gift."

Trader Isfelm waggled her fingers.

"Only a list of mistakes already made. There's no need to make them again."

Padi laughed.

"Very true! Especially when there are perfectly terrifying new errors out there awaiting our attention."

Trader Isfelm grinned.

"We think alike, eh? Maybe not so surprising. I wonder—have you time for one more question? I don't want to keep you from other business—"

"I've still some time 'til my next meeting," Padi said. "How may I serve you?"

"I wonder if *Dutiful Passage* would be willing to take—again, let us make it personal—me aboard, when they leave the Redlands to go back Out." She tipped her head. "I have various skills, which I would of course place at the service of the ship. Or I might go as a passenger, if that was preferred."

Yes, of course. Trader Isfelm *did* intend to go Out. One wondered what the loss of their lead trader might mean for the Iverson Loop, but Trader Isfelm was an astute woman. She would make such arrangements as she found wise and prudent.

Only—

Padi turned her hands palm up.

"This question is for the captain or the master trader, not for the junior trader."

"Of course it is. I'll inquire of the master trader the next time we meet." Trader Isfelm put her notepad to one side, and rose. "I'll send that list of errors to you this evening, Trader, and I look forward to your file of reviews."

"Yes," Padi said, closing her case and rising in her turn. "The adapter kits will be delivered to Transition Point Three within the next twenty-four hours."

"All good. Here, Trader, let me walk you to the door."

Off-Grid
The Tree House

· · · · · · · · · · · · · · · ·

IT WAS A FINE, CLEAR EVENING, AND THE RIBBONS HAD RISEN joyously to their nightly dance.

Tekelia vesterGranz stood on the balcony overlooking the shadow-filled forest, thinking.

The village meeting was scheduled for an hour hence, to be followed, naturally, by a shared meal. As village meetings went, this one bid fair to be lively. The Haosa stinted very little, least of all their emotions, and as a group they tended to feel keenly. The topic of tonight's meeting being the welfare and safekeeping of two small orphans, emotions were certain to run both high and hot.

But it was not the meeting, nor even the children, that occupied Tekelia's mind.

Rather, it was a pair of speaking lavender eyes in a strong, intelligent face, her quick wit, her laughter, and her moments of dense thought.

The press of her fingers, the casual rubbing of elbows, the touch of skin against skin—those were treasures beyond telling, and dangerous, too.

So very, very dangerous.

Tekelia was Haosa; it was no stretch to understand that danger was part of the attraction. Those who lived fully open to the ambient had a fine taste for peril.

And, to say truth, as an instance of Chaos Itself, Tekelia was more than a little dangerous.

Tekelia sighed, leaning elbows on the rail.

The sparkling shadows grew more vivid as the sky darkened toward full night. Soon, it would be time to leave for the meeting.

But Tekelia did not move.

Who knew that touch could be addictive?

Delightful, certainly—and a delight to which Tekelia was peculiarly vulnerable, having been without it for half a lifetime.

Children of Chaos paid for their close relationship with the ambient. They touched no one, and no one touched them, not when the mere brush of a hand would fling a person's essence out from their body into the ambient.

Only, Padi yos'Galan remained stubbornly resident in her body, even when fully embraced, and seemed to feel not even the slightest bit unsettled.

Padi yos'Galan was a trader, from outworld and far away. Traders did not stay in one place. Particularly, young, eager traders did not stay on Colemeno when there were dozens of new markets only waiting for her to open them.

Truly, Tekelia had expected to lose the grace of her touch—eventually. To lose it *now*, for something so trivial as *melant'i*—

No, that was hardly just. *Melant'i* meant a great deal to Liadens, and it was a mark of regard that Padi should wish to protect Tekelia's.

Still, it *was* a trivial thing, for Tekelia to transport Padi to—wherever she wished to go. While teleportation was not a common Talent, those so Gifted tended to be robust. Bentamin, Tekelia had often thought, must be especially strong, to be able to manage the distances he did, working under the Grid. As a Child of Chaos, Tekelia scarcely noticed the Grid's effect, though—

Tekelia blinked.

It would be...an impertinence...to brand Padi yos'Galan a Child of Chaos—no. An inaccuracy. Demonstrably, her touch was harmless, even under the ambient's full blare. However, it could not be denied that she was a very strong multi-Talent, and—perhaps—not *quite* Civilized. Whoever had been given the teaching of her had been strangely reticent, especially in comparison to Haosa teaching. Well. Likely her tutor had been Civilized, and only able to teach as they knew.

Still, there was nothing to say that she could not learn in the Haosa style.

It was, Tekelia thought, with a significant lightening of mood, worth a try.

Colemenoport
Offices of the
Tree-and-Dragon Trade Mission

. . . .

THE MASTER TRADER WAS AT THE DESK WHEN PADI RETURNED to the offices, his attention on the screen and his face austere in concentration.

Padi came forward, put her case on the edge of the desk, took off her jacket and draped it over the back of the visitors chair.

The master trader raised his eyes from the screen.

"Good evening, Trader Padi. You look quite worn out, if you will allow me the liberty of saying so."

"I *am* quite worn out," Padi told him, with feeling. "And surely it's no liberty for one's master to comment on one's condition."

"Former master. You are your own trader now."

"Yet the ties persist," she said.

There was, she noted, no glass by his hand.

"I'm for a cup of cold tea," she said. "May I bring you refreshment?"

"Cold tea sounds delightful," he said, and raised an eyebrow. "You will forgive me if I am out of bounds, but is this perhaps an occasion where cake might be in order?"

"It may be at that." Padi sighed. "Shall I serve at the desk, or the table?"

"The desk, of your kindness. We can sort out these invitations while we refresh ourselves."

The cake was, Padi admitted, finishing a slice and brushing off her fingers, remarkably restorative. She sipped tea. Across the desk, the master trader nodded once, tapped the screen, and leaned back in his chair, glass in hand.

"So, there's your schedule set for tomorrow," he said. "There are a large number of visits."

"There are," Padi agreed. "On the other hand, if Colemeno is to be one of my frequent ports, I should make contacts early and cement them going forward."

"Very true," the master trader said gravely, and lifted his glass, as if in a toast.

"You missed a very interesting interaction at nuncheon, between Councilor ziaGorn and our own Master pai'Fortana, who displayed both forthrightness and grace. We will speak of it more over the meal, so that you may have the benefit of multiple viewpoints of that exchange.

"In the meantime, I am bound to tell you that we have been inept. On Colemeno, biographies, and other business materials, carry, in addition to the principal's name, their Talent."

Padi frowned.

"Why?"

"Why, so that the Civilized will know precisely what it is they are dealing with, when they deal."

"It seems a misuse of *melant'i*," Padi said. "We are here as traders, not as Healers, or, or Witches, or Lucks."

"Very true. And yet—local custom."

"Did Mar Tyn object to having his Talent listed?" Padi asked.

"Very shrewd, Trader Padi. He did, indeed, and waxed eloquent in his reasons. Councilor ziaGorn has promised to send relevant sections of the Council's charter to Master pai'Fortana, so we may hear more of that over the meal, also."

He finished his cake, and set the plate aside.

"I am constrained to put the question in Councilor ziaGorn's stead. Trader yos'Galan, have you any objection to having your Talent listed as part of your biography included in the trade mission's info-packet?"

Padi frowned.

"Let me think on it, please. I note that no one precisely knows what my Talent *is*, which may be a challenge in terms of full disclosure. But, also—it makes me uneasy. I would like to understand why."

"Excellent. There is, as I understand it, no rush."

He lifted his cup.

"How fares Trader Isfelm?"

"Well enough. We agreed on delivery of a dozen conversion kits, to Transition Point Three. I will this evening send delivery instructions to Cargo Master ira'Barti. Trader Isfelm is fixed in her determination to go *Out*. We are in negotiations for Liaden language modules, the most recent edition of The Code, and *A Child's Guide to Melant'i*. There has been an on-faith exchange of information—on my side, the information that language tapes are not quite enough to preserve one's life at Solcintraport; on hers a list of untrustworthy operators to be found along the Iverson Loop."

"There's a good day's trading. *Ge'shada*, Trader Padi."

"Thank you." Padi sighed and sat back.

"You should know that Trader Isfelm approached me in regard to shipping Out on the *Passage* when she leaves Colemeno. I referred her to the master trader and the captain."

"Very good. I have an appointment upcoming with Trader Isfelm. I expect we'll chat about that then. Regarding the language modules."

"Yes, sir."

"Do we know the state of Trader Isfelm's learning equipment? Or if the files we have on offer are compatible?"

Padi sighed.

"Neither of us thought of that," she said ruefully. "I blame a lack of cake."

"Could very well be it," the master trader acknowledged gravely. "I am promised to send the trader some files this evening. I will mention the matter of compatibility to her in the covering note."

"Neatly solved!"

He put his glass on the desk, turned to the screen, and shut it down.

"I believe that your father would like to go home, my child, and partake of an hour's rest, a glass of wine, and a meal before the master trader engages on this evening's work. Are you with me?"

"I am," Padi said, rising and gathering the cups and plates. "I will just put these in the washer."

On-Grid
Cardfall Casino

. . . .

MAJEL CIRCULATED BETWEEN THE TWO MAIN ROOMS, GREETING known clients and introducing himself to those few he did not recognize.

Against expectation, the Yellow Room was open this evening as well, though with limited play. Still, those who paid for access to the elite machines and a moderated environment were accommodated, and if there were fewer machines available to play than usual, they were newer, and more challenging, while the explanation that an up-to-the-minute room master had been installed satisfied the few questions that arose.

There remained the question of how all this was going to be paid for. Granted, if the vids and the experts proved tampering, then half the repair or replacement cost would be borne by the company who had supplied the machines. Still, the casino's share was . . . not trivial.

"Principal ziaGorn!" Majel felt his sleeve caught by Esmir pentOrnil, one of the more demanding, if not *the* most demanding, of Cardfall's regulars. "The Sixes table is closed!"

"So it is," Majel said, his voice reasonable and calm. "I was hoping that I would see you this evening. We are in the process of producing an exclusive card room. Have you time to give me input on our design?"

pentOrnil's eyes widened, and he shifted to slide his arm through Majel's.

"I am at your service, Principal ziaGorn," he said.

"Excellent," Majel said, not entirely untruthful. "Let us go to my booth in the bar, and I will show you what we have in mind."

Off-Grid
Ribbon Dance Village
Meeting Hall

. . . .

"WELL, OF COURSE THEY'LL STAY WITH US!" YFEREN EXCLAIMED. "Where else would the poor wee things go—Ukarn?"

There was a general murmur of agreement with this sentiment, which was no surprise, either to Tekelia or to Village Administrator Arbour poginGeist.

"No one can argue with your instincts," Arbour assured Yferen. "Of course, we wish to shelter and preserve the innocent. The Haosa are rightly known as champions of the defenseless. These children call to our instinct to protect. But the children are not the only vulnerable parties in this."

"What, is Civilization in need of us again?" asked Kencia, who had not much love for those on-Grid. "We had best draw up a schedule of fees, Cousins."

"That has been under discussion," Tekelia said. "But in the case, no—the other vulnerable party is—ourselves."

The response to this was blank silence. The Haosa were accustomed to thinking of themselves as tough, resourceful, and strong.

Nor were they wrong. If they had a fault as a group, it was that they undervalued guile and deceit.

"The children are sent to us by their cousins kezlBlythe, who expected them to fail."

"Yet, they have not failed," Arbour murmured.

"They have not failed," Maradel reiterated from the front row. Tekelia gave her a nod.

"Wherein lies our danger, Cousins. View the matter from the stance of the kezlBlythe. Vaiza and Torin are the last of xinRood, which kezlBlythe has made it their business to eradicate. It has been supposed by the Warden and others who pay attention to such matters, on-Grid, that the kezlBlythe wanted xinRood's fortune."

Tekelia paused and looked over the room. The gathered Haosa were rapt, as who would not be, given such a story?

"Vaiza and Torin are only eight years old. The kezlBlythe stand to gain everything they were thought to want, upon their deaths. The Warden allows us to know, Cousins, that eliminating two small children and their guardian norbear would disturb kezlBlythe sleep not at all."

"Instead," Arbour murmured, "they were sent to us."

Tekelia nodded.

"And the Warden—who is not an idiot—wonders what has, in this last, straightforward matter, kept the kezlBlythe's knife in its sheath."

"Perhaps they thought the Warden was watching too closely, and they would be cheated of their profits," said Yferen.

"Perhaps," said Banedra, "they thought the ambient would do their work for them."

While not out of the kezlBlythe's range, it had a sobering effect on the gathered Haosa. Off-Grid was no place for Civilized children, where even well-shielded and sober adults might become erratic under the influence of the ambient.

"I have examined the children, as Tekelia has. They show no signs of breaking under the ambient," Maradel said. "I speak with Geritsi daily, and with Torin and Vaiza. They are somewhat more subdued than I like to see in children, but that's not surprising, given their losses. They are beginning to trust Geritsi a little, and of course Dosent is a favorite."

A chuckle ran the room at this—what child could resist a waist-high feline who would occasionally allow herself to be persuaded to bear *very good* children on her back?

"So they outsmarted themselves?" asked Tanin the baker. He looked at Arbour. "The kezlBlythe, I'm meaning. If the twins are alive, the kezlBlythe don't profit. The youngers hold what's theirs, even if they're not Civilized."

That was, Tekelia acknowledged, how the law was written, though it was often enough circumvented by the sorts of *qe'andra* the kezlBlythe chose to serve them. However—

"They may have done," Tekelia said. "But, Cousins, I confess to you, I hear a question in the ambient. And the question is:

What do they want? It seems to me that it must be something— other—than the goods that would be theirs, had they only once more extended their hand as they have done many times before."

There was a moment of silence.

"You mean," Banedra said quietly, "that the kezlBlythe want something from us—from *the Haosa*? And that the children are—bait?"

"I fear it," Tekelia said truthfully.

"But—what *could* they want?" Yferen demanded, irrepressible. "Civilization wants nothing to do with the Haosa! We're all ample proof of that!"

Arbour cleared her throat.

"I think, Cousins, that the kezlBlythe may not—quite—be civilized."

Another ripple of amusement ran the room.

"The sense of the village is that Torin, Vaiza, and Eet the norbear will remain with us, where they will be protected and cherished," Arbour said. "Is there more to be said on this topic?"

"One thing more," Tekelia said. "The twins are accustomed to going to school, and they miss the camaraderie and, I gather, the structure. We currently have no other children among us. Were the kezlBlythe not involved, I would suggest that they be sent to the school in Pacazahno, for the basics, and arrange for tutoring appropriate to their Talents, in-village."

"No, that's not eligible," Yferen objected. "If these kezlBlythe are as disordered as you say, we not only endanger our children, but the whole of the Deaf village."

"Agreed," said Banedra, "we cannot use the old solution."

"Why not bring the school here, then?" asked Tanin.

Every Haosa in the room turned to stare at him.

"What?" he said, staring back. "Pacazahno is our nearest neighbor. There have always been good relations between us. Why not bring the children and the teachers here for a six-day together—is school run by six-days, Cousins? It's been some while for me..."

"Merely a detail," Banedra said, leaning forward. "Go on, Cousin. You've given this some thought, it seems."

"Well..." The baker looked embarrassed. "In a general way, the topic interests me. This matter of seeing the children among children and learning what young things need to know—that merely...crystallized what I had been thinking about, in no ordered way."

He took a breath.

"So, as far as it goes, my notion is to bring what teachers and children might like it to us for a six-day together. We have enough spare rooms between us, I think. The teachers will do their usual work, teaching the basics, as Tekelia says, and when those who are Talented go for their tutoring, well—*I* would be willing to teach those who might like it a little about baking. Perhaps there are others of us who might—"

"Yes!" said Maradel. "I will be pleased to teach basic medic skills, if any are interested."

"There's the orchard, for pleasant work, or the gardens," said Yferen.

"Yes," said Arbour. "I think we have the basis of a plan that will limit danger while strengthening our ties with our nearest neighbor. It happens that I have a meeting with Village Speaker joiMore upcoming. I will bring this proposition to her."

"In the meantime," Banedra said, "there's no reason not to share out the basics, so *our* children don't fall behind their agemates. I can tutor in number-craft. Yferen might teach off of his maps." She paused and smiled at the baker. "And Tanin has already volunteered to teach baking."

"Excellent!" said Arbour. "Banedra, will you coordinate?"

"With pleasure," Banedra said. "I'll go tomorrow and speak with Geritsi and the children, to see what they would like, and find the levels and subjects that they have already conquered, so we don't bore them." She paused, brows drawn, and raised a hand.

"Yes?" said Arbour.

"Shall I tell them about the scheme to bring school to them?"

"Let me speak with Konsit and get her reaction first," Arbour said.

"Yes," said Banedra.

"The topic of schooling is being addressed. Is there anything else we ought to talk about this evening, Cousins?"

There was silence for a long count of six.

Arbour stood up from behind the table, and bowed to the room.

"This formal sharing is adjourned," she said solemnly, and then grinned.

"Let's eat!"

Colemenoport
Wayfarer

· · · · · · · · · ·

"EXPEDITER ROOBIOS CAN ASSEMBLE HIS TEAM AS EARLY AS tomorrow midday," Dyoli said. She glanced at Shan. "If the master trader has nothing else for me at that time, I would like to oblige him. Also, I should like to have Mar Tyn with me, if the schedule allows. He has already agreed that he should become acquainted with group presentations, and methods of inventory and fulfillment."

The trade team was at their leisure in the suite's common room, sipping favored drinks, and going over last-minute business before the meal arrived.

Dyoli and Mar Tyn sat together in the double-chair. Padi was curled at one end of the U-shaped couch, Shan and Priscilla sitting near the other end. Tima and Karna were in the two half-loungers, Grad stretched on his side on the floor at their feet.

"Expediter rooBios moves with commendable speed," Shan murmured. "My question would be—can you pull a presentation together so quickly?"

Dyoli's pale brows lifted.

"That will be no trouble at all," she said. "I have reviewed the files the master trader made available to me. I will very easily be able to generalize from those real-time examples. The Grady and the ter'Efferton methods are textbook. I will refresh myself, naturally, but it is not new material."

Shan nodded.

"If you are confident, I am confident," he told her, and looked to Mar Tyn. "Are you quite certain that you are prepared for the heady pleasures of a lecture on delivery protocols and deep inventory, Master pai'Fortana?"

Mar Tyn inclined his head gravely.

"Dyoli has promised that I may leave the room if I am overcome, sir."

Shan grinned.

"A wise precaution. I wonder, have you received the sections from the charter that our friend Councilor ziaGorn promised?"

"I have, and they are very interesting. Civilization appears to consider that Serendipitists have control over their Gift, while acknowledging that accidents may happen even to the most well-regulated person. As that is so, Serendipitists are expressly forbidden from entering casinos and other establishments where"—he paused, eyes narrowed, as if consulting a page that only he could see—"where the ambient may interface with random event."

"Which is remarkably unclear," Padi commented.

"The explanation is certainly not plain," Shan said. "But the prohibition is clear. We do not wish to err against local custom, therefore the Serendipitist in our midst will please remain on the outside of casinos and other monuments to chance."

"I have no desire to ever see the inside of a casino again," Mar Tyn told him fervently.

"Then we have no conflict, though one does wonder what prohibitions might be placed against the other Talents represented among us."

"I wondered the same," Mar Tyn said, "and did a search of the public network. There is a Library of Law and Regulation maintained by the Council of the Civilized, from which I was able to download a copy of the full ruling charter."

He paused and looked a little apologetic.

"I haven't had a chance to read it yet."

"I'm sure you'll find time over the next few days," Shan said gently. "In the meanwhile, might you send a copy of the charter to the whole team, so that we are all informed?"

"Yes, sir."

"Excellent."

"Thank you, Mar Tyn," Padi added. "I must say that I am very confused about this custom, and the underlying assumptions. I heard you were quite stern with Councilor ziaGorn."

Mar Tyn moved his shoulders, looking less happy with this praise from a comrade than he might.

"I had not meant to be *quite* so stern," he said. "I had no idea of the...strength of my opinion until I began to speak. Surely, the custom is not of Councilor ziaGorn's devising."

"Oh, he understood very well that you were not angry with him!" Dyoli said. "Though I thought he was brought up a bit when you claimed him as a comrade."

"What should I have done? A *protected* population?" Mar Tyn's voice was warming, his amber eyes sparkling. "What does that *mean*?"

"That," Shan cut in, "is a very good question, and one that a reading of this charter may clarify for us. If, after we have informed ourselves, we find that we still have questions, I note that we have a liaison who is well versed in local custom."

Mar Tyn subsided, inclining his head.

"Just so."

"I've been thinking," Priscilla said in her deep, calm voice, "of calling Dil Nem down for this projected tour of the yards. He had managed Tiazan's yard on Lytaxin for a time, and will have a better feel than I do for day-to-day operations, what can be made to work, and what absolutely must be replaced or refitted."

"That's a good plan," Shan said. "Indeed, it fits neatly with my own. I have asked Qe'andra dea'Tolin to join the on-port team—Dil Nem may accompany her." He leaned forward to put his glass on the table.

"On the topic of learning more about Colemeno, I've arranged for Portmaster krogerSlyte to escort me to a social history dialogue," Priscilla continued.

Shan raised his eyebrows. "An excellent notion. I look forward to hearing what you learn."

He looked around the room, and gave them all a smile.

"So! The trade mission has not been driven off by the Council, as much as they might wish us elsewhere. Colemenoport itself is eager to explore mutual opportunity, and we have seen enough of interest to justify opening a whole port inventory."

He glanced at those gathered again, his gaze resting on Mar Tyn and Dyoli. "Trader ven'Deelin and Master pai'Fortana are best suited to assist Qe'andra dea'Tolin in her work, unless there is an objection."

"I have no objection," Dyoli said calmly. "As the inventory will be the foundation of the trade office that Mar Tyn and I will manage, it's best for us to be in it from the beginning."

There was a moment's silence.

"Mar Tyn?" Shan murmured.

"It is as Dyoli says. I will be very pleased to do what I may to assist the *qe'andra*, and to—to learn what is needful."

Shan smiled and inclined his head.

"As we are all in agreement, I suggest that it is time to eat."

Alone in her quarters after dinner, Padi refreshed herself, pulled on soft pants and a sweater, and left her hair loose over her shoulders. She stood for a moment, eyes closed, centering herself, before she sat down at the desk and opened her screen.

The hour before the meal, and the meal itself, during which Tima had amused the table by describing the convoluted plot of a serial she and Karna watched together as a relaxation, had done much to restore her energy levels.

While she was not quite ready to march out onto the port to call upon the two dozen vendors who had desired a personal visit from a member of the trade mission, she certainly felt equal to dealing with her correspondence.

She wrote first to Cargo Master ira'Barti with delivery instructions.

Secondly, she wrote to Trader Isfelm, transmitting the promised file of reviews, and passing along the master trader's question regarding the compatibility of equipment.

That done, she opened her inbox.

There were a few general solicitations of the sort that could easily be discarded, which she did, before opening the first item of real interest—a letter from Trader Arbuthnot, who happened also to be her cousin Gordy.

He reported, first, that he had accomplished his separation from Trader per'Cadmie and *Sevyenti* with only a "minor" amount of unpleasantness. He was now on his way via small cruise ship to Napoli, where he would meet *Generous Passage* and her crew.

He was using his *leisure*—she could almost see the irony gleaming between the letters—to bring himself current with station-based marketing and supply, and learning all that he could about his new—his own!—tradeship.

He acknowledged that *Genny*, as she was styled by her captain, was an elder vessel, but hale and eager to be brought out of semi-retirement. She had once been a master trader's ship, so he would enjoy a level of comfort beyond what one might expect of an older ship. Age of course meant less pod-space than *Sevyenti*, but the four she carried were all his—or, rather, Tinsori Light's.

Gordy had written to the light keepers in order to find what items might be particularly welcome, even as he looked for competition and opportunity.

The nearest trade of any kind appeared to be at Edmonton Beacon, and Gordy hoped he wasn't too confident in assuming that a Tree-and-Dragon trade office could do better than *that*, even if Tinsori Light *was* situated at the back end of Away.

Padi grinned. Gordy had been quite oppressed by Trader per'Cadmie, and to find him so full of excitement and plans was a relief. She made a note to mention the letter to Father, and put it aside to answer later.

Next was a letter from Beali Sunderland, a curiosities dealer at Tinbakerport who had been the first client Padi had signed to her own trade-list, when she had been Trader ven'Tyrlit's 'prentice.

The relationship had been advantageous and pleasant. Beali had a surprisingly wide acquaintanceship in markets far from Tinbaker, and Padi had benefited from being added to that web. For her part, Padi had a good eye for the curious and the intriguing. It had been her habit to look out items for Beali, even when, as had become increasingly necessary, she had been required to transship to Tinbaker.

The letter was brief—a congratulation on Padi's ascent to the garnet—a trader in her own face, so soon! Beali said warmly— and a whimsical wondering after Padi's latest route, which had yielded nothing curious for quite some time.

Padi sat back in her chair, lips curved in a half-smile. She did *so* like Beali.

Still, it could not be said that she had been a very consistent source of curios for some time.

While it was possible, even likely, that she might come upon any number of oddities on Colemeno, she could not pretend that she would be a steady source.

It was time to pass her valued client on to another trader, who could give her the attention she deserved.

She pulled up the trade ledger, looking for a particular—yes! It was as she had recalled. Trader Getchell vin'Odri listed a specialty in curios, including in her client list several names familiar to Padi from Beali's web of acquaintance. The two of them ought to deal famously together.

Carefully, she wrote the letters—the first to Beali, thanking her for her many kindnesses to a 'prentice and young trader, and admitting that she was at the moment attached to a market expansion team, and not on-route at all. She promised to keep Beali in her thoughts when she walked new markets, and would contrive to send, when she discovered something appropriate. However, in the interest of a steadier supply, Padi was transferring Beali's information and particulars to Trader vin'Odri of *Nine Moons*, an experienced and devoted purveyor of curiosities of all types.

The second letter was to Trader vin'Odri, providing an introduction and transferring the appropriate transaction records.

Both letters dispatched, Padi glanced at the clock. It was getting late, but there was only one more letter in the queue—and it was from Vanz.

Vanz—Trader Vanz Carresens-Denobli—was her partner in Out of the Dust Limited Trade Partnership. Just before they had come in to Colemeno, she had seen his name in the Guild listing of new traders, and had written to congratulate him. Teasing him a little, she asked when he would be assigned his own ship.

She opened his letter with a smile.

My dear Trader yos'Galan, it began—which gave her pause. Though they had only recently met, they had very quickly become Padi and Vanz, which she found agreeable, as she did having a colleague so very near her own age and estate. She was not at all certain that she ought to encourage *Trader yos'Galan* from Vanz.

Frowning slightly, she returned to the letter.

Your congratulations find me in a quandary—not uncharted space for me, as we're both aware. Clearly, I'm delighted that the Trader was not only able to recall that there was a bit of Guild business pending, but also where he had put the ring for safekeeping. The presentation was made at a small-gather and meeting of the seniors. My mother and aunt were present, to donate the appropriate tears—of happiness, I believe!—and a chorus of my cousins to remark on what trifling gems garnets are.

Padi leaned back in her chair with a soft laugh. This was more in the mode she had come to expect from Vanz. Perhaps the opening had only been a bit of playful chiding for her sally regarding the ship.

She touched the screen, scrolling the letter up.

What I mean to convey is that matters had progressed pretty much as expected, until they didn't.

Padi blinked.

The seniors had various business to discuss at the gather. There was Traveler's Aid to discuss, and some other things, all beyond the reach of a new-made trader and his lowly garnet.

I was called in after a bit, which I had been expecting, because there was the matter of my shares and position in the Family to be settled.

You'll be as astonished as I was to learn that the elders voted me a Daughter's share and responsibilities.

I didn't quite ask the Trader if he'd got the right 'prentice, but that was only because just then my aunt Chasiel, Captain Most Senior, asked what I thought of the Rimedge Loop. I promptly 'fessed that I knew of no such route, but would be pleased to amend my ignorance and write her an analysis.

My mother laughed at that, and the Trader gave me a kindly smile before saying that it was a very good notion Vanz had, to analyze the situation. Vanz being, as the Trader was pleased to say, very solid in analysis.

The sum of all this being that, pending analysis, I may be put on as EvaLee's trader to reopen the Rimedge Loop, which has, so I know now, been Dusted-in as long—or longer!—as the Redlands.

All this to say that I was startled when you followed your congratulations with an inquiry about my new ship. Are you prescient? I never thought to ask.

For the present, not much changes. I'll stay with Nubella Run—*as second trader! My analysis is due to the Seniors before the next Festevalya at Tradedesk, so they can review it before bringing it before the Whole Family Meeting.*

We're on the out-run to the Hacienda now. I have less than half of the adapter kits left in inventory, and am confident of profit, there.

And there's my news. I'm eager to hear more of yours, as time allows it.

Take good care, Padi. I remain your friend and partner—

Vanz

· · · ✳ · · ·

"So far, crew is kept occupied," Danae Tiazan said in answer to Priscilla's question. Danae was first mate and acting captain of *Dutiful Passage*, at the moment in a parking orbit around Colemeno.

"We are on a regimen of repair and brightening, which ought, with judicious scheduling, keep us busy for some weeks. We are considering an adjustment of shifts to accommodate more discretionary time for crew. Second Mate Davis and Librarian Faaldom are together exploring the educational and entertainment modules with an eye toward offering workshops, guided reading groups, viewings of the classic *melant'i* plays, and other such. The modules are—extensive."

It required an active effort of will, not to outright grin at the note of bemusement in the first mate's even voice.

"I believe some of those modules are original with Master Trader Petrella," Priscilla said. Her first duty station on the *Passage* had been as pet librarian, which had put her under Lina Faaldom's authority. She had occasionally been enlisted in file searches, and had noted the size of the entertainment archive more than once.

"The master trader who had *Dutiful Passage* built," Danae said, to show that she knew her lineages, and added, "the same master trader who included a pet library in the initial plans."

"My lifemate suggests that she was concerned of what might happen, should her 'prentice grow bored."

Danae smiled, amusement plain for those who knew what they were looking for.

"Indeed, my own grandmother still tells stories of Er Thom yos'Galan's apprenticeship. It impressed her as few things have."

"So do we all terrify our teachers," Priscilla murmured, and Danae's smile grew wider.

"Indeed. Indeed we do."

She glanced aside, then back to the screen, politely looking toward, rather than at, Priscilla.

"Such stratagems will keep us for . . . some time," she said. "Eventually, however, there will be a call for shore leave. One is well aware that master traders keep their own time. However—"

Priscilla sighed.

"We arrive at my topic," she said. "The master trader has determined that a whole port inventory may go forth, and has called *Qe'andra* dea'Tolin to join the trade mission on-port."

Danae inclined her head.

"I have a copy of the master trader's letter to the *qe'andra*. We will of course have her brought down to you as quickly as possible."

"Yes—about that. Can you spare Dil Nem for a few days? The yard here has not seen upgrades since before the Redlands were engulfed by the Dust, and the yard master would like us to inspect and make suggestions for needed improvements. Dil Nem's experience there—"

"Oh, indeed!" Danae said. "Dil Nem is precisely who you want for that! Will you speak to him yourself, or shall I convey your orders?"

"I'll speak to him when we're done," Priscilla said. "Is there anything else between us?"

"I think not," Danae said. "It is a very peaceful interlude, even if some of us are bemused. Is there anyone else who might be of use to you on-port?"

"I think—" Priscilla began—and stopped, as the screen sparkled, the brightness producing a roar inside her head. No sooner had they appeared than the effects faded, and Priscilla was looking at Danae once more.

"Yes, Captain," the first mate said crisply. "Will you speak with Dil Nem now?"

Priscilla blinked, noting that her head ached. Well, she thought, it had been a long and demanding day. One expected that even a Witch—or a *strong multi-Talent*—might be worn out by such an effort. Only a few minutes more, and she could—would—rest.

"Thank you," she said. "I'll speak to Dil Nem now."

On-Grid
The Wardian

. . . .

BENTAMIN CHASTAMEIR, THE WARDEN OF CIVILIZATION, STOOD in the window of his darkened office, and stared down at the street below.

At last, the kezlBlythe had made an error. There was an eyewitness to Zatorvia xinRood's murder. He had never dared hope for so much. Only—

The eyewitness was—a norbear.

He might have suspected a Haosa joke, save Tekelia had delivered the information with the utmost seriousness.

"Norbears are not sentient," Bentamin had said, and Tekelia raised black eyebrows.

"Are they not?"

"Not by law, is what I mean to say," Bentamin had elaborated patiently. "They are natural empaths, and network builders. They may *seem* to reason when we interact with them, but in fact it is our intelligence that makes their narrative sequential. Tested alone, without a human intelligence translating, there is no proof of sentience."

Tekelia frowned.

"I did consult the law library before I came to you." A sharp glance from one blue eye and one amber. "I know that you are a busy person, Cousin. I may perhaps be wrong, as I am not a *qe'andra*, but it seemed to me that, according to law, the matter of norbear intelligence is far from settled."

Bentamin very much feared that he had blinked. He had studied law, but he was no more a lawyer than was his cousin.

"You will of course do as you see fit," Tekelia said then, rising. "Having just acknowledged that you are a busy person, I

96

recall that I am also a busy person, and must move on to my next duty."

A bow was produced, very fine.

"I bid you good e'en, Cousin. Let us stay in touch regarding Torin and Vaiza."

"Yes. I will begin a search for an appropriate Healer this evening."

"Thank you, Bentamin."

A sparkling swirl of displaced air, and Tekelia was gone.

Bentamin rose and went to the comm unit to place a call to his most discreet agent, to put the search for a Healer into motion.

That accomplished, he stepped to his desk, tapped up the screen and queried the law library.

In truth, he had expected a single, brief cite, which he would dutifully read before he went home to his apartment in the higher floors of the Wardian.

The screen pinged. Bentamin glanced down.

Not one cite.

Dozens.

He sank down into his seat, and opened the first.

He was still at his desk, reading, when Suzee macNamara knocked on his door to ask if he wanted her to stay.

"Thank you, there is no need," he said, sounding distracted to his own ears. He looked up and gave her a smile.

"I have a bit more research to do, then I'll be going home myself," he told her. "Good evening."

"Good evening, Warden," she answered, but his attention was already back on the screen.

When he had at last read the last cite, he rose and went over to the window, where he stared down at the street below.

Not settled, he thought.

Not settled *at all.*

Colemenoport
Wayfarer

· · · · · · · · · ·

THERE HAD BEEN A FEW LETTERS FOR THE MASTER TRADER TO deal with—the most notable from Janifer Denobli, informing him that the Carresens-Denobli Syndicate had approved *Travelers Aid* for Tinsori Light, to assist the light keepers.

It was far more assistance than Shan had supposed would arise from his discussions with Trader Denobli regarding Clan Korval's newest acquisition—a space station from the Old Universe, in very-most need of upgrades.

Unlooked-for or not, the aid was appreciated, and so Shan wrote to Denobli, thanking him warmly, and wondering after any other adventures the trader would be pleased to share.

He offered a brief overview of the trade mission's progress since its arrival on Colemeno, the chiefest in the three-planet Redlands system, while neglecting to mention Old Gods embracing their endings on a weird and twilit hill, with witnesses in a circle around them.

He did recommend the history of the Redlands to Denobli's study, and mentioned that the Small Talents who had arrived so long ago were thriving. Denobli was shrewd; he need say no more than that.

He closed shortly after that recommendation, promising himself the pleasure of writing at more length in the very near future.

Letters dispatched, Shan sat back in his chair and sighed.

He ought, he supposed, to write to his delm, informing them of progress, but really, there had been little quantifiable progress so far, aside from being the first tradeship to arrive at Colemeno after its emergence from Rostov's Dust.

The delm, in fact, had tasked Master Trader yos'Galan with

identifying new avenues of income to replenish Clan Korval's depleted coffers, and so far Master Trader yos'Galan's endeavors had been notable for depleting those coffers even more.

Well, no. In Balance, Master Trader yos'Galan's efforts had not *all* been expensive and inept. There was the new contract written with the Carresens-Denobli Syndicate. That would turn a profit sooner rather than later. And the partnership he had formed with Janifer Denobli would surely begin producing income in a few Standards.

The Redlands, however . . . so far that column was red.

He was somewhat more confident of being able to turn the trick, now that he had begun to dig into the reality of the market. Certainly, there was short-term money to be made in equipment upgrades, current maps, histories, and other such things.

And there was the fact that Colemeno had not been bereft of trade during its time engulfed. The Iverson Loop, serving other worlds likewise cut off from the wide universe by the Dust, had made Colemeno the terminus of their route. The Isfelm Trade Union, in the person of Trader Isfelm, was a principal in that Loop, and the trader was eager to deal.

Given that the systems further in were still somewhat Dust-bound, there was very little doubt that Colemeno could be brought up to scratch, and made to support a combined Korval/Ixin trade office.

What remained was to bring the Redlands into a sensible and useful route. He had spent time with his charts and his routes-books on the way to the Redlands, but so far, he had not—

The door to the room he shared with Priscilla opened, and here came his lifemate herself, wan, and her pattern not so much glittering with energy as spitting sparks.

"Priscilla." He rose and went to her, arms out.

She melted into his embrace, resting her head on his shoulder.

"I am very tired," she stated.

"I see that you are," he murmured, as he scanned her more closely. "Does your head hurt?"

"Only a little."

"Unacceptable," he said, locating the sullen glow of the headache. "Allow me to mend that for you."

It scarcely required more than to think about releasing the pain for it to be gone. There was much to like about Colemeno's effervescent atmosphere, Shan thought; certainly, it made Healing effortless.

In his arms Priscilla sighed, the tension going out of her shoulders. Shan leaned his head against hers.

"I have," he whispered into her ear, "a marvelous plan."

"What is it?" Priscilla whispered back.

"We should seek our bed, and go to sleep."

Priscilla gasped a small laugh.

"I like that plan," she said.

· · · ☀ · · ·

Vanz's had been the last letter in the queue. After a brief struggle, Padi set it aside until she had time to give it the answer it deserved.

In the meanwhile—

She glanced at the clock on the table next to her bed. It was...rather late, according to local time, and tomorrow *would* be strenuous. The path of wisdom led to bed, now rather than later.

So thinking, she closed her screen, and was very shortly thereafter slipping under her blanket.

She turned the room lights off with a word, and settled her head on the pillow, which was scented with something warm and woody. At home, her pillow was scented with lavender, light and sweet, and for a startling moment, she wanted that pillow under her head *now*, and the house full of her kin all around.

She took a deep, calming breath, drawing the woody scent into her lungs. It was not lavender, but it was soothing in its way.

Padi closed her eyes.

...and opened them again, shifting her head, and turning onto her side. She took deep, deliberate breaths; pictured the center of her being as a still silver pool—but it would not do.

The room was too quiet, she thought, and she spoke the command for low-frequency filler sound.

The sound came up to the proper level, and Padi—

Sat up, turned her pillow over, lay down on her opposite side, and waited, rather impatiently, for sleep.

Sleep, however, continued to elude her.

She looked at the clock on the bedside table—and winced.

You might, she told herself carefully, *take board rest.*

Only, board rest borrowed against future energy, and, while beneficial in the short run, was not as restorative as—

It is a very small thing I give; soft, sweet, and infinitely useful to you, Father whispered in memory. There was a delightful taste on her tongue, and a brief glimpse of a pattern in lambent silver, spinning comfort at the back of her mind in the instant before it, too, dissolved.

Padi sighed, and slipped into sleep.

On-Grid
Offices of
chastaMeir and urbinGrant

. . . .

"GODS, HOW PEL WOULD HAVE DELIGHTED IN UNTYING *THIS* KNOT."

Peesha urbinGrant, Pel's partner, ran down the screen one more time, then raised her head to meet Bentamin's eyes.

"I am not Pel," she said softly.

"And yet Pel is lost to us."

"Which, forgive me, Warden, has no bearing on the truth that I am not Pel," Peesha said with a sigh. "Pel was . . . brilliant, fierce, and subtle. I—read and produce documents, and advise clients of their rights and options, according to law."

This was, Bentamin knew, why Pel and Peesha had been partners: Pel to take on those cases that required a mind suited to investigation and innovation, and which might require months to bring right; Peesha to do the painstaking detail work that kept the firm financially stable.

"I understand that your skill set is very different," Bentamin said, gentle in the face of Peesha's dismay. "I ought to have said—had Pel no assistant? A 'prentice, perhaps? Someone who might be able to make a beginning?"

"Well . . . Osha sometimes assisted Pel." Peesha looked back to the screen. "She could certainly open a case file and get these cites in order. I will need to know your purpose for opening the case, Warden."

Bentamin frowned, hesitating, and Peesha raised a hand.

"Do you wish to argue that norbears as a group have seen material harm by being held as nonsentient? Do you wish to argue that native norbears deserve full coverage under the laws of Colemeno? Has a norbear stolen something of value, and—"

"Hold." Bentamin raised both of his hands.

Peesha inclined her head. Bentamin took a deep breath, and lowered his hand.

"What I wish to do is to definitively establish if norbears are sentient."

Peesha frowned.

"But that is not a matter for the law, Warden. That is a matter for science."

"Forgive me. At the moment, it appears that the law is divided on this issue. Thus this delightful knot."

"Yes, exactly; the law is divided. And the reason for that is that the law has been given no support by experts in the field of norbear intelligence. The law must therefore reason with itself whenever a question concerning norbears arises, on a case-by-case basis. We may consult past decisions, but as we see here"—she waved at the screen—"too often the matter to be determined is unrelated to past cases."

Bentamin closed his eyes.

"A definitive study establishing norbear sentience would aid the law immeasurably," Peesha murmured, apparently back at the screen. "And might also aid norbears."

Bentamin opened his eyes in time to intercept her glance over the top of the screen.

"Perhaps if you told me your ultimate purpose," she said, which was reminder enough that Peesha was a Truthseer, "I could be more useful to you. Of course whatever you tell me will be confidential to the case."

You cannot, he told himself sternly, *do this yourself. If it was Pel, you would not hesitate.*

"In confidence, then," he said, meeting Peesha's eyes once more. "There has been a murder committed, and an eyewitness has been found."

Peesha's eyes widened and her lips parted, but she waited for him to say it.

"The witness is a norbear."

Colemenoport
Skywise Provianto

· · · · · · · · · · · · · · · · · ·

PADI DRANK THE LAST OF HER TEA WITH A SIGH, AND GLANCED at the clock hanging on the back wall. Still more than twelve minutes until her next appointment, which was, happily, across the street from the Skywise.

It had been a busy morning, full of names, personalities, and questions, both fearful and intense. Really, it was amazing, the variety of disasters and benefits people either hoped or feared that the trade mission would bring to Colemenoport.

The fearful ones—those who were concerned that long-time, existing arrangements with the Iverson Loop, the Evrits, or the Mikancy Family would be disrupted, or eliminated, by the establishment of a Tree-and-Dragon trade office on-port—Padi found easier to deal with. Tree-and-Dragon would be an *addition* to trade at the Redlands, and would likewise benefit the existing Loops, by providing new goods and a wider market. Aside from being the truth, it was an easy sell.

The intense ones, who assumed that the master trader had a deep plan, and who were inclined to be offended that they were not offered a précis—those were more difficult. Padi could only hope that time would win them to the truth, that, in fact, the Trade Mission was exploratory, and no plans could be made until facts were established.

"Time, Trader?" Tima asked from across the table, and Padi looked to the clock again.

"Time," she agreed, and rose, picking up her case and settling the strap over her shoulder.

The host behind the counter had introduced herself as Bell when Padi and Tima entered. She had placed them at a small table near the back of the room, which was not crowded, brought the trays with commendable dispatch, and perfectly recalled the Tree-and-Dragon account.

She had come back only once, to be certain of the teapot, and to find if more of anything was wanted, and otherwise left them to themselves.

She looked up now as they passed the counter, and raised a hand, palm out and fingers spread, with a smile.

"Good day, Trader. Thank you for your custom."

"Thank you for serving such delicious food, and bracing tea," Padi said. She lifted her hand in imitation of Bell's gesture—and smiled. Colemeno custom demanded a broader smile than Liadens offered to strangers, though not quite so broad as Terran. She hoped she had managed it correctly, as she followed Tima out the door.

Luzant nirAmit met Padi at the door of his establishment. He was an elder, his white hair pulled severely back from his face and held with a sparkling clip. He wore the long vest over loose shirt and pants that was the usual business attire on-port. He also wore an unpleasant expression and failed to return Padi's bow with one of his own.

Padi straightened and met the merchant's cool gaze.

"I'm sent a child instead of a master trader," he remarked. "Am I so poor a thing as that?"

Padi spread her hands, the gesture putting her garnet on display.

"I am Trader Padi yos'Galan, assisting the master trader in the mission to reopen the Redlands to trade. The master trader is very much in demand just now, sir. If he had taken all the requests for meetings in the order received, he could have come to you himself...in perhaps a six-day. Instead, he sent me to you, mere hours after receiving your letter."

"An impertinent child," the elder judged, and Padi swallowed her spurt of temper. If the man was determined to find fault, there was very little she could do, except leave the literature, if allowed, and bow herself out.

"Do you know anything about that operation across the street, where I assume you took a tea break?" Luzant nirAmit snapped.

Padi raised her eyebrows.

"Indeed. It is called the Skywise Provianto. The trade mission has established an account with them, and with several other such businesses around the port, so that team members will always be within reach of a meal, or, as you say, sir, a cup of tea, should it be needed."

Luzant nirAmit considered her out of angry eyes, and turned his hands palm up.

"You're new on port, and likely know nothing about how to go on, coming from the Old World like you do. Be informed, Trader Padi yos'Galan, that the Skywise Provianto is Deaf-owned. All of their employees are Deaf, and they embrace no Civilized business advisor. Now that you have this information, you will be able to conduct yourself fittingly."

Padi recalled Bell's pleasant demeanor and efficient service, so much at odds with the demeanor of the person before her, and was strongly tempted to go back across the street and have another cup of tea until it was time to leave for her next appointment.

It was the thought of that next appointment, and those after it, that decided her approach to Luzant nirAmit. He would stand and argue all day, she felt certain, if she continued to address his spite as rational discourse.

In fact, he was wasting her time, and *that* she did not allow.

She inclined slightly from the waist.

"Thank you for your care, sir. May I deliver this packet the master trader sends to you?"

She pulled it out of the side pocket of her case, and offered it across both palms, as if it were a dueling pistol, which *was* an impertinence, whether the man before her knew it or not.

"Since it's here, I might as well have it," he said, taking the packet up with a frown. "I'll expect to see the master trader himself, the next time I write."

"I will tell him you said so, sir," Padi said truthfully.

She made her bow and escaped onto the walk, Tima close behind.

"Nasty piece of work," she muttered, and Padi sputtered a laugh.

"Yes, wasn't he? Well. We now have an opportunity to arrive at the next appointment respectfully early."

"Or," Tima suggested, "we could walk slow. No sense arriving warm, if you take me, Trader."

Padi sighed.

"I take you," she said. "Thank you, Tima."

On-Grid
Colemeno Historical Society

. . . .

"SCHOLARS, ALLOW ME TO MAKE YOU KNOWN TO PRISCILLA Delacroix y Mendoza, captain of the tradeship *Dutiful Passage*, which has brought to us the Tree-and-Dragon Trade Mission," Portmaster krogerSlyte murmured. She moved a hand in a stylized wave, as if she were connecting Priscilla and the scholars.

"Captain Mendoza, here are Akame sereWai, Historian, and Brun rodaMildin, Sociologist."

"Scholars, I am honored," Priscilla said politely, inclining her head.

"A member of the Tree-and-Dragon Trade Mission," said Scholar sereWai. "Surely, it is we who are honored. What say you, Brun?"

"I say that ideally honor flows both ways," the sociologist said with the same cool amusement she had bestowed upon the more bombastic of the historian's declarations, on-stage.

"Did you enjoy the dialogue, Captain Mendoza?" she asked.

"Very much," Priscilla said truthfully. "I am not as conversant with the removal of the Talents from Liad as I should perhaps be, so I am grateful to Scholar sereWai for expanding my knowledge of that event. Also, Scholar rodaMildin, your account of the joining of the newcomers with established families, and the melding of surnames, to give honor to each, was illuminating."

She smiled. "Traders come to worlds and customs as they are. We are very seldom given a glimpse into the events responsible for those customs."

A server came by just then, offering wine or juice. The scholars chose wine, with enthusiasm. Priscilla took a cup of juice, and after a small hesitation, Portmaster krogerSlyte did as well.

"While the attention of historians is so often focused in the past that the present quite passes us by," said Scholar sereWai.

"Which is why you have partnered with a sociologist," said Scholar rodaMildin. She turned to eye Priscilla.

"While we're speaking of novelties, I may be the first sociologist to have access—your pardon, Captain; I *am* a scholar, and this is how we speak. We don't mean to be rude, only direct."

"I understand," Priscilla assured her solemnly.

"Excellent! Directly, then, I am the first sociologist in more than two hundred Standards to have access to a team of persons from outside of our closed group."

"Hardly closed," objected Scholar sereWai. "Colemeno has trade."

"Indeed it has." Scholar rodaMildin waved her wineglass at him. "However, we have had trade with the same groups for quite some time. Where we do not intersect, our societies, cultures, and mores vary widely. But, where we *do* intersect—at the port, and in the market, we have created a culture that is known and manipulated by both—"

"I believe I have read this book," Scholar sereWai interrupted.

"I believe you have," Scholar rodaMildin agreed blandly. She turned back to Priscilla.

"I wonder if we might keep in touch, Captain? Ideally, I would like to interview you before you become much further acquainted with us, then at intervals until it is time for you to leave us. May I impose upon you so much?"

"I'm certainly willing to see if we can make it work. Must the interviews be in-person?"

"I would prefer so, but I may be able to devise a hybrid system, in order to not overburden either your time or your patience. Let me think on it. May I contact you—through our good friend the portmaster, perhaps?"

Priscilla fingered a card out of her pocket.

"Here is my contact information, locally."

"Splendid! You will hear from me, never doubt it. I would enjoy speaking further just now, but sereWai has seen his editor, and I must circulate or my department chair will be arriving to lead me forcibly away."

She swayed into a bow.

"Portmaster, always a pleasure—and thank you for bringing such an interesting guest! Coming, sereWai?"

The scholars left them. Priscilla sipped her juice and looked about the room.

"Is there anyone else I may introduce you to?" asked Portmaster krogerSlyte.

"I am sure the room is full of interesting people," Priscilla said, "but I've been too long at pleasure. Perhaps another time."

"It would be my honor to escort you at any time, to any event you choose, Captain Mendoza. Please allow me to see you to your train."

"Thank you," Priscilla said. They surrendered their empty glasses to a server, and left the reception hall.

"I should tell you," Priscilla said, as they walked across the sky bridge to the platform. "We will be bringing down two more crew members—our third mate, who was for a time a yard master, and our ship's *qe'andra*, who will, under the master trader's direction, be conducting a whole port inventory."

Portmaster krogerSlyte stopped in the middle of the walk and turned to gaze up at her.

"A whole port inventory!" she exclaimed. "The master trader—he is encouraged by what he sees—but of course, he must be! This is welcome news, Captain!"

"The master trader wishes to proceed properly," Priscilla murmured.

"Yes, yes, of course." The portmaster closed her eyes, took a deep breath, and smiled.

"I have much confidence in the master trader's ability to proceed properly," she said. "But these additional crew—they will wish their own living space. I will open more rooms around your common hall. Also, I will open an adjacent suite of offices, for the *qe'andra's* use. If there is anything else I can do for you or the trade mission, please do not hesitate to ask me."

"Thank you," Priscilla said. "You are very good to us."

"Nonsense! I'm only looking out for my port. And now I fear we must hurry—that rumble is the train coming in."

Colemenoport
Offices of the
Isfelm Trade Union

. . . .

"MASTER TRADER." TRADER ISFELM BOWED FROM BEHIND HER desk. "Thank you for coming to me."

Shan bowed in return, and straightened, raising an eyebrow.

"Surely, it is my part to thank you for agreeing to see me?"

She grinned, and it struck him, how very *much* she resembled his Uncle Daav, Val Con's father—especially that grin, so charming it could melt mountains.

"So we have both said everything needful and polite," she commented, and moved a hand, showing him the chair next to her desk.

"Please, sit, and allow me to offer refreshment. Is your preference ale? Wine? Tea? Cake?"

"No cake, I beg you," Shan said, taking the indicated seat with gratitude. "What will you drink?"

"I've got a fondness for the local ale, especially when there's work to be done."

"Then, by all means, ale."

"Take a bare moment to fetch," she assured him and vanished through the doorway in the back wall.

Shan looked about. In design, the Isfelm Union's office was similar to that which had been opened to the trade mission. However, it was plain that this space had been in use for many years.

There was artwork on the walls—two landscapes and a portrait of a blade-faced dark-haired pilot wearing leather of a long-ago fashion. The tea set on the bureau was not serviceable and retiring, as was the set that had been furnished to the trade mission's office, but outright idiosyncratic, as if the cups had been purchased one at a time by different people, and none of them matching the pot.

"Ah, you admire the honorable ancestor," Trader Isfelm said, coming back to the desk and putting a mug half-full of light amber liquid by Shan's hand.

"Can Ith yos'Phelium, I believe?" Shan murmured.

"Himself and none other." Trader Isfelm raised her glass to the portrait. "Who ran from his duty, to found our family and our livelihood." She cast a whimsical glance at Shan. "Not that it was the *reason* he ran, mind."

She sipped from her mug, and sighed.

Shan tasted his ale, finding it good, and put the mug down.

"Can Ith had been a Scout," he remarked. "Scouts go *eklykt'i* for any number of reasons. Nor would he have been the first of his Line to do so, even so long ago."

"So the records tell us." Trader Isfelm sat, and put her mug aside, her eyes still on the portrait. "Thorough records, so they are, and he didn't stint himself. Though Grandmother Kishara's account would have him at the beck of his luck."

"That's not impossible," Shan said. "Do the records explain the nature of Clan Korval's luck?"

"In some part, by way of warning. They also mention that Can Ith had been born with formidable shields. Those have passed down, apparently unchanged, so I make it policy to be wary of things coming too easy. Though on Colemeno..."

She let that drift off, and spun her chair to face Shan.

"But," she said, "you didn't come here to discuss our mutual ancestor."

"Oddly enough, I did," Shan said. He tapped a finger against his mug. "This is very pleasant."

"Happy you find it so. But—Can Ith yos'Phelium?"

"My daughter tells me that we—that is, we and you—are by way of being 'Dust Cousins,'" Shan murmured.

Trader Isfelm laughed.

"Oh, does she read the romances? Come to that, so do I. But I've done business with Trader Padi. She's too sharp to believe 'em."

"I'm not certain that she has read them, yet," Shan said. "She had a report from a friend."

"Who will surely have told her that, as often as cousins long separated by the Dust find each other in the stories, the odds are—in real life, you understand me—much against it."

Shan had another sip of ale, and put the mug down.

"Here we come to Korval's Luck," he said. "You are not the

first long-lost cousin we have come across in just this Standard Year. The keeper at Tinsori, though his case is somewhat different than your own, has been returned to us."

Trader Isfelm frowned. "Tinsori? I don't—no! I've seen the charts." She raised her mug.

"There was a thankless post, I'm thinking."

When she lowered the mug, she was frowning.

"Given I *have* seen the charts—how did the keeper while his time? There's a couple ghost routes sketched in, but given the space around the station..."

"Unstable in the extreme," Shan agreed. "So unstable that the same keeper has been at his duty for more than two hundred Standards."

Trader Isfelm kept her expression grave, though Shan fancied he saw one eyebrow twitch.

"Stars keep the lad," she murmured. "He's due for some relief."

"Which is on the way," Shan said. "However, my point. Even given the difference in degree, you must allow that two such events inside of a single Standard is—"

"Too strange even for romance," Trader Isfelm finished. She raised her mug in salute. "I'll stipulate it."

"Thank you. We now approach my point, after which I swear I shall leave you to your legitimate work."

"Two traders speaking together is legitimate work by my book," Trader Isfelm said comfortably. She leaned back in her chair. "So, your point."

Shan finished off his ale and put the glass aside.

"I wonder if you indulge in politics."

"As little as possible, to say truth. Mind, being lead trader of the lead trade union stopping at Colemeno all these years, I'm sometimes called to the Council to help them understand certain things. They would have had me advise them on venturing out, once the Dust had danced away." She raised an ironical eyebrow. "Being as they had charts."

Shan took a sharp breath, and Trader Isfelm grinned wryly.

"Yes, but they're groundlings. I had to be about explaining that *space moves*. Not that I was believed. I was sent for special when you came to orbit, to have someone knowledgeable at hand. Which isn't to say that I wasn't eager to come on my own, for reasons I've talked somewhat with Trader Padi about."

"She said that she had advised you to come to me," Shan said. "If you have time, we may also address that topic."

"Oh, I've time," Trader Isfelm said. "But in the case of politics, I stay away."

"You deal with Civilization, then?"

"I deal with *the port*, and such vendors who have come to be partners, and regulars. For the Civilized Council, I'm an outside expert on such things as piloting, and charts, and the fact that the charts they had were more likely to get them killed than naught."

"No one's tried to leave yet," Shan pointed out.

"There's that. P'rhaps they listened, after all."

"The trade mission has been assigned a liaison," Shan said. "A member of the Civilized Council, Majel ziaGorn."

"The Deaf Councilor." Trader Isfelm tapped her chin. "He's an up-and-comer is what I hear from my contacts. When such matters come up, which they don't, often."

"I understand. I wonder—are you considered Deaf by the Council of the Civilized?"

Trader Isfelm blinked.

"Well, they See the shields o'course, but I don't recall it ever came up in conversation. What's to it?"

"Most of the trade mission are Talents. I am a Healer, as is Trader ven'Deelin. Captain Mendoza is a *dramliza*; Master pai'Fortana is a Luck; and Trader yos'Galan has yet to be Sorted. Councilor ziaGorn advised us that courtesy demands we list our Talents in any literature we give out, so that we may be understood 'appropriately.'"

Trader Isfelm was frowning again.

"Not something that I was ever asked about, but—the shields, you know. Basics here on Colemeno is Civilization is the largest group. Two sub-groups. The Deaf—of which Councilor ziaGorn can tell you more than I can—and the Haosa, the Wild Ones, who live apart. The law doesn't permit 'em on-port, and I've not got much to do with the city."

Her frown increased.

"You object to announcing your Talent? They're going to See it anyway—at least, the Civilized will."

"It is a matter of—forgive me—*melant'i*. Trader ven'Deelin, Captain Mendoza, and I have no objection to our Talents being known. We all three have Healing among our skill sets, and will serve if called, that being our training. Trader yos'Galan and Master pai'Fortana are inclined to a different view. They believe that our *melant'i* as traders on a mission must carry all before it. We did not arrive at Colemeno because we are Talents, but because we wish to advance trade."

"It's Civilization you'll be dealing with there, recall it," said Trader Isfelm. "The Iverson Union, me and my brother—we're known. You and yours are new, and—you'll forgive me for saying what you've doubtless already noticed—they're of two, or even three, minds about you."

"I had noticed, yes," Shan agreed. He raised a hand, palm up. "I suppose we will learn as we go. Now—your topic, Trader."

"I fear it's *topics* by now," said Trader Isfelm contritely. "Let me get us more ale."

"So, my first topic, having to do with your main purpose in raising Colemeno, is that the Iverson Union wants to partner with Tree-and-Dragon, and join our Loop into your final design."

Shan raised his eyebrows.

"Certainly, that can come under consideration, once the whole port inventory has been completed."

"I wonder if there's anything we can do, between us, while that work is being done," Trader Isfelm murmured. "Trader yos'Galan impresses me. How if she takes my place on *Ember*, and I take hers on *Dutiful Passage*." She raised a hand, showing palm and wide fingers. "I'm pitching ideas, here, Master Trader."

"I understand," Shan assured her. "You realize that we would need to do a route audit before we can even begin to talk of partnerships."

"Well, I hadn't," Trader Isfelm said frankly. "But now that I do, I'd like to know more. You understand, the routes hereabouts have been set for a long stretch of years. We balance each other—well, the Evrits and the Iversons. Hard to think of a situation where the Mikancy would provide any other than a bad example."

"So they, too, have their place," Shan said, and Trader Isfelm inclined her head.

"True."

"A route audit," Shan continued after a moment, "means that a Tree-and-Dragon trader and a *qe'andra* will go on *Ember* to evaluate the route. Once that is done, we can fairly judge how—or if—we might benefit each other."

Trader Isfelm raised her mug, and considered the contents intently.

"That can be done, surely, while the audit on Colemenoport goes on." She met Shan's eyes. "You and I both know that Colemeno will bring Tree-and-Dragon profit, Master Trader, whether you build a hub here or only braid it into a Loop."

Shan considered her. Such eagerness ought to be rewarded, he thought, even as he lifted a shoulder.

"I will talk this over with my team," he said. "I do advise that, even if we do go forward, there will be some delay, as we will have to send for a *qe'andra*."

"I understand. Let us not lose sight of this, Master Trader."

He would not, so Shan strongly suspected, *be allowed* to lose sight of it, but he inclined his head politely.

"I agree."

He finished his ale, and raised an eyebrow.

"Yes?" said Trader Isfelm.

"I wonder about those charts you have seen," Shan said slowly. "Concerning the ghost routes and Tinsori."

"Old, *old* charts," Trader Isfelm cautioned.

"I have an interest," Shan said, and she laughed.

"In that case, let's discuss them. Why not?"

Colemenoport
Offices of the
Tree-and-Dragon Trade Mission

. . . .

SHE HAD GOT THROUGH THE WHOLE LIST, AND WAS JUSTLY WEARY from her labors, Padi told herself, as they approached the trade mission's office suite.

"I think you might go on ahead," she said to Tima as they came to the main intersection of the hallways. "Unless there's something you need at the office?"

Tima paused, head on one side, and Padi could practically see the security equation running behind her eyes. The building was secure enough that even Grad was forced to admit that the traders might be in the office unattended. In addition, it was attached to the Wayfarer, where their living quarters were, by a security passage.

In fact, it met the previous working definition of a venue safe enough that one-on-one security need not be enforced.

However, the death of Vanner Higgs, and Father's subsequent wounding, had struck the security team to the heart, to the point that they were inclined to be overcareful. And over-care was not, so Padi thought, giving them peace. In fact, it was making them more anxious. It was perfectly plain to see in the mosaic that had formed against the air just behind Tima's shoulder. And, really, Tima deserved peace, and ease, and—

The mosaic smoothed, colors subtly intensifying.

Tima sighed.

"Of course, Trader," she said. "If you need to go out again, just call."

"I'll do that," Padi said softly. "Thank you, Tima. We both did extraordinarily well today."

"We did, didn't we?" Tima grinned. "Your day was longer than mine, with all those questions!"

"But it's what traders do—answer questions."

"Better you than me," said Tima, raising a hand in farewell as she turned toward the hall that led to the Wayfarer.

Padi turned in the opposite direction, toward the trade mission's office.

Truly, it *had* been an arduous day, Padi thought, as she approached the office, and her triumph was that she had learned just why *the port* wanted Tree-and-Dragon.

Colemeno's warehouses were filled to the bursting point. The Dust had slowed manufacturing only somewhat, and there had been a judicious amount of retooling in order to better meet the needs of those ports along the Iverson Loop, but the Loop could not use all of the planet's product. Colemeno *needed* Tree-and-Dragon and its connections to the greater universe of trade.

And wasn't *that* a welcome change?

Padi put her case on the table, went into the kitchen, and withdrew a bottle of tea from the cold box. She cracked the seal and drank, eyes closed, savoring the coolness down a throat parched with too much talking.

Back in the main room, the message-waiting light was blinking.

Padi had another drink of tea, sealed the bottle and left it on the table while she crossed to the comm.

Her father and his lifemate invited her to share the evening meal.

Padi blinked.

A specific invitation to dine together, just they three, suggested that there was a particular topic concerning only them that required discussion. It would not, then, be trade mission business, though it might well be Clan Korval business, or even Line yos'Galan business.

Or, simply a desire to reconnect to themselves as kin. Certainly, the last few days had seen few opportunities for that.

Padi glanced at the clock.

It was just over three local hours before the time they had settled upon for the evening meal. She ought, she supposed, return to the suite. There would still be time to address the most pressing matters of work after she had refreshed herself, and before the meal.

Since she had been planning on returning to the suite this evening, there really wasn't any reason to feel—just a little—downhearted. Was there?

She sent a note to Father, expressing her delight at the prospect of a meal shared with kin, made certain that there were no more messages in-queue, finished her tea, picked up her case, and left the office.

She was walking briskly, her mind somewhat occupied with the topics of the day, when she noticed a slight misting of the air at the turning of the hallway just ahead.

The mist swirled, playfully, and with no transition that the physical eye could follow, Tekelia was there in its place, smile particularly charming, eyes at the moment one blue and one brown, and long dark hair in a neat braid, hanging over one shoulder.

"Padi. Well met."

"Tekelia," she said composedly, as if a sudden jolt of pleasure had not thrilled her. "Well met."

"I've been thinking about our last conversation, and it came to me that there is no need for you to depend upon the Speaker of the Haosa, Warden of the Civilized, or any other person to bring you to where you wish to be. You can bring yourself."

Padi stared.

"I can what?"

"You can bring yourself," Tekelia repeated. "You haven't the way of it, yet, but that's easily remedied. We can begin at once. Open your Eyes and Look at my signature."

Padi frowned, and very carefully opened her Inner Eyes. Her Sight had been less confusing to her since they had come to Colemeno, though she remained wary.

She need not have worried.

Tekelia's signature was quite amazingly plain, unique, and imbued with a sense of *Tekelia* that was as unmistakable as it was indescribable.

"There!" Tekelia said merrily. "All you need do is show that to the ambient, and you will come to me, no matter how far apart we stand."

A bow, and another grin.

"I'll pour the wine."

The hallway was empty.

Show Tekelia's signature to the ambient? Padi thought, frowning, contemplating the fullness of it, bright in recollection.

Well, she thought, very nearly merry herself, how hard could it be?

· · · ✳ · · ·

It was said that a master trader in pursuit of a profit knew neither weariness nor doubt.

This was a patent untruth. More accurately, a master trader *displayed* neither weariness nor doubt, nor any other thing that would give the tempo of the trade into other hands.

Therefore, he had been attentive and sharp through even the last impromptu meeting at the Colemenoport Trade Bar, with a group of small shippers known to Trader Isfelm. Each had Colemeno as an anchor for their Loops, their other anchors being yet Dusted in. They had been quite reasonably anxious about the effect of increased trade at Colemeno, now that it was clear, and had wanted guarantees that they would not lose profit.

That, of course, Master Trader yos'Galan could not give them, though he could, and did, ask each for a précis of their routes, cargoes, and resources.

He and Trader Isfelm had at last quit the bar, both on-route to their lodgings, having taken the shortcut through the office block.

Shan thought he might stop at the trade mission's offices, and then thought that he would not. Truly, it was past time to go home.

They were angling toward the main lobby. He and Trader Isfelm would part there, she continuing to her apartments in the Merchant's Quarter, two streets over, while he went down the security corridor that connected the offices to the Wayfarer.

"Good o'the portmaster to open the big suite to you," Trader Isfelm said now. "Shows intent." They walked a few steps, Shan wondering where this observation would lead.

She glanced at him, face serious.

"Mind, if you're coming to us reg'lar, you'll want to establish your own spaces," she added.

"Indeed so," Shan said, amused. As a result of their earlier discussions, Trader Isfelm had taken up the task of educating him about the port, the markets, and the vendors, with a determination that Shan appreciated. She also showed a tendency to come the elder kin, as if establishing a trade headquarters in a foreign port might be something a bit out of his way, as a master trader.

"Once we are firm, we will look about us for the most favorable location," he added.

"That's the way of it," Trader Isfelm said approvingly, as they followed the hall down to the intersection where they would part. "First one first, then on to the second. Speaking of the same, what did you think—"

She put out a sudden hand, catching Shan's arm and pulling him gently to a stop.

Shan blinked—and blinked again, as he saw Padi at the mouth of the secure hallway across the lobby, speaking with some intensity to her particular friend, Tekelia vesterGranz.

"That's one of the wild ones," Trader Isfelm breathed. "Not allowed at port, is how they write the law here, so best we just don't see them."

This shortly became very easy. No sooner had they stopped than Tekelia bowed—and vanished in a modest swirl of mist.

Shan drew a careful breath, watching as Padi frowned at—or possibly *into*—the air—for an entire minute before vanishing in her turn.

Trader Isfelm dropped his arm.

"You knew she could do that, o'course."

"That?" Shan said, not quite ready to analyze his feelings on the matter. "Not that *precise* thing, no. However, one does wish for one's heir to be remarkable."

Trader Isfelm laughed and continued forward.

"Seems you've got that," she said.

"So it does," Shan said, falling into step beside her. "So it does."

Off-Grid
The Tree House

. . . .

THE AMBIENT WAS...NOT SO VIVID HERE AT THE PORT AS IT was on Ribbon Dance Hill, or even at Tekelia's house on the edge of the wood. There, it was a coruscating rainbow field, saturating everything.

Here, the colors were...dimmer, slower, and somewhat less exhilarating. Even diminished, however, the ambient was there, perfectly apparent to the senses.

Frowning, Padi brought Tekelia's signature to the front of her mind, as if she were trading faces with Lady Selph.

There came a chill, a frisson, an eye-blink of silver, and—

"There you are!" Tekelia said gaily, extending a glass filled with the Haosa's gentle green wine, rather than the sterner ruby.

"Well chosen," she said, accepting the glass with a smile.

They drank. Padi walked to the edge of the porch, to look out over the trees. In truth, it was a pleasing prospect, all the more so for being entirely unlike anything else she had seen today.

"What made you tarry?" Tekelia asked from beside her.

She turned to gaze into mismatched eyes.

"Tarry? When I had to intuit the entire procedure from—own it!—the most minimal instructions possible!"

"Not the *most* minimal," Tekelia protested, holding up a hand. "*Most* minimal would have been—*catch me*."

Padi considered that as she sipped.

"Why do I think that's precisely what the Haosa do amongst yourselves?"

"Because you would do the same, were you Haosa?"

Padi produced a frown that was perhaps not *quite* as stern as she had wished.

"You must have a very odd notion of my character," she said.

"Very likely, as I am myself odd, even among Haosa," Tekelia said equitably, leaning elbows on the rail and holding the glass in two hands.

"Being a Child of Chaos, you mean," Padi said, putting her elbows on the rail as well, and leaning into Tekelia's warmth.

"That, of course. Though standing as Speaker for the Haosa also has an effect."

Padi laughed lightly.

"Yes, I can see that might produce a certain oddness." She sipped her wine.

"Speaking of oddities..." she murmured, "why is the ambient so dim at port?"

Tekelia smiled.

"You have heard it said, I think, that the Haosa live *off-Grid*."

"I have heard that," Padi admitted.

"Civilization—and the port, too—are on-Grid." Tekelia sipped. "Or, I suppose it would be more proper to say that Civilization is *under* the Grid."

"I hadn't realized that the Grid had...presence."

"The Grid is a marvel created by the ancestors, who took their lesson from history. Not many can abide the fullness of Colemeno's ambient field—the First Wave demonstrated that to everyone's satisfaction. However, the ancestors did not wish to abandon Colemeno—and, yes, it has been suggested that this reluctance was an effect of the field."

Tekelia sipped wine, lifted a shoulder and let it fall.

"A discussion for another day. Let it simply be said that the ancestors wished to remain; they wished to live, love, and multiply in a place that was safe for themselves and their children. Therefore, they joined together and created a great weaving of placid energies to shield those who lived beneath it from the— what was the phrase from your guidebook?—the *invigorating atmosphere*? It *is* a weaving they made, thus the ambient falls through, but—filtered—much reduced, less exciting and more malleable for those who see it as a tool."

"Which would be all of Civilization," Padi murmured.

"That is so. We of the Haosa have a far different relationship with the ambient, as you have noted. The amusing thing..."

Tekelia paused to drink wine, and Padi did, as well.

"The amusing thing is, it's said that there were those among the weavers who would now be Haosa, perhaps even a Child of Chaos—or two."

"Do you think that's true, as well as amusing?"

Tekelia looked at her, face serious.

"I do. It's a working of love and mercy, and gave relief to many. The weaving was well done. What is less well done is that we have become...separate. Distrust took root; Haosa and Civilized are not at ease with each other. I don't think that the ancestors intended that."

"Surely they couldn't have," Padi said, straightening out of her lean. "Not with their history."

"The purge of the Small Talents on Liad, you mean." Tekelia slanted a smile at her. "You and I think alike."

"And so we come full circle. Tell me, how will I come back to port if I am to be responsible for my own movements? I grant I could show the ambient my father's signature, but I have—concerns."

Tekelia laughed.

"As I would. But, no. There's another way, which I'll show you, now you're out from under the Grid." Tekelia paused. "Have you time? It oughtn't take an hour, quick as you are."

"Here's a different tune! I thought I had tarried."

"By Haosa standards," Tekelia said, "perhaps, a little. Given that the idea was new to you, and the instructions—I own it!—sparse—you did very well."

"I am mollified," Padi declared. "If the lesson can be taught quickly, I am eager to learn. Father is not the only one who might not wish me to appear, suddenly and unannounced, at his side. However, we need to be aware of the time. I have been particularly invited to share the evening meal in"—she glanced at the timepiece on her wrist—"two and a half hours."

"Well, then, let's get to work!"

Tekelia grinned, held out a hand for her glass—and both vanished, possibly, Padi thought, reappearing in the kitchen.

"First," Tekelia said, "we should go into the great room."

Padi turned toward the windows leading from the porch. Tekelia caught her hand.

"Not like that. Like *this*."

Colemenoport
Port Market Offices

. . . .

"TRADER VEN'DEELIN, WE THANK YOU FOR THE GIFT OF YOUR expertise. You have given us much to think upon."

Chief Expediter rooBios looked around the room, slowly, making certain he made eye contact with each of the twelve persons who had attended Dyoli's presentation.

"May we dare to hope that you will return to us, once we have assimilated the information you presented to us today?"

"I am at your service, sir," Dyoli said, with a slight bow. She, too, glanced 'round the table, though not so intensely as the chief expediter had done. "I believe this meeting is only the beginning of a long and mutually profitable relationship."

"So do we hope, as well," Chief Expediter rooBios said. "Allow me to escort you to the security station."

They had walked to the market that morning with Grad, who had left them in the care of Port Market Security for the day. Now that the day was done, Mar Tyn supposed that they would return to the Wayfarer together, perhaps escorted by one of the Market security officers.

He himself saw very little need for a security escort on Colemenoport, which, by his standards, was rather staid. However, the master trader had been involved in a desperate portside event prior to the time when Mar Tyn and Dyoli had joined the ship. Not much was said about it, only that it had ended with a member of the security team dead, and the master trader badly wounded. The remaining security persons were on their mettle, and they were determined that none of the trade mission should suffer the least inconvenience, much less face actual danger.

"I leave you here in Krai's care, and again, I thank you both for the gift of your expertise."

Expediter rooBios bowed again, and left them.

Krai, tall and lean, looked up from his screen with a smile. "Trader, Serendipitist. Going back to the Wayfarer?"

"Actually," Dyoli said, and Mar Tyn felt a shiver in the air between them. "My partner and I would like to find a quiet glass of wine and perhaps a meal before we return to the Wayfarer. Might you recommend an appropriate restaurant?"

Krai's eyebrows rose, and Dyoli inclined her head.

"Understand that we don't mean to keep you standing by while we enjoy ourselves. Master pai'Fortana and I were only just remarking how very calm and orderly is Colemenoport. Surely, we will be in no danger for an hour or two over a meal?"

"We don't get much trouble," Krai admitted. "Though trouble can happen anywhere."

"Understood," Dyoli said, and glanced at Mar Tyn. "We are not without defenses."

"Hmm." Krai narrowed his eyes, glanced at his screen, and looked back to them with a smile.

"I believe the solution to this riddle is Zephyr's Edge Lounge," he said. "One of our own works security there during the evening hours. In fact, she will have just come on duty. Let me give her a call, so she is aware of who you are, and to find the state of the venue this evening." He raised a hand.

"It is a very safe restaurant in the very calmest part of the port. We don't expect trouble, but we do prepare for it."

"Yes," Mar Tyn said, and Krai smiled at him.

"Only a moment." He stood and went to the comm unit at the back of the room.

Mar Tyn turned to Dyoli.

"What is happening?" he murmured.

"I don't quite know," she answered. "Not a Seeing, but the air is unsettled. Do you feel it?"

"I do," he admitted, and shivered when Dyoli slipped her hand into his. Her fingers were cold, but there was an electricity in her touch that was notable, though it was not exactly the feeling they shared when they were about to . . . interface with the future.

"The thing's done!" Krai announced, coming to them. "Brit will be aware, but will not interfere with your privacy. I'll call

Grad, to let him know our arrangements. It would possibly relieve his feelings if you called him for an escort home, when you're finished."

"Thank you for your care," Dyoli said.

"You're very welcome, Trader. Thank you for reminding us that there's a line between protection and oppression. I'll escort you to the Zephyr and then, I swear, I'll leave you in peace."

Colemenoport
Wayfarer

. . . .

"GOOD EVENING, PRISCILLA."

Shan draped his jacket over the back of the chair in the entry hall, and left his case on the seat.

Priscilla was sitting on the U-shaped sofa, working on a tablet. She glanced up with a smile.

"Good evening," she said. "Sit, and I will fetch wine."

"I am already standing, and in any case would welcome a glass of cold tea. Shall I freshen your glass?"

"Yes, thank you."

She had put the tablet aside by the time he returned and sat down next to her.

He raised his glass toward her with a smile, and drank.

"No toast at all this evening, or is the tea not worthy?"

"The tea is everything that is worthy, and if I were able, I would give it such a toast as might transform it into wine. Alas, I have been buffeted from meeting to meeting since I left you this morning. My wit is at low ebb."

"You might toast to less buffeting," she suggested, raising her own glass.

Shan tipped his head, as if considering the merits of her suggestion.

"I might," he said. "However, I feel strongly that a certain amount of buffeting—even consternation!—works in our favor. We are something new and unlooked-for, arriving at the door of an existing, not to say stagnant, system. It might not have been entirely comfortable, but it was familiar. Our very arrival has thrown order into disarray, widened the horizon of possibility, and kindled, so I hope, the spirit of adventure in the hearts of merchants and council. Really, it's a wonder that any of us can sleep at night."

He put his glass aside, and slid down to let his head rest on the back of the sofa. He closed his eyes, and for a moment merely sat, allowing himself to melt out of the stance, the mindset, the *melant'i* of master trader and into only—Shan.

Eyes closed, he could See Priscilla's familiar and beloved pattern clearly. Even, one might say, with *unusual* clarity. That was Colemeno's particular charged atmosphere at work. It fizzed along his Healer senses, exhilarating and...perhaps dangerous. At least risky. Probably. It might be wise to close his shields entirely, though they were open only the barest amount.

He had never felt less wise.

"Shall I bring you a blanket?" Priscilla asked.

He opened his eyes and turned his head to look at her.

"Will you share it with me?"

"That could be arranged."

"Temptress."

Priscilla considered him, black eyes bright, each ebon curl flashing with energy. Her pattern sparkled—again, the influence of the ambient energies.

"Colemeno agrees with you," he said.

"Colemeno *acts upon* me," she corrected.

"As you say. Tell me how you enjoyed the lecture."

Priscilla raised her eyebrows.

"What do I get in return?"

"An apt question. I offer a précis of my meeting with Trader Isfelm in the latter part of the day."

"Done," Priscilla said. She put her glass on the table, and curled 'round, drawing her legs up onto the cushion as she faced him.

"The lecture was in fact a dialogue between two scholars very well known to each other. They are doing a series, so Portmaster krogerSlyte tells me, and have received good reviews. Scholar sereWai is a historian, and Scholar rodaMildin a sociologist. I feel as though I learned quite a bit, and was entertained as well."

She sighed.

"We attended the reception afterward, and Portmaster kroger-Slyte introduced me to the scholars. I'm...afraid I have promised to let Scholar rodaMildin interview me, as a representative of the first group of unknowns to have raised the Redlands since the Dust's arrival."

"You have been busy. And the portmaster?"

"The portmaster is greatly encouraged to hear that the master trader is opening a whole port inventory. She is assigning additional rooms around our center here, for Jes and Dil Nem. She's also opening an office suite adjacent to the trade mission office for Jes."

"Well. If only everyone was so easy to please."

Priscilla laughed softly.

"How fares Trader Isfelm?"

"Much in her usual style. She made me known to a number of useful persons, and promises more, in the fullness of time. In addition, she advised me to set up my own base, once we become regular here."

"That's good advice," Priscilla said after a moment.

"It is, isn't it?" He sat up and reached for his glass.

"Further on the topic of becoming regular here, Trader Isfelm states that she would favor going forward with a partnership, we providing goods not only for Colemeno, but to the Isfelm Trade Union and the Iverson Loop, which they will take on, and deliver to that portion of their Loop still entangled with the Dust."

"Isn't that rather...soon?"

"It may be. On the other hand, it's also canny. The good trader feels she can trust us, because we are Dust Cousins." He gave her a particularly earnest look.

Priscilla inclined her head gravely. "Of course," she murmured.

"Yes, well. If we go to contract, she will have an existing arrangement in place, which she may then use as a baseline when other traders begin to arrive at Colemeno. In addition, she will have been among the first to contract with Tree-and-Dragon, which she will play to her advantage, or she's not the trader I believe her to be."

"And our benefit?"

"We will have an introduction to trade beyond Colemeno, with the wisdom of an established entity to guide us. Wherein lies the rub."

He gazed down into his glass.

"I have been directed by Korval Themselves to establish *profitable* routes," he said wryly. "Which means that, Dust-kin or merely pleasant fellow travelers, I must insist upon a trade audit."

Priscilla frowned.

"The ship's *qe'andra*—" she began.

Shan shook his head.

"*Qe'andra* dea'Tolin is needed here, and will very soon discover herself with a sufficiency of work. I will this evening send to the delm and ask that Mr. dea'Gauss come to us in our hour of need."

"Mr. dea'Gauss? The *elder* Mr. dea'Gauss?"

"Unless his health does not allow, in which case I believe I may depend upon the delm to find another dea'Gauss who is both brilliant, thoroughgoing, and willing to address an adventure."

"When the *qe'andra* arrives, will you accompany them along Trader Isfelm's Loop?"

He smiled at her kindly.

"Priscilla, you must be exhausted; your wits have gone wandering. The master trader will be continuing his proper work in opening this port, and establishing Tree-and-Dragon as the premier and preferred trade partner."

He sipped his tea.

"Trader yos'Galan will accompany the *qe'andra* on the audit tour."

"Which is why you want the elder Mr. dea'Gauss. Experience balancing enthusiasm."

"Exactly."

"Speaking of Padi," Priscilla said. "Does she plan to share the meal with us this evening?"

Shan sighed, again seeing his daughter frowning at the air before snapping crisply out of sight, appearing to follow Tekelia-*dramliza*. One hesitated to interfere in the private matters of adults. On the other hand, there were expectable standards of courtesy. Such as sending a note to one's parent, acknowledging receipt of an invitation to dine, and regretfully pleading a pressing prior engagement.

"Shan?" Priscilla murmured. He shook himself.

"I am behind in checking my messages. However, it may be that she is promised elsewhere."

It was never wise to try to conceal things from Priscilla who, aside the familiarity granted lifemates, was perfectly able to See his unruly emotions.

"What's happened?" she asked, sharply.

The door to Padi's room snapped open and she strode out, her pattern fairly crackling with energy, and an expression of wide delight on her face.

"It worked!" she said exuberantly. "Oh, this is *excellent*!"

Colemenoport
Zephyr's Edge Lounge

. . . .

THEY SAT IN A GARDEN UNDER A CANOPY STRIPED IN BRIGHT colors that rippled in the warm breeze, sipping the wine that their server had suggested as a pleasant "end of day" vintage.

Mar Tyn was no judge of such things in terms of worth or vintage. Such wine as there had been in Low Port had been sour, or sweet. The sour had been unpleasant in the mouth, and the sweet wine too often was sweet from added sugar meant to disguise the taste of unkinder drugs.

This wine...was pleasant in the mouth, and tasted of citrus and vanilla. He had another sip, and closed his eyes to better enjoy it.

"Now, there's a gentle finishing up to a busy day," Dyoli said. "Our server did not misinform."

Mar Tyn opened his eyes to see her smiling at him.

"A pleasant refreshment," he said, smiling back, and Dyoli laughed.

"You have been studying the master trader, I see. Be warned, my Mar Tyn; supporting that style requires considerable reserves of energy."

"It can do no harm to identify useful phrases and study the best time to use them," he protested. "I don't aspire to the master trader's style. It would look ill on me, I think."

Dyoli lowered her glass and studied him, her expression speculative.

"Not ill, but—startling. If you were a trader, it might do, as an honest advantage, you understand."

Mar Tyn half-laughed.

"Only, I don't understand. What is an 'honest advantage'?"

131

"It is what Master Trader yos'Galan gains with his artless conversation and his air of being, just slightly, foolish. Certain persons fail to see beyond that, or, indeed, to reason their way to the conclusion that a master trader cannot be a fool. Those persons may attempt to overreach. Whereby the master trader has learned something of importance, to himself, and to trade."

"Does your brother practice an honest advantage?"

"He had used to produce an impression of sheltered youth, but he must have refined himself by now. I shall be certain to ask him, when next we meet."

Mar Tyn put his glass on the table, so as not to drink all the wine at once.

"Are we likely to meet your brother again?"

Dyoli's eyebrows rose.

"Certainly, we must. Ixin is a partner in the venture here on Colemeno, and Til Den is the master trader responsible for that. Eventually, he must arrive to see what the contract has produced."

She also put her glass down.

"It will be later rather than sooner, unless Master Trader yos'Galan asks him to come."

"After the whole port inventory, then."

"Oh, surely. Quite likely we will be well set up in the office before we see Til Den again."

"You're very certain of the trade office. The inventory hasn't been started yet."

"The fact that the inventory has been opened means we have progressed a half-dozen steps down the path toward the trade office," Dyoli said. "The master trader must follow the forms, but I do not have the sense that he would have called *Qe'andra* dea'Tolin to the fore if he had not already been convinced that Colemeno will do very well, for Korval and for Ixin."

Mar Tyn leaned slightly forward. Something had brushed against his Gift—an unsettling feeling at best. Yet, he felt no compulsion to rise, or act, or, indeed, to do anything other than sit under the awning in the pleasant breeze, sip wine and say to Dyoli—

"What if, despite everything, it is discovered that Colemeno will not do?" he asked, hearing the urgency in his voice, and wondering if *that* was what his Gift was acting on.

"Dyoli," he said sharply, "are you Seeing?"

She showed him empty hands.

"I am seeing only my love," she said. "As for your question—either the master trader will open the market, or he will not. If he does not, he will move on to his next target of opportunity."

"And we with him?"

"Ah, I see," Dyoli said, her brow clearing. She glanced to the side. Following her gaze, Mar Tyn saw their server approaching.

"Are you content to order a meal and another glass?" Dyoli asked him. "We might continue our conversation at leisure."

Mar Tyn held himself still for a long moment, allowing his Gift time to manifest. Nothing arose.

"In fact," he said to Dyoli, "I am—content. And also hungry."

"That settles the matter, then," she said, and turned, the server having arrived, to ask regarding the evening meal.

Colemenoport
Wayfarer

· · · · · · · · · · ·

THE WILD RUSH OF ENERGY INTO THE ROOM WOULD HAVE BROUGHT Shan to his feet, if Priscilla had not placed a hand on his knee.

"Hello, Padi," she said, calmly. "We were just wondering if you'd be joining us for the meal."

Padi turned, light on her toes, pattern blazing even as the excess energy ebbed.

"I sent to Father that I would come," she said, "and I had told Tekelia *particularly* that there must be a time limit on lessons, as I was promised elsewhere." She looked over her shoulder, finding the clock that dominated the entrance hall.

"Oh, but we did manage it—and I'm not late at all!" she said, sounding less relieved than triumphant.

"Indeed," Shan said. "You are in very good time. Will you have a glass?"

Padi smiled.

"I would like a glass," she confessed. "May I beg half an hour to rid myself of the day's dust?"

"An exemplary notion!" Shan said. "I believe I will do the same. Priscilla?"

"After I call down to be certain of the meal," Priscilla said. "Will Tekelia be joining us, Padi?"

"Tekelia is dining elsewhere this evening," Padi said. "I am given to say that they hope to have all of us to share a meal with the Haosa, very soon."

"That sounds delightful," Shan murmured. Padi spun and reentered her room, rather less precipitously than she had exited, and closed the door.

Shan picked up his glass and glanced at his lifemate.

134

"Only see how inconsistent we are, Priscilla," he said. "We had been distressed when she resisted her Talents. Now, we are distressed when she embraces them." He sipped wine. "Whatever they are."

"And however they may manifest when not being influenced by Colemeno's ambient," Priscilla added. She tipped her head, brows drawn.

"Actually," she said, meeting his eyes, "I think I prefer an exuberant student."

"As do I," Shan agreed. "I only wish I were more certain of the tutor."

"Tekelia has done us no harm, and might be said to have acted generously on our behalf," Priscilla said.

"All true. Well. I had said that my wits were lagging."

He drank the last of his tea and stood.

"I will return, after I have dusted myself off. Possibly my wits will be revived by the process."

"I'll call the kitchen," Priscilla said.

"If one may be bold, Daughter," Shan said, as he poured fresh glasses, "*what* worked?"

Padi was curled into the curve of the sofa, dressed in ship casual: sweater, loose pants, and soft shoes. Her pattern was scintillant, reflecting both pleasure and satisfaction.

She looked up at him, her face relaxed, lavender eyes languid.

"A...technique," she said, and glanced to Priscilla, who was also curled into the sofa's giving cushions, long legs drawn up beside her.

She gave Padi a smile.

"I am," she said, "all ears."

"From which stems my concern," Padi said. "I fear that description may be beyond my scope."

"Come now, Trader yos'Galan!" Shan said, bringing the tray over and setting it in the center of the table. He gave Priscilla the glass of iced mint tea; Padi, the glass of the white. Taking the red for himself, he settled onto the sofa between his daughter and his lifemate.

"I have heard you wax eloquent regarding cogwheels and gear ratios! Surely, you may do justice to a technique which touched you with such joy."

Padi paused, her glass not quite to her lips, expression arrested.

"Joy," she repeated.

"Well," Shan said, apologetically, "perhaps I was mistaken. Priscilla, what aspect would you say adorned Padi's arrival among us this evening?"

"At least delight," Priscilla said. She smiled at Padi. "Are we both wrong?"

Padi sipped her wine, eyes narrowed.

"I will own both joy and delight. As to the technique, it is a . . . mode of travel." She tipped her head as if considering that assertion, then nodded.

"One mode of travel," she said, and met Shan's eyes. "Two formulas for arrival."

Shan inclined his head.

"Yes." Padi sighed. "What one must do is form an image in the mind—either of a personal signature, or a place one has visited. Once the image is perfectly formed, it is shown to the ambient, which—transports one to the person or the place pictured."

She looked down then, and raised her glass, as if to fortify herself against disbelief, or, Shan thought, recrimination.

As strong as her Talent was, Padi had not found it easy to absorb the techniques meant to assist her in its use. This had become a point of frustration to her, and to those teachers who had been available aboard *Dutiful Passage*—including himself. She struggled to build the simplest tools, to hold the most basic shapes firm, and expressed impatience with core concepts. Most of the greater Talents—Healers, and *dramliz* in all their variations—*required* tools, shapes, and concepts to guide them, and to conserve energy, Talent not being a limitless resource.

However, to his Healer's Eyes, Padi's Talent seemed to be precisely that—without limit. When startled or hurried, she did not make a tool, or summon a shape, but merely—*reached* for the desired result.

"I did say," Padi murmured, "that I might not do justice."

"So you did, and we were fairly warned." Shan set his glass aside. "I wonder if you might show me the way of it?"

Padi's eyes widened.

"You're a Healer," she said.

Shan rose, and looked down at her, one eyebrow lifted.

"It can't be helped, you know," he said mildly. "Certainly I have no hope that I will stop being a Healer at my time in life. Will it matter, do you think?"

She blinked.

"I don't know, having just learnt myself. Perhaps we ought better to have Tekelia—"

"Tekelia-*dramliza* is wanted elsewhere this evening," Shan interrupted. "Come, where is the harm? If I am inept or unable, surely all that will happen is that—*nothing* will happen. I will remain here while you manifest in whatever delightful locale you might picture. Once you notice my absence, you can return."

Padi turned to Priscilla, whom he doubted was best pleased with him at the moment.

"Lina said it would take an... appreciable time for his—his Talent—to fully return."

Which was more than Lina had been pleased to tell *him*, Shan thought, crankily. *Vot'itzen*, indeed.

Priscilla moved a hand, to all of his senses utterly unconcerned. "Lina did not foresee Colemeno. He is as well—or better—than he's ever been. I don't think you'll break him. And it would be interesting to know if you can teach him this technique." She smiled. "Please—begin the lesson immediately, so I can have my turn before the meal arrives."

For an instant, Padi looked betrayed. Shan carefully did not smile, but met her eyes gravely.

"Well, Daughter? Is now a convenient time? The meal isn't due for half an hour yet."

She closed her eyes briefly, put her glass down and rose.

"I think," she said, "that I had best emulate my teacher, and begin with this—*catch me*."

She blinked out of sight.

Shan raised his eyebrows.

"I see I've been put on my mettle," he said, and brought Padi's signature to the front of his mind. That part was quite easy, though he remained somewhat in the dark about *showing it to the ambient*. However, if the ambient was, in fact, *ambient*, then surely all one needed to do was to concentrate and—

The parlor smeared away into fog, and he was blinking into Padi's face. They were standing quite close, in the center of her private room.

"I suppose," his daughter said, sounding resigned, "that being a Healer doesn't matter."

"I am pleased to hear you say so," he told her earnestly, even as he did a quick internal inventory. He appeared to be quite unharmed, his heartbeat was steady, his breathing was deep and calm. As best as he could tell, he had expended no energy at all in leaping from parlor to bedroom. Which could not be so.

Could it?

"For the next lesson," Padi said, "you will need to bring the parlor to mind, and show *that* image to the ambient." She paused to give him an appraising look. "It would be best if you picture a section of the room that is clear of furniture or other hazards to footing. I offer this advice from personal experience."

Once again, she blinked out of sight.

It was easier this time—merely a thought, a brief foggy smear, and hey, presto! He was standing beside Padi in the parlor, and Priscilla was rising from the sofa, her eyes sparkling.

"My turn," she said.

Colemenoport
Zephyr's Edge Lounge

. . . .

"THE CONTRACT THAT MY BROTHER AND MASTER TRADER YOS'GALAN wrote between them was for opening the Redlands to trade, and evaluating its suitability as a hub, or multi-route anchor.

"The master trader hopes for a hub, and an expansion of trade in this sector. If he can take that trick, we will be the managers of the combined Tree-and-Dragon and Ixin trade office."

Mar Tyn inclined his head to indicate that he was paying attention, though this was not new information.

"A hub office will also want a trader dedicated to the Colemeno routes—possibly, there will rotating traders, between Ixin and Korval. These are details that must wait upon the port inventory, whereupon the master traders will consult and write another contract.

"In the meanwhile, it would not surprise me if the master trader negotiates a place for Trader yos'Galan for at least one circuit on an already existing Loop. This would not only set her feet on the path to master trader, but will substantially increase the master trader's credibility with the Council."

Dyoli paused to address the *skavaso* soup, which even Mar Tyn could tell was excellent. In fact, his cup was almost empty, as his part had been to listen. He dawdled over the last spoonfuls, while Dyoli caught herself up.

"That was lovely," she said, putting the cup aside with a sigh. Their server came cat-foot to the table, gathered up the cups, and went away.

"If the master trader fails to win his point," he said, "none of those plans will meet reality."

"Very true. And here is where the contract may aid us, my

139

Mar Tyn. It seems very odd to me that the clauses should encompass so much air. There is, you understand, *usual language* which is placed into such contracts, detailing how the resources from each side ought to be accounted, in the case of both success and failure. We being personnel not of his clan, the master trader would have guaranteed to bring us to a port of Ixin's choosing, where we would await our further instructions.

"This contract merely states that, should the mission fail, an evaluation will be performed, and resources disposed as circumstance dictates."

Mar Tyn frowned.

"He could leave us here—the master trader."

Dyoli beamed at him.

"Indeed he could! And will be more likely to do so, if we establish ourselves credibly, beyond our duties for the trade mission."

"Dyoli, would you remain here? Your clan—"

"My clan has become accustomed to my absence. Prior to our meeting, I had my place in the guildhall, as you know. I did visit home, but that was not every day, nor even every *relumma*." She moved her shoulders. "It would have been the same, if I had pursued a career in trade, as Til Den has. Indeed, he is away more than he is home, that being the nature of trade. Should the master trader's plans come to ruin, we may continue as we are. Ixin would be well satisfied, if only I can show that I am gainfully employed, and upholding the clan's honor." She gave him a round-eyed glance.

"Or at least not actively damaging it. And I *will not* hear, Mar Tyn, that you are capable of damaging Ixin's honor."

Their server arrived just then, bearing plates, which she disposed deftly, before refilling their glasses from the bottle, and ghosting away again.

"There will need to be some details arranged," Dyoli said, "such as the timely transfer of my quartershare to our local accounts, but those are merely details, and well within Til Den's scope."

She paused. Possibly, Mar Tyn thought, he was meant to speak, but for his life could think of nothing to say.

Dyoli tipped her head.

"Do you not like Colemeno, Mar Tyn?"

"I like what I have seen thus far," he said honestly, and added, "but we have neither one of us seen very much."

"This is so, but we have time to lighten the burden of our ignorance," Dyoli said. "If it comes about that we cannot support Colemeno, then we may make an alternative plan. We are this evening in the realm of first thoughts, and considering opportunities."

Mar Tyn looked at her.

"Is that trading?"

Dyoli laughed.

"In fact, it is! We will make a trader of you yet, my Mar Tyn."

He smiled and shook his head.

"I doubt I have the aptitude, though I will gladly take lessons from you."

"Then we are in accord," said Dyoli, and turned to her meal.

Colemenoport
Wayfarer

. . . .

SHAN HAD HOPED TO OPEN DISCUSSION OVER THE MEAL, BUT that hope quickly evaporated.

Padi addressed her salad with concentration, devouring it with a dainty ferocity that defeated any attempt at conversation, and reached to the basket for a second biscuit.

Priscilla disposed of her salad and a biscuit with neat efficiency, only checking when she, too, began to reach for a second biscuit.

She raised her head and looked first to Padi, then met Shan's eyes.

He inclined his head.

It was no surprise, really, that Padi was ravenous. Not only had she received lessons in teleportation, she had arrived at home via that means. Then, she had teleported four times across the suite.

Priscilla's increased appetite was also expectable, since she had teleported twice across the suite.

What *did* surprise was that *he*, having likewise teleported across the suite twice, was perfectly satisfied to savor his salad, and would not have considered himself ill-used, if one of his companions had helped herself to the remaining half of his biscuit.

He took a sip of wine. On the whole, he decided, he was relieved to find that Colemeno's pesky field did not transcend *every* law of the universe.

Pushing back his chair, he excused himself from the table, went to the comm and touched the button that would connect him directly with the kitchen.

In short order, he was speaking with Luzant iberFel, the kitchen manager—an excellent person who had made it her business when they had first arrived to find their preferences in

142

terms of foodstuffs, seasoning, and hours—and requested that a sampling of high-caloric foods be sent up.

This required some discussion of what, precisely, his need was.

"My companions have overexerted themselves," Shan said. "They're quite famished, poor things, and—"

"I understand," she said briskly. "We have the basic restorative tray on hand. I'm having that sent up immediately."

"Thank you," Shan said, thinking that of course a planet largely populated by *dramliz* would have developed their own variation of "Healer Mendoza's tray."

"Please tell your colleagues to call down, should they find their own preferences not in the basic tray. We are pleased to customize."

"Thank you," Shan said again. At that point, the food lift chimed, and he closed the call with promises to call again if another tray should be required.

Priscilla was serving out the main course when he returned to table, with the greater share finding its way onto Padi's plate.

She looked up as he placed his burden into the center of the table.

"The basic restorative tray," Shan said to her raised eyebrows. "The kitchen manager asks specifically to be informed of anything you would like to see more, or I assume, less, of, so that she may build on the basics for you."

Padi was rapidly clearing her plate.

Shan sat down and addressed his own meal—fish with lemon sauce. Understated and pleasant.

"Padi, have one of the muffins," Priscilla said, just a little—a very little—Command glittering along the edge of her voice.

Padi fairly snatched up a muffin, and broke it in half.

Shan continued his unhurried perusal of the fish.

He had just finished when Padi leaned back in her chair, apparently sated at last, and looked to Priscilla.

"Healer Mendoza's tray," she said. "But—why?"

"Obviously," Priscilla said, finishing the second high-protein muffin, "because you—and I—expended energy and needed to replenish ourselves."

Padi frowned.

"But—"

"Did Tekelia-*dramliza* not explain the physical costs?" Shan asked, perhaps a touch sharply.

"Possibly there is no cost for Tekelia, who is a Colemeno native," Priscilla suggested.

"I would grant the point, save that Luzant iberFel very quickly grasped the situation, and had a basic tray in the pantry."

"Meaning that the effect and the restorative have entered the common culture," Priscilla said, reaching for her glass.

"I will grant," Shan said, leaning back in his chair, "that Colemeno's long isolation may have eroded the understanding that their situation is—unique."

He raised his glass slightly in salute.

"Which point must be added to our after-dinner discussion."

Padi looked at him.

"After-dinner discussion?"

"Well," Shan said apologetically, "it was to have been a working meal of its kind, but events overtook us."

Padi reached for her wine, and abruptly stopped.

"Tekelia," she said slowly, "had wine waiting for me when I arrived. The last target in our practice runs was the bakery in the village. We each had a slice of savory pie there, and a glass of tea."

"Proving that Tekelia is a native, and that taking care of the energy expenditure is second nature," Priscilla pointed out. "I don't think the failure to give Padi clear warning was—malicious."

"Acquit me!" Shan raised a hand. "I did not say *malicious*."

"Tekelia," Padi said, raising her voice slightly, "is *subtle*, which I discover that I am not. We *did* eat after our exertions. It is entirely my fault if I failed to understand that pie was part of the lesson." She tipped her head, frowning, and sent Shan a sharp look.

"Councilor ziaGorn told us, as well. You recall it, Father, I know. We had been expressing our surprise at how much cake we had encountered, and he said—he said—"

"'No one wants an incident,'" Shan murmured. "'And cake is a very simple thing.'"

"Yes, exactly!"

Shan inclined his head. "Another valid point. We were informed, and more than once. We will therefore know better in future."

"We will," she agreed, "but what *I* want to know right now

is—why were Priscilla and I affected, but not you? You expended just as much energy as we did."

"No, I think not," Shan said. "At least, a self-examination revealed no large—or even minor—expenditure of energy."

"But—"

"You supported his efforts," Priscilla interrupted. "In fact, he *is* a Healer, not a *dramliza*. You may have felt him concentrate on your signature, whereupon your Talent reached out to assist him in accomplishing the jumps." She smiled. "Much like your trick with the stylus, I think."

Padi blinked.

"And that!" Shan said, "would have meant that you worked twice as hard, Daughter, and quite wore through the benefit of your restorative pie at the village." He sipped his wine and put the glass on the table. "No wonder you were hungry."

Padi sighed and closed her eyes.

"I do hope," Shan said, "that this hasn't put you off of leaping from place to place at whim. I found it exhilarating, even as a passenger."

Padi opened her eyes and smiled.

"It was glorious, wasn't it?" she said, softly. "And so—effortless."

"Which leads us neatly into our discussions," Shan said briskly. "Let us adjourn to the sofa. I will bring fresh glasses."

"I will clear the table," Padi said, coming to her feet and beginning to gather the dishes together.

Colemenoport
Zephyr's Edge

. . . .

"SHALL WE HAVE A SWEET?" DYOLI ASKED.

Their waiter had left them alone with the last of their wine, which suited them well, as neither was inclined, just yet, to rise and return to quarters.

Mar Tyn followed Dyoli's gaze. A woman in the livery of the restaurant staff was slowly pushing a mirrored tray past the tables to their right. The tray was crowded with what Mar Tyn supposed must be Dyoli's sweets.

He considered. The meal had been plentiful and good, and he certainly did not feel the need for more food. It had, in fact, been quite some time since he had felt that he had not eaten enough. A sweet would be pleasant, though not at all necessary, only—

There was an itch in the back of his mind.

"Perhaps we should choose enough for all, and take them home to share," he heard himself say with some astonishment.

Dyoli's eyebrows lifted, even as she inclined her head.

"An excellent notion," she said, and raised her hand.

The woman with the sweets tray saw, and turned their way, smiling—

And then not smiling, her face gone ashen and her eyes wide and wild.

"Murderers!" she screamed, and shoved the tray violently toward their table.

Dyoli leapt to her feet and Mar Tyn with her.

"Mind stealers!" the server screamed more loudly, and now other diners were rising, some moving toward them, others backing away.

"Monsters! *Reavers!*"

It was the last word that tipped the scales.

People began to shout, and rushed forward.

The server threw herself at Dyoli, who sidestepped nimbly, her hand falling onto Mar Tyn's arm. She pulled him back with her, as if she might run into the restaurant.

But there was no place to go. Mar Tyn felt the particular electric tingle that meant the Gift that Dyoli and he held together was working, and he swallowed in horror.

They were going to change the future, he knew it.

And people were going to be hurt because of it.

He snatched his arm away, and spun to face the mob at the rear, back-to-back with Dyoli.

"Reavers!" the man nearest Mar Tyn shouted and lunged—

Only to be snatched back by a tall, broad woman in a security vest, who landed light on her feet, grabbed Mar Tyn's arm and Dyoli's and raised her voice.

"Security! The matter is in hand! Everyone resume your seats. The matter is in hand!"

The air warmed, and Mar Tyn was suddenly calm. Very calm. He watched as the effect spread out into the mob. Angry faces became peaceful; tension was shrugged out of shoulders, as people turned back to their tables and their interrupted meals.

He turned his head, and over his shoulder saw another person in a security vest, holding the now-drooping server.

"But they killed Sylk," the server whispered, disconsolate. "They're Reavers."

"Perhaps, perhaps not," said the guard holding her. "You all need to go to the guard house. There's a Truthseer there. She'll sort everything out, never fear it."

Two more uniformed persons were approaching. Port Security, Mar Tyn thought, which ought to have produced concern, if not actual fear, but he was merely calm in the grasp of his captor.

"That's right, now," she said, and adjusted her grip on his arm, bringing him up beside Dyoli.

"Port Security's here, and we're all going to go with them, peacefully."

She began to walk, and they with her.

Colemenoport
Wayfarer

· · · · · · · · · ·

"WE HAVE PERSONAL DECISIONS BEFORE US, WHICH INTERSECT with decisions of trade." Shan gazed at his daughter and lifemate, seated on the sofa. Both looked well fed and alert, which was something of a relief. He sipped his wine and put the glass on the table.

"Firstly, Trader Isfelm, who is, as I believe Trader yos'Galan noted only yesterday, sharp enough to cut, has today proposed a partnership."

Padi blinked.

"Is this why yos'Phelium does not trade?" she asked.

Shan grinned at her.

"You find the trader precipitate?"

"I would," Padi said, "if I had not seen *you* at work, Master Trader." She raised her glass. "I had thought Trader Isfelm bent on going *Out*, as she has it, by any route that presents itself."

"That also seems to be a goal, and is not necessarily incompatible with pursuing a partnership with Tree-and-Dragon," Shan said. "There are other traders involved in the Iverson Loop, including Trader Isfelm's brother, so the family interest is protected, even should the senior trader temporarily remove herself in order to explore opportunity."

"Will she come with us on the *Passage*?" Priscilla asked.

Shan smiled at her. "We discussed it. She proposes to swap places with Trader yos'Galan."

Padi sat up straight.

"Your pardon?"

"Well," Shan said apologetically, "you must admit that Trader Isfelm's bid for partnership has merit, and could prove beneficial

148

to Tree-and-Dragon, the Iverson Loop, and the Redlands. Which means that—"

"I'm to do a route audit," Padi breathed, between terror and amaze, as Shan read it. "I—will need assistance," she said. "*Experienced* assistance."

"Indeed you will," Shan said, with strong approval. "I will this evening undertake to gain experienced assistance for you. There is also, of course, reading—"

"Yes..."

"And a certification course. I will send the module to you. The course is self-paced, and I am empowered to administer the required tests."

If Padi found anything dismaying in the sudden acquisition of a dense course of study in addition to her duties as part of the trade team, she gave no indication of it.

"How soon?" she asked.

"You have time to take the course. Very possibly, the port inventory will be complete before you are called upon to leave us," Shan said. "If your experienced assistance leaves Surebleak upon receipt of my request, he will have some travel before him, Colemeno not being—"

"Conveniently placed," Padi said with a smile. "But we may, in time, make it more so."

"Exactly what I was thinking!" Shan told her.

"Once we have the audit in hand, we will know whether a partnership with the Iverson Loop will in fact be as advantageous as it appears at first glance," he continued. "We may, indeed, wish to offer a temporary partnership, and seal it with an exchange of traders—as Trader Isfelm has suggested. That may be the most graceful route, assuming that Colemeno itself is found to be strong enough to act as an anchor for a Long Loop from our side.

"In any wise, we will assume that, by one route or another, Trader yos'Galan will be departing Colemeno on the Iverson Loop. The *Passage* will certainly depart when the master trader has completed his work. The question arises—do some of us wish to depart sooner? There is no reason that the *Passage* need tarry 'round Colemeno, if it comes to that—"

Beside him, Priscilla sighed, and looked to Padi.

"I've been expecting this," she said, and turned to Shan. "Will I flee to Surebleak so that our child is born in-clan?"

Shan raised a hand.

"Another question—do we wish our child to be born in an *invigorating environment*?"

"The Goddess did say our daughter would encompass marvels," Priscilla pointed out. "Why not begin at once?"

"Priscilla, you terrify me," Shan said with feeling.

"Yes, love, I know," she answered soothingly. "Are we certain that the ambient conditions haven't already had an effect?"

Shan pressed his lips together.

Priscilla nodded. "No. We do not know that. We do not know that our child will be born into a Talent."

"In fact," Shan said, "the only thing we *do* know is that she will be born a child of Korval—which is quite frightening enough."

"There are children born on Colemeno every day," Priscilla said placidly. "I expect they do well enough."

She sipped her tea and turned to look directly into his eyes.

"When the time comes, the captain will take *Dutiful Passage* to the master trader's next destination," she said forcefully. "I will not be coddled. I will not be sent away *to safety*, as if there were any such thing. And I *will not* be a reason for the master trader to stint his work."

Shan blinked.

"Surely you know me better than that," he murmured.

"Surely I do," she answered with a smile.

Shan drew a breath, but whatever he might have been about to say was interrupted by the chime of an incoming call.

Padi rose and went to the comm.

"yos'Galan," she said. "Service?"

"Trader yos'Galan, this is Healer ven'Deelin." Dyoli's voice was sharp, and a bit breathless.

"Master pai'Fortana and I are at the Colemenoport Guard House. We are being held on suspicion of being... *Reavers*. They are insisting upon an official examination. We have previously been examined by Evaluation Expert ringZun, who pronounced us well enough, but that buys nothing from either our accuser or the arresting officer."

Padi drew a breath.

"The master trader will speak with the officer," she said, turning—but Father was already at her side.

"Timin nimOlad, Port Security Officer," said a rather timid

voice. Padi winced. Dyoli's tongue was as sharp as any dagger. Apparently, she had drawn blood here.

"I am Shan yos'Galan, master trader leading the Tree-and-Dragon trade mission," Father said, sternly. "Healer ven'Deelin and Master pai'Fortana are members of the mission. By Guild Law they may have a ranking member of their team with them at any trial or examination."

"Yes, sir." Officer nimOlad sounded almost grateful. "Please do come. Chief bennaFalm has apprised the Warden of the situation. I'm certain he will be pleased to have you here, as well."

"I'll go," Padi said, after Shan had concluded the call. He turned to look at her, eyebrows up.

"You have a reason for making this generous offer, I assume? A desire to tour the port security office? An eagerness to renew your acquaintance with the Warden? A—"

"Tekelia thought you were a Reaver," Padi interrupted. "You are marked by the Healings you shared with Tarona Rusk." She paused to Look—and found the two black threads that marked the association with the woman she understood to have been the genius behind sending captive Talents to Colemeno in order to secure even more Talents for her net of bound power. Civilization and the Haosa had known those agents as "Reavers." Father had cut their bonds, and all the Reavers on Colemeno, and many others, elsewhere, had died, from what Priscilla called "separation trauma."

After, Father had Healed Tarona Rusk of the wounds inflicted on her by the Department of the Interior, and Tarona Rusk had Healed Father of the wounds she had inflicted on him. Those actions had left in his pattern, perfectly visible to anyone with Wizard's Eyes—which was most of the population of Colemeno—two threads that matched the signature that had been apparent in the pattern of every Reaver.

Dyoli and Mar Tyn had been bound to Tarona Rusk, though they had managed to survive the trauma of separation. Their signatures, Padi realized abruptly, would include that same black thread.

"Tekelia," Father said, "was able to be persuaded otherwise. And if I am found to be anathema because of my past actions, then the trade team has its answer, and need waste no more resources on Colemeno."

Padi drew a deep breath, but before she could speak, Priscilla did.

"All Healers know that there must be a certain sympathy between Healer and client. If that sympathy is not present, Healing cannot take place. If it is present, then Healer and Healed become entangled."

She glanced at Father. "I would be surprised to find that lesson had been forgotten here. Also, the signature is quite apparent, for any who can See. Best it's sorted out now."

"Precisely." Father sighed, and turned away. "Well. I to rouse the master trader. We will finish our private discussions at some future point."

"May I at least come with you?" Padi asked quietly.

Father turned back.

"The offer does you honor," he said, with a certain overdone earnestness that Padi knew all too well.

"But I am of more use held in reserve, in case someone might need to pay your bail," she said, moving a hand to show that she understood his position.

Father tipped his head.

"You are despondent. But how if you should be needed to perform a thrilling jailbreak, bringing three of us from captivity to freedom at the speed of thought? Would not *that* be worth doing, Trader Padi?"

It did give one a thrill, Padi admitted, even as she frowned at him.

"I trust you will manage the thing with more subtlety than that, Master Trader," she said sternly, and he bowed his head meekly.

"Your faith in my abilities warms me," he murmured.

On-Grid
Cardfall Casino

. . . .

IT WAS A RELIEF TO ESCAPE TO HIS OFFICE AND THE PAPERWORK waiting for him there.

Majel set the kettle to brewing, and crossed to the desk, bending slightly to tap his screen up.

His mail was—not as much as he had feared, but what was there was dense.

Extremely dense.

The bank had found no breach, and had taken no damage through its connection with the room master. However, the directors were extremely displeased with Cardfall Casino for putting the bank in harm's way, and there would be, so said the letter from his account agent, a Director's Special Meeting called especially to decide if the bank could afford to retain Surda ziaGorn's business.

Majel sighed.

It was all but certain that the directors would find a way to retain his business, the directors being fond of their profits. However, that solution would surely involve new fees, or perhaps a less advantageous interest rate, for Cardfall Casino.

He filed the letter, straightened, and had taken a bare step away from the desk and toward the kettle when the comm buzzed.

"ziaGorn."

"Councilor ziaGorn, it is Padi yos'Galan of the Tree-and-Dragon Trade Mission."

He glanced at the clock. It was not so late as he had thought. Yet—

"How may I assist you, Trader?"

"Possibly, you cannot," she said flatly. "However, I felt that, as our liaison, you should be informed that two of our team—Trader

153

ven'Deelin and Master pai'Fortana—have been taken up as Reavers and brought to the Port Security station. The master trader has gone to stand for them, according to Guild Law. We were told that the Warden will be arriving, as well."

Majel shivered.

Reavers? Say rather, invaders, who had come to Colemeno a-purpose to enslave the lesser of the Talents to their own unknown purpose. The Warden had certified to the Council that the invaders had been vanquished. The Talents were safe from predation, free to lower their shields, and bury the dead—there had been a few of those, though less of their own Talents had died than had the invaders.

And, try as he might, he could not fit the trade team—any member of the trade team—into the pattern of pirates or slavers.

"Councilor ziaGorn?" Padi yos'Galan said, startling him.

"Your pardon. To be accused of being Reavers—that is unfortunate. I will go immediately to support the master trader. Thank you for apprising me of this situation."

"Thank you for your willingness to assist," she said gravely. "I will detain you no longer."

The active light went out.

Majel closed his eyes, took a deep breath, opened his eyes, and turned toward the door.

On-Grid
The Wardian

. . . .

"GOOD EVENING, BENTAMIN."

His Aunt Asta, Oracle to Civilization, was in her library. Lately, he found her in the library more than any other room. He supposed it was better than her former place in the front alcove, where she had sat for hours, watching the street below and the bustle of the Civilization she was bound to protect, but might never join.

"Good evening, Aunt Asta," Bentamin said, moving a stack of books from a chair onto the floor. He sat down, and surveyed her, sitting behind the massive table awash in paper books and readers, her hair every which way and her face rapt.

"Are you still planning to retire?" he asked.

"Well, of course I am," she said. "Civilization no longer needs me."

"Civilization would disagree," he answered. "We depend upon our Oracles."

"Indeed." Aunt Asta shot him a sharp glance. "Even knowing that Long Sight is among the least reliable of Talents, Civilization depends upon its Oracles. There may once have been some value to both sides in that bargain, Bentamin, but time has worn both the need and the value away. Civilization no longer needs an Oracle. Civilization knows quite well what must be done. It is not work that I am proficient in, quite aside from the fact that I am an old woman and have earned my rest."

And she had, Bentamin thought, earned a rest. No one could say that Asta vesterGranz had shirked her duty. She had endured for years as Civilization's Oracle, guiding them through the arrival and death of gods, to name only her most recent triumph. Oracles,

155

after all, did retire. But in the past that had only meant that they were no longer called upon to foretell. They were removed to a more modest apartment in the Wardian, and took up some other quiet work. Surely, they were not allowed to go wandering about the city—Long Sight was a Wild Talent, after all.

And that was perhaps a happy thought.

Bentamin leaned forward.

"How if you were to go to the Haosa for your retirement?" he asked.

His aunt considered him.

"I will certainly visit the Haosa before I go," she said. "But it's my intention to travel, Bentamin. I told you this."

"You did," he admitted. "However, I'm not at all certain that the Council will allow you to—travel, Aunt. They might be persuaded to allow you to go to kin..."

"The Council has no say in what I will or will not do," Aunt Asta declared airily, and reached for her reader.

"Always in the past, when an Oracle was ready to retire," Bentamin said quickly, "a new one arose. I haven't heard of an Oracle waking."

"Nor have I—which proves my point. Civilization no longer needs an Oracle; therefore no Oracle has arisen."

That—made altogether too much sense. Even so, he feared—

"There's no need for you to take this to the Council, if you fear for your credibility," Aunt Asta said gently. "I will be pleased to tell them, myself. In fact, there are a number of things I wish to say to the Council. Mind you, I haven't quite got my destinations fixed. I could, I suppose, remove to Ribbon Dance Village while I'm sorting that bit out—what a useful idea you had there, Bentamin! Thank you. I would not have thought of it, myself, and it's been an age since I've had a good, long talk with Tekelia. How does your cousin go on?"

"Pretty well. It appears that the younger trader has bestowed her affection, and truly, Aunt, Tekelia glows."

"Tekelia has taken a lover! I must meet her! And one of the trade team? That is most excellent, because I really *must* call on Captain Mendoza. I am woefully behind courtesy there, and after *such* a breach! Perhaps I will go tomorrow."

"Go?" Bentamin repeated. "Go—"

Someone rapped on the door to the library, which opened immediately to admit Hyuwen, Aunt Asta's majordomo, carrying a remote.

"Your pardon, Warden, but Chief bennaFalm is calling. He pleads an urgent situation."

Colemenoport
Port Security Office

. . . .

THEY WERE LOCKED IN.

The room was bright, the chairs comfortable, and surely it was far better than standing two alone before an enraged crowd.

"I thought, rather, frightened," Dyoli murmured, as if he had spoken aloud. "Certainly, the desserts server was terrified of us."

"Better she had run, then," Mar Tyn said. There was a limit to what they might say, here, for surely there were listeners. Still, with the door locked, it was a comfort to talk.

"Better, perhaps, for us," Dyoli said. "But not, I think, for her. The grief she carries nearly strangled me—one could not help but feel it! Now that she has been taken up by those in authority, she may be offered a Healing."

Their accuser, one Jayla ezinGaril, had been taken to speak with the Truthseer. Mar Tyn noted, rather bitterly, that *they* had not been offered a Truthseer before they had been locked into a room.

He took a deep breath. Now that the guards were no longer present to enforce calm, Mar Tyn was angry, afraid, and—baffled.

Dyoli had explained that each person had an *inner tapestry,* which was an explication of themselves. Such tapestries were perfectly accessible to those who had the proper Sight.

She had also explained that the Mistress's binding had left a . . . unique mark in his tapestry, and hers, which would also be perfectly visible to those who had the proper Sight.

Not only had they wandered Colemenoport at will for some number of days now, and met many persons, all Talents, some of whom must have been able to See their—*inner tapestry.* Not

158

only that, but they had previously been examined by a specialist recommended by a member of Colemeno's ruling council.

The specialist had pronounced them Healer and Serendipitist, welcomed them to Colemeno, and made no mention of "Reavers."

While Mar Tyn supposed it was possible that they had been dealing only with improperly Sighted persons, surely an expert in evaluating those who were Talented would be so Gifted.

The fact that Evaluator ringZun had made no mention of this mark, nor immediately called Security to come and lock them away, led one to wonder what the desserts server had Seen that no one else had.

Or, Mar Tyn thought suddenly, perhaps the desserts server was distracted. If her grief was as crushing as Dyoli had said, might her reason have suffered?

He glanced at Dyoli, who was sitting with her hands loosely folded in her lap, eyes closed, breathing slow and calm. A meditation, Mar Tyn understood, having seen this before, and did not speak.

He closed his own eyes, thinking back to the moment the server had assaulted them, feeling Dyoli catch his arm. He had felt their shared Talent shiver, and knew they were about to do something—very wrong.

That was why he had snatched himself away, allowing whatever future they had begun spinning to unravel into the overwrought present.

That . . . was not how their shared Talent operated, in Mar Tyn's experience. Certainly, it was not how *his* Talent operated. He had never in his life been able to gainsay his Gift once it had roused, and yet he felt—he *believed*—that he had averted a tragedy.

He needed to talk to Dyoli about this; get her impressions; find if she were angry, or relieved.

But not here, where enemies were listening.

Mar Tyn sighed. Almost, he could wish that the Talent they shared was the ability to speak to each other mind-to-mind, as the Mistress had been able to do with those she had bound closest.

In the meanwhile, the door was still locked, and he began to fear that it would remain so for some time.

"We should be called soon, my Mar Tyn," Dyoli said, calmly.

He looked at her in surprise, finding her with raised brows, and a slightly tipped head.

Yes, well.

Dyoli was a Healer. She would not have heard his thoughts, but she would have *felt* his dismay, very clearly.

His smile was stiff on his lips.

"I find being locked in...stressful," he murmured.

"As who does not? Be of good heart. The master trader will soon arrive, and see the door opened for us."

He might have thought that a fantasy proposed for the interest of their listeners, save at that very moment—

The door to their cell was opened.

· · · ✳ · · ·

The desk sergeant had directed Bentamin to the high-security wing, and did not offer an escort, which was perfectly in keeping with Officer roninPel's character. If Bentamin had insisted, a lesser officer would have been brought forward to perform the honor of escorting the Warden, but there was no need. The Warden knew the way.

The security field glittered across the hallway, a bright amber mist of chorded energies. Should anyone whose signature was not on file attempt to push through, the mist would entangle them and alarms would sound.

The Warden's signature of course being on file, the field faded, allowing him to pass.

Someone ahead of him was shouting. Bentamin paused to listen.

"Didn't you think to mention it?" demanded Security Chief bennaFalm, his voice unmistakable even at a shout.

"No, I didn't think to mention it!" came an answering shout.

Bentamin frowned. He knew that voice, too, though it was not one he had previously heard at such volume.

"They were brought by seelyFaire!" the second voice continued. "Surely, she had Seen! And if—"

Bentamin's frown cleared. Ah, of course. Kayla ringZun. Councilor seelyFaire's pet evaluator.

He moved on, toward the altercation.

"You let known Reavers—"

"They are *not* Reavers!"

"What else are they, Evaluator, with that mark upon them?"

Bentamin stepped into the conference room and leaned against the wall, arms folded across his chest.

ringZun and bennaFalm were both on their feet, shouting across a conference table set with a tea service and cake.

"That mark—" ringZun began, and abruptly stopped. He closed his eyes, and took three deep, deliberate breaths.

"They do bear the sign we had been taught to look for," he said, no longer shouting, though his voice was not completely steady. He raised a hand, apparently to forestall another outburst from bennaFalm, who closed his mouth, and stood silent, glaring.

"However, the thread is not active," ringZun continued. "In both instances it is an—artifact, a relic, a *memory*, if you will, of a relationship. There is no connection; no—energy." Another deep breath. "Scar tissue," he said, and turned the palms of his hands up. "That's all."

"So, they *had been* Reavers?" bennaFalm asked, still angry, but no longer bellowing.

"I think, rather, *touched by* Reavers," ringZun said. "That was my reading, but my reading was cursory, as I have said. Councilor seelyFaire wished me to evaluate their Talents, receptor strength, and sensitivity levels. Which is what I did."

"And what did you find?" Bentamin asked from his lean against the wall.

ringZun turned to face him.

"Warden. I found a classically trained Healer and a Seren-dipitist. Neither seemed overly sensitive to the ambient, though a Serendipitist—"

"Quite," Bentamin interrupted, and looked to Chief bennaFalm.

"I'm told that our guests are being held as high-risk."

"That is correct, Warden. We cannot afford to be careless."

"Certainly not, but now that I am here, perhaps they could be brought out, and given tea, like civilized persons?"

"We are waiting for Master Trader yos'Galan," bennaFalm said stolidly. "When he has arrived—"

"Which he has just done!" a gay voice came from the hallway. Bentamin turned to stare at the tall man, his white hair crisp, his eyes so light a blue they seemed silver in the spare brown face. He was wearing a jacket with the venerable Tree-and-Dragon on the breast, "Dutiful Passage," stitched above it, and below, "yos'Galan."

He was an elegant man, the master trader, and mannered, as he now demonstrated by turning to the portly person who tar-ried at his side with a smile and a slight inclination of the head.

"Thank you, Officer roninPel," he said warmly. "I am sure I would have never arrived so quickly without your assistance."

Officer roninPel made a slightly flustered bow.

"It is—an honor, Master Trader."

"Well, that's very kind of you to say. I expect that I will be quite safe with these gentles, and when we are done, one of them will see me out. Please do take good care of Grad and tell him that we will be reunited as quickly as I can manage it."

"I will do so, Master Trader," Officer roninPel said, as if he were taking a vow.

He bowed again, unsteadily, and left them. Bentamin extended a bare cat-whisker of thought, searching for any influence the master trader might have exerted, but—no. Apparently the man had produced this effect on the famously reticent desk sergeant by force of personality alone.

The master trader stepped into the room, his silver gaze touching each face in turn. He bowed gently to Bentamin.

"Warden, a pleasure to see you. Please make me known to your associates."

Really, the man had too much presence. Bentamin returned the bow, and moved his hand, showing bennaFalm to the master trader.

"Here is Chief Valorian bennaFalm, responsible for keeping Colemenoport secure and safe for all. Chief bennaFalm, Master Trader Shan yos'Galan, who leads the Tree-and-Dragon Trade Mission."

"Chief bennaFalm." The master trader inclined slightly from the waist. Apparently the head of Port Security did not rate a full bow from a master trader, Bentamin thought, amused despite himself.

Chief bennaFalm gave a brusque nod.

"Master Trader yos'Galan. Thank you for coming so quickly."

"I could hardly do otherwise," the master trader said gently, "when you have arrested two members of my team."

He turned toward ringZun without waiting for a reply, and shot an inquisitive glance to Bentamin.

"And this gentle is—?"

"This is Evaluation Expert Kayla ringZun," Bentamin began, but before he could complete the form, ringZun had spun, one hand extended toward the master trader.

"If it comes to that, he bears the same damned mark—twice!"

bennaFalm actually paled. The master trader raised an eyebrow, but said nothing.

Bentamin lifted his hand.

The master trader glanced at him. "Yes?"

"May I verify?"

"By all means. I thank you for asking. We were taught to ask first, at the Hall where I was trained."

ringZun flushed. Bentamin bent his concentration on the master trader's core.

The pattern was rich, beguiling, and, largely, benevolent. The master trader rejoiced in many connections, embracing as he did two vocations that depended upon personal interaction. Bentamin found the particular pattern associated with Healers; the webwork of his Healings surprisingly dense for one who did not practice that calling exclusively. Still, there was nothing that might cause undue—

And there it was. The mark that every Reaver had carried, black, pitiless, and intricate, woven deep into the master trader's core. Twice.

Bentamin Looked closer, finding no active linkage, nor any other dire thing. If he had not himself seen the signature alive and active in others, he would have observed these instances without the least feeling of dismay.

Bentamin withdrew his attention.

"I see the links. They are not active."

"Precisely as it presents in the two persons presently confined in a high-risk room," ringZun snarled.

The master trader looked to Chief bennaFalm.

"Confined?" he repeated.

"The room is very comfortable," bennaFalm began. "Merely it is—"

"Locked," the master trader said sharply. "I insist that my team members be released at once."

bennaFalm opened his mouth; the master trader stepped toward the door.

"Come along, sir. I will accompany you, and guarantee their good behavior."

Bentamin watched bennaFalm, who seemed for a moment as if he would dispute this. It was only a moment, though, before he bowed, and crossed to the door.

"If you will come this way, Master Trader. The high-risk room is just down the hall."

· · · ✳ · · ·

The door opened, and it was the security chief who stood there, looking at them sourly.

Dyoli rose calmly, and Mar Tyn took his cue from her, stepping to her side, but no further, as much as he wished to be beyond that portal.

"Are we," Dyoli inquired in a voice that was mannered without being the least bit courteous, "free to go?"

"Absolutely, you are free to come with us to a very well-appointed conference room and enjoy the refreshments that have been put out!"

Ridiculously, Mar Tyn felt his knees wobble, hearing that voice, not so much well known as impossible to mistake. He took a hard breath and made himself stand straight.

The master trader had, indeed, come.

In fact, he had replaced the security chief in the doorway, and stood with his back against the door, surveying them.

"Trader ven'Deelin, have you been offered insult or taken any harm?"

"Master Trader, I have not."

"Excellent. Please, come forth."

Dyoli moved without hurry, stepping past the master trader and into the hall.

Mar Tyn felt a spike of panic, and breathed it down. The master trader might be willing to trade a mere Luck for a daughter of a High Liaden House, though Mar Tyn did not believe it of him. Dyoli, however, would *not* abandon him. This he knew absolutely, having several times begged her to do just that.

"Master pai'Fortana." The master trader's voice was gentle. Mar Tyn looked up into quizzical silver eyes.

"Is all well with you, Master pai'Fortana?"

Mar Tyn knew better than to lie, but for a moment he was at a loss for truth.

"I am well, sir," he managed, at last, which *was* true. But the master trader would have Seen at least his moment of panic, as Dyoli had Seen his earlier dismay. He ought, therefore, to say more.

"It is only," Mar Tyn continued, "that I do not care to be

locked in." There, that was also truth, though not entirely happy, as he had spent some time locked into a room on the *Dutiful Passage*, just at first.

Master Trader yos'Galan inclined his head gravely. "I quite understand," he said. "You have borne this insult to your liberty with great restraint. Pray, do come forth. The door will not close until you are through."

"Thank you, sir," Mar Tyn murmured. He took a breath, and moved his feet, walking with deliberation, if not calm, passing over the threshold of their cell and into the hallway, where the security chief's glower was utterly eclipsed by Dyoli's smile.

"There you are, my Mar Tyn," she said, slipping her arm through his. "Now let us to this conference room and refreshments. I daresay we will all feel better for a cup of tea."

· · · ✳ · · ·

"In your opinion, Specialist," Bentamin said to ringZun, "are Trader ven'Deelin or Master pai'Fortana dangerous—either separately or acting together?"

ringZun looked goaded.

"You ask if they're Civilized? As I said, neither seemed to be unnaturally excited by the ambient. The Healer's pattern is very structured; much of that will have been imposed by her training, of course. The Serendipitist . . . his Talent is minor at best, his pattern full of air, as one finds with such Talents."

"So, neither is a threat, in your estimation?"

ringZun took a breath.

"Now you ask me to second-guess Chief bennaFalm. I was surprised to find that they were being held so close. However, we are not our Talents, and it is possible that either one could have been carrying a weapon with intent to use it."

"Very true," Bentamin said. "Were they?"

"That, Warden," ringZun said triumphantly, "is a question best addressed to Chief bennaFalm."

That was, Bentamin allowed, the correct answer, and not a bit less irritating because it was.

There was a small sound at the door and he turned his head as Majel ziaGorn paused on the threshold and nodded to the young duty officer at his side.

"My thanks for the escort, Officer."

"It is an honor to serve," the officer assured him, and left.

"Warden. Specialist ringZun." The tone was cool, the bow polite but not in the least obsequious.

"I was told," he said, straightening, "that I would find Master Trader yos'Galan here, with two of his team, who have been ... detained."

"And so you have, Councilor."

The master trader's voice again preceded him. Majel stepped aside, allowing Trader ven'Deelin to enter, followed by Master pai'Fortana, who was followed by the master trader. Security Chief bennaFalm came along behind, and he did not look happy.

"Sit down, please, Trader ven'Deelin, Master pai'Fortana," the master trader said, quite as if he were the host and they his guests. "I'm sure you would welcome tea, and perhaps some cake."

Majel ziaGorn stepped to the table, and poured tea into cups, offering first, not to the Warden of Civilization, who was surely the ranking person in the room, but to Trader ven'Deelin. The second cup went to her assistant, and the third to the master trader.

Only then did he pour for the Warden, Chief bennaFalm, and Specialist ringZun, keeping the final cup for himself as he sat down in the last chair of what had become a very crowded table.

"I am of course very pleased to see you, Councilor," the master trader said. "But I wonder why you are here."

"Trader yos'Galan called to apprise me of your situation, sir," Majel said calmly. "I honor her decision to do so. As the trade team's liaison, my presence is not only appropriate, but necessary."

The master trader inclined his head, then glanced toward the door.

"Ah," said Chief bennaFalm, "Truthseer. Please take your station."

The robed figure bowed and moved to the left, to stand against the wall, hands folded into sleeves and hood pulled close around their face.

The master trader let his gaze rest on the still figure for a long moment, then looked to Chief bennaFalm.

"I require an explanation," he said.

"It is our law that a Truthseer be present when persons are officially questioned. The accuser has already been asked and given her answers."

"Was she offered a Healing?" Trader ven'Deelin asked, sharply, and looked to the master trader. "She was in a great deal of pain. It was...abundantly obvious."

Silence followed this, Chief bennaFalm's face hard. Bentamin sighed and looked to the back wall.

"Truthseer, you may answer the question."

"The offer was made, and refused." The Truthseer's voice was cool and uninflected.

Trader ven'Deelin sagged in her chair.

"I fear for her," she murmured, and raised a hand to the Truthseer. "Thank you for the information."

"I apprehend that Trader ven'Deelin and Master pai'Fortana are about to be questioned," the master trader said, looking around the table. "Are these matters usually handled by a committee?"

Chief bennaFalm looked as if he had bitten into bitter fruit.

"In the usual way of such things, the questions are asked and answered in private. However, the possibility of an incident increases, as you are—"

Bentamin saw him realize that he was about to be inept, and moved a hand.

"As you are strangers to our world and to our customs," he said smoothly, and the master trader awarded him a half-smile.

"Indeed," he said. "Best that we are all informed, so long as my colleagues are willing to answer questions."

"I am willing," Trader ven'Deelin said. Mar Tyn pai'Fortana gave a bare nod of his head.

"The first questions, establishing a baseline," Chief bennaFalm said. "What are your names?"

"Dyoli ven'Deelin Clan Ixin."

"That is true," said the Truthseer.

"Mar Tyn pai'Fortana."

"That is not wholly true," said the Truthseer.

The Serendipitist tipped his head to one side, as if considering the merits of this statement.

"In fact, it may no longer be even slightly true," he said, calmly. "I have not paid my dues to House Fortune in quite some time, a breach that would see me struck from the rolls. The name I bore previously was Mar Tyn eys'Ornstahl."

"That is true."

"What were you doing at Zephyr's Edge Lounge?" asked Chief bennaFalm.

"Sharing a meal," Trader ven'Deelin said.

"And talking," Mar Tyn pai'Fortana added.

"Are you Reavers?" Chief bennaFalm snapped.

As an attempt to unnerve, Bentamin thought, it was a notable failure.

Dyoli ven'Deelin raised her eyebrows.

"What *are* Reavers?" she asked.

"Invaders," Majel ziaGorn said, surprisingly. "They came on purpose to enslave Talents. They bore a distinctive mark, within their own Talent, by which they became known. The Haosa had the hunting of them, until all the Reavers died. There are no more Reavers on Colemeno."

He looked to Bentamin.

"So it was reported to the Council. Have I adequately stated the case, Warden?"

"You have, and I thank you," Bentamin said sincerely.

"The reason the Reavers died," Master Trader yos'Galan said, "is because I cut the ties binding them to *Dramliza* Tarona Rusk. I did this in order to Heal her of dire wounds."

He looked directly at Chief bennaFalm.

"That is why I bear the first of *my* marks. I bear the second because, after I had Healed her, and was dying of it, she went turnabout, and gave me back to myself.

"You will do well to understand, sir, that far from being vandals, these two people are victims, and survivors of a horrific event."

"That," the Truthseer said, "is true."

Colemenoport
Wayfarer

. . . .

PADI FINISHED READING THE INTRODUCTION TO THE AUDITORS manual, and leaned back in her chair with a sigh. Her inclination was to engage with the first chapter, which was not so *very* long, and perhaps take the self-test, but a glance at the clock suggested that she ought to do something more lightsome.

She might, she thought, fetch herself another glass of wine and answer Vanz's letter. *That* needn't consume more than an hour, and surely Father—

Someone knocked on her door. She rose to open it, finding Priscilla, every inch the captain of *Dutiful Passage*, buttons gleaming and face firm.

"The shuttle's down," she said. "Karna and I are going to fetch Dil Nem and Jes. Will you be going out?"

"I'm just about to find a glass and write a letter," Padi told her, and glanced at the room beyond.

"Father *hasn't* come back, yet?" she asked, feeling a sharp twist of worry.

"Not yet," Priscilla said. "It's only been a little over an hour. Untying red tape takes time."

Recalling her own run-in with red tape, Padi smiled ruefully, and turned her hands palm up.

"Time runs differently, when you're waiting," she said.

"I've noticed that myself," Priscilla said dryly. "Hopefully, he'll be here with Dyoli and Mar Tyn by the time I'm back with Dil Nem and Jes."

She nodded, and turned away. Padi stepped out of her room and watched her leave, Karna at her back. The door locked audibly behind them.

Padi went into the kitchen.

Perhaps a cup of tea rather than a glass of wine, she thought, approaching the counter. There would be a debriefing when Father returned with Dyoli and Mar Tyn. Best to be awake for that.

She left the door slightly ajar when she returned, settling behind her desk with a sigh. Putting the teacup on the coaster, she reached for the screen—and checked.

A folded piece of paper—yellow, lined in blue—was lying across her keyboard.

She picked it up, fingertips tingling, and unfolded it.

Good evening, Padi. Are you free to come to me? —Tekelia

She smiled, and reached for her teacup. This was...interesting, and mannerly. No need to disrupt anyone by materializing while they were at study, or asleep, or in some other private moment. Merely send a note, like any other civilized person.

Sipping her tea, she read the note again, and put her mind on how the thing might be done. For surely, this was another lesson, building on those techniques she had learned this afternoon.

First, she needed to write her answer.

She put the page on the desk, smoothed it, and picked up a pen.

I am bound to home this evening. Might you come to me,
for tea? And cake?   —Padi

That done, she folded the paper along its crease, and sat with it on her palm, thinking of Tekelia's desk in the great room, bathed in Ribbon light, and—*pushed* the paper toward that image.

There was a moment of resistance, which might equally have been her inexperience or the effect of the Grid, and the paper faded away, leaving her palm empty and slightly damp.

She had expected something like, but still it startled her into a gasp. Shaking her head, she picked up her cup and sipped.

"I wonder," she said to the room at large, "how one knows if the letter has been delivered."

"When one receives an answer, of course," said a voice grown lately very familiar.

Padi spun in her chair, laughing at Tekelia standing in the

center of her room, dressed much as she was, in soft sweater and pants, and holding a rectangular red tin in one hand.

"I provide the cookies."

"And I provide the tea," she said, rising and beckoning. "Come into the kitchen and choose your blend. I warn you that we will be interrupted. Captain Mendoza has only gone to the dock, to collect incoming crew. Dyoli and Mar Tyn have been accused at the port, and the master trader has gone to—*untie the red tape.*"

"I'll have the spice blend," Tekelia said, surveying the tea case. "Of what are they accused?"

"Of being Reavers," Padi said, refilling the kettle and putting it to warm. She turned.

"I am about to presume upon our friendship," she said.

Tekelia put the cookie tin on the counter and smiled at her.

"I don't mind."

"Well, you might, actually. What I wonder is if you might speak with the security chief or the Warden, and tell them that you have seen the black threads in my father's... pattern, and that he is no Reaver."

Tekelia's brows rose over one blue eye and one brown eye.

"I'd be delighted to perform this service for you, only—the witness of a Haosa is not accepted in law under the Grid."

Padi blinked.

"Whyever not?"

Tekelia's grin showed a certain edge.

"Because Haosa are not Civilized, of course."

"And nor are the Deaf Civilized, so I apprehend! Who *does* Civilization accept?"

"Well," Tekelia said apologetically, "the Civilized, naturally—"

The kettle whistled and Padi turned to pour.

"I suppose I should have spoken to Bentamin after the affair on the Hill," Tekelia said slowly. "But he didn't ask, and I'm not in the habit of volunteering. I *would* have spoken, if I'd Seen Reavers in our midst—Bentamin knows that. I didn't speak, because it seemed to me that the Healing your father performed on the Hill, and its aftermath, were his personal business."

Padi sighed.

"Which is, of course, true," she murmured, handing over the teacup. "I suggest that we make ourselves comfortable on the couch in the great room."

Colemenoport
Transient Docks

. . . .

THE SHUTTLE SAT RESPECTABLY AT DOCK, GANGPLANK OUT, GREEN at-home lights visible above the hatch.

The driver of the secure car provided by the Wayfarer opened the doors, and the back hatch.

At the top of the ramp, Priscilla pressed the button just under the green light, lowering her head somewhat in deference to the scanners.

"Mendoza," she said calmly. "Come to collect crew."

"Greetings, Captain," Dil Nem said, his voice sharper than usual through the speaker. "We're all three on our way out to you."

Priscilla frowned.

All three? she thought, and shivered.

She went back down the ramp to join Karna on the dock.

Dil Nem debarked first, pulling two cases.

He hit the end of the ramp, and saluted.

"Captain," he said, properly. "Reporting for duty."

"Third Mate," Priscilla answered. "You are welcome."

A slim shadow stirred at the hatch, resolving into Jes dea'Tolin, pulling one case, and carrying a second, shrouded in cloth.

Priscilla felt a chill run her spine.

"Captain," Jes dea'Tolin said as she reached the end of the ramp. "Reporting for duty."

"Qe'andra," Priscilla answered. "You are welcome."

She glanced past Jes's shoulder, hoping that her sudden understanding was an error, and that the third crew member would just now—

"I thought it best to protect her from the strange environment," Jes said gravely. "I fear she is a little put out with me."

172

Priscilla eyed the swathed cage, and extended a gentle thought of welcome.

She received the mental equivalent of a disdainful sniff.

"You brought Lady Selph?"

Despite her best efforts, it seemed that her dismay was obvious. Jes pressed her lips together.

"Those were your precise orders, Captain," Dil Nem said. "Lady Selph, and no other, was to come with us, and make our third."

Priscilla closed her eyes, recalling that dropped moment in her conversation with Danae. She took a deep breath, opened her eyes, and took the cage from Jes.

"Welcome, Lady Selph," she said.

Colemenoport
Port Security Office

. . . .

THE MASTER TRADER HAD RECOUNTED HIS MEETING WITH THE Mistress, the death she had dealt his oathsworn, her attempt to attach him, his resistance, and his decision to liberate those others she had attached. It was a tale of some scope, that he laid out with a cool brevity that told Mar Tyn how much the events he spoke of had wounded—and pained—him, still.

He paused after his description of cutting the Mistress's myriad bindings to take up his cup and carefully sip his tea.

The Warden looked to Dyoli and Mar Tyn.

"You were bound to Tarona Rusk, is that correct?"

"Yes," Dyoli said. "The severing of the bonds was...violent," she continued, modeling herself on the master trader's coolness. "I expect there was a multiplicative effect—Mistress Rusk having bound *so many*."

She glanced at Shan yos'Galan, still sipping tea, his face smooth and his eyes distant.

"Master pai'Fortana and I were two of a team of three," she murmured. She was buying more time for the master trader to recruit himself, Mar Tyn realized. She would See the pain Mar Tyn only guessed at. "The separation killed our third outright, and he was accounted the strongest of us."

"To what do you attribute your survival?" the Warden asked.

"To our personal bond, sir," Dyoli answered.

The Warden inclined his head gravely and looked to Mar Tyn. "And you, sir? Did you suffer no hurt from the separation?"

Mar Tyn blinked.

"In fact, I was dying," he said, roughly. "Healer ven'Deelin caught me up and Healed me. She all but died herself in the doing of it."

"I did not die because our bond operated as expected," Dyoli explained calmly.

"Did this Tarona Rusk also die of separation trauma?" asked ringZun.

Master Trader yos'Galan put his cup gently back into the saucer, and met the evaluator's eyes.

"She did not."

"Then she is still at large!" Officer bennaFalm looked as if he might start to his feet and rush off in immediate pursuit. "She could be regrouping at this moment, rebuilding her forces—"

"Forgive me that I was not plain," the master trader interrupted, his cool voice slicing through the other's heat. "I am a Healer. It was obvious to me that Tarona Rusk had been abused by the Department of the Interior, of which I spoke earlier. She had, in fact, been shaped into something she would not have chosen, had she been permitted the counsel of her own mind and heart. That being so, and as I had said, I Healed her.

"After our encounter, Tarona Rusk saw me safe before leaving on a mission of Balance with our mutual enemy," the master trader continued. "I had no more contact with her until we arrived here, on Colemeno."

"Never say she is on Colemeno," Officer bennaFalm almost whispered.

The master trader lifted an eyebrow.

"She is not. However, *I* was on Colemeno and we were, as Evaluator ringZun has said, entangled. I felt her determination to commit self-murder as I stood on Ribbon Dance Hill."

bennaFalm's face relaxed.

"Then she is a threat to us no longer," he said, sounding satisfied.

"She is a threat to *you* no longer," the master trader agreed blandly.

"That," said the Truthseer, "is not a lie, but it allows the questioner to deceive himself."

bennaFalm's face hardened again.

"Is Tarona Rusk, mistress of Reavers, dead?" he snarled.

The master trader sighed.

"She is not. She has forgotten all the evil she has done, as well as all the evil done to her."

"You gave her *forgetfulness*?" ringZun asked, plainly startled.

"Did I not say so?"

"But—where was she?"

The master trader lifted a shoulder and let it fall.

"Somewhat distant from Colemeno, I believe."

Chief bennaFalm closed his eyes.

"Allow me to understand this," he said slowly. "You were able to effect *a Healing* from Ribbon Dance Hill to some undisclosed location, far away from Colemeno."

"That is correct. I expect that the ambient conditions may have given me a boost."

"Doubtless so," ringZun murmured, but bennaFalm had his eye on another target.

"You had this woman in your . . . range, let us say, knew her intention to suicide—and yet you interfered. I ask you why."

Mar Tyn had not thought that the master trader's eyes could become any colder.

"I am a Healer," he said, each word distinct. "There was no need for a woman to die of being betrayed and tortured. I would not have *interfered*, as you have it, had she truly wished to die. She did not. She wished for an end to her own deadliness, and surcease from the pain of her past."

"Truth," said the Truthseer.

The master trader paused, and glanced down. Dyoli took up the pot and poured him more tea.

He inclined his head slightly, but did not pick up the cup.

"Proper therapy in the case was forgetfulness," he said, raising his head to meet bennaFalm's eyes. "She is no longer a threat to Colemeno, or to herself."

"Truth."

"And so she is free to rediscover her potential and create more Reavers, which may again find Colemeno—"

"That is, I think, enough," said Majel ziaGorn, firmly.

Chief bennaFalm turned and stared. Bentamin barely kept his own countenance.

"I beg your pardon, Councilor," Chief bennaFalm said, heavily, "I have many questions yet—"

"As does any thinking being," Majel interrupted. "However, in this case, the questions have gone far afield. What is the purpose of this continued harassment of innocent persons?"

"I—"

"*Are* any of these people Reavers?" demanded Majel of the room at large.

"They are not," said the Truthseer.

There was a brief silence, before Majel spoke again.

"My information was that Trader ven'Deelin and Master pai'Fortana were taken up on suspicion of being Reavers. It has been established that they are not Reavers. Were there additional charges made?"

"There were not," said Chief bennaFalm, sounding sullen.

"You are forcing those found innocent of charges to revisit trauma and pain to satisfy personal curiosity. Neither Colemeno nor justice is served by continuing." Majel turned his head and met Bentamin's eye.

"Warden, I protest on behalf of the trade mission. Further questioning is unfitting and unnecessary."

"I agree," Bentamin said, and looked to Chief bennaFalm—

Who opened his mouth, and closed it again.

Bentamin waited.

Chief bennaFalm sighed, and stated formally,

"This examination is closed. Let the record show that Dyoli ven'Deelin, Mar Tyn pai'Fortana, and Shan yos'Galan are none of them Reavers, and are no danger as such to Colemeno or to Civilization."

Colemenoport
Wayfarer

. . . .

"DID YOUR MEETING END EARLY?" PADI ASKED, WHEN THEY HAD
settled side by side on the couch and each sampled one of the
cookies from the tin.

"It wasn't a meeting, but a party. The village gathered to welcome the two children who were sent to us, and whose care we have
formally accepted." Tekelia half-smiled. "The Haosa are nothing, if
not protective of the small."

"Do people make a habit of giving the Haosa children to protect?"

"It's not uncommon. Whether the thoughts of those who send
them tend in the direction of protection, I can't say."

Padi frowned.

"But—where do they come from?"

"Civilization, of course. Most Haosa are born under the Grid.
I was myself."

Padi paused in the act of reaching for another cookie, and
turned to stare. There was a line between her eyebrows and her
mouth was straight and tense.

Tekelia felt a pang. Of course, Padi yos'Galan would also be
a protector of the small.

"If you please," she said, her voice tight. "I would prefer not
to have a game of *catch me* on this topic."

Tekelia put a hand on her knee.

"Forgive me. I'll try to be straightforward. The case is this:
When a Civilized child is found to have a direct connection to the
ambient, and doesn't require the tools of Civilization in order to
obtain desired results, there are two courses open to the family.

"The first is to send the child to the Haosa, off-Grid, where
they will live among their own kind."

Tekelia paused. Padi was still intent, face taut, waiting.

"Most families prefer to have a Healer seal the unruly Gift away—"

Padi stiffened under Tekelia's hand.

"Seal," she said, and Tekelia looked at her in surprise, seeing that the information had increased her distress.

"I'm an idiot," Tekelia said.

Padi shook her head.

"No. It's only that I have had...personal experience with the sealing away of Gifts, and it was not...happy. In fact, I'm surprised to learn that Colemeno Healers practice such a thing. Every Healer aware of my case begged me to unseal, lest I do myself lasting harm."

Tekelia blinked.

"Why did you seal your Gift away?"

She moved a hand as if brushing the question aside.

"Let me understand this, first. Then it will be my turn to tell a story."

She leaned forward for her cup and sipped, Tekelia following suit. When the cups were replaced, she nodded again.

"We had reached the point in the narrative where fond families make their children Deaf and forgetful in order to keep them safe under the Grid." She blinked thoughtfully. "But the Deaf are not Civilized."

"Yes, but they are *protected*, by their families and by the whole of Civilization. Off-Grid is understood to be a much more dangerous situation, and there are those who would never choose danger for their children."

"Your family did," Padi remarked.

Tekelia laughed.

"Well, vesterGranz and chastaMeir are equally apt to throw out a Wild Talent or a Civilized one. There's my cousin Bentamin, the Warden of Civilization; myself, not only Haosa, but a Child of Chaos; and of course, our Aunt Asta, Oracle for Civilization. Two Wild Talents in two generations—*very* Wild Talents, if I am not modest, and Bentamin is an extremely strong multi-Talent."

"You want me to understand that you are overachievers."

"Exactly!"

Padi took a breath.

"What happens," she said, carefully, "if one of the...sealed away—*remembers*?"

"Ah, well." Tekelia shook off the unfamiliar urge to look away from her gaze. "Suicide is most common, in such cases. Rarely, whole families have been eradicated." Tekelia took a breath.

"But, you see, the Healers are skilled, and it takes an extremely strong will to break imposed forgetfulness, so it happens very seldom."

"It happened in your family," Padi said, and Tekelia smiled at the certainty in her voice.

"Our family knows itself. Not even the least of us can be called biddable."

Padi laughed. "One more thing that we have in common," she murmured, and reached for her cup.

They each had another cookie to finish the tea. Padi put her shoulder against the back of the couch and her knee on the cushion so that she faced Tekelia, her eyes serious.

"Why?" she asked.

"Why what?" Tekelia asked in turn.

"Why is it like this?" Padi burst out. "I understand that the first wave of colonists succumbed to the effects of the ambient. The second wave built the Grid as protection. Does living under the Grid damage Haosa?"

She stopped, face arrested, and leaned forward to take Tekelia's hands in hers.

"I am not harmed by being under the Grid," Tekelia said, squeezing her fingers gently. "At most, I'm slightly irritated because, on-Grid the ambient is, as you noted yourself, less malleable than I prefer. That aside, I can work with it perfectly well.

"As for why—"

The light came on in the alcove, and the outside door chittered slightly.

Padi came to her feet, seeing a flutter of mist from the corner of her eye, but Tekelia was at her shoulder.

Dyoli and Mar Tyn entered the Great Room first, followed by Father, and Grad last of all. Dyoli and Mar Tyn merely looked weary, as well they ought. Father . . .

Father's face was perfectly expressionless, and Padi shivered as if in a chill breeze, as a bland silver gaze passed over them.

"Daughter," he said, perfectly neutral. "Tekelia-*dramliza*."

"Father—Dyoli, Mar Tyn." Padi went forward, hands outstretched. "All of you—sit. You as well, Grad. I will fetch wine and call the kitchen."

"I will fetch wine," Tekelia said, and she threw a grateful look over her shoulder.

"Thank you." She turned back, moving a hand.

"Here is my friend, Tekelia vesterGranz," she said in quick introduction. "Tekelia, you recall my father. Also, we have Dyoli ven'Deelin Clan Ixin, Mar Tyn pai'Fortana, and Grad Elbin."

Mar Tyn and Dyoli bowed, Dyoli in addition murmuring, "Well met, Luzant vesterGranz," before they went to the sofa.

Grad gave a nod, and followed them.

Father remained on the threshold, watching the room with that alien, chilly detachment.

Padi poured a glass of the red and went to him. It was a moment before he inclined his head and took it from her hand.

"My thanks," he murmured, distantly.

"Priscilla went to the dock," she said, meeting his eyes firmly. "She should be back very soon with Dil Nem and *Qe'andra* dea'Tolin." She paused.

"Please, Father—sit down."

It was a relief to see one slanted brow lift slightly. He raised his glass, and took a sip before moving toward the sofa.

Turning, Padi saw that the teacups and the cookie tin had been removed from the table, replaced by a tray holding glasses and decanters. Grad had just poured a glass of the local green, and was offering it to Dyoli.

Padi went to the comm, ordering a plate of sandwiches, and, on impulse, a high-energy tray.

In the kitchen, Tekelia had put the cups into the washer, rinsed and started the kettle, and was putting clean cups onto a tray.

"In case wine isn't what's wanted," Tekelia said, with a nod toward the tea case. "Potent or soothing?"

"Soothing, by all means," Padi said, and took a deep breath. "Thank you, my friend."

"No need for that." Tekelia was measuring tea into the pot, and glanced at her out of eyes that were slightly different shades of blue.

"Your father looks tired. Shall I stay?"

There was a question inside that question, Padi understood, though it took several heartbeats to grasp that Tekelia was asking if Father was—dangerous.

"I've never seen him so—stern," she murmured. "It may have

gone badly, at the guard house. We'll know soon. He will wait for Priscilla, so to tell the tale only once."

The bell over the food lift rang, and she went to open it.

· · · ✳ · · ·

Shan sat at the end of the sofa, wineglass in hand. He needed—or say, he *wanted*—Healspace, but he didn't quite dare it, not in his present state, with the vulnerable around him, and Colemeno's damned ambient—

No. No more agitation. He would be calm. He was a Healer; calm was not beyond him. Though without entering Healspace, it was somewhat more difficult to achieve.

Really, Shan, use your wits, he told himself, and closed his eyes.

A breath, and another, to clear his mind, before he accessed a calming exercise taught to hopeful pilots. He felt himself warm, the sense of abrasion fading somewhat. Yes. That would do. Later, when he and Priscilla were alone, then he would open himself to his lifemate and receive the benediction of her Healing.

He opened his eyes.

The center table had been expanded to its full width, and Padi was just sliding sandwiches and the standard restorative tray onto it, while Tekelia placed teapot and cups.

Padi straightened and looked at him, her face calm, though he could See how worried she was.

"Tekelia was kind enough to bear me company until you returned," she said, by which he learned that she feared some part of his present deplorable state was because he had found her friend with her. That was ill-done of him. He met Tekelia's mismatched blue eyes, and inclined his head.

"Thank you for your care of my daughter," he said, perhaps not as warmly as he might have done, but he had at least offered simple courtesy.

Tekelia bowed in the Colemeno style.

"It is my pleasure, sir." A glance aside.

"Padi? Is there anything else I may do for you this evening?"

"I think not, my friend. Thank you for coming."

Turning, Tekelia bowed to the group at large.

"I am pleased to have met you, and hope to meet you all again, when time is not so dear."

There were murmurs in response, Dyoli producing a nod and

a weary smile. Tekelia moved 'round the couch, heading for the foyer. After a moment, Padi followed.

She hadn't quite put her hand on the plate when the door opened.

Shan looked up as Priscilla entered, bearing a large object swathed in cloth, and a bag slung over one shoulder. He felt a shiver, and leaned forward to put his glass on the table.

Following Priscilla were Dil Nem and Jes dea'Tolin, Karna bringing up the rear. They paused at the side of the sofa, Padi and Tekelia behind them.

Priscilla put the bag off her shoulder, letting it slide to the floor next to one of the half-loungers. She gently placed the large object on the seat of the chair, and pulled the covering off.

Lady Selph was standing tall on her back legs, looking every inch the imperious dowager that she was.

Shan considered her, feeling a chill run his spine, then raised his eyes to meet Priscilla's.

"By my specific order," she said gently, and he felt her chagrin as his own. He closed his eyes briefly, took a deep breath, and rose to bow.

"Welcome to arriving crew," he said, with what cordiality he could muster.

"Allow me to make you known to Tekelia vesterGranz, Speaker for the Haosa. Tekelia-*dramliza*, I bring your attention to Dil Nem Tiazan, Third Mate on *Dutiful Passage*; Jes dea'Tolin, *qe'andra*, and Lady Selph, norbear."

Tekelia produced another bow.

"I am honored."

"Tekelia vesterGranz," Dil Nem murmured, bowing. "Well met."

"Speaker vesterGranz," Jes said, also bowing. "An honor."

Yes, well.

Shan took another breath, looked over the room, and knew in his heart that he had expended his last tithe of energy.

"My children," he said, raising his voice slightly. "It has been a long and exceptional day. Please refresh yourselves. Let us plan to meet tomorrow over nuncheon. Trader yos'Galan, I have three meetings scheduled for tomorrow morning at the office. Are you able to take them for me?"

"Of course, Master Trader."

"Stout heart. I will forward my notes to you. We will also wish to see you at nuncheon."

"Yes, sir."

Priscilla turned, beckoning to Dil Nem and Jes.

"Let me show you to your rooms, and sign you into the apartment's security. You'll be able to order refreshments directly—an ingenious system."

Murmuring, she bustled them out.

"Will you be wanting us, sir?" Grad asked carefully.

Shan shook his head.

"Go and rest, all of you. I assure you that I am going to my room, where I intend to stay for the next eight hours, at least."

"Yes, sir." Grad bowed, and Karna did. Grad picked up a plate of sandwiches, Karna a plate of cookies, and both moved toward Tima's room.

Shan turned a speculative gaze on Lady Selph. She met his eyes, and he felt a fizz of excitement from her. Gods. A norbear. Here, on Colemeno, with its ambient conditions.

"I'll take care of her," Padi said, from beside him. He looked down, seeing worry in her face. "Father. Go and rest."

"Yes," he said gently. "I shall. Thank you, Daughter. I trust you will not allow her to bully you."

"We have quite gotten beyond that," Padi told him. She rose on her toes to kiss his cheek, then stepped back.

Shan turned, felt a brush of intention against his shields. He turned to look at Tekelia vesterGranz.

"I've dealt that trick myself, more than a few times," he said, his voice cool but not, he trusted, uncordial. "Pray, do not think me ungrateful. It is a kindly impulse."

Tekelia bowed, allowing dismay to show.

"Let's both agree that it was a foolish attempt. I've only lately been informed that I'm a blunt instrument, more like a hammer than a loom."

Shan nodded gravely. "So were we all, once. The answer is to practice with your shuttle. Good evening, both."

"Sleep well, Father," Padi said.

· · · ※ · · ·

Padi turned to look at Tekelia.

"Did you try to give Father ease?" she asked, half-unbelieving.

Tekelia sighed.

"I did, and you see how well it went."

"It might have gone far worse," she said. "And he did acknowledge it a kindly impulse."

"So he did. I'm not utterly in disgrace, then."

"I would say not. Here, I ought to see Lady Selph settled."

She moved to the chair, and bowed to the attentive norbear.

"Good evening, Lady Selph. I knew you would find a way down to us."

A chuckle—rather, *the sense* of a chuckle—flowed agreeably through her head as she bent down to pick up the cage. Tekelia already had the bag in hand, and stood to one side, apparently waiting to follow her lead.

Padi turned toward her room.

· · · ✻ · · ·

"Thank you for your assistance, Councilor," Bentamin said, as he and Majel ziaGorn exited the guard house.

"You're kind to style it so," Majel returned, irritation still edging his voice, and blew out a hard breath. "Could he not *feel* the distress coming off of them?"

Bentamin blinked, and looked at him with interest.

"Chief bennaFalm? Possibly not. He's not particularly empathic. If they had been guilty, he might have caught that. But guilt, of course, is heavier and grittier than grief, or distress."

"Is it?" Majel moved his shoulders. "Specialist ringZun surely—"

"Specialist ringZun was not there in an advisory capacity," Bentamin interrupted. "Perhaps I should have intervened earlier, but I hesitate to put the Warden's whole weight onto working systems."

"Yes, of course. Trader yos'Galan did well to alert me. I will call on the trade mission tomorrow, to see if lasting harm has been done. The master trader...it was a terrible necessity forced upon him. That he became by chance a hero of Colemeno..."

Bentamin stirred.

Majel looked to him.

"Yes?"

"Put it to him that way, when you speak to the master trader. I did feel that he carries a burden heavier than the outcome of his deeds may warrant."

"I will express Colemeno's gratitude," Majel said. "Will you report the final outcome of the Reavers to the Council?"

Bentamin frowned.

"We'll have to have the transcript from the room, and—a confidential session, if we don't want the master trader's work disrupted any further."

"Which we do not," Majel said firmly. "It is to Colemeno's benefit to give the trade mission every assistance it asks for, and otherwise to stand aside and let them make their inventories and audits."

"I agree," Bentamin said, solemnly, and inclined slightly from the waist.

"It is late," he observed. "I offer to take you wherever you are next bound."

Majel blinked.

"That is a gentle courtesy," he said. "Do you know Cardfall Casino?"

"I know Riverview Park, across the street," Bentamin said promptly. "It was a favorite morning walk of mine, when I was at university."

"It's a favorite walk of mine, too," Majel said. "I accept your offer of transport."

"Your arm, please, Councilor," Bentamin said, and when they were linked, arm-in-arm, he brought the image of the path curving along the river's edge, under the lumenberry trees, to mind.

A moment later, the street was empty.

· · · ✴ · · ·

"Shan?"

A cool hand was placed gently on his forehead. He sighed as much for the coolness, as for the beloved familiarity of her pattern, soothing abraded nerves, and granting him a tithe of peace.

"Priscilla."

He opened his eyes, and looked up at her, sitting on the edge of the bed beside him, her face tired.

"Crew settled in?"

"They are, yes. I'm assured that the quarters are very pleasant, and that they will wait on you tomorrow at nuncheon. I left Dil Nem ordering up a bottle of wine. Jes allowed that she would welcome a rest before going in to heavy planning."

"That's well, then."

"Yes." She sighed.

"I am sorry," she said, "about Lady Selph."

"One can scarcely be sorry about Lady Selph," he said. "Only, I do wonder how it happened."

"So did I," Priscilla said. "Then, I remembered that I had nodded off—just for a minute!—when I was speaking with Danae, arranging for Dil Nem and Jes to come to us. It had been a long day, and I was tired, and I didn't think anything more of it at the time."

"So you had no notion until this evening?"

"None at all. I'm afraid my shock showed. Dil Nem was very clear that it had been my order—'Lady Selph and none other to be our third.'"

She sighed and looked around.

"Where is the lady?"

"Padi rashly volunteered to act as host, and given my state of mind, that seemed best."

"Yes, of course. About that state of mind—"

She reached down again and smoothed his hair back.

"Are we finished? The trade mission, I mean. On account of being Reavers, or having had congress with Reavers?"

"The security chief might have liked that, but neither the Warden nor Councilor ziaGorn would have it. Not that we are anything like Reavers, which even the chief admitted. I simply had to tell them that I was responsible for the deaths of dozens, including all of the Talents Tarona Rusk sent to Colemeno."

He sighed.

"I found it . . . difficult to have my murders put on display, and my reasons—especially my reasons for allowing Tarona Rusk to live—called into question. One is, so I gather from Security Chief bennaFalm, an idiot."

He waved a hand, deliberately shapeless.

"That aside—the trade mission is free to continue its work."

"Good." She looked down into his face, and he felt her love wash through him.

"I offer," she said, "a healing."

He smiled, and lifted a hand to touch her cheek.

"You, my love, are in no less a state than I am. I will not ask it of you. Let us sleep and take stock tomorrow, to see what can and should be done before I am required to present myself as civilized and peace loving."

"Instead of a bloodthirsty savage from outer space," Priscilla said, nodding wisely. "But, I wasn't clear. I offer a small healing."

She rose, grabbed his arm; pulled him upright, then to his feet.

"I don't say that I'm not tired enough to sleep standing up, Priscilla, but—"

She started across the room, towing him with her.

"We will shower," she said. "After, we will go to bed. And we will sleep."

"You've thought this out," Shan said.

"A small healing," she answered, "is what I offered."

"So you did. I accept."

· · · ✳ · · ·

Padi sat back on her heels and shook her head.

She had freshened the little nest of soft rags in the corner of the carrier, and put pellets, freeze-dried fruits, and a cup of water onto the dining shelf. An image formed inside her head—warm sand and a broad arcing leaf—and Padi shook her head.

"A problem?" Tekelia asked from behind her.

She looked up, moving her hand to show the cage and its regal inhabitant.

"This is not at all what she's used to. Dried fruits, pellets, and still water will satisfy her for an overnight, but I shall have to do better, tomorrow."

"And your tomorrow, as I was privileged to hear, is already quite full of necessary tasks, though admittedly none as important as the lady's comfort."

Tekelia knelt, graceful and smooth, and inclined slightly from the waist.

"Lady Selph, I'm pleased to renew our acquaintance. I offer service. What is necessary to your peace and comfort?"

Padi folded her hands on her knee as images began to flow. Quite vivid, those images, very nearly real in the space between the travel case and themselves.

Running water.

Sand.

Green, growing plants.

There was a pause as those images faded, and a sense of deep thought before another image formed—

A norbear, not any of Lady Selph's shipboard cuddle, Padi

saw—in fact, not a particular norbear at all. Merely the *idea* of
a norbear. Lady Selph wanted company.

The phantom norbear faded away, and Tekelia nodded.

"I understand. I may undertake all but the last of those for
you this evening, if you and Padi allow. An associate is not
something that I may conjure in so short a time, though I know
someone who I think would welcome the counsel of one so much
older and well traveled. I'll make inquiries. In the meanwhile—"

Tekelia looked at Padi.

"Let me solve this for you. I'll be an hour, maybe a few
minutes more."

Padi smiled.

"Far be it from me to deny an eager suitor. I can see you're
quite smitten."

Tekelia laughed.

"Soon."

Mist swirled—and Tekelia was gone.

"Well," Padi said. "I am not a norbear, a fact we have discussed at length. However, I offer a cuddle."

She leaned forward to work the latch; raised the gate and sat
back, arranging herself cross-legged.

Lady Selph stood on her back legs, ears twitching as she
considered the open doorway.

Then she dropped to all fours and deliberately walked through
the door and onto Padi's knee.

Padi thought of flowers in the garden at Trealla Fantrol, and
the feel of the sun on one's face.

Lady Selph accepted those images, giving back the sound of
water flowing, and the movement of fronds overhead.

Padi smiled, put her arms lightly around the lady, and closed
her eyes.

· · · ✵ · · ·

"Mar Tyn."

Here it came, Mar Tyn thought with resignation, and turned
to face Dyoli where she stood at the side of their small dining
table. She had put her wineglass down beside the plate of sandwiches, and was looking at him wearily.

"Yes?" he said. He went to the table and put his own glass
down before reaching out to touch her cheek.

"We might quarrel tomorrow," he suggested. "When we both have our wits about us."

"And likely to do less damage." Dyoli gave him a half-smile. "Only, I don't intend to quarrel, my Mar Tyn. I merely wish to ask why you broke our link at the restaurant. *Something* was building—I felt it—and we might have avoided pain."

"Something *was* building," he agreed. "And whatever it was, it was ill. I—I felt it, like a cold shadow cast over tomorrow."

Dyoli blinked.

"This is new," she said.

Mar Tyn sighed. "These conditions...I had said that my Gift was changing. If that is so, then our mutual Gift must also change."

"Yes," Dyoli said, and reached out to lay her fingertips across his lips. "I have my answer. Tomorrow, we will speak further of this, and—and discover a method by which we may assess these changes. Does that do well for you, my love, or will only a quarrel satisfy?"

Mar Tyn grasped her wrist lightly, moving her hand away as he stepped forward to encircle her waist with his free arm. She moved closer into the embrace, and shivered when he whispered in her ear.

"No quarrel. I have in mind something much more interesting."

· · · ✳ · · ·

Tekelia had not returned by the time Lady Selph had called an end to their cuddle, and Padi had gone to her screen to review the master trader's notes for tomorrow's meetings.

Tekelia had still not returned. It was, Padi thought as she gathered up her robe and entered the 'fresher, rather a relief to find that there was something Tekelia was not able to do with ease and insouciance. She might have been worried that something dire had happened, save for the foolish conviction that she would *know* if Tekelia had fallen into trouble.

And there was an odd fancy, to be sure.

"Go to bed, Padi yos'Galan," she told herself. "You have a very full day tomorrow."

She stood under the shower's gentle rain for a little longer than cleanliness demanded, and sighed when the water cut off, and the walls began to warm.

When she stepped back into her room a few minutes later,

belting her robe around her, Tekelia was sitting on the floor by the window, next to a table Padi didn't recognize.

On the table was a large, transparent enclosure. Padi glimpsed sand, green plants, a small waterfall, a sleeping platform surrounded by leafy plants. Lady Selph was sitting on the table outside of the enclosure, eating a slice of fresh fruit.

"That," Padi said, coming forward to admire it more nearly, "is perfect."

Tekelia looked up with a lazy smile.

"Lady Selph was gracious enough to be pleased. Though it did take longer than I had anticipated. My apologies."

"Completely unnecessary," Padi said. "It is understood that creating perfection takes time."

"You're too good to me."

Tekelia turned back to Lady Selph, who had finished her treat, and was radiating sleepy contentment.

"Now, my lady, you must return to your nest, if you please. I know you remember how to do that."

Lady Selph was seen to hesitate, then dropped to four feet, turned and walked through one panel, which Padi saw now was a clever door. When she was inside, Tekelia touched the side of the enclosure. The gate lowered and locked. Padi leaned closer, and Tekelia caught her hand, guiding her fingers to the pressure point.

"It will not open to her," Tekelia said.

"Wisely done," Padi said, watching the elderly norbear cross the sand to the sleeping platform and disappear behind the shielding leaves.

"I couldn't have done half so well," she added, putting her hand on Tekelia's shoulder.

"I am pleased to be of service," Tekelia said, looking up into her face, eyes at the moment grey and green.

"I'll leave you soon to your rest and your early meetings. Will you take ease from me? I won't be rough, only, as you know, I am not a Healer."

Padi sighed, with a glance at the clock.

"I will gladly accept a friend's kind assistance, but only if you may do so without depleting yourself." She waved a hand. "This must have been expensive of energy."

"It was, but I paused in my labors for a substantial snack, quite enough to see you settled and get myself home."

It was on the edge of her tongue, to say that there was no need for Tekelia to leave, but the clock conspired with the early meetings to convince her otherwise.

She sighed, and went to the bed, slipped off her robe and got under the blanket.

Tekelia came and sat on the edge, taking her hand, and smiling down at her.

"A kiss," Padi murmured, "before you go."

"Another pleasure," Tekelia said softly, and obliged her, gently.

Padi sighed when the kiss was done, nestling into the pillow as Tekelia put a hand on her forehead, and smiled.

"Sleep and rest well, Padi yos'Galan."

· · · ✳ · · ·

She was winsome in sleep, Tekelia thought, drawing back and inspecting the work against the ambient. Satisfied that Padi would awaken rested and renewed, Tekelia sighed, rose, and went to Lady Selph's new abode. That lady was also asleep, a comforter of dreams pulled tight around her.

Tekelia turned again to look at the long form slumbering under the blanket, then thought of the house at the edge of the wood, and the light from the Ribbons dancing over the deck.

Save for the two sleepers, the room was empty.

Off-Grid
Pacazahno

· · · · · · · · · · ·

THE SQUARE WAS MORE THAN USUALLY BUSY WHEN ARBOUR arrived at Pacazahno, and she paused to evaluate the crowd.

The ambient brought her a potent emotional mix of distress, anger, fear, and disbelief, which was not at all Pacazahno's usual atmosphere. And now that her eye had found the pattern, it seemed that most of the busyness was concentrated down-square, near the school.

If there was a problem at the school, Arbour thought, with a little shiver, that was where Konsit would be.

Taking a deep breath, Arbour walked down the square, toward the center of the disturbance.

"But why would anyone smash up our art garden?" a child was asking as Arbour reached the edge of the crowd.

"And the library!" called out a man Arbour recognized as a science teacher.

Arbour hesitated. The emotional soup became thicker with proximity, and it was beginning to act on her. She felt tears rise, and adjusted her shields until the feelings of others faded into the background.

"We don't know why or who, yet," said a firm and very familiar voice. As Arbour had suspected, Konsit joiMore was at the center of the action. "We're going to do our best to find the answers to those questions. I will call the Citizens Coalition, and see what assistance they can give us. Also, I will ask Ribbon Dance Village to send us appropriately Talented Haosa."

"In the meantime," said the woman standing next to Konsit, who Arbour knew for one of the school's three administrators.

"In the meantime, we're asking teachers and students to go to the community building and collaborate on a system to hold classes in that space until the necessary investigations have been made. There will be a whole-school assembly immediately after lunch, to discuss these events."

There was a ripple through the crowd as students and teachers sorted themselves together. Konsit looked around at those who were neither.

"There's nothing to be done right now, except to make sure that the garden and the library aren't tampered with until the investigators arrive."

She turned to the grey-haired woman standing on her other side.

"Constable fuJang will need volunteers to make sure that nothing is disturbed until the investigation is made. Anyone who wants to help, please see her."

There was another ripple as prospective volunteers moved toward the constable. Konsit looked out over the greatly reduced crowd, and said, "The rest of you, please continue with your usual business. As soon as we have any information to share, there will be a village meeting."

A third ripple as those dismissed moved back to their interrupted days.

Konsit turned to Arbour.

"I apologize—" she began, and Arbour held up a hand.

"You have a village to administer and an emergency. No apologies necessary. What happened here? Knowing that will help me decide who to call in for assistance."

Konsit sighed, and threw her hands out, showing Arbour an enclosed area full of broken-off posts and smashed objects.

"It started with an ecology project about durable and weatherproof materials. The children decided that just because they were doing useful research, it didn't have to be utilitarian or dull. So, they made a garden full of weatherproofed art. I have pictures. It really was something to see."

She lowered her hands.

"The other loss is the library. They were thorough—ruined books and broken readers, overturned shelves and furniture."

She sighed again.

"It's just senseless."

"Mischief often is," Arbour told her. "Is there a comm I can use, while you're calling the Citizens Coalition?"

Konsit blinked.

"Yes, of course. You can use Nattie's comm."

Arbour had made her call, and was standing by the window, looking out over the garden. Mischief against the school was unsettling in the extreme, though she would not have been Haosa if she had not seen the opportunity this mischance offered.

The door to Konsit's office opened, and the village administrator came to stand beside her, looking out over the garden with a sigh. Her pattern was showing flashes of tension and dismay, which was expectable, but the strain of those emotions would weary her even before the investigations had begun.

Arbour dared to whisper a small wish of calm Healing into the ambient, and had the satisfaction of Seeing Konsit's tension ease.

"Councilor ziaGorn is not at the Coalition's office this morning. I am promised that my message will be sent to him, and that I should expect a call."

She turned to face Arbour.

"I know we had our usual meeting scheduled for today—"

"Much of which can be put aside until this other matter is solved," Arbour said. With her eye on opportunity, she added, "I do bring one topic that may serve us both, if you have the patience to hear me out."

"Of course I'll hear you out!" Konsit said. "Let me call for a meal to be brought to us out in the garden, so we can be comfortable while we talk."

Konsit heard the tale of Vaiza and Torin out in perfect silence. When Arbour was done, she sat back in her chair and sighed.

"This commuting class seems to solve two problems very neatly," she said. "I don't hide from you that I am *very* unsettled about this mischief against the school. To attack businesses is one thing—wrong, of course, but not on the same level, if you see what I mean?"

"I understand," Arbour assured her. "The art garden and the library—it's too close to the children."

"Yes! And we don't know whether it was merely opportunity— the school was empty—or a warning of worse to come."

Arbour shivered.

"Of course," Konsit continued, "we cannot relocate the entire village, or even the entire school, to Ribbon Dance Village, but a—a commuter class, that would meet your children's needs for companionship and challenge." Her eyes lit. "We would present the opportunity as a challenge to our students—yes, I like this! In addition, developing a method to choose the students who will commute, and designing a curriculum, will distract the teachers and the board from the recent ill acts."

She tapped her finger on her knee, frowning briefly, before looking up and meeting Arbour's eyes.

"I will bring it to them."

"Thank you. Maradel—the village medic—has undertaken to test our two, to gain an idea of their strengths and weaknesses."

"Good, good. I assume she's using the standardized tests. The results will be useful for our planning. I will take this to the board—tomorrow, I think. One of the first things I will suggest is that someone be chosen as a liaison with Medic Maradel. She should expect a call soon."

"Thank you," Arbour said, simply.

Konsit smiled again.

"You and I have been looking for ways to strengthen the ties between our two villages. This may be something that we will wish to continue, even when there are no children at Ribbon Dance."

"In order to get to know our neighbors better?" Arbour suggested, and this time Konsit outright laughed.

"Exactly."

Colemenoport
Offices of the
Tree-and-Dragon Trade Mission

. . . .

MERCHANT VELLATON WAS DARK-HAIRED, DELICATE, AND SOME-
what younger than Padi had envisioned from her reading of the
master trader's notes.

The merchant paused just inside the door, surprise plain on
her face. Perhaps she hadn't received the master trader's message. That, Padi admitted to herself as she rose from behind the
trade table, was the most likely reason for surprise. There were
other, less amiable possibilities, including an attempt to establish
precedence, but until they were revealed, it was best to assume
simple error.

She bowed.

"Merchant vellaTon, I am Padi yos'Galan, trader attached to
the Tree-and-Dragon Mission. It is my honor to assist the master
trader as he requires. I am to convey his regret that he could
not be here for you."

The merchant raised the hand unencumbered by her case,
showing an empty palm and widespread fingers.

"Yes, I did receive his message," she said pleasantly. "I am
to treat with you as I would with him, so he said. You must
excuse my moment of surprise. I had not expected you to be
quite so—vivid."

"Vivid" possibly stood in for "young," Padi thought. If so, it
was a gentle substitution, possibly born of the merchant's own
youth.

"But—no matter! I shall be pleased to deal with you! Please tell
him when next you speak that I offer commiserations and understanding. Business does sometimes pull us in strange directions."

"I will tell him so, ma'am," Padi said as the merchant came forward to put her case on the table.

"I have had enthusiastic reports of you, Trader yos'Galan, from my friend Saru bernRoanti. I think we will deal very well together."

Padi warmed somewhat at that, and offered a smile of her own.

"I hope that we will, ma'am. May I offer tea?"

"Tea would be most welcome," Merchant vellaTon acknowledged, seating herself and pulling the case forward.

Padi crossed the room to the buffet, and drew two cups of tea from the pot. By the time she returned to the table, Merchant vellaTon had the screen she had taken from her case open and active before her.

"If I may ask you to sit next to me, Trader, I think you might find this of interest."

Padi pulled her chair closer and sat down, and Merchant vellaTon moved the screen between them.

"You understand, Trader, that vellaTon Manufactory has been in the business of producing zylon units long before Colemeno and the Dust joined in dance. I have gone through our records and found inventory lists of those days, including what goods we had sent out, and what we had received in return. I wonder if this will be useful to us in our discussions?"

She extended a hand, tapping up the promised inventory list.

"Now, we no longer produce some of these items, not for lack of ability, but for lack of market. With the possibility of once again entering a wider market, with more diversity of taste, we are willing—even eager—to bring the past forward to serve the present."

Padi leaned closer, running a practiced eye down the list, then sat back and picked up her cup.

"You will have to teach me what these are," she said. "And where they went, if you know that."

"With great pleasure, trader," Merchant vellaTon murmured. She had recourse to her own cup, set it aside and opened the details for the first item on her list.

Colemenoport
Wayfarer

. . . .

SHAN DRIFTED AMID WARM CLOUDS, FREE OF CARE, AND IN BAL-
ance with the universe.

Even as he drifted, he knew himself to be on the cusp between
sleeping and waking. Craven, he tried to pull the clouds about
him, as he might the potent fogs of Healspace, but they dissi-
pated even as he reached for them. He would be waking soon,
then, he thought, regretfully, and was on the instant aware that
he had done so.

He didn't open his eyes—not quite yet—but merely lay there,
enjoying the feel of the pillow under his cheek, the weight of the
blanket overlaying him, and Priscilla's long, silken legs entangled
with his. He took a deep breath, drawing in the scent of her hair,
and felt her head shift on his shoulder.

"Good morning, love."

"Good morning, Priscilla. Allow me to congratulate you on
a superlative small healing."

"It was rather a good one, wasn't it?" she said contentedly,
and suddenly yawned, her body stretching against his.

Smiling, he ran his hand down over a warm hip. Priscilla
murmured, and shifted her legs.

He gasped, suddenly much less languid, and she laughed softly.

"May I propose another small healing?" she murmured.

"Oh, I think we're in agreement," Shan whispered, and slid
his hand up to cup her breast.

Off-Grid
Ribbon Dance Village
The News Tree

. . . .

THE AIR SHIMMERED AND SOLIDIFIED INTO A NEAT GROUP OF buildings forming a town square. The sky was opalescent, and a cool breeze touched his cheek.

Scarcely three steps to his right was the news-tree. Bentamin closed the small distance and put his palm against the smooth bark.

He felt a mild electric prickle against his skin, folded his hands together, and composed himself to wait for one of the villagers to join him.

While in Bentamin's experience the wait was never lengthy, it could be as much as ten minutes before someone came for him. As he understood it, the tree conveyed his signature to the ranking person of the moment. He had on previous visits been greeted by the village administrator, the village medic, and by a very tongue-tied person wearing an apron and a quantity of flour.

This time, he had scarcely settled himself before a child's high voice came to him on the back of the breeze.

"I felt it—like an itch inside my head, and the idea of some-body standing at the news-tree!"

"You may have done," a lower, more adult voice made answer. "Sometimes things echo in the ambient. Or, you know, you might have gotten an echo from me—because that is *precisely* what I think it feels like—an itchy notion that there's someone just come in."

"Do all visitors come to the tree?" the child asked then.

"The polite ones do," came the answer. "And here you have a lesson. When *you* go traveling, say to Visalee, or The Vinery, you will be polite and go directly to the news-tree, and wait for someone to greet you."

"But how—" the child began, and then stopped, as the little group of four rounded the corner of the administrator's office: A towheaded young woman in a gardener's smock paced by a large orange-striped *sokyum*, a dark-haired child walking on either side.

The child on the right stopped, and put a hand out to touch the big cat. The child on the left came on another few steps before he stopped, head tipped to one side.

"Hello, Warden Bentamin," said Vaiza xinRood.

"Hello, Vaiza," Bentamin answered, and looked to the child who had stayed with the cat. "Hello, Torin."

"Hello, Warden Bentamin," she answered solemnly.

Vaiza had not used to be the twin to put himself forward, but he appointed himself host, now, and turned to the towheaded woman.

"Geritsi, Warden Bentamin is the guardian of Civilization." He turned back. "Warden Bentamin, these are Geritsi and Dosent, who have been kind enough to let us stay with them at the Rose Cottage."

Bentamin met a pair of humorous grey eyes as the young woman stepped to Vaiza's side, so there were two between Bentamin and Torin, and a guard at her side. Bentamin approved.

Geritsi bowed easily, and not as if she were particularly overwhelmed by his office, or even as if she found his presence unusual.

"Geritsi slentAlin, sir. If you've come for Arbour—Administrator poginGeist—she's away for the day. Vaiza, Torin, Dosent, and I are the greeting committee, but—"

Across the square the door to the clinic opened, and a taller, rangier, and altogether more dangerous-looking woman strolled toward them.

Bentamin bowed.

"Medic arnFaelir," he said. "Precisely who I was wishing to see. Have you an hour?"

The medic came to rest next to Geritsi, and accorded him a nod.

"I've an hour, surely. Will you come into the clinic? It's shielded somewhat."

And would thus offer some protection to his fragile Civilized senses. It was Haosa courtesy, Bentamin understood, and smiled.

"Thank you, I will." He turned back to Vaiza.

"I would also like to visit you and your sister, sir, after the medic and I have finished our business. Will you be available in an hour?"

He didn't see the adults exchange a glance, but he had the distinct impression that they had checked in with each other even before the medic lifted a shoulder.

"We're helping Geritsi with the garden," Vaiza said, perhaps having caught that subtle undercurrent, and opening the way to a polite refusal.

"If you finish weeding the peas, you'll have earned some tea and cookies and a friendly visit," Geritsi said, as if offering a high treat. Bentamin saw Vaiza glance at his sister. She inclined her head, just a fraction.

"Until soon, then, Warden Bentamin," Vaiza said, and dodged around Geritsi to Torin's side.

"Come on! I'll race you!" he said—and they were both off running, the *sokyum* keeping pace.

"I have set a search in train for a discreet Healer from a Hall of good repute who is willing to examine the children," Bentamin told the Haosa medic, after they had each eaten a cookie, and had a sip of tea.

"Yes, Tekelia had said that you would be handling that aspect of the matter," she paused before inclining her head in a fair imitation of courtesy. "Thank you for your efforts on behalf of our children."

Bentamin chose another cookie, and said carefully, "Not only is it my duty as Warden to insure that the vulnerable are protected, but their mother's husband was my cousin; we knew each other well."

"Ah." That earned him a flash of something—perhaps sympathy?—and a murmured, "I'm saddened by your loss."

"Thank you. You should know that I will be visiting the children after I leave you, and will make my own examination, so that I may offer the Healer corroboration."

"Of course."

Bentamin sipped tea.

"In your opinion, Medic," he said.

Her eyebrows lifted slightly.

"All right."

"How critical is it that the children be separated?"

"There's the question, right there. In my opinion, the sooner they're separated, the better. You understand that this work that binds them—the threads are growing tighter, as their patterns grow. A longer wait means more delicate work to unbind them, and more chance of error." She paused, and added, with another lift of her eyebrows, "Understand that I'm not willing to attempt remediation myself even now; the work's that far beyond me."

She sipped tea and put the mug down.

"That understood, we next look at survivability. I'm not familiar with the work that's been done, but I *am* familiar with pattern growth rates and maturity. I'd put it at a Standard, before they start to feel stretched and maybe a little uncomfortable. P'rhaps two Standards, before damage is done." She paused to pick up her mug, and looked directly into his face. "That supposes no new trauma occurs to reinforce the weaving, and that nothing initiates an accelerated pattern growth."

"Soonest done is best, then," Bentamin said. "I agree."

"Let us discuss venue for a moment. A Civilized Healer cannot do her best work in an unshielded environment. I am able to offer a parlor in the Wardian as the most secure—"

"Ineligible," the medic said sharply.

Bentamin felt his own eyebrows lift.

She waved a hand, perhaps in apology.

"Understand that they're our children, Warden, and we won't put them into active danger. You'll know, I think, that Tekelia's got an idea Civilization isn't safe for them."

"There is risk, which is why I am suggesting the Wardian." He paused, and prodded her a bit. "The most secure building in Civilization."

"Scary, too, is what I'm told," the medic said.

"My care is two-fold," Bentamin said to that implied criticism. "I want to distress the children as little as possible. I'm told that they are settling into the village and feel a measure of safety here. However, a Civilized Healer..."

He paused. Medic arnFaelir sipped her tea and put the mug on the table.

"There's a shielded suite at Peck's Market that we use from time to time," she said, moving a hand in an arc from table to shoulder, possibly showing him the surrounding conditions. "We're talking on the level of what we have here, for shielding, maybe a bit more, the market being set at a remove from the Hill."

That might do, Bentamin thought. "May I examine the shielding here?"

"Go ahead. Tell me if you find anything needs patching."

It was a pleasantry, Bentamin thought. Possibly. He opened his shields somewhat wider.

Had he opened so far at his cousin's house on the edge of the forest, he would have beheld swirling ribbons of energy, and been buffeted by sound—Tekelia assured him that the Ribbons not only danced, but sang—and it would have quickly become necessary to increase his protections, though he never completely closed his shields, even off-Grid.

Here under the clinic's shielding, there were a few flashes and flares of color against a pearly aspect. There *was* sound, but subdued, as if someone were singing softly in the next room.

It did not approach the silence available in the Wardian's deepest rooms, nor was it the quiet serenity of a Civilized Healer's examination parlor. But Healers did not always have the luxury of working inside their own parlors, and there were numerous places on-Grid that were every bit as noisy as Medic arnFaelir's carefully shielded clinic.

"It will suffice," he said, drawing his shields closer.

He leaned back and smiled into the medic's dour face.

"I saw nothing in need of repair," he added.

"That's to the good. One or two of ours will be with them, when it's time," she said, and raised a hand as if to stop a protest. "The village *has* taken them as ours, and we protect our own."

The Haosa were great protectors, as Bentamin well knew. He inclined his head.

"That is perfectly understandable, and the condition will be explained to the Healer ahead of the examination."

He sipped his tea, considered another cookie, and decided against. After all, there were still tea and cookies ahead of him.

Colemenoport
Offices of the
Tree-and-Dragon Trade Mission

. . . .

MERCHANT ZERKILIN WAS HER SECOND MEETING.

He arrived slightly beforetime, gravely accepted a cup of tea, and immediately wished to know what precisely would be the role of the merchants of Colemenoport, should Tree-and-Dragon establish itself there. Was there a co-op in the master trader's eye? What would be the membership grades and benefits?

"The trade mission is still in discovery," Padi said, finding herself on firm ground, from the previous day's discussions. "You will be interested to learn that the master trader has decided to conduct a whole port inventory, according to Guild protocol. *Qe'andra* dea'Tolin, who is an experienced trade accountant, trained in the dea'Gauss firm, on Liad, came down to us only last night. I would guess that she will be opening her office and beginning her work tomorrow."

Padi paused, as if weighing whether she should say anything more, then leaned slightly forward.

"Between us, sir—the master trader is keen. Once we have a comprehensive picture of what Colemenoport offers, and what Tree-and-Dragon may offer in Balance, we will bring those insights to the portmaster, the Warden, and the Council. We have been given to understand that the final decision rests with the Council. The trade mission may only propose, though I will say, having seen the master trader at work, if we do propose, it will be with—eloquence."

"The Council are neither merchants nor travelers," Merchant zerKilin said slowly. "They feel their duty strongly, and history has taught them to be...conservative." He glanced at his teacup,

205

but did not pick it up. "May one ask if the master trader might include Colemeno in a route, even if the Council denies what is necessary to shape us into a Loop Anchor?"

"Again," Padi said softly, "the whole port inventory will provide many levels of information. How the master trader will choose to act, if the Council withholds their permissions—"

She moved her shoulders and turned up empty palms.

"We can speculate, sir, but would it not be best to wait until we *know*?"

Unexpectedly, Merchant zerKilin laughed.

"Indeed, Trader! Indeed, that would be the path of wisdom. I am overzealous, I see. But it has been—so long, and there are those of us who see opportunity in change, and do not wish to also see it slip away from us."

"The trade team has much the same attitude toward change and opportunity," Padi said sincerely. "Only, you must allow the master trader to work."

"I will," Merchant zerKilin promised. "And, should the master trader require assistance in his quest to turn opportunity to profit, he may call upon me at any time. For anything."

Padi inclined her head.

"Thank you, sir. I will tell him you said so."

Colemenoport
Offices of the
Isfelm Trade Union

. . . .

IT WAS THE 'COUNTS THAT HAD HER ATTENTION THIS PARTICULAR morning, that having been in the packet come down from *Ember* on the overnight.

Let it be known that the 'counts had never been Chudith Isfelm's favorite side of trade. On the other hand, if she wanted to be lead trader—and she did—the going-over and understanding of the 'counts fairly fell to her.

She carried a mug of ale to the desk, and tapped open the file. Took a sip, and bent to it.

Last half-year profits were strong. That was good, as the current half-year was going to show the effect of *Ember* sitting at Colemenoport, close enough to idle, for as long as it took Tree-and-Dragon to sort out their necessities.

She leaned back in her chair, and had a sip of ale, taking counsel of her favorite corner of the ceiling. If the master trader agreed to let Trader Padi step up to *Ember* sooner rather than later, and she brought along a pod full of goodies from the wide universe, that would draw some interest from those previously disinterested in the Isfelm Trade Union.

Or, she thought, fair-mindedly, it might make no difference at all, habit and tradition being what they were, even—*especially*— 'mong those who rode a Loop.

And that right there was the biggest problem with the routes— all the routes. Calcified, that's what they were, like the Dust had gotten into the deep workings of society and commerce, and froze it all up. By stars, they *needed* Tree-and-Dragon—didn't they just?—to shake everything up, including rigid Looper brains.

She half-laughed.

"It'll be a fine thing indeed to see the Evrits sit down with the Mikancy, and both rise up unmurdered, Chudi Isfelm, but none o'that's getting your 'counts done."

So—inventory. Not much there, she having dropped most of what *Ember*'d been carrying for Brother Jaimy to share out with the rest of the union ships. 'Course, she'd refill from their Colemenoport warehouse before Trader Padi and the Tree-and-Dragon *qe'andra* set off on the master trader's route audit.

And wasn't *that* a fair undertaking? She'd sat up half the night with her screen split in threes like she'd been busted back to 'prentice, reviewing the proper section in the Trade Guild archives the master trader had given her.

Still a lot of study wanted on that front, and she truly hoped that Trader Padi was as bright as she gleamed—and lucky, as well. Though, according to the master trader, that came with.

Well, so. She looked back to the screen.

Accounts owed—only the usual there—and accounts owing, too.

That was the whole thing, then, and done in less than an hour. She reached to sign off—and stopped, frowning at the note at the very bottom of the accounts-owing page.

Passage paid.

Passage paid, right enough—three passengers and light luggage—and they'd never come, had they? The woman had been in a fair frenzy for passage, and canny Trader Isfelm had seen desperation and determination both. Hadn't been anything to do with her, but she'd taken the money, hadn't she, breaking her own rules about passengers *and* cash?

Trader Isfelm would've been satisfied with half upfront, but the passenger wouldn't have it. Paid everything on the nose, and swore she'd be on time.

Only, she missed the time. *Ember* had waited, long enough to make the portmaster testy. There being a strict time limit on that game, eventually *Ember* had lifted.

Chudi'd been in a right swivet about that at the time, turning the thing over and over in her mind. She might've suspected a scam, but she couldn't see how it worked out to a profit.

It wasn't until they'd hit mid-Loop that it occurred to Chudi Isfelm that the passage fee to *Ember* had been *misdirection*, and that *the ship* might've dodged bad trouble. That had been enough to cool her jets, and she'd pushed the matter aside, to think of other things, which was the trader's privilege.

Bookkeeping, though. Bookkeeping never forgets. Done right, the way they did it themselves, bookkeeping didn't lie.

And the fact was that they were carrying someone else's money, and they hadn't delivered what they'd been paid for.

She frowned. It was a sizable amount of money—*passage money*, not goods. Passage money, with no passenger arriving, nor a formal cancellation sent? Nobody'd look askance, if she declared the whole sum forfeit, and set it against operating funds.

Only... it didn't sit easy with her.

In fact, now that it was at the front of her mind again, she didn't feel easy about *any* of it.

That woman—Dust take it, what *had* her name been? She tapped the note on the screen and opened the detail. Right, xinRood. Zatorvia xinRood. Thin and sharp, and so desperate Chudi's own jaw had ached in sympathy.

Below the name, there in the details, was an address in Haven City, and, more to the point—a comm code.

Trader Isfelm reached for the comm.

"kezlBlythe residence," a man's languid voice came out of the comm.

Trader Isfelm frowned, and glanced at the code on the screen.

"Your pardon, Luzant," she said, "I was calling Luzant xinRood about some business we have between us. I must have fumbled it."

Botching a code wasn't a thing she did often—or ever—but she must have done—

"Luzant xinRood is dead," the man informed her, and not as if it was any loss of his.

Chudith Isfelm took a quiet breath.

"I offer sympathy to her family," she said formally.

"Yes," the voice said briskly. "What sort of business?"

She narrowed her eyes.

"Pardon?"

"You said you were calling Zatorvia on a matter of business. I'm her cousin Jorey. Any business she left behind falls to kezlBlythe." There was a pause, before he added, with a malicious edge to his voice, "Did she owe you money?"

"Boot's on the other foot," she said, feeling sharp herself, "I owe her money."

"That's fortunate," the man said. "You can make the transfer to our account. The code—"

"She paid in cash," she heard herself say. "And I'm bound to return cash."

There came a spot of silence, as if he were properly astonished, she thought, and who could blame him?

"Then bring it here," he said finally, and with distinct bad temper. "We're in the directory."

She took another breath, deep and quiet.

"Luzant, thank you for your time and advice," she said, and cut the connection.

Off-Grid
The Rose Cottage

. . . .

COOKIES AND TEA HAD BEEN ARRANGED ON A TABLE AT THE foot of the garden. It was a pleasant place, surrounded by flowers, in the shade of a large and comfortable tree.

It was also rather pointedly *not* in Geritsi slentAlin's house, though they were under her eye, as she continued her work in the garden—Guardian Number One, Bentamin thought, amused.

Dosent the *sokyum* was stretched out by the flowers, seemingly asleep—Guardian Number Two.

"Will you have tea, Warden Bentamin?" Vaiza asked, which was his place, as the youngest at the table.

"Thank you, Vaiza, I would like tea," Bentamin said politely.

The boy stood, hefted the teapot, and poured with a remarkably steady hand. Torin passed the full cup across the table.

"Please, help yourself to cookies," she said, and Bentamin moved a sugar cookie from the center plate to his smaller one, and waited politely while Vaiza poured tea for his sister, then for himself.

He had put the pot down, but not yet reseated himself, when there came a small, intense disturbance in the branches overhead.

Bentamin looked up as a portly, grey-striped body thumped to the tabletop by Torin's hand.

"Eet!" Vaiza exclaimed, and Bentamin bent his head to hide a smile.

Guardian Number Three had arrived.

Eet accepted a cookie, and sat quietly munching while Bentamin made gentle inquiries into Vaiza and Torin's situation.

They both assured him, with differing degrees of enthusiasm, that they were very well at the Rose Cottage, that Geritsi and

211

Dosent were everything that was kind, that they had no lack of people to talk with or visit, though there were no other children in the village at the moment.

"Tanin is going to teach me how to make bread," Torin reported, with the most eagerness she had so far displayed.

"A useful skill," Bentamin agreed, sipping his tea. "And school?"

"Tekelia took that to the village meeting for us," Torin said. "For now, Maradel has been giving us placement tests, so the correct courses can be ordered in."

"We *are* going to stay here, aren't we, Warden Bentamin?" Vaiza asked sharply, as if suddenly understanding where this line of questioning might lead. "We won't be going back into the city, will we?"

Eet put what remained of his cookie down on the table, and settled himself firmly on his haunches. Bentamin met a pair of beady black eyes, and turned to Vaiza.

"Would it be so bad, to go back to the city?" he asked.

Torin bit her lip. Vaiza glanced at her and frowned.

"The city isn't safe," he said at last. "Mother said so. We were going to leave, we had our things in cases, and were waiting in our room for the car to arrive. But then..."

His voice faded out, and it was Torin who said, "But Cousin Jorey killed Mother. And Cousin Avryal said we were abominations. And then we were sent to the Haosa."

Bentamin looked from one to the other, seeing solemn faces, and he dared open his Inner Eyes far enough to see—

The ambient was glitter blown on the wind, distracting, but proximity helped. He saw two patterns, each unique, and then, quite distinct, a third, overlying pattern, anchored in each.

Light flashed, and his Sight fragmented into chaos. With a quiet sigh, he pulled his shields close, and looked back to the children.

"As you guessed," he told them, "my visit has a purpose. I will be engaging a Healer to examine you both in order to be certain that you are quite well."

Vaiza frowned, and glanced at his sister.

"We are very well here, Warden Bentamin," he said, repeating their earlier assurance.

"We are *well enough* here," Torin corrected, and it did not escape Bentamin's attention that Dosent the *sokyum* stretched lazily in her bed among the flowers, and sat up to wash her face. "I—feel different here than I did in the city. There is too much—" She stopped sharply, and flung her hands into the air, as if showing him the Ribbons that were only barely visible in the bright morning sky.

"There is too much," she finished, and looked down at the table.

"Am I not helping you enough?" her brother asked, leaning close. "Torin. Tell me what else I should do."

She reached out and put her hand over his. "You *are* helping me," she said firmly, and raised her head to look at Bentamin.

"Mother told us that we were to help each other. In the city, I helped Vaiza with his lessons and his forms. Here, he helps me."

There was a flicker in the air between them, as a face barely seen. The norbear, Bentamin realized, had entered the conversation.

"Mother," Vaiza said, looking at Eet. "Mother would be proud of us both."

"She would," Bentamin said firmly. "You are strong and courageous. But even the strong and courageous sometimes take wounds—" He thought suddenly of Master Trader yos'Galan.

There was a long pause, before Torin spoke.

"The Healer—would she come here?"

"When it is time, some one or two of the Haosa will bring you to Peck's Market. I will bring the Healer there to meet you."

"Will Tekelia bring us?" Vaiza asked.

"You may ask and see if Tekelia is able to escort you," Bentamin said.

"When?" asked Torin.

"First, I must find the best Healer available. I wanted to speak with you before I went further. Do I understand that you are not opposed to an examination?"

Vaiza looked at Torin; Torin look at Vaiza.

"We are not opposed," Torin said, "as long as Tekelia or Geritsi and Dosent, and Eet, will be with us."

Bentamin inclined his head. "I will make that a provision of the meeting. As soon as I have the Healer's agreement, I will inform Medic arnFaelir, so that arrangements can be made. Is that well for you?"

Another solemn exchange of glances before Torin inclined her head. "Yes, Warden Bentamin. Thank you for your care."

"It is nothing less than my duty," Bentamin told them. "Now, if you will hold me excused, I would like to have a private word with Eet."

Colemenoport
Offices of the
Tree-and-Dragon Trade Mission

. . . .

THE TONE OF THE MEETING HAD EASED CONSIDERABLY.

Merchant zerKilin had several more probing questions regarding the master trader's probable plans for Colemenoport.

He also questioned her closely regarding the protocol of a whole port inventory. Padi was pleased to share with him the relevant section of the Traders Guild guidelines, for which courtesy he thanked her gravely, before making inquiries into what he might do to prepare for Tree-and-Dragon's *qe'andra*.

As their arranged end-time drew near, he took the initiative, closing the meeting gracefully a few minutes early. He very properly asked her to convey his respect to the master trader, as well as his hope that they would soon have an opportunity to sit together and build upon today's beginnings.

He stood, and allowed her to conduct him to the door, where he paused with a broad smile.

"I hope you will not take it amiss, if I should send 'round a case of wine for the comfort of the trade mission—and some sparkling juice, as well, for those times when wine will not do."

It was possible that he thought he was buying access to the master trader with his wine and juice—but it was equally possible that he was merely doing what other vendors at other ports had done—making certain that their name was remembered by attaching it to something pleasant.

Whatever his intent, his manner was graceful, and Padi thanked him for his care before bowing him out into the hallway.

Returning to the meeting room, she refreshed herself, reviewed the master trader's notes for her third and final meeting on the morning, with Luzant Zandir kezlBlythe.

The notes were sparse, and she was quickly the master of them. Rising, she took the used teacups to the little kitchen area behind the main meeting room, refilled the kettle and set it to warm.

She had just arranged the new cups and fresh pot on the buffet when the blue light over the door flashed twice, and a tone sounded.

Her third appointment had arrived.

Padi moved to her place at the table, and remained standing as the door opened to admit a woman with cropped grey hair wearing clothing made in a different style than the port-folk. Merchants and administrators wore a tunic or vest over long pants, and the sort of low sturdy boots favored, so Padi had observed, by those who stood, or walked, for much of their day, no matter the world. The merchants preferred sober blues, greens, and maroons, and a brightly colored shirt beneath the long vest.

Zandir kezlBlythe wore an eye-searing yellow vest decorated with abstract embroidery done in iridescent black cord. The black shirt beneath the vest was some light fabric that rippled and shone like silk; the long flowing pants were scarlet.

Her yellow boots had high red heels, thick soles, and slightly upturned toes.

Padi bowed.

"Ma'am," she said politely. "I am Padi yos'Galan, trader attached to t—"

"Yes," the woman interrupted, her voice sharp and high. "I had the master trader's note. Press of business. Apologies for the necessity of his absence at a prearranged meeting. His second will meet with me instead, and I may deal with her as I would himself."

She paused there and gave Padi a narrow-eyed stare.

Padi kept her face pleasant—and waited.

"Well," said Zandir kezlBlythe, sharpness somewhat lessened. "Perhaps it is a fortunate meeting, Trader. I ask you to pardon a bit of temper. I had set some store on coming to an agreement with the master trader today."

Padi tipped her head.

"I fear the master trader's notes do not mention an agreement, ma'am. May I serve you some tea, and ask you to amend my ignorance?"

"No tea. The agreement has not yet been reached. I hoped to accomplish it at this meeting."

She walked over to the table, pulled out a chair and sat. Padi likewise sat—and said nothing.

Zandir kezlBlythe folded her hands together on the table. She wore an abundance of rings. Colemeno port-folk did not wear rings of rank in the Liaden style. But this woman was not port-folk. It came to Padi that she might, indeed, be a representative of the local iteration of a High House.

"The master trader is presently concentrating his attention upon Colemenoport, as he must. What he may not understand is that he will need contacts—dare I say, friends—in Haven City, in order to realize his ambitions at the port. The kezlBlythe family is known and respected in the city. In short, kezlBlythe wishes to extend to the master trader our friendship, and to become his connection with the key players in the city."

This, Padi thought, was a different order of business than Merchant zerKilin's eagerness. This...was politics. Planetary politics were not for traders to dabble in.

"You may think that the port is the port and the city is not for traders to encroach upon," Zandir kezlBlythe said, as if she had heard Padi's thought. "Here on Colemeno, we have seen a creep of regulation from the Council and the city, into the port."

She paused, her eyes sharp, and her mouth a straight, uncompromising line.

"Tell me this, if you will, Trader yos'Galan—will the trade mission make its final report and appeal to the portmaster or to the Council?"

"To the Council, ma'am. The portmaster allowed us to know that she sits on the Council."

"So she does. One among twelve. The trade mission will need more than one friend on the Council to carry the day. kezlBlythe is in a unique position to provide Tree-and-Dragon with friends on the Council."

Worse and worse, Padi thought, taking care not to let even the hint of *that* thought reach her face.

"The kezlBlythe family is also in a position to connect the master trader with a network of *qe'andra* and accountants, all expert in the laws and practices of city and port."

Zandir kezlBlythe sat back in her chair, as if she had, indeed, completed her pitch and awaited an enthusiastic agreement.

"That is a most generous offer, ma'am," Padi said, "and I am desolate to have wasted your time with this meeting. *Indeed*, the master trader cannot have understood your intention. I can give you no guarantees; nor am I empowered to write contracts on behalf of the trade mission."

She expected another flash of temper. Certainly, the other leaned forward sharply, as if about to deliver a scathing reply. Before she could do so, her brows pulled together. She looked at Padi thoughtfully.

"You may enter into contracts in your own right, however. You *are* a full trader."

"I am a full trader, yes," Padi replied, her voice cool despite the flare of irritation she felt.

"That," said Zandir kezlBlythe, "is good to know."

She met Padi's eyes firmly.

"You will tell the master trader that it will be very much to his advantage to come to my office in the city, so that we may reach an agreement regarding a mutually beneficial business arrangement."

Padi heard a distinct "ping," quite as if someone had thrown a stone against hull-plate, but Zandir kezlBlythe was rising, her business done, and Padi rose with her, not without a certain sense of relief.

She ought to have escorted the guest to the door, but there was no opportunity.

Zandir kezlBlythe turned without a bow or a backward glance, and exited the room.

Padi went to the door and locked it.

Colemenoport
Wayfarer

· · · · · · · · · ·

SHAN WAS DOING UP HIS SHIRT.

It was quite late in Colemeno's morning. He and Priscilla had dawdled in their robes over a positively decadent breakfast, rising at last, and reluctantly, to face what remained of the day.

"We ought," he said, finishing with the last seal, and shaking out his sleeves, "do this again."

"Now?" Priscilla asked, her voice sultry.

He raised an eyebrow and met her eyes.

"There are various commitments already in train," he observed. "I suppose we *might* try *now*. Only, we've just gone to all the bother of getting dressed..."

"You make a compelling case," Priscilla said, solemnly. "Will you sleep with me tonight?"

"Every night for the rest of my life," he told her.

She stepped forward into his embrace, and leaned her head against his shoulder, feeling his arms tighten around her.

"Well."

Shan stepped back, reluctantly. Priscilla shook her hair into order, and reached out to straighten his collar.

"Thank you, Priscilla. It would not have done for me to attend my first meeting on the day looking in the least disordered."

"Who's your first meeting?" she asked, moving to the door just ahead of him.

"Why, Lady Selph, of course. I daresay she's recovered sufficiently from her journey to give me a very severe talking to, indeed."

Priscilla laughed, and opened the door.

Colemenoport
Offices of the
Tree-and-Dragon Trade Mission

. . . .

MAJEL HAD CONSIDERED HIS OPTIONS CLOSELY, AND DECIDED that a personal visit was more fitting to the situation than a comm call. A comm call did not give him the opportunity to assess for himself the state of the master trader's mind, nor did it allow the master trader opportunity to read the depth of Majel's sincerity.

If he found the office closed, he would not have wasted a trip, after all. It had been far too long since he had spoken with the erVintons, and he had already determined to do so when next he was at the port.

The light was on over the door to the trade mission's office. Majel touched the annunciator, and folded his hands before him, waiting.

He waited long enough that he began to think about leaving, seeing the erVintons, and stopping past the trade mission's office again on his way back to the city.

Indeed, he had taken a step away when the door opened to reveal Trader yos'Galan, her face tight and her eyes narrowed. She produced no easy smile upon seeing him, as she had on past occasions, though she did manage a cordial inclination of the head.

"Counselor ziaGorn," she said, and her voice was also . . . less strong than it had been on previous meetings.

"Trader yos'Galan," he answered. "Is the master trader within?"

"There is only myself this morning, Councilor," she said. "Is there something I may do for you in the master trader's absence?"

She took a careful step back, clearing the door.

"Please do come in, and at least allow me to thank you for your service to our team members last evening."

219

Wan expression, narrowed gaze, slowed movements. He knew what this was, Majel realized, and recalled the young trader's antipathy toward cake.

"I wonder," he said, instead of entering the office, "if you have time to come with me to the Skywise Provianto. I am just on my way there, and I thought we might talk together over a meal."

For a moment, he thought she would refuse, and what he might do then, he had no clear notion, but after a moment, she made another attempt at a smile, this one somewhat better, though by no means the expression he had seen adorning her face previously.

"Thank you," she said. "I am partial to the Skywise, and a meal sounds—useful. Let me get my case."

· · · ❀ · · ·

Her head hurt, and she was quite ridiculously tired, as if she had run across the port twice, instead of taking three meetings. Granted, the last had been irritating, not to say actively alarming, but nothing that could account for this sad state.

It was then that she recalled the ping. As if someone had thrown a stone against a wall.

Or a shield?

Padi bit her lip.

She ought to check her shields, she thought, but she did not know how to examine her own shields, and she dared not become beguiled by the ambient, even filtered as it was at the port, with her head aching quite so much.

When the chime sounded, she jumped, and bit her lip, half-inclined not to answer—which really was unworthy of her.

She did look through the door camera first, and opened to Majel ziaGorn, with a sense of relief.

The prospect of a meal at the Skywise had appealed, though she had suddenly been concerned about the walk. Her knees did not feel quite as steady as they should—precisely as if she had run that imaginary race across the port.

By the time she and Counselor ziaGorn had exited onto the street, she was seriously questioning the wisdom of walking any further.

Her companion, however, put his arm energetically into the air, and—sweet relief!—a port jitney came to a stop beside them.

"The Skywise Provianto, please," Counselor ziaGorn said,

supporting her with a hand under her elbow as she climbed into the back seat, before sitting across from her.

"Skywise Provianto!" the jitney driver called out, and they were off.

Her head *ached*.

Padi closed her eyes and accessed a pilot's drill for calmness.

· · · ※ · · ·

The trader had closed her eyes. Majel hoped that she was merely resting. He had heard that, in extreme cases, the afflicted might lose consciousness. He hoped that they were not running too close to *that* outcome, but even if so, the Skywise was the best choice of destination. Bell erVinton was a medic and would surely know what to do.

"Skywise Provianto, Luzants!" the driver called, and Trader yos'Galan opened her eyes.

"A moment," Majel murmured. He descended to the street, offering a steadying arm.

Her eyebrows rose, and he thought for a moment that he had made an error. Then she inclined her head, murmuring, "Thank you for your care," as she accepted his assistance.

Once she was fairly down, he pulled a coin from his pocket and tossed it to the driver, breathing a sigh of relief as he guided the trader into the Provianto—

Before stopping in consternation just inside the shop.

Chairs and tables were flung all about, the sweets cases had been thrown over, and there were cakes and broken crockery spread in sticky confusion across the floor.

Behind the counter were a gathering of people, among them a representative of Port Security, and Bell erVinton. She glanced over her shoulder.

"We're closed, gentles—" she began. Then her eye fell on Trader yos'Galan, and she rushed forward.

"Trader, what has happened to you?"

"I'll ask the same thing of you," Trader yos'Galan answered, rallying somewhat. "Bell, have you been robbed?"

"Robbed, no. Someone wanted to make a point." She glanced to Majel.

"Councilor. Just the person I need."

"I am yours," he told her. "But first—"

"Yes. *First*, Trader yos'Galan, we must tend to you. Come back to the kitchen, it's not so much upside-down there. I have a savory pie in the keeper, cheese, and some cold juice. The sweets were smashed with the case, but never you mind that, good fuel is all you need, as you know and I do."

Trader yos'Galan began to say something—that she would not intrude during a day of misfortune, Majel thought. Bell paid no heed to that, of course, and soon the trader was sitting at the kitchen counter, a plate before her and tongs in her hand.

"Eat, Trader—don't stint yourself," said Bell. "I'll be just over here, speaking with Councilor ziaGorn."

"Done on the overnight," Bell said. "As you see, the kitchen is intact. Security has it down as mischief."

Expensive mischief, Majel thought; yet if the kitchen equipment had been harmed, *that* would have been malicious damage of property, which not only mandated closer scrutiny by security, but also carried an increased fine, when the perpetrators were apprehended.

"The case and fixtures?" Majel murmured.

Bell lifted a shoulder.

"Not enough to level up the investigation. The tables and chairs aren't damaged, just disarrayed. The goods are counted no higher than their ingredients, and unless there's proof of Intent—"

Majel sighed. Intent was subtle, and in the case of mere mischief, often discounted by the Evaluators as excitement attending the acts, rather than a premeditated malicious desire to do harm.

"Could you speak with the security officer about sending a Sensitive?" Bell asked. "If I push, I'll be grilled about who I might have offended, in what way, and offered counseling."

"I don't know about . . . intent," Padi yos'Galan said from behind them, her voice appreciably stronger, "but I tell you, and will be glad to tell the security officer that Luzant nirAmit, across the street, saw it as his duty to inform me that the Skywise was owned by the Deaf, that all the employees were likewise Deaf."

Majel turned to look at her.

She had eaten a little more than half of the pie, and was holding her glass in both hands, elbows braced against the countertop. Her color was better, he thought, relieved.

"After he had done," she continued, "he said he trusted I would *conduct myself more fittingly.*"

Majel glanced at Bell, who met his eyes, her expression bleak, before she moved to the counter.

"Luzant nirAmit is often angry, Trader," she said soothingly. "He remembers the old days, and isn't happy with change."

"Which doesn't mean that security shouldn't talk to him," Padi said. "He's right across the street, and might have seen something suspicious."

"Very true," Majel said, briskly. "It's standard, for security to ask the neighbors if they saw or heard anything." He paused, considering, then touched Bell on the shoulder.

"My casino recently suffered an assault against the machines," he said. "Intent was proved in one of the rooms. It would be prudent to be certain that these two instances are not related."

Bell frowned. "Your casino is in the city, while we are at the port—" she began.

"True," Majel said. "But both of these acts were brought against Deaf-owned businesses. As Chair of the Citizens Coalition, I must be vigilant."

Bell's face cleared.

"Thank you, Councilor," she said.

"Not at all. I'll speak to the officer now. Trader yos'Galan, I'll be a few minutes, only."

"Pray don't rush your business on my account," Padi told him, eyeing the remaining pie speculatively.

Majel bowed and left.

· · · ※ · · ·

"Well, Trader, what *did* befall you?" Bell asked. She had pulled a stool up next to Padi's and poured herself some tea.

Padi had decided against more pie, just at present. She looked at Bell and moved her shoulders.

"I took three of the master trader's meetings this morning. One was . . . fraught, but I was tired out of proportion at the end of it, and coming a headache."

"You expended energy," Bell said, sipping her tea. "Did you not have any cake?"

Padi sighed.

"Here you see my folly. I haven't gotten wholly into the habit of cake. Truth said, I am not half fond. But, in any case, I had done nothing to *exert* myself—meetings are quite calm."

"There are other remedies, if you'd rather not cake," Bell said. "Sweet tea. Cheese. Protein muffins. There's a particular nut-and-fruit bar—in fact, here."

She rose and went to a cabinet with a green door, opened it, rummaged briefly and returned with two bars wrapped in crackling paper, which she put next to Padi's plate.

"Put these in your case. If you find you like them, they're widely available. In the meanwhile, I'll send you a list of beneficial foods from the medic's archive."

She resumed her stool and picked up her teacup, looking at Padi sternly.

"Now, Trader, listen to me. You have become a favorite customer and I don't relinquish those easily. You *must* be vigilant. The ambient acts constantly upon the Civilized, which produces a caloric deficit. Cookies, or a nut bar—those are easy to keep in your case or your pocket, and a cake tin fits neatly into a drawer, which is why it is so often on offer."

Padi blinked.

"The ambient is *always* acting on the Gifted?" she said slowly. "Even under the Grid?"

"The Grid mitigates the effects, but it does not negate them," Bell told her. "You see the need for vigilance."

"I do, yes. I will make certain that I'm better prepared, going forward."

She sighed lightly, and put her empty glass on the counter.

"I am wanted at another meeting, soon," she said. "Tell me what I can do to help you."

"Truly, Trader, Councilor ziaGorn has it in hand. My family is coming to help with clean-up and repair. We'll be open in time to serve the evening menu."

"I thought," Padi said slowly, "that the Deaf were protected."

Bell blinked.

"That is the law, Trader, yes."

"But you and Councilor ziaGorn—as I overheard you just now—you have both seen your businesses assaulted," Padi continued. "And other people, like Luzant nirAmit are . . . angry that you have a business at all?"

Bell said nothing, and Padi felt a pang. To repay kindness by sowing dismay was rag-mannered in the extreme.

"I am rude, and I regret it," she murmured, bowing her head.

"But, we—the members of the trade mission—have been trying to understand—everything! Not only the markets, but the culture, and the law. It is all of a piece, you see. There is a port at which we cannot trade, because planetary law states that only families that are properly headed by a woman may be qualified as a vendor. Had the law stayed in the city, it would have had nothing to do with us, with trade. But the law spilled into the port, you see, and made us untenable. So, we no longer stop there."

Bell took a breath.

"I do see, Trader. I think you want Councilor ziaGorn for this. He has history and law at the front of his mind, whereas I have recipes and catering protocols."

Padi sighed and finished her tea.

"I believe that one of my colleagues is already in conversation with the councilor regarding the issue," she said. She felt considerably better—and not a moment too soon, either. The timepiece she wore vibrated against her wrist, which was the warning to start back to the Wayfarer and the working nuncheon.

She slid to her feet, and bowed.

"Thank you for your aid, and your forbearance," she said. "If it comes about that there is something I may do for you, please do not hesitate to call me. In the meanwhile, I am wanted at my next meeting."

Bell slipped to her feet.

"Don't forget your nut-and-fruit bars, Trader."

"Surely not," Padi said, slipping them into her jacket pocket. "Where may I find a jitney?"

"Right out here," Bell said, moving past her and opening the kitchen door.

Padi exited into an alley, Bell at her side.

"Just up here at the corner, Trader," the other woman said, and walked with her, raising her arm when they achieved the corner.

A jitney pulled over before Padi could draw breath to say thank you. Bell helped her aboard, and stepped back.

"Take good care, Trader," she said.

"And you!" Padi called, but Bell had already turned away.

"Direction, Luzant?" asked the driver.

"The Wayfarer, please," Padi said. She sat back in the seat and closed her eyes.

Colemenoport
Wayfarer

· · · · · · · · · ·

JES DEA'TOLIN STEPPED OUT ONTO THE ROOF OF THE WAYFARER and into an oasis.

Immediately, she felt tense muscles relax, and her jaw soften. She stepped onto a graveled path that ran between mounded banks of pink-and-blue flowers, walking beneath arches of flowering vines, past small pockets of greenery, and a pool fed by a dainty waterfall, populated by green, blue, and orange fish, none of them any longer than her longest finger.

Jes was herself an avid gardener. Before she'd taken to shipwork, she had won numerous awards from the Solcintra Garden Association. Lately, her work with plants had been confined to volunteering in the hydroponics departments of the various ships on which she had served as *qe'andra*. She had been doubly pleased that rotating assignments placed her on *Dutiful Passage*, which had an atrium—a true flowering garden. She spent much of her off-time there, volunteering, or simply communing.

This little park, now, with its cunningly twisty path, and surprising corners—this park had been designed and built by a master. She would have to find who kept it now, and see if they might welcome an occasional extra pair of hands.

She laughed at herself, softly. *You have a whole port inventory ahead of you*, she told herself.

Well, yes. She did. A whole port inventory was no minor undertaking, even for a full team of three. She did not doubt her ability to conduct the inventory, and to produce an accurate report. But it was going to be...challenging.

And there would surely be no time for gardening.

She strolled on, the path now lined with tall, leafless stalks, each topped with a single, perfectly round white flower. They were nearly as tall as she was, bobbing in the light breeze, as if they were dancing.

Her own steps lighter, she continued beneath spreading branches, as the path turned twice, very quickly, before vanishing into a plush lawn. There were a few shrubberies, a few benches, and a riot of bell-shaped blossoms at the bottom of the space, which, Jes thought, hid the end of the roof.

She crossed the lawn to the flowers, and looked over the edge.

Far below was the street, tiny vehicles and tinier figures moving briskly about their lives.

The bellflowers gave off a peppery scent, which the breeze brought directly to Jes's nose. She sneezed—then laughed, as her watch vibrated against her wrist.

Yes, well.

She turned and started back to the door.

· · · ⁜ · · ·

Shan put his hand against the door to Padi's room. The light flashed blue and he entered, walking softly.

The window was unshuttered, allowing Colemeno's daylight to flood the room, and grace the norbear standing tall on her back feet, nose uplifted, like a portly, furry flower.

It was well, he thought, that Padi's note had warned him about the nature of the enclosure Tekelia had provided, else he would have been convinced that Lady Selph stood free at the table's center, with the various accoutrements necessary to a norbear's comfort placed artfully about her.

"Good morning, my lady," he said, dropping to one knee by the table.

She remained in communion with the light for a moment more before settling on to all fours to regard him out of bright dark eyes.

An image formed just behind Shan's eyes—rough black hair pulled back from a round face, and well-opened eyes—one grey and the other green.

"Tekelia-*dramliza*," Shan said. "I have had the pleasure, and I see you have made a conquest."

This sally was greeted with a sense that Tekelia was well mannered and respectful, not at all like some white-haired gadabouts that Lady Selph was too refined to mention.

Shan grinned.

"I am fairly scolded," he said. "I did not make you perfectly welcome last evening, to my shame. I was—a little unwell, and no fit company for anyone, least of all yourself. At least allow that I saw you into the care of those who could—and did!—attend you properly."

Lady Selph marched across the sand to the door panel that Padi had described in her note. She looked at him expectantly.

"I will very shortly be wanted elsewhere," Shan told her.

He received a rather caustic suggestion that it might therefore be to his benefit to open the door *quickly.*

Half-smiling, he touched the lock, the panel withdrew, and Lady Selph walked out of the enclosure and onto his hand. He arranged himself more comfortably on the rug and brought her to his knee.

"I am not at all certain that this environment will ultimately do you good," he began, but there was a face forming behind his eyes.

Vanner Higgs.

Shan felt tears start to his eyes, but the image had called its match without his conscious decision to share. Tarona Rusk, glowing with stolen energy, rose to the fore of his mind. He felt Lady Selph accept the connection, and the information that she had murdered Vanner.

Immediately, he felt the firm press of bodies around him, fur warming fur; heard a deep and steady purr, the sound producing contentment. Peace.

Shan took a deep breath, and another, allowing the purr and the peace to sink deep into his core. It occurred to him that Lady Selph had been uncommonly deft in that sharing, even for so old and canny a lady.

But, there—Vanner had many friends among the crew, some of whom would have sought the norbears for comfort. That Lady Selph brought the topic to him, here and now—Priscilla's small healing had worked considerable benefit, but he was still unsettled by last night's interview at the guard house, and the necessity of revealing himself as a mass murderer.

He felt as if someone had flicked their finger, not gently, against his cheek. It stung.

He raised an eyebrow at Lady Selph.

"Feeling sorry for myself, am I? I suppose it's nothing to you that there were innocents among those slaughtered?"

Another image of Vanner formed behind his eyes, followed

by Tarona Rusk, Priscilla, Padi, Mar Tyn, Dyoli, and—Tekelia vesterGranz.

The Reavers had come to Colemeno to gather Talents into the web of power Tarona Rusk had wielded in service of her masters. They surely would have taken innocents, and it was no stretch to think that they would have assumed Colemeno to be a resource, its people theirs by right. Certainly, Chief bennaFalm had feared as much.

Shan sighed, and inclined his head.

"I understand," he said, softly. "You would have me acknowledge that my actions averted a greater tragedy. I did not have the option of doing nothing; and it was necessary to disarm the enemy I faced."

The imagined touch against his cheek was soft this time, and norbear purrs again filled him with peace.

"Thank you," he said to Lady Selph. "And now I fear I must leave you."

He brought her to the tabletop, and she turned, quite docile, and made her way through the door and into her palatial enclosure.

Shan locked the door behind her, and rose. A wistful image formed behind his eyes—a norbear, no one he knew—the *idea* of a norbear, he thought. Possibly a request for a companion. Norbears could live alone, but Lady Selph had long been part of a cuddle.

"We will send you back to the *Passage* with Dil Nem," he told her, projecting the images of Tiny, Delm Briat, and Master Frodo—her accustomed companions. "But I fear you will be a few days largely alone. We will, of course, visit as often as we are able. You will be pleased to know that we are making many new connections, which we will of course share with you."

She returned no answer to this, but continued her march across the sand to the tiny waterfall and pool. She bent her head to drink, and Shan left her to it.

· · · ✳ · · ·

"*Qe'andra* dea'Tolin, have you a moment?"

Jes turned and smiled at Mar Tyn pai'Fortana. A diffident man, and plain in his manner. She had worked with him and Dyoli ven'Deelin on the info-packet that had been produced for Colemenoport. She had learned then that he had a retentive memory, as well as being quick and certain with his figures.

"The master trader has not yet arrived to call us to order," she said. "Is there something I may do for you?"

He sighed slightly.

"I fear that there is. The master trader..." He paused, as if uncertain quite how to account the master trader. But of course one did not *account* master traders; every one Jes had met—which numbered a fair half-dozen by now—had been an elemental force, and Master Trader yos'Galan more so than most.

She waited. Mar Tyn looked down, then up, meeting her eyes.

"The master trader was pleased to notice that I am able to do sums," he said quickly, "and sent me the Accountants Guild basic course, in case I should like to study, and—certify myself as an accountant. I am told that you are qualified to both advise and test me."

Jes looked at him with renewed interest.

"Have you begun the course?" she asked.

"I read the first two chapters," he said, diffident once more, "and completed the self-tests."

"Do you find the material interesting?" she pursued.

He laughed softly.

"In fact, I do. I am no doubt encouraged by the fact that I did well in the self-tests."

That was perceptive. The course was built to encourage the student. Which did not mean that the first two self-tests would not confound a careless or inattentive scholar.

"I intend to continue," Mar Tyn pai'Fortana was saying. "However, I fear that I will need assistance as I progress—and also someone to administer the section tests. I do not want to importune you—"

She moved a hand.

"It is true that I will be busy—we will all be busy, I collect! But if you can find time to study, I can find time to assist you and to administer the tests. In fact, if you won't think me too odd, I believe I will find it...soothing to reengage with the basics."

"I understand, I think," he said. "Constant challenge is wearying."

She laughed, surprised.

"Exactly!" she said.

· · · ✳ · · ·

"Portmaster krogerSlyte has made an office suite available to the *qe'andra's* team in the mercantile complex," Priscilla was saying. "She sent me the room number, and the door code this morning. She also asks that Jes contact her directly, if there's anything at all needed to make the space as efficient and pleasing as possible."

"The portmaster is gracious," Jes murmured.

"The portmaster," said the master trader, "has been a staunch ally. I note that she speaks in terms of the *qe'andra's team*, and while I would very much like to produce two—or two dozen—additional *qe'andra* to assist you, that is beyond my power."

"Two dozen would be rather too many," Jes told him calmly. "I had anticipated the need of tapping local resources. Early this evening, I have an appointment with Fenlix clofElin, who chairs the Colemenoport Business Association. She assures me that she can give me a vetted list of qualified *qe'andra* on the port."

That, Padi thought admiringly, was quick work. She did not know Jes dea'Tolin well. The *qe'andra* kept herself very close. Padi had met her in hydroponics once or twice, and had seen her tending plantings in the atrium, as a volunteer gardener.

As a *qe'andra*, the accounting and analyses she had completed on Padi's behalf had been meticulous. The master trader spoke highly of her abilities and accomplishments, but Padi had not been quite prepared for this decisive action.

The master trader inclined his head and reached for his glass. After a moment, Jes spoke again.

"In terms of assistants who are nearer to the mission, I wonder if I might ask Trader ven'Deelin and Master pai'Fortana to come into the *qe'andra's* office—perhaps on a rotating half-shift? I know that the master trader's team is spread very thin—"

The master trader raised his hand.

"The whole port inventory is pivotal; the trade team cannot come to a decision without it. It is my part to be certain that you have the assistance and resources that you need in order to perform the inventory properly and in a timely manner. Indeed, if *my* assistance on a rotating half-shift will make your work smoother, I will arrange my schedule to accommodate yours."

Jes blinked, and Padi didn't blame her. On its face, it seemed preposterous that a master trader would propose that his duties on port were second to...anything.

Looked at twice, however, it was perfectly proper. The master trader needed to know if and how this port could serve him. While there were matters of trade for him to pursue on Colemenoport, until the whole port inventory was completed and understood, he could make no commitments, and do very little in the way of business.

All the while *Dutiful Passage* sat in orbit. Losing profit.

Padi shivered. She had understood that the bid for the Redlands had been . . . a risk. Now, quite suddenly, she realized just how high the stakes were. If Jes's work revealed a flaw; if the master trader's leap did not prove a profit . . .

"Thank you, Master Trader," Jes said. "I will call upon you if necessary. In the meanwhile—"

"In the meanwhile," Dyoli interrupted, "I propose that I come into your office full-time, if the master trader agrees, and if it will serve you, Jes. As you know, I am nothing like a *qe'andra*, but I do know how to read ledgers and inventory sheets."

"Your assistance would be most welcome," Jes told her, and looked past Dyoli to Mar Tyn. "Master pai'Fortana? This touches upon our earlier discussion, and the study you have recently embarked upon. A 'prentice in a busy office learns much, even if it seems that one's head will whirl away."

Mar Tyn smiled his slight smile.

"I had just been thinking how I might ask you to allow me to assist you full-time," he said.

Jes raised her hand. "You must have time for your studies. Since you have solicited me as a mentor, I will share that I hope to see you complete the second level by the time the master trader makes his decision regarding this port. I insist that this goal is every bit as important as completing the inventory in a timely manner."

"I agree," said the master trader, and nodded at Mar Tyn. "Master pai'Fortana, consider yourself 'prenticed to *Qe'andra* dea'Tolin."

Mar Tyn looked aghast. Dyoli fairly beamed. Master Trader yos'Galan waited.

After a moment, Mar Tyn cleared his throat, and leaned forward in a seated bow.

"Master dea'Tolin, I stand ready."

"Excellent," Jes said calmly. "This evening, you will accompany me to the meeting with Chair clofElin. In the time between the end of this meeting and our departure, I would have you work through as much of the third chapter as you are able. If you complete it, take the self-test, and send it to my screen. Be ready to explain what you have read."

"Yes," Mar Tyn said simply.

"That being settled," said the master trader, "do we have more business?"

"I have information for the whole team and security," Padi stated.

"Speak, then, Trader Padi."

"Yes, sir." She glanced around the table, her eyes lingering on Priscilla, before she brought her attention back to the center of the table.

"We are all informed regarding the ambient conditions of Colemeno, which increase the...abilities of those of us who are Gifted. We have recently discovered that it is necessary to refuel with carbohydrates or protein after we have exerted ourselves. The need is so prevalent, that it has left an imprint on society. You will find that cake is always on offer, in order to limit what our liaison Councilor ziaGorn is pleased to style *incidents.*"

She paused to have a sip from her glass, and looked 'round the table again. Mar Tyn gave her a smile, as if in encouragement.

"This morning, I learned that the ambient does not *only* interact with us when we use our Gifts. It acts upon us *constantly*, even when our Gifts are quiescent."

She looked to the master trader.

"This means that one can be doing nothing more ambitious than taking three meetings of various levels of complexity, and arrive at a caloric deficit. I am told that this looks like exhaustion. It *feels* like exhaustion, in my experience, with a touch of headache."

The master trader's eyebrows rose slightly, but he said nothing.

"Even under the Grid, here at the port, or in the city, those of us who are Gifted—and our friends—must be vigilant, and always have the means to balance our caloric outgo in our pocket, or case."

She put the fruit and nut bars Bell had given her on the table.

"These were suggested by Bell at the Skywise, who is a medic, as a satisfactory substitute for cake."

There was a small silence after she had finished. Grad shifted in his seat, glancing around at his teammates.

"Security will watch for signs of exhaustion, and mention it, when noted," he said.

"That will be most helpful," the master trader said. He looked to Priscilla, then away. "Trader, will you source those fruit-and-nut bars?"

"Yes, sir, I will."

"Splendid. Have we any other topics of conversation?"

He looked around the table. No one spoke.

"Then I believe we have our tasks laid out before us. Let us adjourn and go to work. Trader Padi, attend me, if you please."

Colemenoport
Skywise Provianto

. . . .

PORT SECURITY HAD LEFT AFTER ASKING ONLY A VERY FEW additional questions, for which Bell suspected she should thank Majel ziaGorn. He had stayed with her, picking up chairs and tables, while she called the lockmaker and the security firm. Coming back from her calls, she found him cleaning the newly righted display cases, his vest hung on a peg by the door, and his sleeves rolled. She brought out a broom and began sweeping up the ruined pastries, the two of them working in companionable silence, until her family arrived, and respected him into superfluity.

She was in the midst of a discussion with Aunt Jaynis regarding whether they should offer an abbreviated menu for the evening trade, or buy ready-made meals from the market to resell, when Bell saw a movement from the side of her eye.

Turning her head, she saw Majel ziaGorn, his red curls disordered, take his vest down from the peg and slip it on as he stepped toward the door.

"A moment," Bell said hastily to Aunt Jaynis, and rushed to see him out.

"Councilor, again, thank you for your assistance," she said.

He laughed lightly.

"And, again, it was not a pleasure, but certainly my duty, to be certain that you were not left alone in the aftermath of violence, and to do what I might to reorder chaos."

She sighed, wanting to deny "violence." But, there—cases had been overturned, goods had been destroyed, and—far worse—someone had managed to come into the shop while it was locked and warded against intruders.

He raised his arm for a jitney, and sent a glance to her face.

"If you need further assistance, please don't hesitate to call me," he said. "If I'm not at my office, I'll be at the casino. A message left in either place will find me."

"You're too good," Bell began, but here was the jitney and he was stepping forward to claim his ride, though he paused a moment to look back to her.

"Not at all. Be well, Surda erVinton." He stepped into the jitney, and said, "The train station, please."

Bell watched him out of sight, turned to go back inside, and nearly fell over the elder standing there.

"Luzant nirAmit!" she said on a gasp. "I did not see you, sir!"

"Yes, it was obvious that your thoughts were elsewhere," he said, with a strong frown. "Surda, I have just come from giving testimony at the guard house. The officer in charge assured me that you will be given a copy of my affidavit and the Truthseer's Guarantee. I regret that I saw nothing that will be of use in finding those who authored this attack against your business. I opened my security cameras to the investigation. They may be more helpful."

"Thank you," Bell said, wondering at this outburst of civility. "Our own cameras were depowered."

Luzant nirAmit blew out a hard breath.

"Rascals," he muttered. "I must ask, Surda, were there any injuries?"

"No, none. We close at night port, of course." And the damage had been done before she had arrived in the early hours of day port, to start the bread.

Briefly, she wondered how near she had come to interrupting the making of mischief, and shivered.

Luzant nirAmit gave her a knowing look.

"It's distressing in the extreme to find that one's space has been violated," he said solemnly, "and to think how matters might have fallen out differently, but for an accident of timing..."

His voice drifted off, face closing into the hard, angry mask—and softening again.

"Surda erVinton, I know that I have not been of much use to you, or your business. I have, in fact, allowed the past to poison the present. I am old, and I have lost much. But those truths do not excuse me from doing my duty to life and to the common good. Therefore, Surda, I ask to be allowed to serve you in this matter."

Bell went back a step. Was he suggesting—*what* was he suggesting?

The old man lifted both hands.

"Understand me, not in the way that your mother knew. There were abuses, I am aware, and more than enough anger on both sides. I mean to honor the code by which I was raised—that obliges me to offer my Gifts where they will be of use, and to not be shy of accepting an offer in kind. Our Gifts are not the same, by which we learn that we were meant to support each other."

He blew out a hard breath and bowed, creakily.

"So my grandmother taught me, and I am ashamed that I allowed myself to set that teaching aside for so long."

Bell drew a deep breath. It was, she told herself, an honorable offer of assistance. Only—

"Truly, sir, I don't know what you might do for us. We've had Port Security, and the specialists and a Sensitive. You've given your statement to the Truthseer, and allowed access to your cameras. It seems to me that you have been more than generous."

"Generous—no. I've done what duty demanded, as I do now when I offer to examine your locks." He glanced at the undamaged door. "Am I correct in supposing that they were able to unlock the door?"

"Yes," Bell admitted. "We've called the lockmaker."

"Of course. I don't propose to manipulate the lock, only to Look at it. It may be that I can identify a flaw in the current making. At the very least, I may give you a description of what is there so that you may compare it to the lockmaker's account."

Bell glanced past his shoulder and saw Aunt Jaynis in the window, hands raised and a faint look of alarm on her face.

An honorable offer of assistance, Bell told herself again. And, besides, it seemed clear that the old gentleman would not be easy until he had done something that satisfied his need to be of use.

"Thank you, sir. If you would examine the lock, and tell me what you See—that would be most helpful."

His face eased, and he bowed again.

"Excellent," he said. "Thank you, Surda."

Colemenoport
Wayfarer

. . . .

"DO I LEARN THAT YOUR MEETINGS PRODUCED AN 'INCIDENT,' Trader?" the master trader asked, as he settled behind his desk.

Padi sighed.

"I believe it is more accurate to say that my own inattention and antipathy to cake produced an incident," she said, sinking into the side chair. There was an ache just behind her eyes, as if she had bruised the inside of her head.

"If Majel ziaGorn hadn't come by to see you, recognized my state, and swept me off for a meal, I don't know what might have happened. I am ashamed to own that, left to myself, I probably would not have thought of cake, as I hadn't extended myself, particularly." She paused, considering that last sentence.

"Unless exercising patience counts."

"Did you exercise prodigious amounts of patience? I swear to you that they all seemed convenable, in correspondence."

She laughed, and lifted her hands, showing empty palms.

"And so they were...mostly. Shall you like a report now?"

"If you find it convenient," he said politely. "May I give you something to drink?"

"If you please, a glass of the white."

"Done."

He crossed the room. Padi closed her eyes and reviewed a simple board rest exercise. When she opened her eyes, the master trader had resumed his seat.

"If it is not perfectly convenient to report now, I will make time later," he said, bringing his glass to his lips.

Padi reached for her own glass, sipped, and looked up at him.

"I think it had better be now," she said. "Though I may cry off for an hour or two, after."

238

"Self-care is very important," he said solemnly. "So I am told."

"I have heard the same," she agreed, matching his tone, "from a source that I consider impeccable." She had another sip of wine and put the glass aside.

"So—my report, if you will, Master Trader. I will of course forward my notes, and other information entrusted to me to your screen."

"Of course. Please proceed, Trader."

"Yes. My first meeting was with Merchant vellaTon, representing the vellaTon Manufactory, and was most informative. She had order and fulfillment records from before the Dust arrived, which she thought might be of use, going forward. She did need to teach me what it was that vellaTon manufactured, and current markets must be researched, but in all, it was a satisfying and productive meeting. I found Merchant vellaTon to be sensible and meticulous. We share a connection with Saru bernRoanti at the port market."

She paused.

The master trader inclined his head.

"The second meeting was with Merchant zerKilin. He was altogether eager, wished to know if Tree-and-Dragon would be establishing a co-op, and what the fee structures might be."

The master trader laughed.

"Yes sir, and so I told him. He eventually found himself able to agree that it was best to allow the trade team time to work, so that we might all know the answers to his questions. He promises to have his records in perfect order and available to Jes immediately she calls for them. He will also be sending a case of wine and another, of juice, to the trade team's office, of his kindness."

She sipped her wine.

"He was perfectly well mannered and convenable, after we managed to ford his enthusiasm," she added. She leaned back in her chair, and closed her eyes.

"And the third meeting?" the master trader prompted.

Padi opened her eyes, and sat up straighter.

"Your pardon," she murmured.

"The third meeting was with Zandir kezlBlythe of Haven City. Very high in the instep. She was put out at first; it seems she had determined that she *would* sign an agreement with the master trader today, which of course was not possible. I think that she may be quite accustomed to getting her way."

She paused, weighing her next words.

"She sold hard. Her theme was that it will be necessary for the master trader to have good contacts in the city, in order to succeed at the port. She allowed me to know that the master trader will need friends on the Council, and that she is able to deliver those friends to him. She also said that she will connect the trade team with a network of highly-qualified *qe'andra* and accountants in the city."

She paused, closing her eyes again, briefly, feeling quite disoriented.

Really, she was exhausted, despite Bell's care and the nuncheon she had just eaten.

She opened her eyes, and took a breath.

"I was to tell the master trader *particularly* that it will be very much to his advantage to call on Luzant kezlBlythe in the city, so that a mutually beneficial business agreement may be made."

She paused, noting that her headache had eased somewhat.

"She left quite soon after. I was sitting quietly, attempting to recruit myself, when Majel ziaGorn arrived, wanting to speak to you, and thereby brought me to Bell—oh!"

She sat up suddenly, bringing herself up short.

"When we arrived at the Skywise, it was to find that mischief had been carried out against the premises. Port Security was present. Bell swept me off to feed me, while Councilor ziaGorn dealt with the officers on her behalf. I never found what he had wanted to speak with you about, Master Trader. Forgive me."

"I will call him," the master trader said, as her father shook his head.

"You are wilting before my eyes, Child. Have you business on port today?"

"No, sir," Padi said. "I had thought to hold myself at the master trader's word."

"And as you have heard, the master trader awaits the outcome of the *qe'andra's* work. It is perfectly possible that I will also rest, after I have called Councilor ziaGorn."

Padi nodded. "The information that the ambient exercises our Gifts constantly..." she began.

"Is disquieting in the extreme," Father finished. "We will talk of it later. Indeed, I mean to speak with Priscilla, and also write to Lina. But you, my child, will go and rest. Now."

"Yes, sir," said Padi gratefully, and left him.

On-Grid
Cardfall Casino

. . . .

MAJEL ZIAGORN STEPPED OUT OF THE 'FRESHER, HAIR DAMP AND disorderly. He was barefoot, and had pulled on soft pants and a comfortable old shirt.

He was, he realized, hungry, which was unfortunate in its way, as it brought back thoughts of the Skywise Provianto, and, more particularly, Bell erVinton.

Not much hope in that direction, my friend, he told himself kindly, as he moved to the comm. The erVintons and the jakValins had been port-folk since before Colemeno had properly had a port. The chances of them marrying into the city were slim at best.

"Principal ziaGorn," Erbet's deep voice came out of the comm, "what can we be pleased to serve you, sir?"

"A hearty nuncheon, if you will. I wonder—is there bean stew today?"

"And fresh-baked rolls, still warm," Erbet's voice dropped, as if he were sharing a secret. "I'll send that up ahead, shall I?"

Majel's stomach rumbled, and he smiled.

"I think you'd best do that. And a bottle of ale, please."

"Done. A moment only."

Indeed, Majel had scarcely reached the kitchen when the food lift's bell rang. He opened the door, and slid out the tray, carrying it to the table.

He broke open the roll, inhaling the aroma of new bread, and sampled the stew with a sigh of satisfaction.

The bowl was half-empty when the comm chimed. He paused, and glanced at the countertop monitor. The code wasn't familiar. It might be a constituent, though most called his office at the Sakuriji. The comm chimed again. He had another spoonful of stew and decided that he would call back.

Another chime, another spoonful of stew. A click.

"Councilor ziaGorn, this is Shan yos'Galan. I find myself in your debt twice over."

Majel leapt up and darted into his office, touching the comm's receive button.

"Master Trader, how may I serve you?" he asked, only slightly breathless.

"By accepting my gratitude for your timely assistance to my heir this morning," the master trader said. "Also, it comes to me that I was rather abrupt last evening, and failed to thank you for your assistance to me and mine."

"There is no debt, sir; I was pleased to serve," Majel said, and caught himself with a half-laugh. "No, *that* failed of being what I meant to say. In truth, when Trader yos'Galan called me last night, I had no idea what I might do, except stand in support. That I was able to materially assist you and yours was... gratifying. This morning—it was fortunate that I came by. Once I had understood what had happened, then of course I did what I might."

"Of course," the master trader repeated softly. "Councilor, you must forgive us. I think that we did not mention to you that we're rather trouble-prone, as a kin-group."

"Korval precipitates unlooked-for events," Majel said, recalling ivenAlyatta.

The master trader laughed. "An excellent summation. I ought to be more adept, but local custom trips us all, so I will ask: In your estimation, are we in Balance?"

Liaden Balance was a fearsome thing, from what he had learned from reading history. Best not to be caught in those calculations.

"In my estimation," he said firmly, "yes, Master Trader, we are in Balance."

"I accept your estimation; no debt lies between us," the master trader said, his voice formal, as if he were delivering a ritual phrase. There followed a silence not quite long enough for Majel to wonder what he ought to say next, before the master trader spoke again.

"We come now to my second reason for calling," he said, sounding his usual affable self. "Trader yos'Galan tells me that you had particularly come to see the master trader. She is quite put out that she forgot to ask what your business was."

Majel sighed.

"Indeed, sir, I had hoped to speak of this in person."

There was a very small pause.

"Shall I come to you, then?"

"I would not put you to so much inconvenience. I had only wondered, sir, if you have considered that your actions, which you spoke of last night, mean that you have done Colemeno and all her people an immeasurable service. If you will speak of debt, it is we who are in yours."

Silence.

You should have waited until you were with him again, Majel told himself, and drew a deep breath.

"I do not mean to say that we were without protectors—the Haosa and the strong Talents would surely have vanquished those Reavers who had come to us, but at what cost? And, if, as seems likely to me, the first wave of Reavers were followed by a second, forewarned—lives would have been lost, innocent and Reaver alike. Indeed, I see no solution to the emergency that would not also have produced dead innocents. It may be, sir, that yours was the kindest of all possible solutions. People died, but far more survived."

More silence.

Majel closed his eyes.

"Forgive me," he said, his voice slightly unsteady, "if I have been too bold."

There came a slight sound, as if the master trader had imperfectly stifled a laugh, or a sneeze.

"Boldness counts, to dragons," he said. "As it happens, I have received similar counsel from another source. I note that it has long been known that self-Healing is the most difficult."

"Yes," Majel said, relieved. "One always holds oneself to a higher standard than any other person."

"We understand each other. Was that the whole of your mission to me this morning?"

"It was, yes."

"Then I will leave you in peace, Councilor. Thank you for your care."

"Sir," Majel said—but the master trader was gone.

Slowly, he went back to the kitchen to find the last of the bean stew cold.

The light over the food lift was on, which meant that the rest of his luncheon had arrived.

He had scarcely taken two steps in that direction when the comm chimed again. A glance at the monitor showed the number of the Citizens Coalition's office.

"Duty calls, Councilor," he said aloud, and went back to his office to answer the comm.

Colemenoport
Skywise Provianto

. . . .

"WHAT HAPPENED HERE IS THAT SOMEBODY SPOOFED THE LOCK," the lockmaker told Bell. He shrugged. "It happens."

Bell considered him, very aware of Luzant nirAmit standing just behind her at the bar in the private party suite, which doubled at need as a conference room.

"Spoofed the lock," she repeated now, looking hard into the lockmaker's face. "And how was that done, precisely?"

The lockmaker didn't quite roll her eyes.

"Complicated to explain when the energies involved aren't intuitive," she said, which was very nearly diplomatic. "Some folks are mimics, see? And some of those folks have ... time on their hands, and mischief on their minds. They can see the lock we made for your door, and they can see the key—"

"Which is, so you told me at the time, my personal signature," Bell said.

"That's right. If you got their attention for some reason, they could study on you, make a replica of your signature—now, that's a lot of work, and there's not many who have the skill or the patience. But, like I said, it does happen, and we're insured against it, so you won't be out of pocket for the new lock—"

"And this new lock," Bell interrupted, "will it be built properly?"

The lockmaker stiffened.

"Understand what I'm saying, *Surda*. There was nothing wrong with *the lock*. It was the fact of somebody spoofing it that got them in. The lock worked just fine."

Bell looked to Luzant nirAmit.

"Surda erVinton asked me to inspect the lock, as I am able to perform that service for her," he said, still maintaining his

245

secondary position. "I agree that the lock performed its function perfectly, accepting the signature it was given. Locks are simple things, and may only react to the data they are offered—open or remain closed."

The lockmaker's shoulders eased.

"However," said Luzant nirAmit.

The lockmaker stiffened again.

"I only wonder why you provided Surda erVinton with *quite* so simple a lock," Luzant nirAmit said temperately. "A single-signature lock, even in so peaceable a quarter of the port—seems to beg for those who have mischief on their minds to expend a little effort in pursuit of their...fun. Do you not make two-level locks, Luzant? Ought I to advise Surda erVinton to seek another Fabricator, or are you able assist her in her goal of keeping her business secure?"

"With all respect, Luzant, Surda erVinton is Deaf. How do you imagine that she will produce the interactive pattern?"

"Many years ago, one of my mother's acquaintances had a two-level lock. The first was a passive recognition system, as you had installed for Surda erVinton. The second-level verification was a plain-tech handprint. Neither system was perfect, alone, but used together, they stood faithful guardians for many, many years."

The lockmaker blinked.

"Signature and tech," she repeated, staring at some point beyond Bell's right shoulder. "I have seen articles, which were inconclusive—as you mention, Luzant, the tech-side of that equation is not proof—only—"

She looked to Bell.

"Surda erVinton, do you carry a pocket comm?"

Bell produced a small smile.

"I am a member of a large and busy family, Luzant. Yes, I carry a pocket comm."

The lockmaker squinted once more at the far wall, as if assuring herself that she had solved a difficult sum completely.

"Here is what I propose, then. I will install a new signature lock, coupled with an electronic repeater. When you approach, the lock will read your signature. If it is found to be a match, the release will engage, but, instead of unlocking the door, it will trigger a call to your pocket comm. Press answer, and the lock will disengage. If you do not press answer, the lock will remain in force."

"And if the call does not arrive?" Luzant nirAmit murmured.

The lockmaker looked serious.

"If the call does not arrive, then my advice to Surda erVinton would be to withdraw and call our service, to which she already subscribes as a valued customer. We will dispatch a technician, or call Security on the Surda's behalf. She would remain at a distance to await our assessment." The lockmaker gave Luzant nirAmit a bold look. "We do not endanger our customers, Luzant."

"I am pleased to hear it," he murmured. "Surda erVinton, are you satisfied with this two-level lock proposed by the Fabricator?"

"I am," she said. "It is in line with what we discussed, sir, after you had inspected our current lock. I do wonder, though"—this to the lockmaker—"how quickly this new lock may be installed."

"Surda, it will be installed before you close for Night Port. If it is not, I will overlock the door with my own signature. In the time between, I will have our own security personnel add the Provianto to an hourly sweep until the new lock is installed and improved. Do these arrangements satisfy, Surda?"

"They do, I thank you," Bell said.

The lockmaker tarried a few more moments, taking measurements and readings, and departed.

Bell turned to Luzant nirAmit.

"Thank you, sir, for your assistance. I am grateful."

"Thank you, Surda, for allowing me to help," Luzant nirAmit said. "If there is anything else that will benefit from my intervention on your behalf, I beg you will allow me to assist again."

He bowed.

"And now, I bid you good day, Surda."

He bowed once more, and left her, not waiting for her escort to the door.

Colemenoport
Wayfarer

. . . .

PADI WOKE ALL AT ONCE, AND FLOPPED OVER ONTO HER BACK, staring up at the pale pink ceiling while she took stock.

She felt...better, and doubtless would feel more improvement, once she had taken a shower. Intending to do just that, she threw the blanket back, noting as she did so that she was hungry.

Rising, she turned toward the 'fresher, paused, and went, instead, to the comm.

"Service, Trader?" came the easy query from the kitchen.

"Would you send a—restorative tray to my room, please?"

"Right away, Trader." That was considerably sharper.

"Thank you," Padi said, and tapped the connection off.

She had scarcely gone two steps back toward the 'fresher when the delivery bell chimed.

At least eat a muffin before you shower, she told herself, changing course yet again. *After all, Trader Padi, no one wants an incident.*

When at last she had showered, and dressed in ship's casual, she carried what was left on the tray across the room. Lady Selph was waiting for her by the door to her enclosure. Padi set the tray down, took up a cross-legged seat on the floor, and pressed her finger against the release.

Lady Selph strolled out onto the table, and accepted the piece of fruit Padi offered her with regal grace.

Padi chose a piece of fruit for herself, and they ate in companionable silence for a few minutes. The nuance Padi received from the elderly norbear was pensive consideration, which suited her own mood.

When the fruit was gone, Lady Selph posed a question. Padi blinked, and looked again. It took a moment to realize that what she was looking at was herself, asleep, hair flung about the pillow every which way, and one arm outside the blankets, resting on her stomach.

"Well you might ask," she said to Lady Selph. "It happens that my meetings were very trying, and I failed to eat appropriately."

Lady Selph allowed it to be known that eating was very important.

Padi laughed.

"Yes, so I am learning. But you remind me that I have faces for you. Here—"

She lifted the norbear to her knee, and carefully visualized Merchant vellaTon. When she felt Lady's Selph's acceptance, she formed an equally careful image of Merchant zerKilin, which was likewise accepted.

When it came to Zandir kezlBlythe, however, matters went askew. Padi found an unexpected difficulty in providing what might be termed a "fair copy" of Luzant kezlBlythe.

She struggled to be accurate, but the image would not come right. When there finally came a pressure of paw against her wrist, she had produced a severely sharp-faced woman with narrow, avaricious eyes, the whole image sticky, as if it had been made out of honey.

She felt Lady Selph put her attention on this travesty for a long moment. Then came the query.

"Well, she was the last," Padi told her, "and I expect that I was already feeling the effects of not having eaten a sufficiency of cake. I had quite the headache by the time she was done with me."

She paused, frowning down into Lady Selph's furry face.

"I think she tried to *push* me," she said slowly. "The most peculiar sensation, and—and I thought I heard a sound, like a rock bouncing off a hull."

Lady Selph allowed it to be known that pushing people was rude.

"Indeed it is. My shields—I suppose I will have to ask Father to look at them for me, or perhaps—"

Lady Selph wondered why Padi could not tend her own shields.

Padi glared at her.

"Because I'm an idiot and don't know how to see them," she said, hearing the snap in her voice. "It's quite ridiculous. All I need is a mirror, only—"

She stopped, and took a deep breath, her attention focused inward, where the oddest fancy had formed...

Lady Selph allowed it to be known that she wished to return to her apartment.

Padi saw her safely inside before rising, and going across the room to the full-length mirror next to the closet.

She paused, looking at herself, hair loose along her shoulders, eyebrows pulled, mouth straight.

"All I need," she said aloud, "is a mirror."

She opened her Inner Eyes.

Sparkling ribbons of color filled the surface before her. The reflection of the frowning woman faded under their assault, until they, too, faded, giving place—and for the second time, she Saw her own shields.

Pewter they were, not silver, but for all their lack of shine, they put forth a steady, lambent glow. The shape suggested dragon wings, with a fretwork that evoked knots of flowering lavender. There was a dent in the upper right quadrant—damage from a previous attack—which her shields had turned.

Slightly to the left of the old scar, was a new one. Padi leaned closer. The old scar looked as if someone had thrown a boulder against her shields, with considerable force.

The new scar—looked as it had sounded, Padi realized. As if a stone had forcibly struck her shields, and bounced away. There was a dent, and a black smear around it, like carbon.

It would, Padi thought, be quite enough to give one a headache, to be hit with a stone thrown with such force.

Of course, it would need to be repaired, Padi thought, staring at the reflection. As if the thought were the action, she saw the dent fill and smooth, though the black stain remained.

That will need to be polished clean, she thought, *very* carefully. Color swirled in the mirror.

When it faded, Padi beheld her shields once more, repaired and glowing from within.

Carefully, she considered the scar from the first encounter. Her reason for leaving it...apparent to those who had the proper eyes to See it, had been that it would serve as a warn-away. Who would attempt a person whose shields had held against such an impact?

But it would seem that Zandir kezlBlythe hadn't even *Looked*, but merely let fly with her malicious pebble. Perhaps she had only wanted to give Padi a headache, in punishment for not being the master trader. If so, she had succeeded.

Padi stepped back and gave her shields one more inspection, finding them as strong as ever.

Satisfied, she closed her Inner Eyes. This time there were no colors in the mirror before the reflection of the woman in ship's casual appeared, her face relaxed and her frown retired.

Padi sighed—and sighed again.

She was hungry.

Off-Grid
Pacazahno

. . . .

THEY HAD VISITED MOST OF THEIR USUAL TOPICS AFTER ALL, sitting in the sun in the pleasant garden and eating the meal that had been delivered from the common kitchen.

It was as Arbour was taking her leave that the office window opened and Nattie put her head out.

"Konsit, Majel ziaGorn of the Citizens Coalition is returning your call of earlier today."

"Ah," said Arbour, taking a step to the side, but Konsit looked at her and raised a finger—*wait*.

"Please tell Councilor ziaGorn that I will be with him in a moment," she said. Nattie withdrew. Konsit looked to Arbour. "If you have time, that is."

"I have time, and the garden is still pleasant," Arbour said, and sat down again on the bench.

Konsit smiled and went inside.

It wasn't too many minutes before she was back again, carrying two tall glasses of lemonade.

Arbour, who had been communing with the ambient, roused herself, and looked up.

"Thank you," she said, receiving her glass with a smile.

Konsit was tense again; and more than tense, she was worried. Arbour considered, but decided against whispering another well-wish into the ambient. Konsit had a village to administer and folk to protect—a certain level of tension and worry were not inappropriate in the case.

"The chair of the Citizens Coalition will be coming himself. He says that there have been . . . a number of acts of mischief directed at Deaf business in Haven City."

252

Arbour frowned.

"That's unsettling. Does he think those are related to this?"

Konsit smiled wanly.

"Well, that's what he hopes to establish, of course. He'll be bringing investigators—Talents." Konsit took a breath. "The Haosa—"

"The Haosa," Arbour interrupted, "will be pleased to support the efforts of the Citizens Coalition's investigation."

The other woman's relief washed over Arbour like a shower of warm rain.

Konsit did not trust the Civilized Talents from Haven City, Arbour thought. Come to that, neither did she, and especially not off-Grid.

"The people I have called to help you should arrive within the hour. I'll wait, if you'd like that, and make introductions."

Another wash of warm relief.

"I would like that, very much. In the meantime, I called a few people, and if you are able to talk to them for a few minutes about your idea for students and teachers to come to Ribbon Dance Village, I think that will be helpful, and get the project started."

"Soonest begun, soonest done," Arbour said lightly, and sipped her lemonade. "I'll be pleased to talk with them, of course."

Colemenoport
Wayfarer

. . . .

PADI SAT BACK IN HER CHAIR AND CLOSED HER EYES.

She had sourced the fruit-and-nut bars, and ordered a sampler pack, answered her mail, and sent the master trader a note, desiring to know what he would like her to do for him.

The answer to that note had just come back.

Take the rest of the day off.

Really, it was unprecedented. Perhaps her eyesight was suffering under the assault of too much cake.

She opened her eyes.

There on the screen, the master trader's message, wonderfully brief.

Take the rest of the day off.

One did not write to master traders and ask if they were feeling quite themselves. One assumed that the master trader understood the meaning of his words.

Take the rest of the day off.

Padi took a deep breath and opened the desk drawer where she kept her stationery.

Off-Grid
The Tree House

. . . .

FOUR HAOSA, ONE TALENTED IN BACK SIGHT, ANOTHER IN PSY-chometry, and two Persuaders, had been called to Pacazahno by Arbour. There had been vandalism at the school, which was a near-enough miss that Tekelia shivered on hearing the news.

More news was that Majel ziaGorn, the Deaf Councilor himself, was to survey the site, with his team of Civilized Talents, and evaluate the damage.

That was worrisome, in Tekelia's opinion. Unless they were very proficient with their shields, or of relatively low Talent, Civilized investigators were more likely to make a muddle than forward discovery.

Still, however problematic bringing a Civilized team with him might be, it turned out that Councilor ziaGorn had a very good reason for going to Pacazahno himself.

Deaf businesses had been assaulted in the city and the port, and the Chair of the Citizens Coalition, who was likewise Majel ziaGorn, was naturally curious as to whether the mischief at Pacazahno was linked to those other events.

And that was, in Tekelia's opinion, a very good question, indeed. Which was why the screen was presently displaying the *Haven City Tattler*'s Offenses Against Civilization Log.

It was notable that the casino owned by Majel ziaGorn had been targeted several times, as well as a catering service on the port. Over the last half-year, there had been a growing number of reports filed by Deaf-owned businesses, of what City Security was pleased to dismiss as "mere mischief."

"Mischief" had a monetary value, which Tekelia—and apparently the perpetrators of the incidents reported—happened to know.

It sounded as if the vandalism at Pacazahno went beyond "mischief"—even if a children's art garden was dismissed as valueless, the destruction of a library—

There came a knock at the door.

Tekelia looked up from the screen, and asked the ambient who it was.

The signature that came back was that of the Warden of Civilization.

The knock came again, rather a diffident knock. Perhaps Bentamin had decided that Tekelia's privacy was worth something after all.

A third knock. Tekelia pushed back from the desk.

"Do come in, Bentamin, and have done with that infernal noise!"

"I spoke with Medic arnFaelir," Bentamin said. "She suggested the suite above Peck's Market as an appropriate venue for the Healer's meeting with the twins."

Tekelia moved a hand, indicating that Bentamin should go on.

"Yes. After that, I spoke with Torin and Vaiza. They were able to accommodate a meeting with the Healer, and asked that you act as their escort."

"If they want me, then of course I will," Tekelia said, wondering if this was the reason for Bentamin's visit.

"I told them to ask you." Bentamin sighed. "I did see the— artifact, it seemed to me. Very intricate work, so far as I could tell in this atmosphere." He leaned to the desk, plucked one of Entilly's cookies from the tin, and ate it, frowning down at the floor. Tekelia waited.

"After I had spoken to the twins, I spoke to Eet," Bentamin said at last, raising his head and meeting Tekelia's eyes.

"He was—compelling in the extreme. I have no doubt what he saw, and that he *did* see it—it was no dream, Cousin."

"No, it wasn't," Tekelia agreed. "I am convinced that Eet saw the deed done."

"Yes, well."

Bentamin sagged back in the chair, looking up to Tekelia, who was leaning against the desk.

"So compelling did I find Eet's witnessing, that I immediately went to Peesha urbinGrant, who I have engaged to give me legal advice, particularly on norbear sentience. I described the event as Eet had seen it. Peesha is a Truthseer. When I had done, she asked me who was my witness, and were they being kept safe in the Wardian."

Bentamin closed his eyes.

"I told her that the witness was with the Haosa, and that it was the norbear I had told her of, previously. She said—"

Bentamin stopped. Tekelia waited.

Eventually, Bentamin looked up.

"She has no precedent. Even beyond the issue of norbear sentience, which has not been established on Colemeno, a norbear has never been called to testify. They are not, you understand, *forbidden* to testify, merely they haven't done. And if we put Eet before the court to produce his evidence, it will most likely be called a mistrial, and we will not see justice done."

Tekelia sighed.

"What we want is for kindly Cousin Jorey to confess."

"That would save a good deal of trouble," Bentamin said politely. "Any idea on how to make it happen?"

"Let me think on it," Tekelia told him. "In the meanwhile, has a date been set for the Healer?"

"I'll be speaking with her this afternoon. As soon as we're firm, I'll let you know. Remember that the children are to ask for your escort themselves."

"Oh, yes," Tekelia said. "I'll remember."

Silence fell then, with Bentamin back at his study of the floor.

The soft *pop*! of displaced air was therefore quite audible.

Tekelia looked down at the desk, and the folded sheet of paper, lying where there had been nothing only moments before.

The paper displayed the distinctive pattern of its sender, which faded quickly into the ambient. Tekelia picked it up and unfolded it.

The handwriting was also distinctive, and the subtle scent, as well.

To my considerable astonishment, the master trader has commanded me to take the rest of the day "off." May I hope that you are in similar straits, and that we may celebrate together?

Padi

Tekelia laughed.

"There's a rare sound," Bentamin said. "What's afoot?"

Tekelia looked up, still smiling.

"Padi sends that she has been ordered to spend the rest of the day in leisure, and is at a loss as to what she ought to do."

"And she wrote to you for a tutor. Clever woman." Bentamin rose with a smile, and bowed.

"I will leave you to your lessons, Cousin. Thank you."

Tekelia frowned.

"Whatever for?"

"For listening," Bentamin said simply—and was gone, the ambient swirling briefly, and settling.

Smiling again, Tekelia called a pen to hand, and bent down to answer Padi's note.

On-Grid
Wayfarer

. . . .

SHAN LEANED BACK IN HIS CHAIR AND CLOSED HIS EYES.

Truth said, he was not looking forward to his next interview. A prudent man might very well decide not to engage with the subject at all.

His *melant'is—none* of his several *melant'is* allowed him to turn aside. Nor was he a fool; his first sally onto this particular field had left him bruised. To broach it twice was on its face an act of folly.

And yet, the master trader valued his captain; Thodelm yos'Galan valued a skilled and fertile adult of the Line; Shan valued his lifemate beyond all reason.

And that must stand as both his excuse and the *melant'i* from which he broached this, again, with Priscilla. Oh, the master trader might order, and Thodelm yos'Galan thunder, but any wounds would be dealt to living hearts.

He opened his eyes, pushing the chair back—and paused as the computer chimed. He had mail. Perhaps it would be complicated mail, requiring hours—days!—of research.

He tapped the screen.

Disappointingly, the note was very brief, requiring no research at all. Merely his daughter wished him to know, as the master trader had granted her the rest of the day off, that she was going to visit her friend Tekelia, who had proposed a picnic by the river. She expected to be home for tomorrow morning's working breakfast.

A picnic by the river, he thought. How agreeable that sounded.

He closed the letter, and sat for a moment longer, considering. He could not provide a river, but a picnic on the rooftop

259

garden was well within his reach. It seemed a well-enough day, outside the window. And surely a pleasant meal in convivial surroundings was the least a man could do for his lifemate before opening the door to strife.

He leaned to his computer again, wrote a brief note, then reached to the comm to call the kitchen.

"Good afternoon, Priscilla."

He had spread the rug on the plush grass at the side of the pool. A miniature waterfall provided both music and a pleasantly damp breeze. A bottle of cold tea was set out, and the glasses ready; the rest of the feast yet hidden in the pretty basket provided by Luzant iberFel, who was apparently no stranger to romance.

"Good afternoon," his lifemate answered, looking wryly at the rug. He stepped forward and helped her down to it before taking his place nearer to the basket.

"Tea?" he asked.

"Tea would be splendid," she said.

He poured, offering her the first glass, which she held in both hands. Shan tapped it lightly with his.

"To my love," he said.

Priscilla smiled, and drank, then settled somewhat, leaning lightly against him, and sighed.

"This was a good idea."

"I wish I might say it was original with me, but I owe all and everything to Padi, who informed me that, released for the rest of the day by the master trader, she has chosen to picnic by the river with her friend Tekelia. It sounded so agreeable that I determined at once that we deserved a similar treat."

"You're not wrong," Priscilla said, reaching to put her glass on the flat stone wall enclosing the tiny pool. "Do you think those little fish are edible?"

"Possibly, they are. However, we do not need to test the theory, or indeed exert ourselves in the slightest. Luzant iberFel has packed enough to feed the entire trade mission."

"Because," Priscilla murmured, "no one wants an incident."

"I daresay that thought might have been in her mind."

"Speaking of incidents," Priscilla said. "Padi's news regarding the known behavior of ambient conditions on those who are Gifted was...unsettling."

Shan caught his breath. He would have rather they had enjoyed the meal first, and an hour of contentment together. But here was the trade on the table, waiting for his answer.

"Extremely unsettling, I would say. So unsettling that, in face of reason, I find myself forced to ask you again, my love—will you withdraw, at least to the ship?"

Silence.

Priscilla took up her glass, and sat holding it against her knee as she gazed out over the pond, and the pretty little waterfall.

Shan retrieved his glass and sipped, waiting.

At last, Priscilla moved. She raised her glass, sipped tea, and turned her head to meet his eye.

"Yes," she said. "I'll withdraw to the ship. If you come with me."

Off-Grid
The Tree House

. . . .

THE AMBIENT SWIRLED, BRIGHT AND JOYOUS, AT THE CENTER OF the great room, subsiding nearly at once, leaving behind Padi yos'Galan, wearing a sweater that very nearly matched the lavender of her eyes, with a pair of tough brown pants and boots. She was cradling a bottle of wine against her breast.

Tekelia smiled.

"You *are* bold, to bring wine through the ether."

Padi frowned slightly. "I thought I ought to at least contribute something to the festivities," she said. "Has it gone off, do you think?"

"No, I think we'll find it very good," Tekelia said. "Only be aware that the ambient occasionally excites wine. Bottles have exploded upon arrival."

Her eyebrows lifted, and she looked down.

"Well," she said. "I see that I was lucky. How very unlike me."

This, Tekelia had learned, was a joke. Clan Korval as a kin group had, as Padi previously explained, an . . . interesting relationship with random event. It was not quite a Talent, but potent nonetheless.

"Now that you are safely arrived, we may begin your exploration of leisure." Tekelia waved at the basket sitting on the desk. "Only put your contribution into the basket—"

Padi frowned again.

"But—we risk an explosion. To be lucky twice—may happen, but truly, it is not at all wise to depend upon fortunate outcomes."

"Very true," Tekelia agreed. "However, the chances of the bottle exploding are significantly reduced, if we walk to the river."

She glanced over her shoulder, through the wide windows that gave onto the deck.

"Walk?"

Tekelia stepped forward to take the bottle from her hands, and turned to tuck it into the basket.

"Yes, walk. Do you mind? It's an easy trail, and pleasant, I promise you."

"Well, then," Padi said, taking Tekelia's hand. "Let us by all means walk to the river."

The path meandered beneath the arcing branches of the trees, sometimes wide and sometimes thinner, depending on the importunities of low-growing shrubs.

In fact, it reminded Padi of the path to the Tree Court at Jelaza Kazone, and she smiled as Tekelia took the lead through a particularly overgrown section.

When the path widened again and they were walking side by side, Tekelia slanted a look at her.

"At the risk of sounding as if I wish you to work, I wonder if you know how norbears are accounted, out beyond Colemeno?"

Padi frowned slightly. "Accounted?"

"Perhaps the better question is, 'Are norbears considered sentient? Is their word good, and their evidence weighed equally with the evidence given by other sentient persons?'"

"Oh." Padi sighed. "Norbears...are difficult," she said. "Some worlds ban them altogether. Others welcome them. They are occasionally—I suppose you would say *employed*—as by some offices of the Pilots Guild. Lady Selph and her cuddle are part of the pet library on the *Passage*, where their function is to divert, amuse, and, to an extent, Heal. I was myself sent to Lady Selph to be Sorted. However—"

She took a deep breath, and let it out in a hard *puff*.

"However, those are all to do with norbears being *empaths*. Sentience"—she shook her head, and met Tekelia's eyes, one brown and the other grey—"I don't know. Perhaps, somewhere, norbears are considered sentient and their testimony allowed to weigh. Shall I build you a search?"

"Now, that *does* sound as if I've given you more work," Tekelia said.

She moved her shoulders.

"Building the search should take no more than five minutes. Sorting the results when they return might be a lengthy process..." She grinned, and stopped in the center of the path, swinging around to face Tekelia.

"I have a proposition."

"Tell me," Tekelia said, matching her grin.

"I will construct the search and set it to work. When the results return, you will be the one to sort them. Have we a bargain?"

"We do! It's only just that I sort the data, since the question is mine."

"Then I will build the search—tomorrow."

"Thank you."

"It's no trouble at all," Padi said.

The path ahead was narrow again, and Tekelia stepped forward to lead the way.

When they came together again, Padi had a question.

"I wonder why you are interested in norbears." She smiled. "Aside from being on Lady Selph's string."

"Who could not admire so staunch and upright a lady?" Tekelia said gaily, then lifted a hand.

"As it happens, the children who recently came to us have lived all their lives with a norbear—one Eet. We wish to make sure that his rights are properly observed."

"I see. Perhaps he should meet Lady Selph, to pick up pointers," Padi said. She meant it as a joke, but Tekelia answered her seriously.

"I hope that can be arranged. Eet isn't a cub, but his scope has been limited."

Padi blinked, then shrugged.

"Well, why not, after all?"

Tekelia smiled.

"Exactly."

Colemenoport
Wayfarer

· · · · · · · · · ·

"COME WITH YOU?" SHAN REPEATED. "YOU TEMPT ME, LOVE, never doubt it, but the master trader holds me in thrall. Until this port is proven—"

"Nonsense," Priscilla said briskly. "I heard the master trader say only this morning that he could not proceed until the whole port inventory was completed." She paused, head tipped.

"It's true that he also put himself at the *qe'andra's* service, in case she should need papers sorted, but I think she would understand, if the master trader put it to her that he was returning to the *Passage* to have his health evaluated by the medic and the ship's Healer."

She paused, as if awaiting an objection, and Shan obligingly said, "But I'm not ill."

"You may not recall it, my love, but you hadn't fully recovered from your adventure on Langlast when we arrived on Colemenoport. You came on-planet, opened your shields, and the ambient has buoyed you ever since. We know that the ambient acts on us, and in some measure amplifies our Gifts. What we *don't* know is if it heals."

Shan raised an eyebrow.

"I assume from this that you intend to repair to the ship for a medical evaluation and consultation with the ship's Healer, as well," he said.

"Yes."

"Excellent. However, I feel compelled to note that this path has a curve at the end. For instance, if the medic and the ship's Healer find me to be in good health, I would expect to return to Colemeno in service of the master trader's business."

"Of course," Priscilla said calmly. "And, if I am cleared by the medic and the ship's Healer, I'll also return to Colemenoport, and the captain's duties to the master trader."

She met his eyes, and smiled.

Shan sighed, and shifted so that he was lying across the rug, his head in his lifemate's lap. He closed his eyes, and after a moment, he felt her brush his hair.

They remained thus in communion for some minutes before he spoke again, eyes still closed.

"Priscilla."

"Yes?"

"You drive a hard bargain."

"I'll take that as praise."

He snorted lightly.

"What will happen, I wonder, if one or both of us is found to have taken harm from Colemeno's ambient conditions?"

"Then we will formulate a decision based on the known data," Priscilla answered serenely. "It's *why* we collect data isn't it?"

"Altogether too reasonable," he murmured. "Nor must we overlook the fact that standing at the head of a whole port inventory in the master trader's absence will look well in Trader yos'Galan's file."

"Of course not. Does this mean that you agree?"

"Do you know? I think it does."

"Good. Are you going to sleep, or should we find out what Luzant iberFel thinks is appropriate to a romantic picnic on the roof?"

"Oh, the basket, by all means!"

He sat up, and turned, so that he was kneeling before her, their faces at a level.

"Before we eat, I have a proposal."

"Yes?"

"Yes. I propose that we seal our bargain with a kiss."

"Oh," said Priscilla. "We wouldn't want to ignore tradition, would we?"

On-Grid
The Sakuriji
Council Chambers

. . . .

"THANK YOU, WARDEN CHASTAMEIR, FOR YOUR REPORT," SAID Chair gorminAstir. "Before the Council moves on to its next order of business, I wonder—is the Oracle for Civilization quite well?"

Bentamin inclined his head, carefully. He had been expecting this question to arise rather sooner, and had prepared for it as best he could.

"Asta vesterGranz enjoys her usual robust health, Chair gorminAstir."

"Good, good. It has been so long since she has had a word for us that I feared she might be ill."

"You speak with the Oracle every day, Warden?" That was Councilor tryaBent, who surely knew the answer to that question. Bentamin recruited himself to patience.

"The Warden's list of mandated duties includes a daily consultation with the Oracle."

But the famously ill-tempered councilor was not to be put off so easily as that.

"Yes, it is. I merely wondered if you were doing your duty."

That was forthright, even for tryaBent—and it was, Bentamin acknowledged, a perfectly reasonable question.

"I am doing my duty, ma'am. If you doubt it, you may take testimony from the Oracle's staff, or pull the Wardian's security tapes."

"The Oracle has been at her post for a number of years now," azieEm said, cutting off whatever might have been tryaBent's answer. "Gifts do wear out, as we all know. If the Oracle's Eyes are closing, ought we instate another, and allow one who has served for so long to return to her family?"

azieEm was one of the younger councilors. While an awareness of her youth made her timid, Bentamin had found her
thoughtful, and forward-looking. She of course honored history
and tradition, but did not always look for answers there.

"In fact, the Oracle has spoken of retirement," Bentamin said
carefully.

"Retirement?" seelyFaire exclaimed. "How should she retire?"
azieEm turned to look at her.

"Asta vesterGranz has exercised her Gift to Civilization's benefit for many years. Why shouldn't she retire, bearing our very
great thanks for her service?"

"An Oracle might retire," said Chair gorminAstir, "but in
the past, a new Oracle has arisen first." She looked to Bentamin.

"Has a new Oracle arisen, Warden?"

"Not to my knowledge," Bentamin admitted. "The present Oracle
has suggested that this is because Civilization no longer has need."

"What!" cried tryaBent. "Ridiculous! *We* are the judge of what
Civilization requires, and an Oracle who does her duty is a necessity! Chair—"

She rose abruptly, and bowed to the table.

"Chair gorminAstir, I suggest that what we have here is a
case of malingering. The Oracle has grown tired of duty, and is
withholding information from the Warden, and thus from the
Council, because she wishes to *retire!*"

"Sit down, Coracta," the council chair said, and when she had
done so, added, "Do you have a course of action to propose?"

"Chair, I propose that the Oracle for Civilization be called
to this chamber at our next meeting, so that she may explain
herself to us."

"I agree," said seelyFaire. "There has possibly been a misunderstanding. Even more than that, the Oracle's duty is to
Civilization. As the representatives of Civilization, the Oracle is
ultimately accountable to us."

Chair gorminAstir looked around the table.

"Does anyone else wish to speak to this issue?"

"I think it will be very helpful to us to see the Oracle and
listen to what she may have to say to us," said azieEm. "Our
Warden has been a faithful go-between, but as has been said,
the Council is ultimately responsible for both the Oracle's duty
and Civilization itself."

Councilor targElmina shifted, and leaned across the table to address Archivist ivenAlyatta.

"Has it ever been done, that the Oracle came to the Council?"

The archivist frowned.

"I'll research it. It seems to me that, in the very early days, the Oracle didn't just report to the Council, but was a sitting member."

"Ridiculous," tryaBent muttered.

"Other discussion?" asked the council chair.

No one spoke.

"Very well, we will vote. All in favor of inviting the Oracle for Civilization to visit the Council at its next meeting, raise your hand."

Bentamin looked around the table. All had raised their hands, with the exception of Majel ziaGorn, who had sent that he was required at Pacazahno, on business of the Citizens Coalition.

"The question passes," Chair gorminAstir said. "Warden, will you please extend the Council's invitation to the Oracle?"

"Yes," Bentamin said. "I'll speak to her this evening."

Off-Grid
Coosuptik River

. . . .

LEISURE, PADI THOUGHT DROWSILY, WAS REALLY QUITE PLEASANT.

They had eaten a substantial snack of bread, cheese, and nuts, and sampled the wine, which had not, she found with relief, been spoilt by journeying through the ether. In fact, they had been everything that was indolent, and had made a game of asking questions about each other, turnabout, until Tekelia had leaned close, and kissed her.

That had been agreeable, so she kissed Tekelia, and one sweet pleasantry had led to another, until here they lay on the rug under the trees, with the river plashing quite nearby, Tekelia's head on her shoulder.

There came a soft sigh, and Tekelia murmured, "I am going to miss this."

"What? Having the afternoon off?"

"Well—yes, but more so, this."

Tekelia raised their clasped hands, so that she could see brown fingers and gold, interwoven.

Padi felt her breath catch.

"Padi?"

She wriggled, and got herself sitting upright, assisted by firm hands, leaning forward to look into a worried face and eyes that were both dark brown.

"Is there," she said suddenly—"Tekelia, is there *no one* else?"

Tekelia sighed. It was no use to pretend misunderstanding. By now, Tekelia knew how to value Padi yos'Galan. A game would be met with scorn; a failure to answer would only have her ask again, less gently. One did not toy with Padi yos'Galan; nor lie to her.

"Why do you sigh?" she asked now. "Have I been inept?"

"I sigh because the truth is melancholy," Tekelia answered. One hoped that the truth did not make one into an object of pity. "There is no one else, no."

Lavender eyes grew stormy, and Tekelia felt a shiver in the ambient. Not pitied, no. One had gained a protector.

The realization was—odd, as was the emotion it engendered— not shame, Tekelia thought, but joy, that she cared so much. Also, sadness, because—

"What is, is," Tekelia said gently to those fierce eyes, and fiercer spirit. "I am a Child of Chaos, Padi. More ambient than physical."

"Bah," Padi said decisively, and bent to kiss Tekelia's brow, laying one cool hand along their cheek.

Leaning back, she shook her head.

"That is not the ambient, my friend. It is Tekelia."

"And I am proven by history and by testing to be an instance of Chaos itself," Tekelia said, voice sharper than her care deserved. "This is not whim, but fact."

Padi's regard was steady, though Tekelia could not name the emotions that boiled in the ambient between them.

"Are there others?" she asked eventually.

Tekelia frowned.

"Others? The Haosa—"

"Other—*instances of Chaos*," Padi interrupted.

"None that I am aware of," Tekelia said slowly. "In theory, it is possible that there is another—or even two—at a more distant remove, who have not stepped into the fullness of themselves."

Tekelia paused.

"I had a mentor, when I arrived—another Child of Chaos, who taught me what he could of our condition."

Padi leaned forward.

"Did you never touch?"

The thought of what might come forth from such a touch made the blood run cold. Tekelia took a deep breath.

"It was not considered . . . wise."

The ambient crackled with Padi's anger.

"You were born Civilized, you said. Surely you didn't— *discorporate* people—while you lived under the Grid?" She caught her breath on that, her gaze sharp enough to cut. "Was that why you were sent—to the Haosa?"

Sharon Lee & Steve Miller

"Nothing so dire." Tekelia reached out and lightly traced one high, delicate cheekbone, marveling at the softness of her skin.

She sighed and leaned into the touch.

"Tell me," she said. "Why were you sent to the Haosa?"

"If I am to do that," Tekelia said, reluctantly sitting back from her, "I will want another glass of wine, and some cheese."

Padi turned toward the basket. "Fortunately, we have those to hand."

"I was sent to the Haosa for the usual reason: My tools did not work properly. Had I not been able to make tools at all, then I would simply have been pronounced Deaf, or at least Low Talent, and allowed to remain much as I was, save I would no longer be given tool-building lessons. If I was Low Talent, I might have had a curriculum in control, but nothing more dreadful than that."

Tekelia sipped wine, and looked out over the river.

"No, the difficulty, you see, is that I could make perfectly adequate—even quite beautiful—tools. Only they didn't work. Also, I could lift any object brought to my attention by my tutor, hold it, spin it, or send it to Metlin, without so much as thinking about building a tool."

Padi raised an eyebrow.

"*Did* you send something to Metlin?" she asked seriously.

"I think not," Tekelia answered, "but that's not to say I couldn't have done." A sigh and a wry look.

"It looked black for me at that point, but it was clinched by my cousin Camafy, who has a rare genius for irritation. I lost my temper, and it could have gone ill for us both. Happily, there was an elder to hand who saw the whole, and was able to deescalate the event."

A deep breath.

"That, however, did prove me out. Clearly, I was Haosa—noncompliant and a threat to Civilization."

"And so you were sent away," Padi finished softly.

"So I was," Tekelia agreed, "and it was not, in all, a tragedy. Some of my off-Grid cousins weren't only sent to the Haosa, but cast out of their Civilized families. Contact with my family never lapsed; my birthright still flows into my drawing account every half-year, with the proper increase when I came of age."

"But you are not Civilized," Padi pointed, dryly, "and may not live under the Grid."

"But, then, I don't *want* to live under the Grid," Tekelia countered, and she smiled.

"The children who just came to us are in much worse case," Tekelia continued. "Far from making certain that they are well cared for and not in want, their kin has made a petition to declare them—the last of their family—a failed Line. They've also filed to transfer all of the children's property to themselves."

Padi's eyes narrowed.

"One knows what to think of their kin. Have the children no recourse?"

"Some recourse. A failed Line must be proven, and the proof hasn't been made. The petition to strip them of their rightful property, as you say, shows us the quality of their kin."

Tekelia considered the ambient, which was still inclined to be stormy in Padi's orbit.

"Such petitions have been filed before, and the Council, to its credit, most often disallows them. In particularly egregious cases, a substantial fine has been leveled against the petitioners."

"Hitting them where it hurts." Padi sipped her wine, and looked to Tekelia.

"That was a very effective diversion," she said.

"Thank you," Tekelia said modestly.

"Did you never try," Padi said slowly, "to touch someone... on-Grid?"

"Until recently, I had no subjects that I was willing to lose for the experiment."

Padi laughed.

"So the greedy cousins are good for something after all?"

"Unfortunately, the greedy cousins are Civilized, and I don't care to be the out-of-control Wild Talent who brings Civilized discipline down on the Haosa."

Padi sighed.

"It's complicated, isn't it?"

"Wouldn't you be bored, if it wasn't?"

"You know me too well," Padi said.

"And I would like to know you better," Tekelia answered. "I believe you owe me a story."

Padi raised her eyebrows.

"What story?"

"The story of why you locked away your Talent."

"Oh," Padi said. "That story."

She drank off what was left of her wine, and put the glass aside, then turned a critical eye on their arrangements.

"Do you mind sitting with your back against the tree, and your legs before you?"

"Like this?" Tekelia made the necessary adjustments.

"Exactly like that," Padi said, and stretched out on the rug, resting her head on Tekelia's thigh.

"If I am going to tell *that* story," she said, looking up into Tekelia's face, "I am going to be comfortable."

"That seems fair," Tekelia said gravely.

Padi smiled, and took a deep breath.

Off-Grid
Pacazahno

. . . .

FOUR HAOSA HAD ARRIVED SO PROMPTLY KONSIT THOUGHT THEY must have flown, and had been introduced by Arbour as Yferen, Maybri, Chalis, and Uri.

"Welcome," Konsit said warmly. "Thank you for coming so quickly."

"Pleased to be able to help," Maybri said, "though not pleased you've had trouble, Speaker joiMore."

"At least nobody was hurt," said Yferen, and then looked sharply at Arbour. "That's so, isn't it, Arbour? No one was hurt?"

"As far as we know, property damage only."

"Everyone is accounted for and healthy," Konsit added. "We made certain of that, first. Would you like to eat something? The village kitchen has set up a buffet. I'll take you over, and show you the cottage we've opened for you—it's directly across the square."

"I will be going back to Ribbon Dance," Arbour said. "Before I go, Konsit—Maybri and Uri are Persuaders, and may be of use to Constable fuJang, and also with the team coming in with Councilor ziaGorn. Yferen is a Back-Seer, and Chalis is a Psychometric. They may be able to find a thread of your mischief-makers."

"It'll look like I'm just sitting in one spot, maybe having a bit of a nap," Yferen told her earnestly. "What I'll be doing is sorting back through recent events at the art garden—" He broke off and looked at Chalis.

"Is that best, do you think, Challi?"

"Yes, you take the art garden, and I'll start in the library. If things were tossed around and smashed, they may very well remember who did it. The art garden would have seen a great deal of daily excitement, so best you start sifting."

275

"Right. If you get something in the library, we can try to match it to the garden. In the meanwhile, I'll try to pinpoint the time."

Konsit looked from one to the other.

"You'll be looking at what happened *last night* in the art garden?" she said, hearing how uncertain her voice was.

Yferen laughed.

"Sounds daft, doesn't it? Easier to do than to explain."

"Yferen has a strong and accurate Gift," Arbour said gently. "You can trust him to use it for your benefit."

"Yes, of course," Konsit looked at her, feeling her uncertainty fade. She took a deep breath.

"Thank you for all of your help today."

"Didn't we agree that neighbors help each other?" Arbour asked, with a smile. "Now, I really must be getting back, and these four"—she made a show of eyeing each one of the Haosa in turn—"had best have something to eat, and then get to work."

Off-Grid
Coosuptik River

. . . .

"I MAY HAVE ALREADY MENTIONED ONCE OR TWICE THAT MY kin-group, Clan Korval, is rather prone to falling into scrapes."

"I believe you have said something on that point," Tekelia murmured, smoothing a hand over her hair.

"Yes, well. It happens that some years ago, Uncle Val Con fell into a scrape that was remarkable even by our standards. I shall gloss most of it, as it would take longer than we have left in the day to lay it all out. The important point is that things went from bad to worse, and from worse to dire, whereupon the first speaker invoked . . . an emergency protocol. Part of that protocol had the clan's very youngest, and the very oldest, retiring to a safe place while the remainder—who are very resourceful, but few in number—undertook to resolve the problem."

She took a breath and lifted a hand. Tekelia obligingly wove their fingers together, and Padi brought their joined hands to her breast.

"Hidden as secretly as possible, then, were two elders, two halflings, and three children. Quin was eldest, then myself, then Syl Vor, who was considerably younger, and two infants."

She paused again, and Tekelia felt her tension crackling in the ambient.

"If telling this story distresses you, I needn't—" Tekelia began, but Padi held up her free hand.

"It will distress me, because it is a distressing story. But, I wish to tell it, because you wanted to know why I had sealed my Gift away, and what was the result of doing so. I . . . feel that you should know these things, not only to know me better, but in case it should in some way help those who have their Gifts sealed away, in order to keep them *safe*."

"I understand," Tekelia said, and settled more closely against the tree.

"I will try to fly the route quickly," she said, lowering her hand to place it over their clasped hands.

"It was, as you of course have understood, a very tense time. We had our regular lessons, and accelerated piloting courses, and accelerated self-defense. I was Quin's co-pilot, as we kept the order amongst us; Syl Vor, the babies, and the elders were our passengers. It was our duty, pilot and co-pilot, to present a calm face, and to learn everything that we could that might ensure our survival."

She paused for another deep breath.

"Well. All was as it was, and one morning I woke, earlier than the rest, to find that the things on my bedside table were—floating. I blinked, and they tumbled down, with clatter enough to wake Quin, who accepted that I had flailed about in my sleep, and I lay there, trying to convince myself that it was an anomaly. My father, as you know, is a Healer, and his youngest sister is...a very powerful *dramliza*. In the usual way, it would have surprised no one to find that I had a Gift.

"However, we were not in the usual way; there was neither Father nor Aunt Anthora, nor a Healer Hall, to teach me, and, to say the thing and get it done—I decided that, for the sake of calmness, and our ultimate survival, I would not deal with— whatever it was.

"So, I put it in a closet."

"Of course you did," Tekelia murmured, and Padi laughed, rueful.

"Of course I did," she repeated. "After a time, we were liberated from our retreat, only the clan's great enemy had not been quite entirely vanquished. I came to my apprenticeship under the master trader somewhat later than I ought to have, and it seemed intolerable to me that my rightful training would again be set aside while I was trained in a Gift I had no wish to have."

"So you kept it locked away."

"I did. And I suspect that it will come as no surprise to you to learn that, over time, it cost me more and more energy to keep that door locked."

She paused again, and closed her eyes. Tekelia saw a pattern take shape in the ambient, and felt Padi's tension ease.

She opened her eyes.

"Eventually, the situation came to the attention of my elders, who begged me to throw down the walls and become wholly myself. By then, I own, I was afraid for what might happen—which turned out to be very reasonable."

She stopped abruptly, her breathing somewhat ragged, the grip of her fingers very nearly painful. Tekelia breathed into the ambient, warming it, sending calmness swirling 'round Padi's pattern. She sighed, and relaxed slightly.

"Would you," Tekelia asked, "care for another glass of wine? Or some water?"

"Water, please," Padi said, releasing Tekelia's fingers and sitting up.

Tekelia reached into the basket and took two blue-glazed pottery cups. Padi took them in hand, and Tekelia went back to the basket, withdrawing a cold bottle.

Tekelia filled each cup, put the bottle away and accepted the cup Padi held out.

For a moment, they simply sat with each other, sipping water, listening to the breeze in the trees, and the murmur of the river.

"Speaking of sending something to Metlin . . ." Padi said after a time. "I threw something, inadvertently, and I still don't know where it landed. Father offered that it may have gone back in time, where it might have forcibly struck the original owner in the head. He seemed to find the notion quite cheering."

Tekelia grinned.

"Can you describe this object?"

"Oh, indeed! A flat stone disk, blue and green swirling 'round each other. Neither ugly nor beautiful, though I always thought it a trifle sullen. Father used it as a coaster on his desk. Perhaps that was its original use."

"You sent it to me," Tekelia said.

Padi stared.

"Your pardon, I—what?"

"In fact, it did hit me in the head—not hard! I'll return it to you this evening—I should have done so before this, but it quite slipped my mind."

"But, why—forgive me. Why would it have come to you?"

"I must have been close in your thoughts," Tekelia said. "The ambient tends to operate like that."

"But there was no ambient! I was sitting in the master trader's office aboard the *Dutiful Passage*, doing a lesson in raising an object—and the object offered for raising was that disk. Then—there was a disturbance. I was startled, and—quite lost track."

"If there was no ambient, where did you get the energy to throw the disk?"

Padi shook her head. "My teachers would have it that my Gift draws on my personal energy, as would any physical activity."

"Oh." Tekelia drank water and set the cup aside. "In any case, you may have it back this evening."

"Thank you. I'm sure Father will be delighted to see it again." She sighed and put her cup next to Tekelia's.

"There is a little more to the story, if you care to hear it."

"I would very much like to hear it."

Padi nodded.

"Matters stood in equilibrium for some while. I contrived to ignore my Gift, though the price of keeping it contained was becoming dear.

"And then—we were on-port, and agents of the clan's enemy found us. Father was—badly wounded. I tried to hide from those who were sent to capture me, and when that failed, I killed them. Two people. I killed them with my Gift."

"Padi—" Tekelia reached out, but she shook her head.

"Very quickly now," she said, breathless again. "The energy of my Gift breaking free threw me into a closet, and I was quite at a loss, until I realized that the dragon I had released was nothing more fearsome than myself." She sighed. "That my Gift *was* myself—a portion of the whole, without which I was a stranger to myself. Which is of course what my elders had been telling me all along."

She let her breath out in a huff; the ambient swirled with mingled humor and sadness.

"The arrival of my Gift created new problems, though none particularly deadly. I am, so I am told, *very bright*. Not even Priscilla can See me well enough to Sort me, and I am not at all adept at making tools."

"So you were sent to Lady Selph for Sorting?"

"In fact, and I will say that Lady Selph does not find me so much bright as dense."

Tekelia laughed, and Padi did.

After a moment, she said, "You see why I wanted to tell you."

"I do, and I thank you," Tekelia said. "I have another question."

"Ask."

"Would you like to go back to the house?" Tekelia asked, and allowed the ambient to heat in a different way.

Padi laughed.

"Yes," she said. "Yes, I would very much like to go back to the house."

Colemenoport
Colemenoport Business Association

. . . .

"OF COURSE, THE ASSOCIATION IS HONORED TO BE ASKED TO assist Tree-and-Dragon's work. Our members practice the generally accepted accounting principles, and are well versed in all of the mercantile arts. Given Colemeno's situation until just recently, we have of course not been called upon to assist in a whole port inventory, so there is a lack of expertise—"

Chair clofElin paused, as if unsure how to proceed.

Mar Tyn sympathized, but Jes dea'Tolin was not so handicapped.

"A whole port inventory is not so common an undertaking that I would expect to find expertise on any world," she said easily. "Happily, the Accountants Guild has produced a kit, and trained the tradeship *qe'andra* to oversight, and compilation.

"What I hope to find is from three to six independent port accounting firms willing to enter into a short-term contract with the Tree-and-Dragon Trade Mission. Compensation will be to port business association scale."

Fenlix clofElin leaned forward, eyes wide, as if she were an inept gambler, Mar Tyn thought, who had just made Scout's Progress in piket.

"Those are—very generous terms," she said. "The kit—" Words seemed to fail her.

"As soon as six accountants have agreed to assist us," Jes said, apparently understanding the unspoken question, "I will convene a seminar. We will all go over the kit, and make certain among ourselves that there is no question about the tasks, or the protocols."

She paused. The other woman said nothing.

"Yes," Jes murmured. "You must know that we are constrained by the master trader's necessities. He has set an ... ambitious schedule for the completion of work. It is not by any means impossible, but it will require diligence."

"I understand," Chair clofElin had found her voice again. "I will send a bulletin to our members this evening, *Qe'andra*. To whom should interested parties address themselves?"

"To my apprentice, Mar Tyn pai'Fortana," Jes dea'Tolin said, as if it were quite usual, and not the least bit ridiculous. Mar Tyn managed to not turn to stare at her, and in only a moment had regained sufficient wit to reach into his sleeve, and offer his business card across the desk.

"Thank you, Apprentice pai'Fortana," Chair clofElin said. "I will include your information in the bulletin."

"Thank you," Jes said.

"We are honored. Is there anything else I may do for you, *Qe'andra*?"

"In fact there is. The master trader had asked me to give him particulars on the kezlBlythe firm."

"The kezlBlythe firms," Chair clofElin murmured, with just the slightest emphasis on *firms*. "They are not under port jurisdiction, being based in the city. You would need to apply to my opposite number at the Haven City Business Association. I will be pleased to give you an introduction."

"That would be most helpful, thank you."

"Of course. May I serve you in any other way?"

"You have done everything I could have hoped for," Jes told her, rising from her chair. Mar Tyn likewise rose. They bowed, and Chair clofElin did them the honor of rising and showing them to the door herself.

Off-Grid
Pacazahno
. . . .

MAJEL WAS WEARY.

In the end, he had chosen a team from the Cardfall's staff, they being the people he knew. That had involved appointing Seylin, his chief of security, a strong Talent and a trained security officer, as head of the team, and directing her to bring whomever she needed to make a thorough investigation.

Seylin had chosen Ander, their lesser Sensitive, and Beni, their eldest bouncer.

"We're going to be working with shields up," Seylin told Majel. "It's plenty noisy, even at Pacazahno. Ander's been studying the security course with me—and doing well at it, too. Beni's got a fine eye for a detail, and I haven't seen the trouble she can't handle, yet."

So they left, leaving Nester, Seylin's second, in charge of security, and Mily, the night manager, in charge of operations.

They had come to Pacazahno in the late afternoon, been shown the damage, and the team presented to Constable fuJang, who took them in charge.

The village manager—Konsit joiMore—had then escorted him to the school, where he heard the tale of the vandalism from the teachers and students who had found it. After, he had returned with Konsit to her office, where she called for tea, and upon its arrival sat down in her chair with a deep and gusty sigh.

"Your pardon, Councilor," she said, sitting up straighter.

Majel held up a hand, forestalling any more apology.

"I'm weary myself, and my day has been nowhere near as adventurous as your own."

"Adventurous," she repeated. "One tends to forget that adventure is so tiring. We're usually much more relaxed here in the village."

284

"It was good of the Haosa to send Talents to assist you," Majel said.

"Ribbon Dance Village has always been a staunch friend of Pacazahno," she answered, and waved a hand toward the tea tray.

"Please pour for yourself, Councilor. No disrespect intended."

"Of course not," Majel said, rising. "May I pour for you, as well?"

He saw her hesitate on the edge of refusing on account of his rank, but then her face relaxed into a rueful smile. "Thank you, sir, for your courtesy."

"It's the least I can do," Majel told her with perfect truth. "What will you have in your cup?"

"Tea, and only tea," she said. "I'm a simple woman."

Majel smiled, and poured, handing her the first cup. He kept the second—tea and only tea—for himself, and returned to his chair.

"If I may ask, what are your plans going forward?"

"Outside of the investigation, you mean? Ribbon Dance Village has offered to host a few teachers and some compatible students. They have a pair of children in care, and no one near their age. The proposal would have our children and teachers go to Ribbon Dance for a half-month at a time, perhaps. Regular school will be held, supplemented with life skills taught by the Haosa, who depend on technology even less than we do here. The educators have been talking it over today, and I get the sense that they think it will not only be workable, but beneficial. And it will build closer ties with our neighbors."

"That sounds a very good notion," Majel said. "I've lately come to think that the Haosa are our better allies."

"Better than Civilization you mean?" Konsit sipped her tea. "I remember when we were Protected. My parents lost their business, thanks to a corrupt mentor. They packed up everything they had left, my brothers, me, and the cats, and hired a truck to take us to Pacazahno, without any idea of how different it would be. How rugged, compared to Haven City. But there was the other thing, living among people who are like you, and experience the world as you do, and don't believe you to be..."

She looked aside, biting her lip.

"Lesser?" Majel offered. "Disabled?"

"Either or both of those will do," Konsit said, and sighed

again. "Now, sir. It is coming late, and there's no more for either of us to do until we're called. There are several families who have room for a guest, if you don't mind being separate from your people—"

"I'll be going back to the City this evening," Majel said. "My team knows their work. I expect them to be of use to Constable fuJang, and to understand when they are no longer needed, or if they are more hindrance than help. If—"

There was a clatter outside, and Nattie threw the door open.

"Your pardon, Konsit—Councilor. Constable fuJang is calling from the library. He says that Ander found a match."

Off-Grid
The Tree House

. . . .

THE STAR HAD SET AND THE RIBBONS WERE COMING INTO THEIR own, dancing across the darkening sky.

Padi leaned on the porch rail, wineglass held loosely in one hand. She was wearing Tekelia's extra robe, and her hair was loose to the wind's caress.

Tekelia was likewise *en déshabillé* and careless, radiating a sleepy contentment that reminded Padi forcefully of a satisfied cat.

"It's a shame that one cannot see the Ribbons at the port," Padi said lazily.

"Ah, but Civilization does not wish to be reminded of the wilder aspects of their environment," Tekelia said. "It's not only light pollution that keeps the Ribbons dim."

"The Grid?" Padi asked, and Tekelia raised the wineglass in salute before drinking off what was left.

"Civilization deeply distrusts the ambient—the unregulated ambient, I should say."

"I still don't understand why that is," Padi murmured, leaning companionably against Tekelia's shoulder.

"Well, history," Tekelia said. "You know the First Wave failed; and the reason it failed is because the ambient acts differently upon those who are Gifted. Some thrived, but others—broke. Some merely killed themselves; others preyed upon their neighbors. There was a general lack of understanding of the invigorating atmosphere. By the time the survivors understood what was happening, and figured out how to shield, so they might control the effects, the colony was in danger of becoming nonviable."

Padi shivered, not only because the air was growing cool.

"Civilization is the child of the Second Wave," she said, carefully.

"The Second Wave had the survivors of the First Wave to teach them," Tekelia said. "But incidents did still occur, one of them quite horrific, and I will *not* relate that story this evening. If you are curious—which of course you are—the account is available from the library."

"No one wants an incident," Padi said, turning her head to look into Tekelia's eyes. "It's what people say, when they offer the cake."

"So they do, and it is true," Tekelia said. "But cake is not a preventative. Some still broke, though not as many. To shorten the tale considerably—a group of Greater Talents at last realized that the constant assault of the ambient was the danger, even for those whose shields were strong. This realization produced the idea—and then the reality—of the Grid. On-Grid, the energy loss is more manageable. Off-Grid, we must be on our mettle."

"So it *is* dangerous, to live off-Grid. The families who chose to Deafen their children are right in that."

Tekelia turned a hand palm up, palm down.

"Right and wrong. The ambient *is* a natural condition. As with any force of nature, it must be respected. Not all people are suited to live out in the open, constantly buffeted by nature."

Tekelia paused.

"I should say that Haosa as a class have a taste for risk. I don't know if that's an inborn trait that allows us to live more comfortably off-Grid, or a result of living off-Grid.

"We also tend to be—more exuberant in our emotions. Bentamin tells me that, to him, it seems as if the Haosa are always—playing. He disapproves, you understand."

Padi laughed, recalling the stern Warden of Civilization.

"Of course he does."

A shout intruded into the small pause following her laughter. A shout from rather high up.

Padi straightened and stared into the sky. A small figure shot past the dancing Ribbons—and again came the shout.

"What is that?" she asked.

"Who," Tekelia corrected. "I believe it must be Kencia."

"But—Kencia can fly?"

"Oh, yes. As to why Kencia is choosing to fly just at this moment, and in such a state of hilarity—there's a Ribbon Dance tonight."

A Ribbon Dance.

The phrase thrilled, and she looked to Tekelia, who was still staring up into the sky, amused, she thought.

Tekelia turned to meet her eyes.

"There will be a surfeit of food, a number of people in various stages of exuberance, gossip, games, and dancing. Would you like to go?"

"Yes!" Padi said with decision.

Tekelia laughed.

"Of course you would."

"Do *you* want to go?"

Tekelia swayed a bow.

"Of course I do."

Off-Grid
Pacazahno

. . . .

"IT'S THE SAME!" ANDER WAS SAYING, SOMEWHAT WILDLY, AS Majel and Konsit joiMore arrived in the library. "I swear it's the same, but—"

"Gently, gently . . ." Seylin had her hands on the boy's shoulders, not only offering comfort, but to keep him in one place. As it was, his feet were shifting, as if he were dancing.

"Ander," Majel said, standing next to Seylin. The boy turned his head, eyes wide.

"Principal ziaGorn."

"That's right," Majel said, keeping his voice smooth and soothing. "Can you tell me what you Saw?"

"The same Intent, sir, as was in the Yellow Room, and there's, there's—"

Tears started in the boy's eyes, and Majel was about to direct Seylin to take him to find some rest, when two persons burst into the room, and rushed toward them.

"Yferen and Chalis," Konsit joiMore murmured in his ear. "Two of the Haosa who have come to help us search."

"Someone found a hint, is what we heard," said the male of the duo.

"I did!" Ander called out. "Please, are you a Sorter or, or a Healer? I—I've seen it before, the Intent, but now there's so much more fixed to it, and I don't know—"

The other boy held up his hands.

"Neither Healer nor Sorter."

Ander let out what sounded like a small sob.

"No, nothing's lost! You've Seen it, and you've got it tight in your head, I See you do. Challi an' me'll help you tease it out,

290

but first you've got to eat something! You're right on the edge, Cousin. It won't do to fall over, now will it?"

Majel felt Konsit leave her place at his shoulder. He heard her cross the room, and open the door, shouting down the hall to Saffel to bring sandwiches and cakes, on the run!

"But I'll forget—" Ander protested, his feet moving more desperately against the floor. Majel saw Seylin increase her pressure on his shoulders.

"No," said the female of the pair—Chalis, Majel told himself. "You won't forget. Was it one of these machines that was tainted?"

"Yes—that one!" Ander pointed at the mess of broken readers. Majel looked, though he could not have said which particular unit was meant, but Chalis appeared to have no such difficulty.

"And now you've told me and Yferen," she said crisply, "so the memory's triply safe."

"But—"

"Trust us to know our own Gifts," Chalis said firmly. "You *must* eat, and so ought we, if we're to go to work."

"Be good and then some to solve this thing tonight. I don't like the idea of bad Intentions in the school like this," Yferen chattered on, easing closer to Ander, around Seylin's opposite side. He glanced down at the boy's busy feet, and looked up with a smile.

"It's a fine night for a Ribbon Dance, Cousin. Thank you for coming to help us when you could've been dancing." He turned his head then, at the sound of something being wheeled rapidly down the hall, with an accompanying clatter of pottery.

"We'll eat in the hall!" Chalis called, moving to the doorway. "Thank you, Saffel."

"Welcome, welcome. You need else or more, just holler."

"We'll do that—Yferen?"

"Coming," said Yferen, and he turned his head to look directly at Seylin.

"You'll want to eat something, too, Civilized. Those're fine shields, but they don't come for free."

Seylin blinked, and inclined her head.

"You're perfectly correct. Thank you for your care. Ander—"

"That's the thing, Ander," Yferen said, smoothly sliding an arm around the boy's waist. "Let's dance us over to some of Saffel's fine food, and a big mug of sweet tea..."

Seylin stepped back, taking her hands from Ander's shoulders, and Yferen swept him into a showy spin, and began, indeed, to dance toward the door.

Ander laughed, matching step, and the two of them vanished into the hallway in Chalis's wake.

Seylin turned to Majel.

"Cousin?" she said, carefully.

Majel held up his hands.

"One discovery at a time, my friend. Go, and have something to eat."

Off-Grid
Ribbon Dance Hill

. . . .

DRESSED AGAIN, AND HAIR NEATLY BRAIDED, PADI AND TEKELIA stepped out onto the deck. Tekelia was carrying the basket from their picnic, now refilled.

Padi went to the rail, looking out over the trees. There was still a smear of light on the horizon, but overhead the Ribbons were brilliant.

"Shall we walk?" she asked.

"One does not walk to a Ribbon Dance," Tekelia said, holding out a hand. "Will you allow me to bring you, as my guest?"

"Surely, I'm nothing else, if not your guest," Padi said willingly. Tekelia's hand was warm, and she felt a frisson of excitement as their fingers met.

"So, we go," Tekelia said softly.

Fog swirled; there was a moment of chill airlessness, and an eruption of sound and color as Ribbon Dance Hill snapped into being around her.

"So, we arrive," Tekelia said, and Padi stood very still, feeling an unfamiliar fizzing in her blood.

"Tekelia!" The shout was from somewhere nearby, but Padi did not see who of the many dancers crowding the hilltop had called.

Tekelia lifted the basket high, possibly an answer to that welcome, and moved off at an angle to the dancing, to a group of tables, each groaning under a burden of baskets, plates, trays, tins, bottles and jugs.

Tekelia found a place to put their basket, then turned to face her.

"Are you all right? One's first Ribbon Dance can be a bit overwhelming. No shame, if you'd rather we go back—"

"No," Padi said. "I hadn't quite expected—but I *want* to stay, at least for a while." She took a breath, listening to the sound of voices, woven round with music, that seemed not all to quite come from the musicians she could see at the center of an exuberant circle of dancers.

"Keep hold of me, do," she said, around the effervescence in her blood. "I feel that I might rise into the sky."

"I'll hold you close if you have no need to fly," Tekelia promised. "Let's go 'round and find who's here."

"Tekelia!" Another shout, this produced by three persons, arm-linked, swaying toward them from out among the dancers.

"Tekelia, well-come! Who is this—somebody in from Visalee?"

"Padi, I make you known to Kencia, Stiletta, and Klem, as mad a threesome as ever you'll find, and Ribbon-drunk to boot."

"Untrue!" protested the one Padi thought was Stiletta. "The Ribbons are barely risen! Even Klem can keep a cool head this early."

Tekelia moved a hand.

"If you say it, Cousin. Now attend me: Here is Padi yos'Galan, trader attached to the Tree-and-Dragon Trade Mission, and my guest."

"Oho! In from the port!" Kencia said wisely. "It's a wilder wind blows here than ever ventures under the Grid, Trader."

"So I've noticed," Padi said, squeezing Tekelia's hand.

Stiletta caught that motion, and hooted. "I expect the trader could teach you three or six things, Kenny, if you were able to learn them!"

But Kencia was leaning forward, straining against his companions' arms, brow knit, squinting at Padi as if he were trying to see her through fog, or from a very great distance.

"*Not* Haosa," he said, definitively.

"Not Haosa," Padi agreed. "Korval."

"Is that it? Not something you see every day, in any case." Kencia straightened with a grin, still arm-linked to his companions. "Welcome and good dancing! If Tekelia gets tired, you come and find us, eh? We'll see you merry as never was!"

"I'll bear that in mind," Padi said politely, as the three wove away toward the laden tables.

"Ribbon-drunk?" she murmured, as Tekelia led her toward the cluster from which the music she heard with—*with your ears*, Padi thought. Which was an absurd thing to say, only she *was* hearing that other music, on another level altogether, that transcended mere hearing.

You're hearing with your Inner Ears, she told herself. *Priscilla said that you could hear ambient noise.* And certainly the ambient was noisy in this locality!

The dance snaked in and out, crossing itself, pulling tighter to the musicians, then dancing away again. The dancers were hand-linked, some laughing, some singing, and some, Padi noticed, not quite touching the ground.

Hand-in-hand with Tekelia, she drifted closer, her feet taking up the rhythm, as the dancers swept past, their gaiety contagious. She laughed aloud, dancing forward, Tekelia her willing partner. The line swept past, quite close now, and several of the dancers crying, "Join in! Join us!" so that Padi laughed in answer. The last of the line swung out, grasping her free hand, crying, "Dance with us, lady!"

Perforce, Padi danced, Tekelia's hand warm in hers, buoyed by the music and the excitement in the air.

The musicians had put their instruments down and gone off to the tables, as the line broke apart into separate dancers, and followed, laughing still, and some still floating.

Padi sighed, and turned to smile at Tekelia.

"That was splendid," she said. "Thank you."

"No, surely I should thank you," Tekelia said earnestly.

"Whatever for?"

"For my first time link-dancing."

Padi stared.

"Have you never—" she began, and then stopped herself, remembering—

"We should eat," Tekelia said, tugging her toward the tables.

She blinked.

"Already?"

"Already." Tekelia smiled. "Is your blood fizzing?"

"It is! And yours?"

"Of course. It's a Ribbon Dance."

Padi approached a tray of sliced cheese and bread, and hesitated.

"Try something else, if that's not to your liking."

"No, it's only that I really feel that I must be anchored or rocket into the sky."

"I can eat one-handed, can't you?"

"I suppose I'll find out," Padi said, spying the next tray, full of small sandwiches. She had one of those up with her free hand, and devoured it in two bites, suddenly ravenous.

A second sandwich quickly followed the first, and she might have been astonished at herself, if she had not seen Tekelia reach for a third and positively gobble it down.

"Tekelia!"

That shout was accompanied by such a bolt of joy, Padi felt her eyes tear with it.

Tekelia turned, and Padi, too. A small boy was running toward them, pulling away from another child, and a woman, who were not going to catch him before he careened into Tekelia, and—

A large plush shadow leapt from the right, between Tekelia and the onrushing child. The boy shouted, wordless. Padi saw him try to stop, but his momentum was such that he stumbled, grabbing onto the cat's broad shoulders to save himself from the fall.

"Dosent!" he cried, lifting a face quite red with laughter. "You got in my way!"

"And well that she did so," Tekelia said calmly. "Good dancing to you, Vaiza."

"And to you," the child gasped, half undone with speed and with laughter.

"Vaiza!" The second child had arrived. "You were going to hug Tekelia! You know that's not allowed!"

"But that lady is holding Tekelia's hand!" Vaiza countered, just as the woman arrived, round cheeks pink, and her hair coming down from what had been a knot at the top of her head.

"She is holding my hand," Tekelia said. "But it doesn't follow that you can do the same. All our Gifts are different."

Padi felt a tug on her hand and stepped forward.

"Padi, this is Vaiza xinRood, Torin xinRood, Geritsi slentAlin, and Dosent."

"Good dancing, all," Padi said politely.

"This is Padi yos'Galan, of the Tree-and-Dragon Trade Mission," Tekelia finished.

"Good dancing, Trader," Geritsi said with a broad and generous smile. "I would like to stay and talk with you, but I fear I'd better get these scamps home and in bed. Ribbon-drunk, indeed."

It seemed to Padi that this was only half-true. Vaiza was quite merry, but Torin was positively wilting, her eyes heavy and her shoulders slumped.

She was not the only one who had noticed.

"Have you sampled any of Emit's sandwiches?" Tekelia asked the twins. "I've just eaten three, and Padi matching me. I recommend you have some before we finish the whole plate."

"That's right," Geritsi said, putting a hand on Torin's shoulder. "You'll feel better, when you've eaten something."

Tekelia slipped to one side. Dosent the cat yawned, and Vaiza ducked under her chin to reach the table.

"They look good, Torin. You should have one."

"And you," said Geritsi, coming to his side.

"I will in a minute," Vaiza said, dodging past her to stand in front of Tekelia.

"Tekelia, Warden Bentamin says he will be taking us to a Healer, to see how we are faring."

"That's very kind of Warden Bentamin."

Vaiza paused, as if he might argue that point, then blurted, "Warden Bentamin said we could have someone from the village with us. Will you come?"

"I would be honored. Do we know when this event will occur?"

"Not yet. He needs to find the right Healer and talk with her."

"Well, then, how's this for a plan? As soon as Warden Bentamin lets you know the day and time he has set for the meeting, send to me, so that I can be sure to be there with you. Will you be asking anyone else from the village to go with you?"

"Geritsi and Dosent," Torin said, her voice surprisingly strong.

Tekelia looked over Vaiza's head to Geritsi. Padi saw her incline her head. "Of course, we'll go."

"Then that seems fairly settled," Tekelia said. "You will now eat something, please."

"Yes!" Vaiza said exuberantly, and lunged for the sandwich plate.

Off-Grid
Pacazahno

· · · · · · · · · · ·

MAJEL HAD GONE BACK TO THE CITY, LEAVING ANDER IN SEYLIN's specific care, with instructions to bring him home, when their business was done.

Halfway through the—meal, Seylin supposed she ought to style it, though she had never in her life seen so much food vanish so quickly, and into so few people. Beni arrived with another laden tray and two more Haosa, introduced as Uri and Maybri.

"There's been a breakthrough, is what the good constable told us, Cousins," said Uri, choosing a slice of cake from the plate.

Chalis swallowed what seemed to be an entire sandwich and washed it down with tea, waving her free hand in Ander's direction.

"A stroke of luck," she said, lowering the mug. "Cousin Ander here works at a casino in the city that recently saw some mischief done against it. He caught an Intention, but it was too dim under the Grid for him to read it close, or to feel out any associations."

Uri gave Ander a nod and a smile.

"Things are a deal brighter hereabouts," he said. "Good catch, Cousin."

"Thank you," Ander said indistinctly around his fifth sandwich.

"Not only did he catch the Intention," Yferen said, taking up the tale, "but he was able to identify the strongest source. Challi might be able to tease out a face, and I might be able to scrape off a time, so we can get an inkling as to what went forth in the garden."

Seylin sighed, and looked at them clustered around the food trolley. Beni was also eating a sandwich—more out of politeness than need, Seylin thought, and then laughed inwardly. She had herself accounted for four sandwiches, and was seriously considering having a slice of cake with the last of her sweet tea.

Costly shields, indeed, she thought, just as Yferen put down his plate.

"Are we ready, Cousins?"

"Ready," said Maybri. "How can we help?"

"On standby, I should think," Yferen said, with a glance at Chalis, who inclined her head. "Challi and Ander will need quiet to examine the Intention found, and to see are there others. I—"

"I may be of use," Seylin said, moderately, "in the room. There may also be physical clues, and I am trained in security procedures."

There was a pause, as Chalis and Yferen exchanged a glance. Chalis turned to look at Ander.

"Seylin is my supervisor," he said. "She will have to report to Principal ziaGorn what she's witnessed. She should be there."

"Nice, tight shields," Yferen added, looking at Chalis. "Oughtn't to bother what's there or the reading of it."

"They are impressive, those shields," Chalis agreed. "All right, Civilized, you're in, but you keep just as quiet as you are right now. It's finicky work, and that room has years of echoes in it."

"Before, I'd like to try something out in the garden with Cousin Ander, if the rest of you will stand between us and the curious," Yferen said.

Chalis frowned.

"What's in your mind?"

"I want to try a projection. It's a Ribbon Dance night. Might get something."

Chalis tipped her head to one side consideringly, then looked to Ander.

"Cousin, are you willing to participate in one of Yferen's mad schemes? I'll tell you, he's famous for them."

"And no blame to you if it doesn't work!" Yferen said earnestly. "It's only a notion of mine—which I *am* famous for, and also for the fact that they so seldom bear flowers. Still, Cousin, it *may* work—I've seen it done and so has Challi. If it does, that puts us nearer to finding who made this mess. If it doesn't—well." Yferen moved his shoulders in what was almost a dance move of itself. "We tried, as we must."

"I'm willing," Ander said, "but you have to know that I—am not a strong Talent. It comes and goes, and I don't know any techniques—"

"We're well off-Grid here, Cousin. You may find things go easier for you."

There was a pause, as if Ander had only now understood what "cousin" might mean.

"All right," he said, squaring his thin shoulders. "Let's try."

The last daylight had long since faded, and it ought to have been too dark to see in the remains of the school's art garden.

And yet, there was more than sufficient light to see, though it flowed and flickered through all the colors of the prism. Seylin stopped to look up at the broad ribbons of light flowing across the night sky, bright enough to cast a shadow before her.

"They're beautiful," Ander said sharply, stopping and craning upward. Yferen stopped next to him, and turned his face up as well.

"They are that, Cousin," he said gently. "They are that."

He took a breath, as if looking away from the dancing Ribbons pained him a little, and said, briskly,

"Now, Cousins, and Beni, too—stand between us and the curious. Challi, with Ander, please. Civilized, if you're to witness to your employer, stand aside and keep those shields snug."

"Yes," said Seylin, and to Ander added, "I'm also here for your protection, Ander."

"I know that," he said with a small smile. "Thank you, Seylin."

On-Grid
The Wardian

. . . .

ASTA VESTERGRANZ PAUSED THE READER AND RAISED HER HEAD, as if an unexpected sound had reached her in the quiet depths of her bookroom. Mist momentarily obscured the shelves, then faded, leaving a rectangle of exceptionally clear air, rather like a window from which one could see... endless possibility.

"Oh," she said softly, and made a mental note to ask Hyuwen how one went about acquiring cases.

The window faded; the shelving returned. Asta blinked. She glanced down at the reader, marked her place, and rose.

Best she ask Hyuwen now, before she forgot.

She had gone perhaps a dozen steps down the hall, when Hyuwen appeared from the direction of the front hall.

"Ma'am," said her majordomo. "The Warden apologizes for arriving outside of his scheduled hour, but he bears a message from the Council that he felt ought to be delivered at once."

The Warden, not her nephew—and on official Council business. Asta sighed. Blast the Council. Still, she had better see the Warden, who was, after all, only doing his duty.

"Please bring Warden chastaMeir to me in the alcove, Hyuwen," she said. "Find if he would like tea, and if so, bring a tray to us."

"Yes, ma'am." Hyuwen vanished back down the hall.

· · · ✷ · · ·

He hadn't stopped to change out of his robes of office. He hoped that this formality would send the message that he was there in his official capacity, as the agent of the Council of the Civilized, and that he would be greeted by the Oracle to the Civilized.

301

That would be the best outcome.

However, there was always the chance that the robes and the invitation both would irritate his Aunt Asta.

That was, Bentamin admitted to himself, the more likely outcome.

In either case, his visit was likely to be short, so he declined the offered tea, and followed Hyuwen to the alcove, with its large window overlooking the nighttime city streets.

Asta vesterGranz stood before those very windows, looking out at a freedom that would never be hers, whether the Council someway forced her to shoulder her duty once more, or saw her retired to another, less luxurious, apartment in the Wardian. An Oracle, after all, was a Wild Talent, and could hardly be set loose into the very heart of Civilization.

Bentamin paused on the threshold.

"Good evening, Oracle."

The woman at the window tipped her head slightly to one side, before calmly turning to face him.

"Warden," she said mildly. "To what do I owe the pleasure?"

"Duty," he told her. "The Council of the Civilized directs me to invite Civilization's Oracle to the next meeting of the full Council, in three days."

"Ah. May I know the Council's topic, in order to properly prepare?"

"The Council is concerned by the lack of insights flowing to them from the Oracle. They wish to find if your Gift has run dry, or if there is another reason for this lack."

"They want to know if I'm malingering," she said, crisply. "Of course they do. Did you speak to them of my retirement?"

"I raised the topic. The sense of the Council is that retirement of the present Oracle must coincide with the arising of a new Oracle. Since a new Oracle has not arisen—"

"Civilization has no further need," she said, with obvious patience.

"I did tell them that this was your stance," Bentamin answered, his own temper flickering.

"Did you? What did they say?"

"I believe Councilor tryaBent said, 'Ridiculous.'"

The Oracle to Civilization laughed.

"Poor things. New ideas are so difficult."

Bentamin sighed, and cast the Warden aside.

"Aunt Asta. Will you have a Healer before the meeting? A report regarding the state of your Gift might be seen—"

"As a preemptive move from a malingering Oracle, which would force the Council to send me to their own chosen Healer," Aunt Asta interrupted. "No, my dear, if I'm to be examined, let it be only once."

"They will not allow you to retire, unless and until they are presented with a new Oracle. Even should that occur, they will not—Aunt Asta, you will never be set free to travel."

She tipped her head.

"Are you certain of that, Bentamin?"

"Yes," he said. "If it falls to the Council to decide, you may be removed to another apartment inside the Wardian, and you will no longer be called upon to exercise your Gift. That is what happens to Oracles who retire."

"That is what *has* happened to Oracles who retired," Aunt Asta said tartly. "Unless they died."

"Aunt Asta—"

"There, Bentamin," she said, her voice suddenly soft. She came forward and raised a hand to his cheek.

"Don't fret, dear. I've been wanting to talk to them, you know."

"Yes," Bentamin said. "I know."

Off-Grid
Pacazahno

· · · · · · · · · · ·

THE TWO HAOSA AND BENI ACTING AS A SCREEN, THE OTHERS arranged themselves at the center of the garden. Yferen stood to the left, Chalis to the right, with Ander tucked between them. Not wishing to disturb the work, yet conscious of her duty, Seylin stood half a dozen steps to the left and behind the threesome. It seemed to her that the colorful air was slightly...thicker just a step or two in front of them, as if a tiny, localized fog was rising.

"Now, Cousin Ander, be as easy as you may. All I want you to do is to think about that Intention you Saw back there in the library. Just let it rise to the top of your thoughts—no pushing or straining—no reprisals if this doesn't work. It's only a mad notion, after all."

Seylin caught herself nodding, and looked at Yferen with new respect. Ander was standing quite still, scarcely seeming to breathe. The air before the three of them continued to thicken, picking up a swirl as it shaped itself into—into something Seylin had never seen before, but was instantly recognizable for all of that—ill-will bled off of it, and determination, an intention to frighten and subjugate. To rule.

"Nasty bit of anything," Chalis commented, low-voiced. "I've got it."

"I've got it," Yferen said. "Going to try for the other one. If we can hold the match in the ambient, that might be useful, even if we can't fix the signature."

"Don't wear him out," Chalis cautioned.

"No, we'll feed him again before setting him to help you sort the library," Yferen murmured. He took a breath, and spoke again in that easy, transfixing voice.

"Now, Cousin Ander, you remember that first Intention, back at your workplace. Think of that now, just that. I know it'll be muddy, but let's just try."

Thick air swirled again and this time the sensation of malice was so strong that Seylin gasped.

"That's pure hate, that is," Yferen said. "You all right, Civilized?"

"Yes, only—surprised."

"That's three of us, anyhoot. I think we've seen enough, Challi."

"I agree."

"Fine then, Cousin Ander," Yferen said, loudly cheerful, "I think you and Challi ought to get a snack and then get busy in the library. I'll take a look around out here."

Ander shook himself.

"Did I help?" he asked tentatively.

Chalis laughed and patted him on the shoulder.

"You helped most wonderfully, Cousin! And, you're witness to one of those rare occasions when one of Yferen's notions not only bore a flower, but an entire bouquet."

"Mock me," Yferen said mournfully, and Chalis laughed again.

"When haven't I? Come on, Ander, let's grab some cake and tea. Coming, Civilized?"

"Coming," Seylin answered.

Off-Grid
Ribbon Dance Hill

. . . .

THE RIBBONS WERE WELL UP IN THE SKY, THOUGH NOT SO FAR that Padi could not feel their caress, and a certain sense of lightness.

There were fewer dancers on the hill, now; the musicians' circle was empty. The dancing itself was less frenzied, and more intimate, as if the Ribbons now bestowed benediction, after the intoxication of their rising.

Padi and Tekelia danced together, moving to the song of the Ribbons, Padi's hand on Tekelia's hip; Tekelia's hand on her shoulder.

They had eaten, several times, and danced again. They had wandered the edges of the hillside, pausing for introductions, and to watch a display of acrobatics, involving meters-high leaps, sky-tumbling, and leisurely wafts, as if the athlete reclined on the back of a zephyr.

The music changed. Padi swayed closer to Tekelia, smiling into eyes that were blue and amber.

"Tired?" Tekelia asked.

Padi considered. She ought by rights to be very tired, she thought. Rather, she found herself...content, and full of a potent, malleable energy.

"Not tired," she said, "and I wonder—"

She paused, looking up into the Ribbon-washed sky.

"What it is that you wonder?"

"I wonder if I *could* fly," Padi said.

"To fly at a Ribbon Dance is both dangerous and beautiful," Tekelia said, seriously. "Both attract the Haosa, of course, but I feel I should warn you that unexpected things may happen if you give yourself to the sky."

"And yet," Padi said, "I feel that I must. I locked myself away for so long, that it seems...churlish to deny my Gift a flight, if it is able to go so high."

"Oh," Tekelia said, softly, "I wager you will go as high as your heart will take you."

Startled, Padi brought her gaze down from the sky just as Tekelia dropped her hand, and stepped back, arms spread wide.

"Follow your heart. Nothing holds you."

And, indeed, nothing did.

Padi's heart lifted, and the rest of her followed—it was simple and as exhilarating as that. Color bloomed around and within her; she laughed with the joy of it.

She danced there in the plain air and sky, while the Ribbons swirled above and about, curling round her waist, her arms— broad lavender ribbons, and lacy silver ribbons. Somewhere in the distance, someone was singing, and almost—*almost*—she could hear the words—

"How high will you rise?" a familiar voice called, and she spun, Ribboned and enraptured, to face Tekelia, who was dancing with streamers of crimson and gold.

"I think this is high enough," she said, not even glancing down to see how far she was above the ground.

Guided by what impulse she could not have said, except that it seemed to come from the base of her spine, where she had been taught that her Gift resided—she caught the end of a lavender ribbon and extended it.

"Tekelia, dance with me."

Around them the Ribbons flared, edging Tekelia with living flame.

"I will dance with you in joy," Tekelia said, extending the end of a bold crimson ribbon. "Will you also dance with me?"

"In joy," Padi promised, and knew it for truth.

Off-Grid
Pacazahno

. . . .

"YOU DON'T HAVE TO GO BACK, YOU KNOW," YFEREN SAID TO ANDER.

They were sitting together at one of the tables set out in the village square, Chalis having thrown them out of the library as "all aglitter," and choosing Seylin to help her with the finicky detail work of finding which of the damaged devices remembered its abuser most clearly.

Ander took a bite of cake, chasing it with a sip of sweet tea. He glanced up, first to the sky, where the dancing lights were still visible, though not so close as they had been. He sighed, and smiled, and lowered his gaze somewhat to meet Yferen's eyes.

"Would I stay here?" he asked, genuinely puzzled.

"No! Why would you stay here? Well." Yferen waved his hand, interrupting himself vigorously. "Understand, if you want to settle at Pacazahno, it's not a bad choice. Might be a bit more comfortable for you, now I think, coming from the big city—there's more people, is what I mean."

"More people than where?" Ander wondered.

Yferen laughed.

"Here I am, making a hash out of it. Should've waited for Challi. Maybe not, though. She'll bring your boss's eyes and ears, and this ought to be private—between cousins."

"All right," Ander said equitably. "Why not start again? I'll listen tight."

Yferen laughed.

"That's a go! What I mean to say is, if you want to come with us to Ribbon Dance Village, rather than going back under the Grid, we'd be pleased to have you. Me and Challi got plenty of room—you can guest with us 'til you see how the Haosa suit you."

"Haosa," Ander repeated softly, and Yferen sipped his tea by way of being sure he didn't say anything to cut off Ander's thinking.

"Why would the Haosa want me?" Ander asked.

"Why wouldn't we?" Yferen countered.

"Because my Gift is weak, and I'm not—not proficient. I don't like to be a burden, you see. I have a job in the city, and I support myself. I'm learning the first-level security module, which is interesting. Seylin says I have an aptitude."

Yferen took a breath, and counted, like he promised Challi he would before he said anything wild. When he made twelve, he smiled, and reached out to touch Ander's knee.

"I don't know what you look like in the shadow of the Grid, Cousin, but sitting right here, right now, you're a warm, steady fire. You grabbing that signature so quick—I was impressed, but that's nothing. *Chalis* was impressed. You might be light on control, but there's those among our cousins who would gladly teach you. While that's going on, you could look about for what you'd like to do."

He hesitated and pulled his hand back.

"Or you might want the city and what you know—that's . . . I'm not trying to make your choices for you, Cousin Ander, only to show that there's more choices than what you're given in the city."

"Thank you!" Ander said. "Thank you for your care. Are you going back tonight? Do I have time to think?"

"All the time you want to think, and a better man than I am for doing it."

Yferen turned his head, looking across the square to the school.

"Here comes Challi and the Civilized."

"Seylin," Ander said. "Her name is Seylin."

Yferen caught his eyes, and bowed his head slightly.

"Seylin," he repeated. "I'll remember that."

Off-Grid
The Tree House

. . . .

TEKELIA LAY IN THE DARK, PADI WRAPPED CLOSE; HER HEAD ON one shoulder, and her breathing slow and calm. Her pattern would have her not quite asleep, but drifting in that direction.

Tekelia ought also to be seeking sleep, but could not resist one more look within at the several shared threads, tasting the joy, support, and light that each offered, and which brightened every hour. And there among them, the newest, sparkling with courage, strength; love and protection. Broad, close-woven lavender, it was altogether a marvel.

One did not quite feel worthy.

Go to sleep, Tekelia thought, sternly, and felt Padi stir.

"What color were your eyes," she asked, "when you lived under the Grid?"

Tekelia felt a small shiver in the ambient, as if the question were dangerous, and, Haosalike, smiled into the darkness.

"Brown," Tekelia said. "They were both brown."

Colemenoport
Wayfarer

. . . .

HER BEDROOM SNAPPED INTO BEING AROUND HER, BITTERSWEET, and Padi sighed, casting a thought to Tekelia, as, on Liad, one might throw a flower to a favorite.

Something warm returned along the line of that thought—a sense that Tekelia was pleased to accept her token, and wished her a merry day.

Padi laughed, and spun toward Lady Selph's residence. The norbear was curled tightly into a pile of grass, a scrap of soft fabric tucked protectively against her belly.

Father must have made her a doll, Padi thought, with mingled worry and amusement.

She retreated without waking the elderly lady, and entered the 'fresher, emerging very shortly to pull on proper trade clothes. Leaving her jacket on the end of the bed, she leaned over her computer, tapping it awake to check her messages—and abruptly sat down.

There was an urgent message from her father at the top of the queue; and an urgent message from the master trader just below it.

Both? Padi stared. What could possibly have happened, that *both* her father and the master trader deemed it urgent? *Something at home*, she thought, breath caught, and throat tight, the faces of her kin flickering before her mind's eye. Had the Department of the Interior made a strike? Surebleak was little more than a backworld, defenseless against—

A wave of half-humorous commonsense washed through her, and Padi shook her head.

"Yes, of course," she murmured. "No need to panic until we read what's been written."

Shaking her head, she opened the first letter.

Her father desired her to ping him when she had returned home; and to meet him on the roof.

The master trader desired the same.

Well. That was puzzling, but not necessarily alarming.

Padi sent the pings and glanced down the message queue, finding no urgent business—nor anything from Vanz or Gordy. Which just meant that they were busy—as she was.

She closed her eyes for a moment to better see the Ribbons dancing across the night sky—and felt a breath of quiet joy like warm lips pressed against her cheek.

Smiling, she returned the salute, and rose to put her jacket on.

She found him at the far end of the garden, one booted foot on the parapet, elbow across thigh, gazing out over the port.

He was also dressed for trade, though his jacket was folded atop a basket sitting on the nearby stone table. The breeze was running fingers through his hair, and his face, with its strong nose and decided chin, was in profile quite forbidding. Around him—Padi frowned, squinting somewhat—yes, there *was* a small, color-shot tumult surrounding him, as if they were Ribbons, dancing.

"Good morning, Father," she said gently.

The pensive figure at the wall drew a breath and sighed it out before straightening and turning toward her with a smile.

"Good morning, Daughter. Allow me to congratulate you on an early return."

"I wanted to be in time to check my mail before the team's breakfast meeting."

"Ah, the breakfast meeting! That has been put back to a luncheon meeting. I hope you are not too cast down to have only myself as a companion in breaking your fast."

"I'm always happy to be with you, Father," Padi said, her eye drawn to the roil of color outlining him.

"Perhaps not always," he said, moving toward the table. "I seem to recall a few occasions when neither of us was particularly happy with the other."

"Well, but that must be so, mustn't it?" Padi answered. "In any association as long as ours, there will be times of differing opinions. Given our lineage, I think we can agree that we've fallen in much more often than we've fallen out."

"I think you may be correct," Father said, shifting his jacket and opening the basket. He rummaged briefly and turned, holding two vacuum cups.

"I hope you will find the local morning wake-up brew acceptable," he said, handing her a cup.

"More than acceptable," Padi assured him. "I fear I'm developing a fondness."

"It's pleasant to have favorites on this world or that," Father said, raising his cup. "It makes a return that much more delightful."

He set his cup down and began to unload the basket.

"You ought to know that your proposed picnic with Tekelia-*dramliza* resonated so deeply that Priscilla and I had one of our own, up here by the waterfall. These"—he flourished a bowl before setting it down on the table—"are left over. Luzant iberFel treasures heroic notions of what constitutes a romantic meal for two."

Padi thought of the quantities of food she had consumed yesterday, and smiled.

"She doesn't want an incident," she said, taking a covered bowl from Father's hand, and setting it on the table.

"I daresay that's it," he said, removing another bowl. Padi took that, as well, and he dove back into the basket, emerging with plates, and two sets of utensils wrapped in napkins.

"Well, there. Serve yourself, Daughter."

She did so, even taking a slice of cake onto her plate before sitting down. Father was still choosing his meal, and again her eye was drawn to the dancing outline—

"Am I casting an unusual shadow?"

Padi blinked, and met a quizzical silver gaze.

"I hardly know," she said truthfully. "I've not seen it before, but, right now—there are colors all about you, like—like an aura. Or as if the ambient is...excited in your presence."

Father lifted an eyebrow, and turned to his plate.

"When I was quite a boy," he murmured, "I had used to see 'sparkles' around people. Disconcerting to my elders, of course, at least until I learned that not all such beauty could be clasped in the hand."

Padi blinked, recalling Ribbons dancing overhead, and how she was able to extend her own particular lavender ribbon, and receive Tekelia's crimson in return.

"Did you have a pleasant day off, Daughter?"

"It was extremely pleasant. I may have to make a habit. In the evening, we went to the Ribbon Dance, which was—exceptional. I met a great many people and—I can fly."

He glanced at her.

"Can you, indeed? Will that be your preferred mode, going forward?"

Padi frowned, and brought her attention within, seeking the surety of the night before—and finding it sadly absent.

"I think it may have been an...effect of the ambient, on the Hill, you know, with the Ribbons risen."

"Perhaps you will show me, someday," Father said, and returned to his meal.

Padi did the same, accounting for everything she had taken, including the cake, and picked up her cup.

Father pushed his empty plate away, raised his cup and shook it lightly.

"I fear we have outpaced our resources. There is bottled water in the basket, if you're thirsty."

"I'm well enough for now," Padi said, and hesitated.

"Do not hold shy, Child," Father murmured. "What would you say?"

"The master trader also sent that he wished to speak with me," Padi said slowly.

"And you were naturally wondering what the tiresome fellow has to say for himself. I ask a few minutes indulgence, yet, before the master trader. I would first like you to know that Priscilla has agreed to return to the *Passage*—"

Padi jerked upright.

"She *has*?"

"Well you might be astonished. But, yes, she has agreed that it is prudent to have a wellness examination done by our Healer and our medic. Once we know how matters stand with her and the child, we will see what further decisions must be made."

He paused, one eyebrow lifting somewhat.

"Now, I believe we must have the master trader. For you see, Trader Padi, Captain Mendoza's capitulation came with a price. She—rightly!—pointed out that her lifemate had taken severe wounds which had not healed by the time we raised Colemeno. She also pointed out that, upon discovering the exhilarating effects of the ambient, her lifemate—unwisely, perhaps, but understandably—chose to operate with his shields open, at the same time the master trader embarked on an ambitious course of preliminary market evaluation."

He paused. Padi became aware that she had been holding her breath, and filled her lungs.

The master trader extended his hand, palm down, and rocked it back and forth.

"These facts, combined with the information that Colemeno's ambient conditions act as a constant systemic stress, has made Captain Mendoza anxious regarding her lifemate's health. As she put it—very succinctly, so I thought at the time!—'We do not know if the ambient heals.'"

Padi stared at him.

"But—are we giving up on Colemeno? The inventory—"

"Tut, tut, Trader yos'Galan, where are your wits? Of course we're not giving up on Colemeno. The inventory, as you point out, has only just begun, and I assure you that it was not invoked in a spirit of play."

"No, sir, of course not," Padi said, "but—"

He raised his hand, the master trader's amethyst glinting.

"I anticipate you, I think. I did pledge myself to assist *Qe'andra dea'Tolin*. I have discussed the situation with her, and she assures me that she will have help aplenty, and has released me from my promise."

"Oh," Padi said inelegantly. Her heart was racing, but her brain was curiously bemired, as if it could not quite draw a conclusion, when it was perfectly obvious that Father and Priscilla were going back to the *Passage* and the master trader was—

"You can't be leaving *me* in charge of the trade mission!" she exclaimed.

The master trader looked abashed.

"Your pardon, Trader. I ought to have first inquired if you are ill or incapacitated. I ask you to forgive my lapse, and put these questions now before you. Please do honor me with your usual frankness."

Padi glared at him.

"I am perfectly well—*more* than perfectly well, sir! But you must recall that I have only very recently come to wear the garnet. Colemeno is my first experience of trade missions and opening a new port. A whole port inventory is, is—a textbook exercise to me!"

"As it once was to me," the master trader said soothingly. "I learned the particulars in the field, when Master Trader Er Thom was moved to explore Jitsu as a potential hub."

Padi blinked.

"Jitsu? Jitsu isn't a hub."

"No, it's not," the master trader agreed. "Its inadequacies were revealed by the whole port inventory."

"Was Master Er Thom very put out?"

"Disappointed, certainly. Jitsu did look likely from a moderate distance, and it would have solved several knotty transshipping problems. He went on to open Vanilette as a hub, and solved the freight-transfer difficulties by buying into one of the bounce stations at Ebra's Pearls, for the cost of upgrades."

He moved a big hand.

"I, the garnet new on my finger, learned from Jitsu, as did Master Er Thom. It is my expectation that you will learn from Colemeno. I do allow that we are somewhat shorter on staff than we were on Jitsu, but the concepts and the protocols remain the same. Now, as then, we are fortunate in our team, and I anticipate..."

He paused, casting a glance upward, as if searching for storm clouds in the bright sky.

"I anticipate that there is *no more chance than usual* of something going amiss," he said, meeting her eyes.

Padi took a breath.

"That is not," she said, "very comforting."

"It was meant for honesty. You seem alarmed, Trader. I wonder—ah! I see what it is! You are concerned that you will be flying alone! Nothing could be further from my intent. You must know that, while I repose the greatest confidence in you, and know you to be the equal of any challenge, I will not leave you bereft of both my person *and* my advice. It would be quite unlike me to withhold my advice, would you say?"

Padi met his eyes.

"In fact, it would be wholly unlike you," she agreed, beginning to feel more settled in herself.

The master trader smiled.

"I think it only fair to warn you that I will want detailed reports, according to a schedule that we will have in place before the luncheon meeting. Understand me, Trader Padi—I will expect you to discuss your actions and the reasons for those actions in depth. In return, I promise I will not hold shy of sharing my experience, my opinions, and my necessities with you."

Padi closed her eyes, quickly reviewing a piloting exercise meant to impart calm in stressful situations.

Opening her eyes, she said, "That is *somewhat* more comforting."

"I exist to solace you, Trader Padi."

"Yes, certainly, but—"

"Do *you* wish to give up Colemeno, Trader?"

"No, sir, I do not!"

"It pleases me to hear you say so. Whom do you propose to stand as Trader-in-Charge in the absence of the master trader, if not yourself?"

And that was the question, wasn't it? Padi thought. Put thus, it, too, was rather comforting.

"There is only me," she admitted.

"Why, yes. How perceptive of you. Have we an accord?"

Padi sighed, and extended her hand, palm up.

"Master Trader, we do."

"Excellent," he said, and placed his palm against hers.

"I propose that we remove to your office to formulate a detailed plan, so that we may present an orderly transfer at the luncheon meeting."

The master trader sat back.

"Priscilla and I will be going up to the *Passage* this evening, which I do realize is rather soon," Father said. "However, neither the captain nor the master trader is in much demand at the moment. Lady Selph will return to the *Passage* with us."

"No," Padi said. "No, please leave her."

"She does miss her cuddle, you know, which she might have seen as a fair trade, had there been new contacts available to her. To be confined to a cage, no matter how splendid, and all alone—it must be dreadfully flat for her."

"Yes, I see, but—there is someone who may be in need of her counsel." She took a breath. "Ribbon Dance Village has come to stand guardian over two children, orphaned. The kin that remain to them are more interested in gaining their property than caring for them. They have all their lives been attended by a norbear, and the village wishes to—honor his rights. Lady Selph may be able to assist norbear, village, and the children, too. I would like to put the problem to her, and see if she has an interest. If she would rather return to the ship, then of course, she should go."

"I see. By all means, place the matter before her."

"Also, I have undertaken to build a search regarding norbear sentience for Tekelia," Padi continued. "Tekelia will sort the results."

"...and will come to stand as an elder before the sorting is through. Norbears are a...complicated subject."

"I had feared as much," Padi admitted, and looked up into the tame and Ribbonless sky.

"It is very pleasant out here," she said. "However, if you are leaving tonight—"

"Yes. There is work before us."

They had repacked the basket, and were turning toward the door before Padi recalled one other piece of business.

"Father, I have something for you," she said, pulling the blue-and-green stone coaster out of her pocket.

He received it with both brows well up.

"Truth told, I never thought to see this again," he said. "Where did you find it?"

"I sent it to Tekelia," Padi said, and moved her shoulders. "Tekelia says that they must have been close in my thoughts, and offers that the ambient very often operates in such a way."

"The ambient," he murmured, slipping the coaster away into his pocket.

"Had Tekelia any insight regarding how the ambient might have invaded the *Passage* while it was yet some distance from Colemeno?"

"No, sir."

"Well," said Father. "That's encouraging."

On-Grid
The Sakuriji

. . . .

MAJEL SLIPPED INTO HIS SEAT AT THE COUNCIL TABLE, THE LAST
to arrive. Despite three cups of wake-up, he was feeling...some-
what less than alert.

Worse, it was the Council of Claims this morning, which
he found a challenge even on a good day. He was, in his off-
hours, reading the minutes of previous Claims meetings, but as
a new councilor, he was not—could not be—conversant with
precedent, law, or when—and why!—it was permissible to vary
from precedent. In fact, he, with azieEm, was more a spectator
at the Council of Claims than a participant. Most often, he had
a headache by the time the session was finished.

Today, for a novelty, he had a headache before the session
had begun.

"Let the record show that all councilors are present to review
current claims and petitions," Council Chair gorminAstir stated.
The bell rang, silver-bright. Majel winced.

"We have before us a petition from the kezlBlythe family to
find xinRood a failed Line, and an accompanying petition, that
xinRood's assets be transferred to kezlBlythe, last of kin."

She looked up from her screen.

"These petitions were filed at the municipal level, and the City
Council ought to have handled them. However, the city chose to
send both to the Council of the Civilized for resolution, citing
the kezlBlythe's standing as one of the foremost families in the
city and Civilization. In short, the City Council did not feel itself
able to rule appropriately on these petitions."

That was rather odd, Majel thought, leaning back in his chair.
The kezlBlythe were a force in Haven City; one could hardly do

any kind of business without bumping into them or their interests. Still, there were other prominent families and cooperatives, and the City Council did not hold shy of judging them appropriately. Or so one hoped. Why should—

"Quite right," seelyFaire said briskly. "The kezlBlythe deserve the honor of having their petitions reviewed at the highest level. They *are* a prominent family and Civilization owes them much."

Majel blinked, his gaze crossing that of the Warden, who looked similarly amazed, and just as worn down as Majel felt.

"All honor to the kezlBlythe," azieEm said in her soft voice, "but surely the City Council has precedent to guide them. The law must apply equally to all."

That was encouraging line of thought. Majel made a note to seek azieEm out and get to know her better.

"Sometimes there are compelling reasons to sidestep precedent," seelyFaire said. "Doubtless, the City Council saw that this was one of those instances, and did not wish to be perceived by other prominent families as having a preference."

"If the City Council should not have preferences," azieEm persisted, "how much less should the Council of the Civilized have preferences?"

"The Council of the Civilized exists *precisely* because sometimes, there is reason to circumvent precedent."

"I see that Councilor seelyFaire has given some thought to this matter," Chair gorminAstir said, dryly. "Have all present read the petitions under discussion?"

A general wave of assent flowed 'round the table.

"The petition to find that xinRood has failed seems to me precipitate," said ivenAlyatta. "Observably, the Line has *not* failed. There are two children, both in good health."

"And Haosa," tryaBent growled. "Proof enough of failed genes."

"Is it established that the children are alive and healthy?" Portmaster krogerSlyte asked.

"Yes," said the Warden. "I saw them myself very recently. We had tea and spoke of their mother."

"Clearly then, the children are the proper holders of the property left by their parent," said azieEm, her timidity overcome by what appeared to be outrage. She turned to the Chair. "Chair gorminAstir, I ask for instruction: Why were these petitions not dismissed at the municipal level?"

"I suspect it may be as Counselor seelyFaire suggested—that the City Council feared being seen as partisan."

Majel blinked. So, the City Council was protecting itself? That was not altogether unbelievable. The kezlBlythe *were* known to be sharp in their practice of business, and those who sat on the City Council were themselves in business. As were some of those who sat on the Council of the Civilized.

tryaBent, for instance, was old in textiles, and enjoyed the custom of the elite families. Which made it doubly interesting that she spoke now.

"If the remaining xinRood are among the Haosa, they have no need of whatever might be left of the family fortune. The Haosa live communally."

"They do," said the Warden, "but communities need funds to survive."

"Why should the xinRood fortune fund the Haosa, when kezlBlythe will invest in Civilization?"

"It would do no harm," seelyFaire said, as one granting a major concession, "to give the children a stipend so that they may buy themselves comfort off-Grid."

"Nor would it do any *harm*," the Warden said, very cold and precise, "to admit that the petitions have no merit, follow well-established precedent and deny them."

"Of course the petitions have merit! They would not have been filed if the petitioners did not believe their case had merit!" seelyFaire was playing at being aghast, Majel thought, with her hand pressed to chest. "And as for partisanship, Warden, it is well known that you have been stalking the kezlBlythe for years. Have you found any evidence of wrongdoing?"

There was a long silence. seelyFaire smiled.

"You have not," she said, with satisfaction. "Now, the Council may decide the amount of the stipend, and—"

"I propose—" Majel raised his hand.

"I am speaking!" seelyFaire snapped.

"Yes, but *I* am interested," said the council chair. "What is your motion, Councilor ziaGorn?"

"I move that the precedents be entered into the record," Majel said.

Silence greeted this, then ivenAlyatta laughed softly.

"Second."

"This is a waste of time," said seelyFaire.

"Only a matter of good housekeeping," said Portmaster kroger-Slyte. "Third."

"I call the vote," said gorminAstir crisply. "Those in favor of entering the precedents for finding a failed Line and for redistributing the property of Lines found to have failed into the records of this proceeding, raise your hand."

It carried, with only seelyFaire and tryaBent voting against.

Five minutes later the next motion, to deny both petitions, put forth by ivenAlyatta, also passed, along the same lines.

Majel sighed and sat back in his chair, unaccountably relieved.

He noticed that his head wasn't hurting any more.

Colemenoport
Wayfarer

. . . .

THE LUNCHEON MEETING HAD GONE WELL. NO ONE HAD DEMANDED
to know if the master trader was feeling *quite* himself, or suggested
that, perhaps, Trader yos'Galan was, just a bit ... inexperienced.
Indeed, everyone behaved as if the entire preposterous undertaking
was quite in the usual way, Trader yos'Galan entirely capable, and
themselves perfectly satisfied with the new arrangements.

After the meeting, Padi went to her room to speak with
Lady Selph.

Dowager on knee, Padi related the story of the norbear guardian, his two charges, and their deplorable kin. She had the sense
that Lady Selph absorbed this history with great seriousness, and
was inclined to the cause of the other norbear.

"The norbear's name is Eet," Padi finished, handing Lady
Selph a slice of fruit. "Tekelia particularly hoped that you would
be willing to speak with him."

Lady Selph indicated that she would be pleased to do so.

"Well, but there is this other thing," Padi said apologetically.
"Father and Priscilla are returning to the *Passage* this evening.
They know that you are lonely, a little, away from your cuddle,
and they have offered to take you with them. Of course I will
miss—"

Lady Selph *harrumphed*—at least Padi heard something very
like "harrumph" inside her head.

"Do I take that to mean you would rather stay?" she asked
humbly.

Lady Selph allowed it to be known that this was so. Padi
obviously needed her. Also, she was interested in getting to know
Tekelia better. As for Eet the norbear—it could very well be that

he would benefit from shared dreaming, and she therefore professed her willingness to travel to his location.

"Tekelia will be pleased to bring Eet to you," Padi told her, trying not to think of Lady Selph escaping onto Colemeno.

Lady Selph gave as her opinion that Tekelia was an excellent person. Further, she was pleased to find that Padi thought so, as well.

An image of a broad red ribbon formed in the place in her head where norbear communication happened. Bright and brash, it was threaded through a tapestry already bold with color, and rich with associations. Lady Selph's admiration of the red ribbon expressed itself in a purr.

Padi blinked, and leaned slightly forward, as if that would help her see more clearly.

"I—is that *me*?" she asked, remembering how she had Seen Vanz's pattern, in Healspace.

Lady Selph admitted that it was, indeed, her, and much more pleasing than previously. When Padi yos'Galan had first caught the attention of Lady Selph's cuddle in the pet library, her pattern had been unsettling—there came a flash behind Padi's eyes, of the same brilliant tapestry, but constricted, whole sections knotted up with iron-grey thread, and the rest beginning to show signs of pulling—of unraveling.

Padi caught her breath.

"As bad as that?" she murmured, and felt Lady Selph pat her wrist.

She was given to know that Padi yos'Galan was well on her way to becoming a properly integrated person, and that Lady Selph trusted that she would continue to improve herself, so that one day she might also teach.

That did seem...unlikely, Padi thought, and caught the impression of a sniff from Lady Selph.

Padi grinned.

"If you will return to your residence," she said formally, "I will let Father know that you have decided to stay, in an advisory capacity."

Lady Selph allowed herself to be placed on the approach to her abode, and ambled back within. Padi pressed the lock, and got up to give Father Lady Selph's decision.

✳   ✳   ✳

"Hello, Padi," Priscilla said, looking up from the screen in the common room. "Looking for Shan?"

"In fact, I am—" Padi changed course, to perch on the chair at Priscilla's right. "Is he engaged?"

"He's resting," Priscilla said. "Is it something I can help with?"

"Yes. I've spoken with Lady Selph. She's decided to remain here, to advise Eet the norbear, and to flirt with Tekelia."

"That sounds like an enjoyable curriculum," Priscilla murmured, reaching to her screen and tapping it twice before she turned in her chair to face Padi. "I could almost be persuaded to stay, myself."

"Only then Father wouldn't go to the *Passage*," Padi said. "This *is* about getting Father to the *Passage*, isn't it?"

"It's about getting your father a medical check-up, yes," Priscilla said, unperturbed. "It's fortunate that he gave me a bargaining chip."

Padi laughed.

"Has he realized that?"

Priscilla raised her eyebrows.

"He *is* a master trader."

Padi blinked.

"That's disturbing."

"I'd say *prudent*, myself. He does have a good understanding of his faults."

Padi laughed.

Priscilla tipped her head, and gave Padi one of those narrowed glances that meant she was looking beyond the physical world.

"May I be insufferably rude?" she asked.

"I'd like to see that," Padi said with a grin.

"I'll take that as a yes. I See that you've acquired a bright new connection, which is already rude, you know. I might not be able to help Seeing it, but mentioning it without having permission to Look isn't done."

"Lina gave me that lesson," Padi said. "By coincidence, Lady Selph just showed me my...my life-tapestry, with the red ribbon woven in. I'll prevent you from committing another rudeness by telling you it's a token from Tekelia. Lady Selph approves, but, then, she's sweet on Tekelia."

"Lady Selph is an excellent judge of character," Priscilla said. "Now, I'll tell you that this ribbon puzzles me. It's connected to your core—I mean to say that it's an integral part of you. It doesn't seem to be a lifemating, but I'll admit that it's difficult for me to See clearly here. I wonder if you'd tell me what it *is*."

Padi stared at her for a long moment, during which she felt a whisper of affection, and received the suggestion that Tekelia might come to her.

She did not do anything so gross as say, "No," but merely let it be known, as Lady Selph might do, that she was well enough.

"Padi?"

She took a breath.

"We went to the Ribbon Dance," she said slowly. "In retrospect, I was likely what is known locally as Ribbon-drunk. I rose into the air, the better to be among the ambient. From there, I asked Tekelia to dance with me, and offered a ribbon—"

She paused, frowning, seeing the moment again, and feeling her Gift warm.

"I believe that the ribbon I offered was—me. *Of* me." She moved a hand, impatiently. "Lavender. Tekelia offered a ribbon in turn—crimson, as you See—asking if I would dance."

She raised her eyes to meet Priscilla's warm, dark gaze.

"We each accepted the other's ribbon, and—we danced."

Priscilla nodded, but said nothing.

Padi sighed.

"We're—there's an—awareness. Not unpleasant, or intrusive. Something like talking with a norbear." She smiled suddenly. "Only not as bossy."

Priscilla laughed.

"I understand that you've made a formal connection with Tekelia," she said.

"And you'll tell Father so?" Padi asked shrewdly.

"Of course," Priscilla said serenely.

"I will find out how formal," Padi said. "It—didn't occur to me to ask, last evening."

"Who thinks of such things in the middle of a party?" Priscilla asked, and tipped her head. "Would you like a glass of wine?"

"Do you know?" Padi said. "I think that I would."

On-Grid
Haven City
Judiciary Center

. . . .

THIS HAD PROBABLY NOT BEEN A GOOD IDEA, TRADER ISFELM reflected, as she took the lifter to the fourth floor.

On the other hand, having decided to preserve *Ember*'s honor, like the starry fool she was, that beside having taken a strong and everlasting dislike to Jorey kezlBlythe over the course of a five-minute comm conversation, what remained to her was planetary law, Zatorvia xinRood having been a fully Civilized citizen of Colemeno.

It had taken her some time with the directories to find the right office, and then some back-and-forth with various of the denizens, until it was decided, by the fourth paper pilot, that it would be best if she came in person, with documentation, and the amount to be refunded.

So, here she was, in full trade dress, case in hand, pledged to meet a paper pilot who was going to probably charge her a fee to give the determination that the refund belonged to Jorey kezlBlythe.

You're a fool, Chudi Isfelm, she told herself, as she came up to a door bearing the legend, DEATH DUTY, INHERITANCE, AND POST MORTEM PAYMENTS.

She did consider turning on her heel and walking away. The money could be set against ship's ops.

Only—even standing in this strange hall, facing a sign that fair shouted wasted time and fees levied—it didn't sit right with her. Zatorvia had two children, as she'd learned from rummaging around in various public databases. The passage fee was considerable. Happen the kids could put it to good use.

"Right, then," she said, and pushed the door open.

On-Grid
The Wardian

. . . .

BENTAMIN CARRIED A GLASS OF WINE WITH HIM INTO THE WIN-
dowed alcove that, like Aunt Asta's, one floor up, looked out over
the city, and the street below.

The Wardian was tall, the apartments situated in the upper
floors, so that the view swept over lesser structures, all the way
out to the horizon line, where the ambient broke against the edge
of the Grid in a constant chromatic barrage.

Beautiful, violent, and ever-changing. The ambient, that had
divided them into Us and Other, as surely as the old world had
done.

Bentamin sighed, and sipped his wine.

It came to him—had come to him during the meeting of the
Claims Court, even as seelyFaire had accused him of persecut-
ing the kezlBlythe—that he was no longer fit to be the Warden
of Civilization.

He examined the thought as he might examine any piece of
evidence—coldly, and with more attention to fact than feeling.
The untamed ambient continued to storm the Grid's edge, but
Bentamin's Sight was turned inward.

Finally, he stirred, lifted the glass and drank his wine off in
one quick gulp.

seelyFaire was correct, coming and going. He was partisan.
It was his duty as Warden to guard Civilization against such
errors as the kezlBlythe represented. Worse, he shared with his
mother the belief that the Haosa and the Civilized were one
people divided by—*a method*. Both Civilized and Haosa used
the ambient. What difference if the Civilized built tools, while
the Haosa did not need them?

His mother had not hoped to see a Haosa sitting on the Council in her lifetime, but she *had* thought that Bentamin would see it. He had shared that optimistic goal, especially after Durella vinsEbin had clawed her way onto the Council and blocked every effort to restore the patronage system, gathering such allies as krogerSlyte, targElmina, and the late montilSin to her side.

And perhaps the Haosa *might* have seen a councilor installed. He had been hoping to persuade Tekelia to sue for an advisory seat, as the Speaker of the Haosa government. Such as it was.

Though the patronage wars were alive with seelyFaire and tryaBent, still Bentamin thought he might have managed to see a Haosa seated, if not voting, on the Council. krogerSlyte had been receptive, and ivenAlyatta. One didn't quite know what to make of azieEm, but she had not outright rejected the idea. Though recently seated, Majel ziaGorn showed signs of being an ally worth having—

Then the Reavers arrived.

Civilization credited the Haosa with having vanquished the Reavers, the existence of Shan yos'Galan having not yet come to Colemeno's attention. It should have been the perfect time to see a fully-invested Haosa councilor seated.

But the demise of the Reavers, while largely acknowledged to be a satisfactory outcome, had the unfortunate effect of reminding Civilization that the Haosa were—

Dangerous.

Even ivenAlyatta, the most liberal among the seated councilors, had suggested that it might be wise to "wait a bit."

And, now that seelyFaire had cast out the idea that the Warden of Civilization was *partisan*—the wait became longer still.

No, he corrected himself. The wait became interminable.

seelyFaire had done damage—real damage, and he had no doubt she had intended to do so.

He was no longer an asset, to the Council or to Civilization, which he was sworn to protect.

He was a liability.

And he was not only a liability to goals long held dear. He was a liability to Aunt Asta.

The more liberal councilors might, indeed, allow the Oracle to retire. But not even the most liberal would allow her to leave the protection of the Wardian. She was not safe for the Civilization she had worked to protect for so many years. He thought he might have been able, before, to argue that she be allowed to go to the Haosa, though it would have been tricky. The Oracle had Seen secrets, after all, and it could not be supposed that she had forgotten them.

Bentamin sighed. In two days, Asta was to go to the Council for her reprimand. She would, he thought, do herself no good by speaking her mind, as she doubtless would do. gorminAstir was tolerant, especially of those who had done duty unstintingly, but her patience had a limit.

No, Bentamin thought, it would be best for Aunt Asta if she did not meet with the Council.

He could, at least, arrange that.

On-Grid
Haven City

. . . .

JES WAS PUTTING THE RIDE TO THEIR APPOINTMENT AT THE
Haven City Business Association to use by quizzing Mar Tyn
on the study material he had completed. He had come to expect
this of her, and owned that he would have been disappointed,
had she not turned to his lessons.

In fact, he had only last night finished Module Five: Balance
sheets and financial statements. Before he began, he had felt
himself on firm ground. After all, Dyoli had him busy notating
profit-and-loss statements submitted by on-port businesses. So
great was his confidence, that he opened the module rather late
in the evening.

As he should have expected, the form was more nuanced
than the relatively simple task Dyoli had given him had revealed.
He stayed up behind-time in order to wrest the last bit of
understanding from the material, and had been pleased that the
rescheduled breakfast meeting had given him time to reread,
and take the self-test.

He was beginning to find the material challenging, but much to
his own surprise, that only made him more determined to become
its master. If he had considered the matter at all, he would have
predicted that he would become disheartened as the work grew
more demanding, and eventually fail to open the next module.

But here—Master Trader yos'Galan, Dyoli, and Jes herself were
perfectly convinced that he could—that he *would*—complete the
course, take the certification tests, and stand up as an accountant. It was as if their belief in this outcome buoyed him, and
lent him resolve.

So it was that he was in the middle of discussing the derivation

of income statements from raw balance sheets, when his Gift...
shivered.

His voice died in his throat, and he could swear he saw
sparkling ribbons dancing away into the future, and...fading.

"Mar Tyn?" Jes said, her voice sharp enough to gain his attention, but the fit had passed; the ribbons dissolved. He turned to
look at her.

"My Gift stirred," he said. Of course, Jes knew he was a Luck,
but he thought that she did not apprehend the whole of it. Very
few did, after all.

"Are you in pain?" she asked.

"No. It was a momentary sensation, gone now. I suppose
it might have simply been a...reaction to the"—he waved his
hand in an arc over his head—"conditions. Forgive me for being
distracted."

"I understand that it is a distracting circumstance," Jes said,
and awarded him her half-smile. "At least that much. I depend
upon you to tell me if you require assistance, and what would
best serve you. I am not at all Gifted, as you know, but I will
do my best."

"I thank you," Mar Tyn said, genuinely touched. "I will tell
you, if I am able to do so, if I should require assistance."

She looked at him askance, and he braced himself for an
inquiry regarding what his Gift may have *done*, precisely, but all
she said was, "You were discussing financial statements, for our
mutual edification. Pray continue."

"*Qe'andra* dea'Tolin." The receptionist rose from behind her
desk, her hands clasped before her breast; her demeanor anxious.

"Chair tayKorat is desolate that he cannot keep to the agreed-
upon time, but an emergency has called him away. He wishes
you to know that he would have missed you for nothing less. He
commends you to Sub-Chair hanEsis, who is extremely knowledgeable. The Sub-Chair is available and—"

"And will be pleased to assist the *qe'andras*," a new voice
stated from Mar Tyn's right.

He turned to see a woman in business dress, her pale hair cut
so short that it stood up from her head like a brush. A cluster
of gemstones glittered in her right ear.

She inclined from the waist in the Colemeno style.

"Pinfer hanEsis at your service."

Jes inclined, likewise in the Colemeno style.

"Jes dea'Tolin, *qe'andra* in service of the Tree-and-Dragon Trade Mission." She straightened and moved a hand in Mar Tyn's direction. "One's apprentice, Mar Tyn pai'Fortana."

"I am honored, *Qe'andras*. I will do my utmost to answer every question, and to find those answers that I may lack, and deliver them to you."

"That is exactly what I was hoping for," Jes assured her, and the other woman smiled.

"Then, please, come with me to the meeting room, and I will be honored to do my best for you."

"As you may have heard," Jes said, after they had been properly seated, the tea served and the cake offered, "the trade mission has undertaken to do a whole port inventory. To accomplish this within the master trader's timeline, we will need assistance, which I hope to hire from city-based firms."

"I will be pleased to make recommendations and supply introductions," Sub-Chair hanEsis said. "I will need a specific list of tasks and the master trader's timeline."

"Yes, of course. However, the master trader entrusted me with a specific inquiry regarding a firm in the city which was recommended to him. I wonder if we might address that first, so that it is not forgotten in the larger discussion."

"Certainly. What is the name of the firm that was brought to the master trader's attention?"

"kezlBlythe," Jes said, and picked up her teacup.

Mar Tyn saw Sub-Chair hanEsis—flinch, her eyes narrowing, and her mouth pinching tight. He was not entirely certain that Jes had seen that reaction—or no, she must have done, because she put her cup aside and tipped her head slightly in that way she had when something *interesting* had happened.

"You know of this firm?" she asked.

"Of course, everyone is aware of the kezlBlythe," Sub-Chair hanEsis said, recovering herself somewhat. "To call them a firm, however . . . more properly, they are a network, operating under private oversight. The overseeing association does have a membership in our organization, and I can of course supply contact details."

"Thank you," Jes said. "I will see that the master trader receives that information."

She leaned forward slightly, and smiled her professional smile.

"Now, we come to the meat of the matter," she said, sounding almost gay. It was not her usual mode when addressing business, but Mar Tyn saw it have an effect on the woman across the table. Her tension vanished entirely, replaced by an answering gaiety, and Mar Tyn wondered if, despite her protests, Jes might not have a Gift.

"Pursuit of a whole port inventory requires that all businesses on-port provide financials, stock inventory, specialties, and, in the case of Colemeno, any trade records from the time before Rostov's Dust interjected itself. What we need are knowledgeable, working accountants to accept our collated data, crunch our numbers, and generate reports to our specifications on, I will be frank, a very tight deadline."

Jes paused to sip tea.

"Historically, it has been Master Trader yos'Galan's preference to—"

The door to the meeting room opened abruptly. Sub-Chair hanEsis started, and Mar Tyn felt his own muscles tense. Jes dea'Tolin merely glanced up, as cool as a glass of water.

A man entered the room hastily, his complexion high, and his smile too wide. Mar Tyn felt a flicker along nerves long attuned to his Gift, but it subsided without acting upon him.

"*Qe'andra* dea'Tolin!" the newcomer exclaimed, with an extravagant bow. "My apologies, most profound! To have kept you waiting for me—inexcusable, I know it, and yet I beg your indulgence."

"*Qe'andras,*" Sub-Chair hanEsis said, with restraint, "allow me to make you known to Calven tayKorat, Chief of the Haven City Business Association." She looked to the man in the doorway.

"Sir, here are *Qe'andras* dea'Tolin and pai'Fortana, from the Tree-and-Dragon Trade Mission."

"Yes, yes, of course," the man said, coming forward and pulling out the chair directly across from Jes. "Again, Qe'andra dea'Tolin, my apologies."

"There is not the slightest need to apologize," Jes told him. "Sub-Chair hanEsis has been most helpful. We had been discussing the need for reputable firms to accept data from us, and refine it to our specifications."

"Hah. Quite a bit of data, I'm thinking, if you're collecting from every vendor and manufacturing interest on-port. I will not mince words, *Qe'andra* dea'Tolin—you want to contact the kezlBlythe Association and enter into a working agreement with them. They have an extensive network, and a great deal of weight in the city's business—"

"Indeed, sir, I was just telling Sub-Chair hanEsis of Master Trader yos'Galan's preferences. He prefers his team to work with small, reputable independents. We are not in need of weight in the city, merely trained professionals, whom we will pay at their established rates. Sub-Chair hanEsis was about to generate a list of such firms for me, as I understand it?"

Sub-Chair hanEsis blinked, then inclined her head. "It will take only a moment, *Qe'andra.*"

"But that's not at all necessary," Chair tayKorat said, leaning across the table, one hand sliding forward, as if he would actually place it on Jes's wrist. She picked up her cup, and he withdrew his hand.

"The kezlBlythe Association can receive your data at one point, distribute it and your instructions throughout their network, then collect and compile the results as you desire. You must see that such a system will save you time and effort. I have heard that the master trader's timeline is short—"

"It is ambitious," Jes said calmly, "but not unreasonable." She put her cup down, and folded her hands neatly on the table, out of range, Mar Tyn noted, of Chair tayKorat's reach.

"As to the kezlBlythe Association, sir, you represent them well, and they sound most efficient. However, they do not meet the master trader's specifications."

The man smiled, and leaned forward confidentially.

"As to that, surely the *qe'andra* in charge of a whole port inventory may decide for herself what will serve the mission best. All honor to the master trader, and absolutely his deadline must be met. But surely his preferences regarding details are secondary to your own?"

Mar Tyn did not snort. Or laugh.

Jes preserved a perfectly calm face.

"A master trader's preference is never whimsical," she said solemnly. "But in the case, the Accountant's Guild recommends the precise approach I have described as optimum."

Chair tayKorat was seen to wilt slightly.

In that moment of relative peace, Sub-Chair hanEsis pulled a data-key from her screen, and stood to offer it to Jes.

"Here is the list you requested, *Qe'andra* dea'Tolin," she said, "with ratings, specialties, and rates. If there is anything else—"

Jes stood, and Mar Tyn did, too, on the principle that business was done, and that it was best to be gone before Chair tayKorat recruited another argument, or asked for the return of the data-key.

"Thank you," Jes said, handing the key to Mar Tyn. "I appreciate your assistance. We will leave you to your work, now, Sub-Chair hanEsis."

She stepped away from the table, and the Sub-Chair came around to accompany them. At the door, Jes turned and bowed in the Colemeno mode.

"Chair tayKorat, I am pleased to have met you, sir."

"*Qe'andra.*" He rose and bowed. "If I may assist you in any way, or if, after all you will wish an introduction to the kezlBlythe Association, only call me."

They were back in the car and on the return route to the port before Jes looked at Mar Tyn, her expression speculative.

"It was very fortunate, I think, that we were able to meet with Sub-Chair hanEsis prior to Chair tayKorat's arrival," she said blandly.

Mar Tyn took a deep breath, recalling that moment when his Gift had shivered, and the dancing, sparkling ribbons.

"Yes," he agreed, "that was Luck, indeed."

Off-Grid
The Tree House

. . . .

THE COMM CHIMED.

Tekelia looked up from the screen with a frown. Comm calls were something of a rarity, and usually presaged an emergency.

Chest tight, Tekelia rose, crossed the room, and touched the receive switch.

"Yes?"

"Tekelia!" Aunt Asta's voice was positively brilliant. "I'm glad I caught you at home. Could you come to me, please?"

Tekelia glanced over a shoulder, to the screen and the letter from Blays, Visalee Village's Counsel to Chaos. There was much to think about in that letter, and while an answer would have to be made soon, it was by no means urgent.

"Shall I come to you *now*?" Tekelia asked.

Aunt Asta laughed.

"*Now* would be perfect. I'm in the library."

The library table held two large, and three smaller, cases, a tea service, and a tin of Entilly's cookies.

Aunt Asta was sitting by the tea service. At Tekelia's arrival, she smiled, and picked up the pot to pour.

"There you are, dear! Sit, refresh yourself, and tell me about your lover."

Tekelia paused in the act of pulling out a chair to consider her.

"Did you bring me here *now* in order to pry into my affairs?"

"Not at all, dear," Aunt Asta said placidly. She placed the full cup, poured another, and looked up.

"Tekelia, do not *loom*. I do indeed have a use for you, but I thought we might indulge in gossip over tea."

337

"Before we get to the heart of the matter. I see." Tekelia sat down, and tasted the tea, deliberately not looking at those cases.

"Who told you that I had a lover?"

Aunt Asta beamed.

"Why, Bentamin, of course. He said you *glow*, and I see that he did not exaggerate! One of the traders, I think?"

Tekelia sighed. "I wonder if Bentamin can be persuaded to take a lover, so we could gossip about him."

"That will be a worthy topic, when it occurs." Aunt Asta pushed the cookie tin forward. "However, it has not yet occurred. Until it does, we may talk about *your* lover."

Laughing, Tekelia chose a cookie.

"Her name is Padi yos'Galan Clan Korval. She is brilliant and brave; thoughtful, snappish, loyal, Liaden, witty, and altogether astonishing. If I sound besotted, I am."

"I must meet her," Aunt Asta stated, sipping tea.

"I will try to arrange it. Understand, her first business is to do with the trade mission, and it keeps her twixt dance and daggers. It may be an abrupt meeting, and not long."

"That will do," Aunt Asta said, with vast serenity. "Is she a Child of Chaos?"

Tekelia swallowed the bite of cookie hastily, and washed it down with tea.

"She interacts with the ambient like a Haosa. She tells me she hasn't been Sorted. Possibly, she's too bright for her teachers to See properly."

"I may be able to help there," Aunt Asta said. "If she permits, of course."

"Of course," Tekelia said politely, setting the cup down.

"Now that we have discussed my lover—Aunt Asta, why am I here?"

"I need help moving," she said simply, and waved her hand at the cases.

"Moving where?"

"To Ribbon Dance Village—or so I hope! I tried to call Administrator poginGeist, but I was asked to leave a message."

"Arbour had business away; she'll be back in the village tonight, and would have returned your call tomorrow."

"Which may well have been too late. I have...a feeling that I ought to move—*soon*."

Tekelia sighed.

"I think you'd better tell me from the beginning."

"Yes, you're right, of course." Aunt Asta refreshed their cups. "I am retiring from my position as Oracle to the Civilized."

"Has another Oracle arisen?" Tekelia asked carefully, beginning to get a glimmer as to the reason for haste.

"Civilization no longer requires an Oracle. Let us say that I have Seen it."

Tekelia looked at her.

"Have you? Seen it?"

"I have seen that Civilization will end, and also the Haosa," Aunt Asta said, quite calmly. "But we can speak of that later. First, I must move—myself, and those things which I cannot be without. Hyuwen will pack the rest into storage."

"And you need to move before Bentamin has time to notice?" Tekelia asked. "Aunt Asta, we're in the Wardian."

"So we are," she agreed, sipping her tea. "And you came to me here, in the Wardian, because I invited you, thereby circumventing the wards."

"Very true, and entirely separate from removing you—and your cases!—*from* the Wardian."

She sighed.

"I told Bentamin that I am retiring, and that my ultimate goal is to travel. He was horrified, of course, poor child, and made the suggestion that perhaps I might retire to Ribbon Dance Village, as a sort of reflexive compromise."

"And now that you've had time to consider it, you think it's a very good notion, as a first move."

Aunt Asta smiled.

"Exactly. And it must be done before Bentamin, having likewise had time to think about it, realizes that he has given me leave to go."

Tekelia looked at her in awe.

"Aunt Asta—"

"Look at the wards," she interrupted.

But Tekelia was already examining the dense weaving of Rule and Intent that made the Wardian the impregnable fortress it was.

The weaving was exceptionally dense with regard to the Oracles, who were Talents of no inconsiderable strength. Not a few previous Oracles had objected to being imprisoned in the

Wardian, a Wild Talent at the heart of Civilization. Tekelia looked to that portion of the wards that specifically tied Aunt Asta into the Wardian—and blinked.

There was a gap—a very tiny gap, in that large and complex weaving. But there was *give.*

Tekelia could work with *give.*

"Tekelia?"

"I See it."

Tekelia rose.

"If we're to do this, then *now* is hardly soon enough. I will take you first. You may have to reconcile yourself to the loss of your cases."

"Hyuwen will put them on one of the trucks to Peck's Market, if you can't manage them, dear." Aunt Asta rose with a smile. "I did try to plan for contingencies."

"Of course you did," Tekelia murmured, considering the wards again. It was going to be tight.

But not impossible.

Stealth, however, was out of the question. Tekelia sighed. Well, so be it. Certainly Aunt Asta had earned a rest—even the Warden thought so. The give in the wards proved that.

"Just a moment, dear," Aunt Asta said. "I'll bring Entilly's cookies."

There was a small scraping sound as the lid was put on the tin. Tekelia smiled as Aunt Asta stepped near.

"You'll guest with me this evening," Tekelia said. "We'll talk to Arbour tomorrow."

"Whatever you say, dear," Aunt Asta said meekly.

Tekelia laughed, and reached for the ambient.

It took long seconds to make the connection, but eventually it came firm. Tekelia thought of the great room in the house at the edge of the trees.

Mist swirled.

The library was empty.

Colemenoport
Transient Docks

. . . .

IT WAS CHILLY ON THE DOCKS, AND THE LIGHTS PRODUCED A red glare overhead.

Shan helped Priscilla out of the car, retrieved the picnic basket, and stood with his hand on the door.

"Are you still content with your bargain, Captain?"

She raised her eyebrows.

"Are you in the habit of second-guessing your work, Master Trader?"

He huffed a laugh.

"I deserved that."

He closed the door, dismissed the car, and turned, offering his arm.

She took it, and they walked up the ramp together.

"Will you open for us?"

"Of course."

He bowed her ahead of him when the hatch opened, pausing on the threshold for a moment, looking up at the hard red glow, feeling the sweet, bright sparkle of the Gift at his core. Then, lest he seem to be hesitating, he stepped into the shuttle.

The hatch closed behind him.

Off-Grid
The Tree House

. . . .

"BUT THIS IS LOVELY!" AUNT ASTA CRIED. SHE OPENED THE COOKIE tin and held it out.

"Sit down, dear, and have a few cookies."

Tekelia was already sitting, awkwardly, on the edge of Padi's desk. The ambient glittered and shouted, as if in joyous welcome; the sudden weakness passed. Tekelia sighed, and took a cookie from the offered tin.

"Yes," said Aunt Asta, putting the tin down on the desk by Tekelia's hand. She drew a deep breath, lifting her face as if into a gentle rain.

"This . . . is beautiful," she murmured. "If I go no further, it will have been enough."

She lowered her head, and Tekelia saw tears shining in her eyes.

"Thank you, my dear. It was a heroic effort, and I ask no more from you. I can do without my cases for a few days."

"I don't think it will be as long as that," Tekelia said, taking a third cookie.

Aunt Asta tipped her head.

"No?"

"No." Tekelia sighed and stood. "I was not quiet, getting us out. I imagine Bentamin might have heard something."

"Oh," said Aunt Asta. "But—"

She was interrupted by a *thump*—really quite subdued—as a large case appeared on the floor near the bookcase.

A second thump accompanied the arrival of the second large case, neatly placed next to the first; followed in short order by two of the smaller cases.

This was followed by a tight, energetic swirl of mist that

melted quickly back into the ambient. The Warden of Civilization had arrived, carrying the last, and smallest, case.

"Bentamin!" Aunt Asta exclaimed gladly. "How thoughtful of you." She picked up the tin and walked forward to offer it. "Entilly's cookies. Please, refresh yourself."

"Thank you, Aunt Asta." Bentamin placed the case carefully by the others, chose a cookie, ate it in two bites, and reached for another. Tekelia thought he looked more worried than angry, and wondered if that was a good sign, in terms of Aunt Asta's removal from the Wardian, and, indeed, Civilization.

On the other hand, he *had* brought the cases.

"My thanks, as well, Bentamin," Tekelia said. "I couldn't quite manage it all at once, and going back wasn't possible."

"Of course not," Bentamin said. "The loophole in the wards collapsed as soon as Aunt Asta was removed." He sighed and took a third cookie.

"You might have exercised some subtlety," he said.

Tekelia laughed.

"Have you *looked* at that working? If you'd left a bigger hole, Cousin, I might have managed subtlety, but I didn't care to risk our aunt."

"You could have reduced the risk to nothing, had you left her where she was."

Tekelia blinked.

"Have another cookie, Bentamin; your thinking's still uneven. It *was* you who created that loophole, or am I blind as well as unsubtle?"

Bentamin sighed, and took another cookie, which he all but swallowed whole.

"The loophole was mine," he admitted. "Aunt Asta has earned her rest."

"And the lack of a replacement Oracle?" Tekelia said.

Bentamin looked goaded.

"Civilization does not need an Oracle," Aunt Asta said firmly.

"She Saw the end of Civilization and the Haosa," Bentamin told Tekelia. "If that is an accurate Seeing—"

Tekelia glanced at Aunt Asta.

"Long Sight is open to interpretation. Context matters, as I believe we were both reminded only recently, Bentamin."

"We were, yes. It was an apt reminder."

He threw his hands wide, and looked to Tekelia.

"Will the Haosa have her?"

"She was ours from birth. However, as Speaker for the Haosa, I must protest the Warden's new policy of casting his difficulties off-Grid. The Haosa are not your remote storage. We govern ourselves, and, just as we have no voice on the Council of the Civilized, the Council has no voice here."

Bentamin's face relaxed into a smile.

"*There* is the ferocity I value," he murmured. "I will of course make a report to the Council. They would never have let her go, but getting her back—that, as you point out, Cousin, is much more problematic."

Tekelia looked to Aunt Asta.

"The Haosa exist to be Civilization's bugbear."

"Unfortunately true," Bentamin said. "Civilization needs to find its courage."

Aunt Asta came forward, and placed a hand on Bentamin's arm.

"Tekelia is exhausted, Bentamin, and ought to rest. I will make sure of it, no fears there. In the meanwhile, do, please tell the Council what I told you."

"I intend to do precisely that, Aunt," Bentamin said, and bowed. "Good day, both."

Mist swirled, and he was gone.

Colemenoport
Transient Dock

. . . .

THE PILOTS HAD CHECKED SHUTTLE SYSTEMS, VERIFIED THEIR
equations, and notified the ship of their intention to arrive.

That done, they opened the picnic basket.

"I wonder," Shan said, after the tea had been poured and the
nut-butter sandwiches unwrapped, "if you have anything to tell
me regarding Padi's situation."

Priscilla raised her eyebrows.

"Padi is perfectly apt and capable," she said.

Shan sighed and shook his head. "I'll tell you what it is,
Priscilla, you've been spoilt by keeping company with persons
of questionable character."

"I don't think there's any *question* about your character,"
Priscilla commented, wide-eyed. "Do you?"

"Utterly ruined," Shan said mournfully. "What will I tell our
daughter?"

"I look forward to learning that."

Priscilla took a bite of her sandwich, washed it down with
tea, and smiled at him.

"I did Look, as you asked me to do," she said. "I confirm a
heart-link, but I can't confirm a lifemating. Padi allows me to
know that she and Tekelia agreed to dance together, and shared
ribbons. It being, as I was told, a Ribbon Dance."

"Of course," Shan said politely.

"Speaking of Looking," Priscilla continued. "I saw no sign of
a new strike against her shields."

"Which either means that it wasn't there, when I thought I
Saw it, but was an artifact of the ambient. Or, I suppose Tekelia
might have repaired them."

345

"Or Padi might have repaired them," Priscilla added.

"True. She is coming to good terms with her Gift, which must be counted as profit." He sighed. "I suppose that Padi will eventually allow us to know if Line or clan has obligations toward Tekelia, or Tekelia to us."

"I did get the impression that she was going to speak with Tekelia," Priscilla agreed. "Local custom..."

"Indeed," Shan said. "Local custom."

He finished his sandwich and drained his glass of tea.

"Are you wishing anything more from the basket, Pilot, or shall we file our intention to lift with the Port?"

"I believe I'm done for the moment," Priscilla said, extending a hand to touch his wrist. "It will be pleasant to be home again."

He smiled.

"So it will."

Colemenoport
Wayfarer

. . . .

THE WATERFALL WAS A DELICATE LITTLE BEAUTY. IT HAD BEEN built in a staircase design, and each of the three streams woke music in the stones.

Padi crossed the grass to the low wall, put the basket down, and leaned over to run her hand through the water, smiling at the flow of cool silk over her skin.

She looked up, seeing a glimpse of the port's red sky through the interlocking branches of the surrounding tall shrubberies, or miniature trees.

Yes, she thought. This would do.

Straightening, she shook the water from her hand as she moved two steps forward of the wall.

"Tekelia," she said.

Behind her, the water sang its pretty song. The grass rippled and the breeze stroked her cheek, wanton.

Mist swirled.

Tekelia smiled.

"Hello, Padi."

"Hello, Tekelia. Thank you for coming to me."

"Thank you for calling me. Is Captain Mendoza displeased?"

"Only curious, I think," Padi said. "I appear to have leapt before looking, again. Truly, it's becoming my defining trait. Now that I've leapt, however, I wonder if you might explain to me what it is we *did*."

"Did when?"

Padi laughed.

"There is that," she acknowledged. "The specific inquiry was in regard to our exchange of ribbons last night."

Arms out, she spun, snatching up the basket, and holding it aloft.

"I have wine, cold tea, cake, cheese, nuts, fruit, and cinnamon-fruit bread fresh from the oven. Will you share with me?"

"Gladly." Tekelia looked 'round at the dusky little glade. "Shall I fetch a blanket?"

"There's no need to exert yourself," Padi said. "There's a table, just along here, and a view that you will, perhaps, find interesting."

"By all means, lead on," Tekelia said, taking her arm.

"This is a view," Tekelia allowed. They had left the basket on the table while they approached the edge of the roof. Padi stood sensibly on the ground, but Tekelia leapt lightly to the top of the wall.

"It might be Metlin's sky, red and Ribbonless."

"I was thinking that I preferred the Ribbons, too," Padi said. "I came here first, thinking that I might see them."

"No, you won't see the Ribbons from inside Civilization," Tekelia said softly. "Though, if you're high enough, you can see the edge of the grid."

Padi spun on her heel, looking about them. "How high?"

"Oh, the Wardian," said Tekelia pointing off into the red distance. Padi leapt on the wall, bracing herself against one shoulder, and sighting along the line of Tekelia's finger.

"The tallest building in Haven City," Tekelia said.

"Is the roof accessible?" Padi wondered, and felt a ripple of amusement that wasn't... quite hers, as the shoulder moved under her hand.

"It's also the most secure building in Haven City," Tekelia added.

"Well, then," Padi said. "Perhaps not tonight."

"I agree. This day has held enough excitement for both of us, I think?"

"It certainly has for me," Padi said, dropping lightly from wall to grass. Tekelia landed beside her and they walked hand-in-hand to the table.

Padi opened the basket and laid out the little feast while Tekelia poured the wine.

When they were at last seated, leaning companionably against one another, Padi said, "If you please, Tekelia—what precisely did we accomplish in our exchange of ribbons?"

"We agreed to dance together," Tekelia said promptly. "I see now that I ought to have stopped to make certain that you hadn't only meant for the Ribbon Dance. It can be undone, but—"

"Priscilla said your link was an integral part of me, now," Padi interrupted. "It was so marked to her Inner Eyes that at first she thought we were lifemates." She met Tekelia's eyes, and said sternly, "I recently had a lesson in what the *undoing* of such links may cost. I'm guessing that *undoing* a connection so intimate that Priscilla mistook it for a lifemating, would hurt one or both of us. I don't willingly hurt you, my friend. I only wish to understand what we have between us."

Relief—again, not quite her own emotion—washed through her.

"Does it strike you as ... interesting, how quickly we became ... as we are? Are you normally so easily attached?"

"As to that, I hardly know," Padi said slowly. "Are *you*?"

"Historically? No. Though I do dance with others."

Tekelia sipped wine and set the glass aside.

"Open your Eyes."

That meant her Inner Eyes, once a proposition that made Padi acutely anxious, and might take several minutes to achieve.

She had found it a simple matter, at Tekelia's house, to open her Inner Eyes, and more difficult, under the Grid. This time, however, it was effortless, and Padi wondered if it was a matter of practice showing profit, and if it would remain so easy when she was gone from Colemeno.

Do you go—soon? Tekelia asked, but not aloud. Padi turned on the bench to stare.

"I heard that inside my head!"

"Yes, of course," Tekelia agreed, largely unsurprised. "We dance together. Now, look, do you See my pattern?"

It was impossible not to See Tekelia's pattern. Padi took a deep breath, trying to make sense of a weaving rich with emotion, afire with color, as if Tekelia contained a Ribbon Dance at their core.

"Do you See the green-and-yellow ribbon?" Tekelia asked.

Padi made an effort—and gave a small gasp of surprise as the green-and-yellow ribbon became quite apparent, as if the act of Looking had brought it forward.

"I See it," she said, and added, as certain of it as she was of her own name, "That is Geritsi."

"So it is. Can you trace it?"

Padi could, and did, noting how supple the ribbon was, how it interwove with others of the threads and ribbons that made up the tapestry that was Tekelia.

"These other ribbons—you also dance with them?"

"Quick, Padi yos'Galan," Tekelia said, approvingly. "Yes. Now, if you will find your own ribbon that you gave to me..."

It was no sooner said than she had it, boiling with an energy that was rather embarrassing, after the cool order of Geritsi's connection.

"Trace it," Tekelia murmured, but Padi's Inner Eye had already followed the lavender ribbon from the misty edges of Tekelia's tapestry to the very center, where it plunged into the heart of the weaving—and vanished.

"We are an impetuous family," Padi said, resignedly. "I think I did say so."

"And I told you that the Haosa love danger."

"We were both fairly warned."

"Look now to your pattern, if you will, and find the ribbon I gave to you..."

It was like...blinking, Padi thought. Tekelia's pattern faded, and the small bold weaving she had been shown by Lady Selph rose before her Inner Eyes.

Only—it was not so small. Rather, it was misty at the edges, very like Tekelia's pattern, and if it was less dense, the connections she did have were steadfast and tightly woven.

The crimson ribbon rose to her attention, and she followed it until it plunged into the core of her pattern, and disappeared. Into her essential self.

"The other ribbons are part of a network," she said slowly. "The ribbons we share are—"

She paused, groping for the concept—

"They are dedicated," she finished. "But what do they *do*?"

"An excellent question!" Tekelia said gaily. "I have no idea. I do agree with Captain Mendoza, that this is no lifemating—we do not make a third complete pattern between us. We are intimately connected, and complimentary, but beyond that, I know nothing more than—we dance."

"We dance," she murmured, "with each other."

"Yes," Tekelia said, and Padi felt a light touch against her cheek. "You should withdraw now, and eat. Here—"

She closed her Inner Eyes. Before her on the table, mundane sight showed her a plate filled with really too much cheese, a slice of the still-warm bread, nuts, and—a slice of cake.

"Thank you," she said, picking up a piece of cheese.

"No one wants an incident." Tekelia took a slice of cake from the tin.

"I believe I have not told you that my Aunt Asta has retired from her duty, and come to live in Ribbon Dance Village," Tekelia said. "She is staying with me for a day or two, until a suitable cottage is found."

"That happened today?"

"It did." Tekelia smiled. "It has been a full day, now that I think of it."

Padi sighed, and took up the slice of bread.

"I felt that you also had some tumult in your day," Tekelia said delicately, reaching for the bottle and refreshing their wineglasses.

"Does that disturb you? To...*feel*...me?"

"Not at all," Tekelia said, and leaned over to kiss her cheek. "It's an honor to dance with you, Padi yos'Galan." The whisper put warm breath against her ear, and Padi shivered.

"I only wonder what made your day unsettled," Tekelia asked, sitting back. "If you would care to tell me."

"Well. Father and Priscilla have decided to return to *Dutiful Passage* for medical examinations. I am therefore thrust forward as head of the trade mission, and director of the whole port inventory. That was—unexpected, and, truth told, I am still waiting for them to say that it was only a test."

"Maybe it is," Tekelia said.

"Oh, there's no doubt there! Only, I feel that they are quite serious about returning to the ship."

She paused for a sip of wine, and broke off a corner of cake.

"I spoke with Lady Selph, who is eager to interview Eet, and to deepen her connection with you. Also, I built your search and set it running. You should be warned that Father tells me you will be an elder before you finish sorting the results. Norbears, it turns out, are difficult."

Tekelia laughed.

"Yes—wholly surprising," Padi agreed.

"*You* should know," Tekelia said, "that my Aunt Asta wishes to meet you—Bentamin told her that I have a lover, and she's delighted. She also offers to Sort you, if you wish it."

Padi looked at her empty plate in puzzlement. Surely, she hadn't eaten *all* of that food? She picked up her wineglass, and looked to Tekelia.

"It's a very kind offer. If she does not find me too bright, or too stupid, I would welcome her Sorting."

"I'll tell her so," Tekelia said, glancing up at the sky—then laughing softly.

"No Ribbons to help me know the age of the night." The comment was rueful.

"I expect it's late," Padi said, rueful in turn. "I have early business, of course, and ought to retire. Will you stay?"

Tekelia sighed.

"I should like nothing better, but I should make sure that Aunt Asta hasn't done anything—rash."

Padi lifted her eyebrows.

"Is she prone?"

"She has until very recently lived both on-Grid and under the constraints of the Wardian. Today was the first time she's been off-Grid, and while hers is a Wild Talent—"

"Yes, you had best make certain that she hasn't fallen into a scrape," Padi said.

She rose, and together they repacked the basket.

Standing side by side at the edge of the roof, they looked out over the port and finished the last of the wine.

Tekelia sent the empty glasses back to the table, and turned to Padi, putting warm, firm hands on her shoulder.

"Until soon."

"Until soon." Padi leaned close to bestow her kiss.

Tekelia stepped back, Padi feeling reluctance that this time seemed to echo her own.

Mist swirled and she was alone on the roof, shivering in a breeze suddenly gone cold.

Sometime later, as she lay in bed, Padi closed her eyes, feeling Tekelia's warm glow at the center of her.

Chiat'a bei kruzon, she thought.

Dream sweetly, Tekelia answered.

Padi was still smiling when sleep took her.

On-Grid
Cardfall Casino

. . . .

MAJEL SAT BEHIND HIS DESK AND CLOSED HIS EYES.

He had spent much of his day, from very early, immersed in databases: the private member reports of mischief filed with the Citizens Coalition; reports of mischief against the Deaf recorded in the newspaper's Offenses Against Civilization, comparing the number and kind of events that went unreported; Port and City Security's response to those events that had been reported, and any fines or judgments made before each case was closed.

On a whim, he had also called up the database of Deaf-owned business, noting the recent wave of closures.

Head ringing with data strings, he had spoken, first, to Bell erVinton and Konsit joiMore. Both had agreed—reluctantly, in the case of the village administrator—that the community should be informed of the mischief that had been brought against them.

He had then spoken to the Advisory Board. They had agreed that it was prudent to call a meeting of the Citizens Coalition. The notice was being sent out even as he sat, trying to recruit himself.

Majel yawned, suddenly and prodigiously. He would be wanted on the floor in a few hours. Perhaps he should go up to his apartment and take a nap.

Another yawn overtook him.

Definitely, he should take a nap.

He had just pushed his chair back when the intercom pinged. "Principal ziaGorn, Security Head atBuro and Sensitive makEnontre are here to see you."

Majel took a breath, recalling Ander as he had last seen him, hectic and luminous.

"Of course, I will see them," he said, and settled back into his chair.

"We have the signature of the most...intense vandal," Seylin said. "We've also identified three other signatures of persons who seem to have accompanied the first. Speaker joiMore is consulting with her advisers concerning the best course of action. She is, understandably, concerned about calling in Civilized law enforcement or security teams."

"Of course," Majel said, considering Seylin closely. He read the signs of exhaustion, but there was something more, too.

"I will be happy to brief you, Principal ziaGorn, on the options open to the Speaker and her village. But, first, you should hear Ander."

Majel looked to the Sensitive, who seemed more rested than either of his elders, if rather more apprehensive. He was taller, Majel thought, and then realized that the boy was sitting up straight, rather than in his usual slump.

"Ander," Majel said gently, "are you well?"

"Principal ziaGorn." Ander cleared his throat. "I'm as well as I ever have been, here under the Grid, but now I know what it feels like to *really* be well, so it feels as if I'm—not ill. Just...dull."

Majel inclined his head. "I believe you said that your Sight was much improved at Pacazahno."

"I—yes, sir; it was. And that leads me to what I need to say. I—I'm going off-Grid. Leaving my job here. If you want me to stay until you can hire—"

"Wait." Majel held up a hand. "Ander, you don't have to—"

"I want to!" the boy burst out. "Everything was *so clear*, and I could do things—All my life, my head has been full of fog—everything at a distance, and so...difficult. Off-Grid—the fog burned off. I'm *not* stupid; I'm *not* useless. I can do what I was *meant* to do. Yferen and Challi have said I can live with them, and that the—that my cousins at Ribbon Dance Village will teach me what I need to know to make the best use of my Gifts."

Ander stopped, gulped, and finished at a whisper.

"I want that, sir."

"Of course you do," Majel said, around the knot in his own throat. "We all want to make the best use of ourselves. If you've found teachers, I have no complaint. You should, absolutely, be taught. But what I wonder is this—*must* you resign your job here at the casino? I know that you've been studying security protocols with Seylin. Are you interested in continuing with that?"

Ander bit his lip.

"I—yes, sir, I am. It's fascinating, and Seylin says I'm good at it."

"He is," Seylin put in.

"But, this other thing—I feel it has to come first."

"I understand," Majel said. "What you need to do is sort priorities."

Ander frowned.

"Sir?"

"I value your service," Majel said. "You're a good worker, attentive to detail, and you've been studying to acquire new skills. I can only believe that knowing the boundaries and shape of your Gift, and its most efficient use, will be beneficial to you—and so to me. I would like to offer you an alternative to leaving my employ. Will you hear me, or are you quite set on going?"

"No—yes! I would like to hear an alternative. Only, I don't know how long it will take—to learn my Gift."

"Understood," Majel said briskly. "What I propose is that you take a vacation—perhaps four weeks. Go to your cousins and learn whatever they can teach you. I will keep your position open, and you will draw full pay."

"It may," said Ander doubtfully, "take longer than four weeks."

"What I ask is that you come to me at the end of four weeks. We'll talk; you'll tell me of your progress, and your intentions. Perhaps by that time, you will be able to work part-time—one week on, one week off? Something of that nature. You might ultimately decide that it's best to resign from the casino and live among your cousins full-time, but there's no need to leap into chaos all at once." He smiled faintly. "The smart gambler always has a back-up line of play."

Ander's answering smile was tentative, then more assured.

"I accept your alternative, sir."

"Thank you," Majel said gravely. "When do you go to your cousins?"

"This evening. The night lorry will take me as far as Peck's Market. Yferen will meet me, and we'll go to Ribbon Dance Village together."

"You have this well in hand, then." Majel inclined his head. "Thank you for telling me your plans and for being receptive to negotiation. I look forward to seeing you in four weeks and discussing your progress and plans."

Ander's smile this time was broad. He stood and bowed.

"Thank you, sir," he said, adding in a rush, "I didn't really want to leave my job."

He turned to Seylin.

"Thank you, Seylin, for everything you've done for me."

She snorted lightly. "You do well, you get more responsibility. That's how I run *my* floor."

Ander laughed, bowed once more, and left them, the door closing quietly in his wake.

Majel looked at Seylin. Seylin looked at Majel.

"We should—" she began.

"Both get some sleep," Majel finished, firmly. "You may brief me on the options available to Pacazahno at mid-shift. I'll leave word with Nester that I'll be coming down to the floor late this evening. You may wish to leave a similar word."

"Already done," Seylin said, rising with a sigh. "You look dreadful, by the way."

"So do you," Majel said cordially.

He stood and walked around the desk, waving her ahead of him.

"Come along, old friend. Let's put our plan into action."

On-Grid
Haven City

. . . .

"DENIED!" AUNT AVRYAL REPEATED, STARING AT AUNT ZANDIR. "For what reason?"

"Precedent."

Aunt Zandir all but spat the word—in quite the rage was Aunt Zandir—and whirled to stalk down the length of the room.

"Well, the City Council is made up of fools, and always has been," Aunt Avryal said. "We'll appeal to the Upper Council."

"No, we will not! That favor has already been done for us. Finding itself unable to *appropriately rule* on our petitions, the City Council sent them on to the Council of the Civilized for resolution."

Aunt Zandir spun on her heel, stalking back up the room, anger boiling off of her.

When she reached the top of the room, where Aunt Avryal lounged, she stopped and glared down at her.

"The Council for the Civilized refused to rule xinRood a failed Line. There are two members still hale, and healthy, and living among the Haosa, thus the Line is no failure."

Aunt Avryal frowned.

"They're still alive?"

"So the judgment against us states. It seems that no one less illustrious and meddlesome than the Warden saw them only recently, spoke with them, and found them healthy and thriving."

Aunt Avryal said nothing. Aunt Zandir took a deep breath.

"The transfer of fortune was denied because the brats are still alive, and will need their assets to support them."

"Ridiculous," said Aunt Avryal. "How many trees can they possibly want to buy?"

"There wouldn't be any problem with the transfer if the brats were extinct," Jorey said from his lean against the wall.

Zandir spun.

"You! *You* are the author of this disaster, you and your too-willingness to create extinction! First Pel, then Zatorvia—there was no reason *either* needed to die. It never occurred to you that *I* had a plan! I could have put Pel to very good use. I *planned* on putting him to use! But *you* found it far more amusing to kill him.

"Gods know, Zatorvia was a weak instrument, but she was well in hand. We could have used her to our advantage, but once again I found *my plans* shattered by—you!"

She had stalked closer to the place where he leaned, her rage burning white-hot against Jorey's Gift.

"You are no longer an asset to this family. While I might support a fribble, I will not tolerate an active liability. It is inconvenient that the Council has ruled against us. However! If the brats are still alive, they may yet be of use to us."

"How can they possibly be of use to us," Aunt Avryal demanded, "off-Grid, savage, and unschool—"

"Let them settle," Aunt Zandir said, walking back toward the center of the room. "Let them form links and associations among the Haosa. Then, we'll see where our advantage lies."

She paused, her eyes narrowed in thought.

"I can *almost* See it," she murmured, and suddenly came back to herself, spinning on her heel and striding back to Jorey. He felt her Talent claw against his insides, and bit the inside of his cheek to keep from crying out.

"If you create one more difficulty for me or fail to follow your instructions in any way, I will see that you are not only Deafened again, but burnt, as well. You will be *nothing*, do you understand me?"

Her touch was white-hot; she would shrivel his lungs with her heat.

He gasped in a breath of cool air. He was not, he reminded himself, afraid of Aunt Zandir.

He was only afraid of what she could do.

"I understand," he croaked.

She stared at him for a long moment, then with a final slash of her Talent, she spun and strode away, leaving Jorey wilting against the wall, bleeding from the wounds she had inflicted.

Colemenoport
Offices of the
Tree-and-Dragon Trade Mission

. . . .

SO FAR, PADI THOUGHT CAUTIOUSLY, TRADE MISSION MATTERS were going well, despite the absence of the master trader.

Of course, they had only just met for nuncheon—Padi, Jes, and Dyoli, that was. Dil Nem and Grad had set off early for the yards. Mar Tyn, Karna at his back, was delivering solicitation packets to the list of accountants who had written wishing to know more of Tree-and-Dragon's accounting necessities.

Padi had initially lent herself to the task of bringing the *qe'andra's* suite into usefulness, until it became plain that she was superfluous, and left Jes and Dyoli to it, after gaining their agreement to join her for nuncheon in the trade office.

She had been happy to hear Bell's voice when she called the Skywise to order the meal.

"Is everything well?" she asked.

"Everything's well, Trader, thank you for asking," Bell said.

"Did they find who was responsible?" Padi asked, which was perhaps too familiar of her.

"Security couldn't find anything to identify those responsible," Bell said calmly. "As it was only mischief, they've retired the complaint."

Padi bit her lip, remembering the overturned display cases and sweets ground into the floor.

Mischief.

"How may I serve you?" Bell asked after a moment, and Padi shook herself into order.

"I need a working nuncheon for three, boxed meals for four, fresh fruits, and cake. Credit the trade mission's account, if you will."

"Very good, Trader. I can have that sent 'round inside the hour. Is that convenient?"

"That will do well for us," Padi said. "Thank you."

"It's a pleasure to do business with you, Trader. Take care, now."

"Take care, Bell," Padi said, and closed the connection.

She sat for a moment, wrestling with the urge to call Majel ziaGorn and demand that he speak to Port Security and inspire them to do better—but surely, it was none of her concern, out-world as she was.

A deep breath, then another, before she reviewed a piloting exercise meant to impart calmness.

Opening her eyes, she leaned forward to tap up the screen and review the morning's correspondence.

"The office suite is entirely functional for three," Jes said, as they finished their meal. "My hope is that Mar Tyn will return to us with six letters of interest in hand. I would like to start the initial phase of regularizing data no later than tomorrow evening."

Padi glanced at Dyoli, who seemed perfectly calm, and back to Jes.

"You hope to have your six possibles by this evening, teach the module tomorrow, and have everyone at their desks by tomorrow evening," she said. "That seems...ambitious."

"Surely you understand that the master trader's timetable has been ambitious from the first," Jes said. "It is my part to match him."

She raised a hand, as though Padi had been about to speak.

"You perhaps do not realize how well the traders have per-formed the preliminaries. Colemenoport is generally inclined toward the mission; we have the goodwill of the portmaster, the market master, and many of the vendors. While I understand from the master trader's briefing that there are those who see opening to trade as a risky business, even they would rather see it handled by Tree-and-Dragon, with their knowledgeable and personable traders, than some other, unknown quantity."

Padi raised her eyebrows.

"It's perfectly true," Dyoli told her. "The comm only came online this morning, and we're already getting calls from port vendors, wanting to know how much and what kind of data they should send. For the moment, we're asking them to be patient—"

"But I should send a memo," Jes said, and cocked a speculative eye in Padi's direction. "In fact, you might assist with this, Trader. You of course have a contact list—"

"I do," Padi agreed, "but if you want to reach everyone, you'll want the market master's list, and permission, I think, to send through the official port network."

"Yes—that is well thought," Jes said. "I would rather not waste time with people debating whether we are legitimate."

"I am on good terms with the assistant market manager," Padi said. "After we're done here, I'll see if she has time for me. The port market is extremely interested in opening trade, and well disposed toward the mission. If Saru can't provide what we need, I'm confident she will be able to send me to the proper source."

"I will then leave that piece with you. After we are done here, Dyoli, I want you to review the compilation kit. We will go over any questions. Our goal is to have you fully conversant with the methods involved, as you will be interfacing with the contractors here on port."

Dyoli inclined her head. "I understand," she said.

"So. I will put together the port memo, and also the solicitation letter to the city firms, for Trader yos'Galan's review."

Jes leaned back in her chair, and smiled at the two of them.

"Do you know?" she said with what seemed to Padi to be simple happiness. "I've missed this."

Dutiful Passage
Colemeno Orbit

. . . .

"WELL," SHAN SAID, OPENING HIS EYES, "THAT WAS EMBARRASSING."

"Aside being covered over with rue," Lina said, from somewhere in the vicinity of his left shoulder, "how do you feel, old friend?"

Well, that was the question, wasn't it? Shan thought. He took a breath, and reached for Healspace.

It bloomed around him in misty swirls of teal and peach, cool, and refreshing. A thought brought his pattern forward, and he smiled to See it; the links that had been broken, reformed; the evidence of abuse faded, and overgrown with vibrant color.

"Shan?"

The mist pirouetted, and Shan opened his eyes to find Lina's face bent above him.

"I feel perfectly well," he told her. "What's more, I *am* perfectly well."

"I agree," she said, and her smile was wry. "As a Healer, I find you in astonishingly good health. Still, you know, fainting in the hallway is not the done thing, and Keriana would have you stay here until she arrives."

"Priscilla," he said, then, and of a sudden recalled it. The two of them, having debarked, walking from the shuttle docking toward the main hall. He had felt a moment of lightheadedness, and before him had seen Priscilla falter, straighten—and falter again.

He had leapt to catch her, and had somehow contrived to hit his head.

"I didn't faint," he told Lina. "Priscilla fainted."

"If you will quibble, then, yes—Priscilla fainted. You only lost your balance, and knocked your head. You will wish to know that you succeeded in cushioning Priscilla's landing, and that no harm was done to the decking."

"And why did Priscilla faint?" he asked, though he could feel the links that bound them, vibrant and strong, and heard her voice whisper inside his ear, *I'm fine, love*.

"It would appear that Priscilla fainted as a result of a sudden drop in her blood pressure. She is, as you may be aware, pregnant."

"I did know that, thank you," Shan said, evenly, and felt Priscilla smile.

"Keriana has initiated a suite of tests," Lina said, impervious to irony. "After all, you both wished thorough checkups."

"Thus, the plan goes forth. Am I allowed to sit up, do you think?"

"I think you had best remain lying down until Keriana has done her checks," Lina said.

Shan sighed.

"Since you are here, amuse me," he said. "Has my Gift been replenished?"

"Largely so, to my mind," Lina said. "I gather that you have Colemeno's effervescent atmosphere to thank for this."

"That was another thing that we hoped to discover by returning home. Colemeno's ambient conditions are—remarkable. I felt that I had recovered myself almost immediately we came onto the dock, and made the decision not to shield."

"That was impetuous," Lina said, and raised her hand. "Not that I am surprised, you understand."

"Impetuous to a fault," Shan said mournfully. "It has always been so."

Off-Grid
The Tree House

. . . .

ARBOUR HAD SUGGESTED LILAC COTTAGE, DIRECTLY ON THE VIL-
lage square, as possibly suitable to Aunt Asta's needs.

Tekelia, following them to the cottage, with its signature lilac
shingles, privately thought it would prove ineligible, given the
amount of traffic on the square. Aunt Asta after all had lived retired
in her apartment in the Wardian, seeing only staff and the Warden—

"Oh! This is delightful!" Aunt Asta proclaimed, turning in
the center of the great room. She crossed to the large windows
looking out over the square, and the group of cousins slowly
assembling to see who had come among them.

She turned to Arbour.

"Will they visit, do you think, or will they be shy?"

Arbour laughed. "They're Haosa! Of course they'll visit!" She
paused. "If you'd prefer a quieter location—"

"No, I declare this a perfect situation!" Aunt Asta swept out
of the great room, down the hall, accompanied by a clatter of
doors being opened—and calling out her delight at the back room
with its windows overlooking the garden and lawn.

"That will be my library!" she declared, arriving back at the
front. "Thank you so very much, my dear. I hope you won't be
a stranger here."

Arbour grinned. "I'm Haosa, too," she said.

Aunt Asta laughed, and took herself outside, down the path
to the cluster of cousins loitering there.

"Good morning!" she said blithely. "I am Asta vesterGranz,
and I will be living here. All of my things are at Tekelia's house.
Who of you might be willing to help me move them?"

✴   ✴   ✴

They had all trooped back to Tekelia's house, cousins and hand wagons in train. Tekelia had retired to the porch with a glass of wine, to give Aunt Asta adequate scope for direction, and the willing movers room to work.

So much for assumptions, Tekelia thought, looking out over the trees. Of course, Aunt Asta had lived retired, but she had done so by Civilization's command, not her own free choice.

Indeed, it appeared that Aunt Asta quite *liked* people—only hear her chattering and laughing with her willing helpers.

Tekelia sipped wine, and smiled, and reached within to touch a particular lavender ribbon. Padi felt the touch, and sent a ripple of affection, well laced with contentment. Tekelia sent the same, and withdrew to the trees, the porch, the wine.

In the great room, the bustle continued. Tekelia leaned elbows on the railing and considered less pleasing things.

Bentamin would be duty bound to report the Oracle's retirement to the Council. The next meeting of the Council of the Whole, according to the *Tattler*, was tomorrow. It was certain to be an uncomfortable meeting, Tekelia thought, and wished that there was some way to be certain that Civilization would not be appointing a new Warden as part of the proceedings.

"Tekelia?" Aunt Asta called from the great room.

Tekelia stepped through the door.

"Here, Aunt. What's to do?"

She laughed.

"I came to tell you that everything is packed into the wagons and made secure. We'll be leaving for my cottage now. I am promised a meal at Stiletta's house, and Klem tells me that her sister has already been in to dust and open the windows. She also sent for more bookshelves, which should be in place by the time I arrive. So you see I'm very well taken care of, and you mustn't worry about me."

Tekelia smiled.

"You carry all before you, Aunt Asta. I'll try not to worry, though I hope I'll be allowed to visit now and then?"

"I insist upon it! In fact, if your arrangements allow, visit this evening with your Padi." Her gaze grew distant for a moment, as if she were contemplating something just beyond Tekelia's shoulder. "Yes, this evening will be very good."

Her gaze sharpened, and she looked to Tekelia's face.

"That," she said, "felt . . . rather odd."

"The ambient does interact with our Gifts," Tekelia said. "It may take some getting used to."

"I look forward to becoming accustomed," Aunt Asta said. "Until this evening, my dear."

"Until this evening, Aunt Asta."

On that, she was gone, clattering down the outside stairs as gay and as heedless as a child.

Colemenoport
Offices of the
Tree-and-Dragon Trade Mission

. . . .

JES'S HOPE IN MAR TYN HAD NOT BEEN MISPLACED. HE HAD returned to the office while Padi was with Saru, bearing not six, but eight letters of interest from port accountants.

"Which is precisely what we want," Jes told Padi. "Depend upon it, some one or two will wash out of tomorrow's workshop. If we can retain six—or even four—we may proceed with confidence."

The proposed vendor memo, which arrived on Padi's screen mere moments after that discussion, was a lesson in clarity and precision. She sent it on to Saru, as arranged, to be distributed via the official network to all of Colemenoport.

That done, and the mail queue being momentarily clear, Padi rose, intending to make herself a cup of tea.

A tone sounded, and the light over the doorway flashed twice.

Padi sighed. She had no appointments scheduled. On the other hand, the whole port knew where the Tree-and-Dragon Trade Mission had its offices; she and the master trader had labored to make that so.

She opened the door.

"Good day to you, Trader Padi," Trader Isfelm said cordially. "I hope I'm not too late to do business."

The trader was looking somewhat less buoyant than usual, and she was carrying a case under one arm.

"It is, so my master taught me, never too late to do business. Though I do warn you that if you must have the master trader, he is not to hand."

"Wanted on the ship for a day or two," Trader Isfelm said wisely. "Sent me a note to say so."

367

"In that case, please do come in. I was just about to make some tea. May I offer you a cup? Or perhaps—"

"You know, tea would be a treat," Trader Isfelm said, stepping into the office. Once over the threshold, she paused, and sighed.

"Are you well, Trader?" Padi asked, for this was not at all in her usual style.

"Well enough. Well enough. Only I've been dealing with city folk the last while, which I make it my bidness never to do, and it's put me out of temper." She offered Padi a one-sided smile. "Nothing to do with you, Trader."

Padi closed the door, and waved her hand at the conference table.

"Please sit and rest, Trader. The tea will be a moment or two."

When she returned to the office, bearing the tray, Trader Isfelm had put herself at the center of the table, case open before her.

Padi paused, seeing what appeared to be the edge of a flat chart. Such things were old, and rare, and by rights ought to be resting in a carefully maintained archive, while copies were made available to those with an interest.

She put the tray down at the end of the table, poured two scant cups, but did not put them out, and opened the cake tin.

Trader Isfelm watched these arrangements with grave approval.

"The master trader had an interest in some charts I'd seen back before I learned how to pack a pod. Ghost routes, the space at Tinsori, and suchlike. I said I'd look 'em out for him. Found the old files in deep backups, right about where I figured they'd be, given when I saw 'em first.

"Then I remembered we had the flats—family story is that Can Ith bought 'em—had some idea of trading out toward Tinsori. Not much sense to that notion, given the space and the station. Anydays, took a bit to figure what Brother Jaimy might've thought to be appropriate storage. Just put my hand on it this morning.

"Now."

She reached into a jacket pocket and produced a data-key.

"That's a fresh copy of the files," she said. "The master trader can have it with my goodwill. Like I told him, these are old, *old* charts, not safe for navigation. You understand me, Trader Padi?"

Padi bowed slightly.

"I understand you, Trader Isfelm," she murmured. "The master trader is a pilot; as I am."

"Just making sure. Dragons aren't so common in my life that I want to put any at risk."

"Thank you for your care," Padi said solemnly.

Trader Isfelm laughed.

"That's right. Now. If the master trader might be interested in antiquities, there's this, right here..."

She stood to remove the carefully folded plas-sheet and set it to one side while she shifted the case to her chair.

Then, slowly, and with great care, she began to unfold the flat.

"Take hold here, if you would, Trader," Trader Isfelm said. "It saw some use before it came to us, and sitting in a box all this time's only made it more fragile."

Padi held the edge indicated while the trader finished unfolding. She took a step back, so the sheet had no wrinkles.

"Let's put 'er down now, Trader, nice and slow..."

The chart settled gently to the tabletop. Trader Isfelm crossed to the control panel and brought the overhead lights up. Padi leaned over the chart, finding the legend and the key, rendered in Old Trade. A particular phrase caught her eye, and she leaned closer.

"Rim's Edge Route," she read slowly—and blinked.

"That's the one caught me, too, back when." Trader Isfelm was at her side, leaning over the chart, tracing the route with one finger not quite touching—

"Right. Didn't think I'd made that up. Not an imaginative child." She angled her finger toward a particular point on the chart, still not touching it.

"Jump point fixed by Riley's Tavern. Riley's Tavern's sun went out of sequence 'bout the time this chart was drawn."

"Which doesn't mean the Jump-point collapsed," Padi murmured, more to herself than to Trader Isfelm. She was thinking, recalling Vanz's letter—*my aunt Chasiel, Captain Most Senior, asked what I thought of the Rimedge Loop.*

"Surely not," she said.

"Hit a resonance, Trader?"

"More likely just a coincidence," Padi said, straightening. She moved down to the tea tray, Trader Isfelm with her. They each took up a cup.

"I cannot say that the master trader will want the flat chart. I will ask him, when we speak next. In the meanwhile, please hold—"

Trader Isfelm raised her hand.

"I'd rather you hold it, Trader. Had deuce's own time finding it; almost like it was hiding from me."

Padi considered. Her experience of Trader Isfelm did not encourage her to believe that this was a setup for under-dealing. Best to treat it as fair business, then.

She inclined her head.

"I will keep it in the safe here, if you wish," she said. "Understand that I cannot promise the master trader will—"

"Understood, understood. Might not be in the market for old flats. No deposit necessary, Trader. In fact, it's me should be giving you a coin, for taking up storage. Let's have some cake. After, we'll both see it put into your safe, I'll give you a coin, you'll give me a receipt and that'll all be done proper."

"That sounds to be a reasonable approach," Padi said, and picked up the pot to warm their cups.

On-Grid
The Wardian

. . . .

"WARDEN, THANK YOU FOR AGREEING TO SEE ME SO QUICKLY," Majel ziaGorn said, stopping just over the threshold to bow.

The Deaf Councilor looked breathless, Bentamin thought as he rose from behind his desk to bow in return. One might even say that he looked worried.

"When you invoke the safety of Civilization," he said, lightly, "what else could I do?"

Councilor ziaGorn did not take the joke. If anything, he looked more worried.

Bentamin allowed himself to taste the other man's emotions. Worried, indeed. All but sick with it.

"Will you have tea?" Bentamin asked. "It's a fresh pot. Also, I have cookies."

"Tea and cookies would be most welcome, I thank you," Majel said, and Bentamin felt the shiver of his relief in being offered something so commonplace.

"Excellent." Bentamin came 'round the desk, and moved a hand to show his guest the two comfortable chairs with the table between. "Please sit and relax." He went to the buffet.

It was only a moment to pour. He carried the cups to the table with his own hands, which was courtesy.

Majel murmured something that might have been thanks, but Bentamin had returned to the buffet, opening the drawer—and realizing his error. The cookies were Entilly's special sort, which acted directly on one's Gift.

On the other hand, he thought, considering the inner tumult Majel ziaGorn was attempting to contain, they surely couldn't do any harm, and the man clearly needed some surcease. Bentamin opened the tin, and set it in the middle of the table.

"I hope you don't mind homemade," he said, taking his seat. "My cousin keeps me well supplied."

"You're fortunate in your cousins," Majel said politely. He took a blue-iced cookie, and bit into it.

Bentamin took a cookie iced in yellow, and ate it, attentive to the pattern of the man opposite him.

His own cookie brought the accustomed flicker of energy, and an outspreading sense of peace.

The effect seemed to be the same for his guest. Bentamin did not See the flare of a Gift engaged, but he did See the burden of worry lighten somewhat, as Majel visibly relaxed in the chair across from him.

"Your cousin is a good baker," he said, and Bentamin would almost have suspected him of irony.

He sipped his tea and put the cup on the table, Majel doing the same.

"Now," Bentamin said, "how may I serve you?"

"By listening," Majel said promptly. "After you have listened, if you would care to advise me, I would be grateful. There are..." He hesitated, took a breath and offered a wry smile.

"There are very few people that I may talk to about this matter."

"Then I am honored to be one of the few," Bentamin told him, and settled deliberately back into his chair.

"I'm prepared to listen."

"I'll be as brief as possible," Majel told him. "First, a question: Were you aware of the damage done at the school in Pacazahno?"

"I was not. Was anyone injured?"

"No. The library was torn apart, and an outside art installation under the care of the students was destroyed. Both events occurred in the small hours of the morning; no one was injured."

Bentamin drew a hard breath. No children had been injured, but—mischief against a *school*?

"I mention this as the latest in a growing number of incidents of mischief done against Deaf-owned property and business," Majel continued.

"The security logs—" Bentamin began, and Majel held up a hand.

"The Citizens Coalition keeps a database—several databases. From them, I learn that barely half of the mischief done in the last year has been reported by the victims."

"Why? Security can't find those responsible and deal with them appropriately unless the crime is reported."

Majel sighed. "We aren't talking about crimes. We are talking about mischief-under-the-law. Both Port and City Security consider investigating such things a waste of their time, and have a tendency to blame the victims for a lack of understanding and a failure to employ basic protective measures, because they are Deaf. In short, it is less exhausting to clean up the mess and move on, than it is to call Security."

He paused for another sip of tea, glanced speculatively at Entilly's cookies, but did not take another one.

"I saw this dynamic in action just recently, when the Skywise Provianto was the victim. Port Security was diligent, but it was clear their stance was that Bell—Surda erVinton—had forgotten to engage the lock, thus providing *an opportunity.*"

Bentamin sighed, loudly. Majel's mouth quirked.

"Yes. I was able to prevail upon them to pull the camera records and make a fuller inspection of the damage, but even so, it was ruled mischief—regrettable, but no crime committed, and nothing to identify the... mischief-makers."

"And the lesson learned from such things is that the perpetrators of the mischief will not be pursued," Bentamin said. "Why report an event, when the only outcome will be insults and more inconvenience. I see."

Majel sighed.

"This brings us to the incident at Pacazahno. The village administrator called upon her neighbors at Ribbon Dance Village for assistance in the aftermath of the... mischief. A team was sent—two Persuaders, a Psychometric, and a Back-Seer. They were able to pinpoint when the event took place, the state of minds of the perpetrators—which, as I understand it, was not that of exuberant youth, but rather mature purposefulness."

He paused, and sent Bentamin a wry glance.

"We come now to the part of the tale where I may only repeat what I've been told, and hope that it makes sense to you."

"I understand," Bentamin assured him. "Please continue."

"Yes, well. I am told that a signature has been isolated, which matches a signature found at my casino, when it was targeted. This signature carries an aura of specific and intense hatred.

"I am told, and the village administrator also, that there are methods by which this signature, which has been Seen by several Haosa, a Sensitive in my employ, my chief of security, and also... imprinted on at least two readers that were smashed in the library—it is said that there is a way for this signature to be... traced. To a particular individual."

"There are methods, yes. It's fortunate that the Psychometric was able to isolate tainted devices. The village administrator—"

"The village administrator," Majel interrupted, "is not inclined to bring Civilized Security personnel into her village. When we last spoke, her intention was to work with Ribbon Dance Village to develop an early warning system and to upgrade the security at potential high-risk targets—her office, the medical center, the community kitchen, the school. She felt, strongly, that if Security were to find the person whose signature has been identified, and fined them for mischief, that would be... an invitation, let us say, for more—and more serious—mischief to be done at Pacazahno."

Majel tipped his head and met Bentamin's eyes.

"For what it may be worth, my own security chief agrees with her."

Bentamin drew a careful breath.

"If a complaint is not made, then justice can't be done."

"If a complaint is made, justice is scarcely done in any case," Majel said, sharply. "The fine for mischief is negligible, and in the case of an actor who *hates* Deaf..."

He caught himself and moved a hand in apology.

"Your pardon, Warden. I'm aware that you are not the cause of this."

"Not personally, no," Bentamin said dryly. "May I ask why you brought this to me, if not to make a complaint?"

"I had hoped for advice," Majel said slowly. "The mood of the Coalition is dissatisfied. There's talk of a strike—"

"A strike?"

Majel sighed.

"The Deaf are aware of their lack of standing, in society, and under the law," he said dryly. "The sense of the Coalition is that Civilization does not properly understand the many ways in which we contribute to the health and prosperity of all. It's thought by some that a coordinated shutdown—every Deaf business to close and every Deaf worker to stay home—may usefully demonstrate our worth to Civilization."

"You don't agree?"

Majel moved his shoulders.

"We need allies, in order to effect change from within the system. We risk alienating the very people who might help us, if we strike."

Majel ziaGorn had a good deal of solid political sense, Bentamin thought.

"If I take this to the Council, with seelyFaire ever seeking a way to return to the Patron System..."

He flicked his fingers, and sat back, mouth tight.

"Have you spoken to krogerSlyte?" Bentamin asked. The portmaster was Majel's most reliable friend on the Council.

"Not yet. I thought of you, because this is what your office was formed to do—to ward Civilization from dangers external and internal. We have a dangerous situation, where members of one group find it acceptable to prey upon members of another group—and community protections have failed."

"That is the mandate of the Warden's office," Bentamin agreed. "But I must have cooperation—reports must be filed, evidence shared. If trust can't travel that far, then there's very little I can do. I agree that taking the matter as it's now shaped to the Council would be an error. There may, however, be another way, that may win you more allies and friends."

"I welcome your advice."

"ivenAlyatta will be your best resource for this. The woman knows everything—or can find it in the archives before you draw three breaths. She also knows a great many useful people. What you will wish to bring to her is data—how many businesses in the city and port are Deaf-owned? What is their net worth? What percentage do they make up of the port and city's worth? Who are the exceptional members of your Coalition—include artists, as well as business people. If she likes you and finds your project worthy, our archivist will put you to work drilling down for even more. The initial data that you will bring to her is to demonstrate that you understand the task you have taken in hand."

"I understand," Majel said. "I had also been thinking of azieEm, who has had some interesting things to say of late."

"I would advise a private meeting with ivenAlyatta before anything—data in hand, mind! By all means ask for her impressions of your fellow councilors. You'll be entertained for hours."

For the first time in this meeting, Majel smiled.

"I'll be certain to ask."

He rose, and bowed.

"Warden, thank you, for listening and for your advice." He paused with another odd glance at the tin. "And for sharing with me your cousin's very interesting cookies."

Bentamin rose and returned the bow.

"I'm pleased to have been of service," he said, truthfully. "If you can persuade someone to give me access to one of the tainted devices, I might be of more help to you."

"I'll see what I can do. Ultimately, it is Administrator joi-More's decision."

"And I gather that she would not welcome a call from the Warden of Civilization."

"Not at this time, I think," Majel said, politely.

"I understand."

Bentamin walked his guest to the door and saw him out.

When the door had closed, he stood for a moment, looking at the tea things without seeing them, and thinking about—norbears.

Civilization did not even recognize the Deaf as fully functional persons. What chance had he, really, with his norbear eyewitness to murder?

Colemenoport
Offices of the
Tree-and-Dragon Trade Mission

. . . .

PADI READ AND APPROVED THE LETTER JES HAD PRODUCED. IT was her plan, explained in the accompanying memo, to send the letter to each of the firms on the list provided by the Haven City Business Association, outlining the work to be done, and soliciting contractors. She thought to send this solicitation over her signature as *Qe'andra*-in-Charge of the Whole Port Audit, unless Trader yos'Galan wished to sign it, as Overseeing Trader.

Padi laughed, and reached to the keyboard, assuring Jes that her letter was both clear and compelling, and that it should absolutely go over her signature.

"I am, as the master trader was before me, willing to assist you in any matter, but I believe I am not so much overseeing your work, as removing myself as an obstacle."

That done, she turned to the results of the search she had built for the Rimedge Loop, which had returned so many tangled threads that she despaired of sorting them.

Perhaps she ought to simply write to Vanz.

Or . . . perhaps not yet. If the master trader had an interest in the Rim's Edge Route—but, there, the cat was already out of the bag, if the two routes were, indeed, the same. Had not Captain-Aunt Chasiel set Vanz to study the route? The master trader had shared his hopes for the Redlands with Trader Denobli, who had been Vanz's master. Trader Denobli, being, according to the master trader, nothing like a fool, had doubtless begun looking about him not only for profit, but for ways to sustain and grow the new-forged business alliance between his Syndicate and Tree-and-Dragon.

No, the route was no secret, however it was rendered. What fell to her was the same duty that had prompted Trader Isfelm. She opened her mail queue, and addressed a letter to Vanz.

My very dear Trader Denobli.

I write, briefly, not to inform you that Master Trader yos'Galan called for a whole port inventory of Colemeno, and immediately removed himself to the Passage on other business, leaving me to oversee the daily work, nor to allow you to know that I will be conducting a formal audit of the Iverson Loop as soon as the necessary qe'andra *arrives to assist me, assuming that I pass the certification course.*

No, discussion of these events must wait until such time as I may do them full justice, possibly over a bottle or two of wine when next we are in the same port.

Instead, I write to tell you that I have recently seen a chart—a very old chart. Among the routes illustrated is, if my Old Trade has not betrayed me, the Rim's Edge Route.

I was, naturally, struck by the similarity between what I am assured is a ghost route, and the Loop that you are to reopen.

I do not ask you to give me confidential information. I merely pass on the warning that was given me—to be cautious regarding the markers, and most especially the Jump-point hard by Riley's Tavern.

She paused, considering what else—

The comm chimed.

Padi tapped "receive."

"Tree-and-Dragon Trade Mission, Trader yos'Galan speaking. Service?"

"Good evening, Trader yos'Galan," said a warm and welcome voice. "This is Tekelia vesterGranz. May I speak to Padi?"

She laughed.

"Are you studying *melant'i*?"

"I thought I had best, as it means so much to you. Was my form correct?"

"Perfectly. You might also have said, 'Hello, Padi; it is Tekelia.'"

"I'll remember. I wonder—are you free this evening?"

"I'm just finishing a letter. I'm told the *qe'andra's* office will be working for some hours yet, but that I need not hold myself at their word. I do need to visit with Lady Selph, but after—"

"After will suit," Tekelia said. "May I come to pay my respects to the Lady? Or will that be too much company?"

"Surely you know that you are preferred over myself. Also, I believe her to be quite capable of sending one or both of us off, should we prove—"

She stopped, caught by a notion.

"Do you know?" she said. "I think she would welcome a visit from Eet, if that might be possible? She did elect to stay, rather than rejoin her cuddle on the *Passage*, but I know she is lonely. Father made her a rag doll, but I daresay it isn't the same."

"I'll see if Eet is at liberty. How will we arrange ourselves?"

"I'll finish my letter and go home," Padi said. "If Lady Selph is receiving, then I will—I will whisper," she said, feeling her cheeks warm.

She felt a shiver of laughter inside her head, even as Tekelia said gravely, "That sounds like an excellent plan. I will await your whisper."

The call ended.

Smiling, Padi turned back to her screen, and read what she had written.

It was well, she decided; she had done honor to Trader Isfelm's concern, shown care for her business partner, and her friend, and hinted only *very* lightly that she was willing to learn more.

She leaned to the keyboard again.

Take good care, Vanz.

Padi

Two taps sent it into the queue to be uploaded to the *Passage*, from which it would be dispatched.

Padi shut down the screen, and crossed the room to get her jacket.

On-Grid
The Wardian

. . . .

IT WAS DONE.

Bentamin leaned back in his chair.

He had examined his motives; he had weighed the probable harm that would come from doing nothing, against the possible good that would come from doing—something.

He had weighed possible outcomes.

Innocents were in it, but they were well guarded. His quarry would either stampede—or stay the course, leaving him to wait, and watch for the next error.

And hope that there wasn't another murder in it.

Colemenoport
Wayfarer

. . . .

"GOOD EVENING, LADY SELPH."

Padi unlocked the door to the norbear's residence. Lady Selph marched out, stopping at the edge of the table and rising to her back feet.

Padi lifted her to one knee, keeping her hands firmly against portly norbear sides. Lady Selph settled down, with the suggestion of a sniff, followed by a query.

"It was a moderately pleasant day, yes," Padi said. "Jes is quite the dynamo. I would hardly have credited it, had I not seen it for myself. And I must say that sending Mar Tyn to hand-deliver the contractor solicitation letter was a stroke worthy of the master trader himself."

Another query formed, and Padi laughed.

"Restful? Well, perhaps not, but very effective, and interesting, too. Surely you've seen her in the Pet Library?"

Lady Selph agreed that she had previously been acquainted, though slightly, with Jes, adding that she had never seemed half so busy then, and had smelled pleasantly of growing things.

"That was probably your good influence at work," Padi told her. "I wonder, do you care if Tekelia—and Eet, too, if his duty allows—call on you just now?"

Lady Selph let it be known that Tekelia was always welcome. In the case of Eet, she had been anticipating his arrival ever since Padi had discussed his situation with her.

"I had only wanted to be certain that you were of a mind to entertain," Padi told her. "Allow me a moment."

But instead of simply whispering "Tekelia," she paused. There were other resources available to her now. She ought to make a study of them all.

So.

She concentrated, as if she were about to show Lady Selph the face of a new acquaintance, and—*thought* the words, *Lady Selph will be pleased to entertain Tekelia and Eet.*

It seemed she heard a hum, as if of a wire in the distance, and a tug at the base of her spine. She turned her head in time to see the mist dissipate and Tekelia stand forward, a strap slung over one shoulder, supporting a bag from which a quizzical furry face peeked.

"You heard me," she said, absurdly pleased.

Tekelia grinned.

"As you see. Now—"

Tekelia came forward to kneel next to Padi, and put the bag on the floor before them.

"How do you think it best to proceed?"

"I think," Padi said, "that Lady Selph ought to greet Eet on her own ground, so to speak."

She put her hands around the lady's ample middle and lifted her to the table. Lady Selph immediately entered her residence. Padi then turned to the bag and its wide-eyed occupant.

Carefully, she offered her signature, as Lady Selph had taught her. She felt Eet accept it, and offer his own, which she accepted in her turn. Before she could ask permission to lift him to Lady Selph's level, a face took shape, very slowly and carefully, in the space behind her eyes.

A dark-haired woman, thin face dominated by a pair of sparkling blue eyes. There was a taste of sorrow attached to the image, and Padi felt tears start to her eyes.

"I do not know her," she said, gently.

The image faded. A second arose—strong faced, and long nosed, with dark, decided brows.

"That is Trader Isfelm," Padi said, offering her own image of the trader as she had been this afternoon.

Eet accepted the match with a sense of satisfaction, and Padi took a breath.

"I think we had best allow Eet and Lady Selph to have their coze," Tekelia said. "There will be time to exchange acquaintances later. Padi will lift you, if you allow it."

On the heels of this came a rather acid observation that Lady Selph had no fresh fruit to hand.

Padi laughed, and looked to Tekelia. "Do you mind calling down to the kitchen?"

"Not at all." Tekelia rose, and moved to the comm.

Padi reached into the bag and got a grip on Eet, who was a good deal thinner than Lady Selph, and wiry, where she was accustomed to norbears who were decidedly plump.

She placed Eet on the table, and sat back carefully, hands hovering on either side, in case he should suddenly bumble off at a tangent. Indeed, he hesitated, sitting on his haunches, and shifted, as if he would turn away—and just at that moment, Lady Selph, standing inside the entrance to her residence—chirped.

The effect on Eet was immediate and telling. He went to all fours and all but ran forward, not stopping until his head was pressed against her belly.

Lady Selph chirped again, and Padi felt a wash of what might have been concern.

"Here we are," Tekelia said, putting a tray on the floor on Padi's left. As she might have expected, there were sandwiches, a pot of tea, cake—and a small saucer of freshly cut fruit.

Tekelia put the saucer inside the residence, and locked the door before settling back and giving Padi a smile.

"We should eat something."

"So I gathered."

Padi chose a sandwich, and shifted slightly, so that she leaned against Tekelia. "I had completely forgotten to ask where we are called to, this evening."

"And I should have told you without prompting. My Aunt Asta moved into her cottage today. She would very much like to meet you."

"And Sort me?"

"It's possible that's also in her mind. I should tell you that she Saw something with regard to meeting you this evening."

Padi lifted her eyebrows.

"Shall I be disturbed?"

"Disturbed . . . no. But it's always wise to be cautious around an oracle."

Padi laughed and took another sandwich.

"I will bear that in mind," she said. "Now, before I forget—"

She rolled to her feet and went to the desk. Returning, she held a data-key out to Tekelia.

"The results of the search on norbear intelligence," she said. Tekelia smiled.

"That was very quick! Thank you."

"You won't thank me when you open it," Padi said darkly, and glanced into the residence. The norbears were at the saucer, each busy with a piece of fruit.

"If you will hold yourself at Lady Selph's word," she said to Tekelia, "I will change into something more suitable."

Tekelia was sitting on the end of her bed, back toward Lady Selph's residence, when Padi came out of the 'fresher. She had taken her sartorial cue from Tekelia, who was dressed neatly, but unexceptionally, in sweater, sturdy pants, and boots, and had pulled her hair back into its usual tail.

She paused, looking over Tekelia's shoulder to Lady Selph's residence, where she saw the saucer, but no norbears.

Padi sat down next to Tekelia.

"Tell me they have escaped together in a ship left Eet by his grandsire, and they mean to set up as pirates of the spaceways."

Tekelia laughed softly.

"No, how could I? Not that I don't think they'd do well persuading people out of their goods."

"Oh, born to lawlessness, never doubt it," Padi agreed. "But I see no norbears in that cage."

"They're under the platform. Listen and you'll hear them," Tekelia said, adding, "not too closely. Eet had a great need to unburden himself, and I felt that I was...an unwanted third."

Padi concentrated, as if she were about to present Lady Selph with a new face for her collection, and there, indeed, was a swift murmuring, interspersed with flashes of things seen: a shelf crowded with bric-a-brac; a swirl of mists; Torin's face—

Padi withdrew her attention.

"I see," she murmured. "Do you think we ought to leave them together while we call on your aunt?"

Tekelia sighed.

"I promised Torin and Vaiza that I would return him to their care when I came to see Aunt Asta."

"Ah. Well, then, how do you propose—"

But just at that moment, there came a sharp suggestion that Eet was needed by his children.

"I should never have doubted," Padi said wryly, and came to her feet. She approached the residence, Tekelia at her side. Lady Selph and Eet were just inside the door. Eet was holding Lady Selph's doll tightly against his chest.

Padi touched the lock. Eet stepped out onto the table, the doll still cuddled close, and climbed into the bag Tekelia held open. Lady Selph stood inside, watching.

When Tekelia lifted the bag to settle it over a shoulder, she turned and marched back in to the residence, passing the saucer that still held some fruit as if it wasn't there.

Padi extended a tentative thought of comfort.

In return, came a flash of teeth, and sharp reminder that Padi beware of predators.

Off-Grid
The Lilac Cottage

· · · · · · · · · · · · · · · · · ·

LILAC COTTAGE HAD LARGE WINDOWS ALONG THE FRONT, THROUGH which could be seen... quite a number of people. Voices and laughter drifted out of those generous windows, and music, too.

"She cannot possibly want to see me this evening," Padi said, staring at the scene before them. "There's no room even for Eet."

"Eet at least must enter. I promised Vaiza and Torin faithfully to have him back to them this evening, and last I had heard from Geritsi, they were determined to join the Opened House Party."

"Opened House Party?" Padi repeated.

"Indeed, yes. Whenever an empty cottage is reopened to a new resident, there must be a party, else we would not be Haosa. Lilac Cottage was opened to Aunt Asta this morning. She immediately met three of our cousins in the square and enlisted their aid in shifting her belongings. They grabbed carts, while a fourth volunteered to dust and air out the house."

Tekelia paused as a particularly loud round of laughter burst from the open windows.

"The sister who was readying the house called in more bookshelves from the village holdings, and, there being no reason to keep it secret, let it be known that the Oracle for Civilization was home at last. Cousins began arriving even before she had returned with the carts, so she had ample help in getting unpacked.

"More came as news spread, bringing food, of course..."

"And presto! An instant crush, and your aunt the hostess of the season," Padi said.

More laughter spilled through the windows, followed by a bright glissade of music.

Padi hesitated. Tekelia settled the strap of Eet's bag over one shoulder.

"I must certainly go in and exclaim over the new arrangements and assure myself that my aunt is well, and not overtaxed by all these people."

Padi took Tekelia's hand.

"Lead on, my friend, and I will do my best to follow."

As they approached the front door, two people came out from the house, and looked up with glad cries.

"Tekelia! Padi! Well met!"

Stiletta and Klem from the Ribbon Dance, Padi remembered, and produced a wide Haosa smile.

"Well met again," she said.

"I warn you, Cousins," Klem said, "the whole village is inside that house. You might fare better out here on the path. Someone's bound to see you and bring out a tray."

"No, but Tekelia will want to make certain that we've done well for Aunt Asta—" Stiletta gave them an owlish look. "She said that we were all to consider her our aunt, and she would consider us all niblings, open to her care and correction."

"Grace and threat in one neat sentence," Tekelia said. "Don't say you weren't fairly warned."

"Never," Stiletta vowed, and tugged on Klem's arm. "We promised Kencia our aid in the night garden."

"That's right, work calls!" Klem said gaily, and off they went at an angle to the path.

"The night garden?" Padi asked, as they moved toward the door.

"I'll show you," Tekelia said. "Though perhaps not tonight."

Hand-linked, they walked down the path and through the open door. Just inside, Tekelia paused, a move with which Padi sympathized entirely.

It *was* a crush, the room awash in people, with a particularly dense knot at the back, where, Padi strongly suspected, Tekelia's Aunt Asta would be found.

Well, she thought, taking a breath, *best to get on with it. After all, we* were *summoned.*

Her companion, however, still tarried. Padi looked at the side of Tekelia's face, then out over the room again, seeing it as might someone who was constrained not to touch any other person.

It would, she conceded, be tricky, and with the stakes so high, even someone as matter-of-fact as Tekelia might need a moment to plan.

"I could," she said, leaning to Tekelia's ear, "go first, and break trail for you."

At that moment, a clear voice overrode the general racket.

"Tekelia, well met!"

Tekelia's fingers tightened around hers, and she looked back over the room to see that people were—shifting.

The crowd condensed and a path opened before them. Tekelia stepped forward, and Padi, too, watching as the way continued to open.

They're afraid, she thought.

No—that was not exactly correct. There were smiles aplenty, and nods of acknowledgment as they passed. Padi recognized faces from the Ribbon Dance, felt their affection wash warm against her heart.

They were afraid, she realized, but not of Tekelia. Tekelia was welcome, indeed.

No, they were afraid of *touching* Tekelia—of the *outcome* of touching Tekelia.

And if she thought back, who at the Ribbon Dance had crowded Tekelia? Who had taken Tekelia's hand? Padi yos'Galan, and none other. It was only the crowded venue that made their restraint more obvious this evening.

Padi felt something flicker in her breast—not quite anger and not quite pity, but some complicated mixture of both. What did it do to one, she thought, as they moved down the room, to always have people withdraw from you, to never be offered a hand, to always be on guard against an unintended contact? The smiles and gestures of welcome did not obscure the fact that people were drawing away.

"There you are! Padi, it's good to see you again!"

Geritsi slentAlin stepped into their path. Her hair this evening was done in a very proper knot, held with an ornate comb.

"Geritsi, well met," Padi said, and glanced about. "But where is Dosent?"

"Home. She does not care for large crowds."

"She may have a point," Padi said, and Geritsi laughed.

"I was just thinking the same thing. But, here—Aunt Asta

had just now asked if you had arrived," she said. "I thought I'd felt Tekelia outside, and volunteered to lead you in."

"We were outside, but the way opened and now we are inside," Tekelia said. "Where is my aunt?"

"The back parlor."

Padi eyed the mass of bodies between them and the doorway she barely glimpsed in the back wall.

"I'll lead you in, never fear it," Geritsi said.

"We are in your hands," Tekelia said. "Where are Vaiza and Torin? I promised to deliver Eet back into their care."

"They're attending Aunt Asta," Geritsi said, "she's the tonic they need, I think. I heard Torin laugh."

"She is a force, my cousin Bentamin has long sworn it." Tekelia glanced to Padi.

"Shall we go on?"

"I would not see you forsworn; therefore, you must return Eet to the children. If Geritsi will guide us—"

"You can place your faith in me," the other woman assured them.

"Then, lead on," Tekelia said, and squeezed Padi's fingers.

The back parlor was less peopled than the great room, most of them clustered near the center, where an elder lady with an untidy mass of grey-shot dark hair tumbling about her shoulders sat in a large chair, a child leaning against each knee.

"Tekelia!" she exclaimed gladly. "I had quite given you up!"

"You said this evening, so we have arrived on time," Tekelia pointed out. "And you don't seem to have been short of company."

"Oh, my dear, no! They are taking such very good care of me! I'm quite overwhelmed."

Tekelia smiled at the children.

"Hello, Torin. Hello, Vaiza."

"Tekelia!" the boy said gladly. "It's good to see you!"

"Hello, Tekelia," the girl added, with a solemn smile.

"I have Eet here. Are you ready to receive him, or shall I take him to Geritsi's house?"

"I'll take him," Torin said, stepping forward.

Tekelia held the bag out. She took it and peered inside.

"He's sleeping," she said softly, "and he has—is that a dolly?"

"It is," Padi said. "Lady Selph gave it to him. My father had made it for her, because she had left the rest of her cuddle on our ship, and he thought she might be lonely."

"But now Lady Selph is lonely again," Vaiza said, stepping to his sister's side, and peering into the bag.

"I'll make her a new doll when I go home," Padi said.

"Now, my loves," Aunt Asta said, reaching out to touch small hands. "I must ask you to go with Geritsi, so that Tekelia, and Padi, and I may talk in private."

"It's time you had something to eat," Geritsi said, picking up on her cue. "And I know Feyance had promised to show Torin his mandola. Both are in the kitchen, so I think we have our direction."

"Goodbye, Aunt Asta," Vaiza said. "Can we come to see you tomorrow?"

"I think that might be arranged—or, you know? I'll come to see you. I haven't met Dosent yet."

"Good! Torin and me'll make cookies for you!"

"I look forward to that," Aunt Asta said as she rose from her chair. Geritsi caught each twin by a hand and led them into the crowd.

Tekelia looked at Aunt Asta, eyebrows up.

"In private?"

"No one can hear anything in all this roar," Aunt Asta said comfortably, and turned, holding out a hand.

"You must be Padi. I remember seeing you on Ribbon Dance Hill that night. A woman on fire, you were. I am so very pleased to see you again. I am Asta vesterGranz."

Padi put her free hand out, and found it pressed between two soft, warm palms.

"I'm pleased to meet you, too, ma'am," she said honestly. Her hand was pressed again, and released.

"You must call me Aunt Asta," the elder lady said, comfortably. "One cannot have too many niblings." Her eyes narrowed somewhat. "And you are still on fire, I see! Oh! And Tekelia—"

She turned, hand extended, and cupped Tekelia's cheek.

Behind her, Padi heard a sharp sound, as those nearest them drew in a collected, horrified breath.

Tekelia's fingers around hers were viselike; shoulders rigid.

Asta vesterGranz merely leaned closer and kissed Tekelia's cheek, before stepping back, her smile beatific.

"Aunt Asta—" Tekelia's voice failed for a moment, then came back, shaky but sharp.

"I cannot believe you took that risk."

"But there was no risk at all, was there, my dear? Padi centers you."

"You don't know that!"

Aunt Asta's brows pulled together.

"Don't I? You know, it *is* very noisy in here, and I'm so unused to crowds. You're quite right that I might have not understood what I Saw."

And that, Padi thought, was a hit worthy of Father.

"There's quite a pleasant green space just behind the house," Aunt Asta continued. "My library overlooks it. Why don't we all three go out where it's cooler and there are less people, and I can be certain of what I'm Seeing?"

Padi waited, feeling the grip on her fingers ease, and a certain settling in the air between them.

"Yes," Tekelia said mildly. "By all means, let's go outside."

Outside, there were flower beds bordering a wide green space, and a sweet-scented breeze, bearing music on its back.

Near the center of the space was an open-sided pavilion, sheltering a table and some benches. Aunt Asta led them there, and settled onto one of the benches, patting the space next to her.

"Padi, will you join me? Tekelia, draw that other bench closer. Now, isn't this much cozier than all the din inside?"

"It is," Tekelia said, having moved the bench forward without actually touching it. "I'm only aquake to learn what must be private."

"Well, Padi's Sorting for one, thing—ah, food and drink arrive. Thank you, dear."

"Thank Geritsi," Tekelia said.

"Whom you asked to see us supplied," Aunt Asta returned. She smiled up at the two lanky persons approaching, one carrying a tray of various foods, the other a pitcher and glasses.

"Thank you both!" she said happily. "Now, don't go before you tell me your names."

The older of the two grinned and bowed. "I'm Yferen, Aunt Asta."

The other, who seemed much younger, ducked his head in a sort of half-bow. "Ander, ma'am. I'm—new."

"Well met both! Ander, my dear, please do call me Aunt, or Aunt Asta."

The boy's smile transformed his face.

"Yes, ma—Aunt Asta. Thank you."

"Not at all. I'm new, too, you know. We must have tea together soon, and share our impressions. Right now, I have some private business with Tekelia and Padi."

They both bowed this time, and strode away, Yferen putting his arm around Ander's shoulder.

Aunt Asta drew a deep breath and turned on the bench to face Padi.

"Before we continue, I must say that I remain deeply mortified by the use to which I put Captain Mendoza. I would very much like to apologize. Do you think she might come to me—at her convenience, of course! I would go to her, but having once gotten away from Civilization, I feel that I ought not to go back."

"I'm certain she would like to meet you, ma—Aunt Asta," Padi said, catching her error in time. "However, she has accompanied my father, her lifemate, up to our ship for a few days."

Asta vesterGranz patted her gently on the knee.

"At her convenience, my love! I am completely at her service."

"I will give her your invitation," Padi promised. "I will be speaking to the ship tomorrow morning."

"That is very well, then," Aunt Asta pronounced. She tipped her head.

"Tekelia tells me that you have yet to be Sorted. I believe I may be able to perform that service for you, if you like."

"My elders and my teachers all set great store by Sorting," Padi said. "The situation has been that I have been too...bright for them to See properly. I have been given basic lessons and forms, and I do not hide from you that I am not a very apt student. I do begin to think that, if we only knew what my Gift is, more applicable lessons might be offered, and I would become—more apt."

"Exactly!" Aunt Asta smiled. "It's important to know your strengths, so that you might build on them properly—and also to know your weaknesses, so that you may protect yourself."

She stood, and smiled gently down at Padi.

"Stand with me now, that's right, and only rest your hands in mine. If Tekelia would provide us with some quiet—thank you, dear. Now, if you please, Padi yos'Galan, open your shields so that I may See you."

The last person who had undertaken to Sort her had not asked so gently, nor had Padi been so well disposed toward them.

She opened her shields, and saw Aunt Asta's eyes widen, even as she smiled.

"You brook no nonsense, do you, my love? Well, now, what do I See?

"A little Foresight, but not enough to disrupt your peace of mind. A strong aptitude for Healing—you will want to take training there—it's a gentle and useful Gift."

"My father is a Healer," Padi said.

"Then you will have a mentor close by. That's good. I See that you have a deep relationship with luck, and a strong sense of reality. Neither of those is a Gift; however, they form the framework through which your Gifts operate. I expect that is how you are able to center Tekelia and neutralize their most chaotic aspect. I can See the shape, but I do not wholly recognize it. You may, indeed, be the bearer of a new Gift."

She moved her hands away from Padi's.

"You Look like Haosa to me, Padi yos'Galan. Your Talent acts directly upon the world; you require no tools to focus your will. You must be very careful about the energy you expend—your teachers will be able to address that with you."

Padi looked past Aunt Asta to Tekelia, who was sitting calmly, listening, certainly. Her sense, through the link they shared, was that Tekelia was interested, but not at all distressed.

"Excuse me if I have not quite understood," she said to Aunt Asta. "You seem to say that my Gift exists to—center Tekelia."

"Certainly, your Gift does center Tekelia," Aunt Asta said.

"Yes, but, ma'am—I hadn't known of Tekelia until very recently, and Colemeno only slightly longer. It was far more likely that Tekelia and I would never meet than that we would. Had we not, what of my Gift then?"

"An excellent question!" Aunt Asta exclaimed. "We are not our Gifts; our Gifts are only a part of the wholeness of ourselves. You are a very strong multi-Talent, with a great deal of scope. It will fall to you to decide how much, and what sort, of training you wish to take in order to be the best Padi yos'Galan you can contrive to be. I do counsel you to take training as a Healer. Not only is it a good and useful Gift, it can be too easily misused in ignorance, and real harm done."

Padi inclined her head. "Of course, I don't wish to cause unintended hurt."

Aunt Asta laughed.

"No, any harm you do will be intentional, I warrant! Let the good you do be intentional as well. You have a long discovery before you, my dear—how I envy you!"

She stepped to the side.

"Now, children, I think we should eat something—and Tekelia, you may let the ambient in again."

On-Grid
Cardfall Casino

. . . .

"PRINCIPAL ZIAGORN, MAY I SPEAK WITH YOU A MOMENT?"

Majel turned. The person before him was not a regular, though she looked slightly familiar. She was dressed with propriety, the only odd thing being the boutonniere of baccata sprig, with three tiny red berries showing.

Perhaps she was in mourning, Majel thought. He smiled, as befitted the host, and inclined his head.

"Of course," he said affably. "How may I serve you?"

His interlocutor glanced from one side to the other. The main room was busy at this hour, and apparently her topic was not for public consumption.

"Shall we go to the bar?" he asked.

She smiled.

"Yes, thank you."

Majel led his guest to the far end of the bar, where the acoustics had been managed to allow private conversation.

"May I give you wine?" he asked.

His companion held up a hand.

"If I might have a glass of water?"

"Certainly." He leaned forward to signal Mardek, who arrived almost immediately with a pitcher and two glasses half-filled with ice. He glanced at Majel's guest, but made no sign of concern, and went back to his station at the center of the bar.

Majel poured water into glasses.

His guest drank thirstily, while Majel studied her more closely.

"Thank you," she said, putting the glass down. The look she turned on him was quizzical.

"You don't remember me," she said.

"I've been thinking that I *ought* to remember you," Majel said, "only I don't quite—"

He blinked.

"The last chizler," he said.

She smiled.

"In fact, the last chizler," she said, gravely, and that, Majel thought, was why he had not placed her. Her demeanor with Seylin after being taken off the Sixes table, during the interview, and when she was escorted from the premises by City Security, had been tolerant and self-possessed. This gravity hardly became her.

"I came," she continued, "to give you that guarantee. I *am* the last chizler, of an arranged set."

She slipped the baccata sprig from her buttonhole, and laid it on the bar by his hand. "I offer my sorrow, for the damage I and mine did to you and yours."

He glanced down at the sprig. Three berries, he recalled, meant sorrow and guilt.

He looked back to his guest.

"We did apprehend you," he pointed out.

"Indeed you did, but did you apprehend those we covered for, by drawing attention away from the Yellow Room?"

"Not yet, no, though we did find and repair the damage."

She reached to the pitcher and poured herself another glass of water.

"I," she said, after the glass was filled, "am Deaf. My associates, whom you also apprehended, are Deaf. We were paid to create a diversion at the Sixes table on five separate occasions. Our employer was not Deaf."

She took a long swallow from her glass and put it aside.

"It was a risky contract, but it paid well, and income had lately been slight. Our purpose was to draw floor security, and patrons, to the Sixes table at certain set times, which meant that we had to be caught, our faces and names recorded. But, since the casino sustained no loss, we were only cited as mischief-makers, which, as you know, falls off the official records at the end of a half-year."

"Very true."

Majel had a drink of water.

"You are telling me this for a reason," he suggested.

"Yes." She took a breath. "As I said, we are all five of us Deaf. We attended the emergency meeting, heard of the mischief against the school, and the request for data of previously unreported incidents of mischief to be sent to the Coalition. And it occurred to us—as it should have previously—that *ours* were the names and the faces Security had recorded. That not only would we be found, when it transpired that the action we covered materially harmed this casino, but it would be also a case of Deaf preying upon Deaf. City Security, having their criminals in hand, will not look further, for a Civilized organizer. Nor will they give much credit to Deaf criminals seeking to implicate a respected Luzant."

Majel raised his glass—lowered it to stare at her.

"You can identify this respected Luzant?"

"Yes, Principal ziaGorn, I can, and I will. He is a regular player here. He did not give us a name, and he took some care to alter his features, but he did not alter his clothes—and I saw him twice on the evening when I played at Sixes. I took care to remember the face he wears here."

Majel glanced down, saw the sprig of baccata with its three red berries, and picked it up to slip into his buttonhole.

"What shall I call you?" he asked.

"Elza, Principal ziaGorn."

"I am pleased that you came to me with this, Elza. Would you like a tour of the floor?"

She smiled.

"I would be delighted," she said.

Colemenoport
Wayfarer

· · · · · · · · · · ·

"GOOD DAY TO YOU, TRADER PADI! HOW DO YOU GO ON?"

"No, surely, that is for me to ask!" she protested. "How are you, Father?"

"Tolerably well, my child. Lina has of course scolded me. Keriana has made some tests, and promises that she will make more. Priscilla has ransomed herself to Lina so that I might speak with you, and hear all your news. So, tell me, are you well?"

"Yes, of course," Padi said, somewhat surprised. "I should tell you that Tekelia's Aunt Asta did the kindness of Sorting me."

"Did she, indeed? And what did she find?"

"She counsels me to train as a Healer, as I have sufficient of that Talent to be *good and useful*. Also, I have Foresight, though not enough, she says, to disturb my peace. For the rest of it, she thinks I may bear a new Gift. It is at least nothing quite like she has Seen before. She would have me be a very strong multi-Talent, and to her Sight, I am Haosa—able to interact directly with the ambient, with no need to build tools to focus my will."

She paused, and added, "At the moment, the apparent best use of my Gift is that I center Tekelia."

There was silence, longer, Padi thought, than lag could account for.

"Aunt Asta tells me, as you have yourself, that we are not our Gifts, and that I have a long and interesting discovery before me."

"I see. I will, I think, wish to call upon Tekelia's aunt, to thank her for her service to us."

"She would welcome that. Indeed, she wishes that Priscilla might come to her, when it is convenient. She feels she owes an apology."

"Well, then, we will make a party of it!" Father said gaily. "How does Tekelia go on?"

"As ever, I think. It will perhaps comfort you to know that Tekelia does not believe we are lifemated, only that we dance together...more intimately...than those others Tekelia dances with. And, do you know, that may be my Gift in action."

"So it may. What interesting developments, to be sure. I look forward to your explorations and discoveries."

Padi frowned at the comm, but before she could ask what troubled him, he spoke again.

"May the master trader inquire into the progress of the whole port inventory?"

"Yes, certainly. Jes and Dyoli are even now instructing the eight interested accountants in the subtleties of sorting the raw data we are already receiving from vendors on-port. A solicitation letter has been sent to the suggested firms in the city, and Jes is confident of a similar outpouring of support."

"This sounds like excellent progress," the master trader said. "And on the trade-side?"

"The port inventory seems to have cast trade into the shade," Padi said. "I have a few appointments today. Yesterday's most notable transaction was supplied by Trader Isfelm, who has found the old charts she had spoken to you about. She supplies a data-key, gratis. She also showed me the flat chart from which the copy on the key was taken. The tale is that it had been purchased by Can Ith yos'Phelium, who had an eye on the routes around Tinsori, for trade. It is presently in our office safe, and Trader Isfelm has given port-rate for storage."

"Well! Please send the data from the key to me. What does Trader Isfelm wish for the flat chart?"

"She would offer it to the master trader as an antiquity, sir."

"I see. If she is content to leave it in our safe, I will look at it when I return to port," he said. "I expect that the data-key will provide what I may need."

"Yes, sir," Padi said. "I have...additional information."

"Do you? Please, Trader Padi, enlighten me."

"I recently had a letter from Trader Vanz Denobli, telling me, in part, that upon achieving his garnet, and a daughter's share, he was given to study the Rimedge Loop, which had long been closed due to Dust, for a possible reopening. Trader Isfelm's chart details, among other things, the Rim's Edge Route."

She thought she heard the master trader say, very softly, "Ah."

"I have written to Vanz, sir, telling him about this chart, passing on Trader Isfelm's caution that it is not a navigation tool. The trader gave me to know that the star that nourished Riley's Tavern had long ago become unstable, but there has been no recent word of the Jump-point, hard by, doubtless because of the Dust."

"Doubtless so. Very well, then, Trader. I have no interest in the flat chart. I suggest, but do not insist, that it may make a handsome present from you to Trader Vanz, to celebrate his recent successes."

Padi raised her eyebrows.

"It might, at that," she said. "I will speak with Trader Isfelm."

"Excellent. Is there anything else I should know, Trader Padi? Have you a need for the master trader's counsel on any topic?"

"At the moment, I think not," she said. "All must await the outcome of the inventory, and *Qe'andra* dea'Tolin has that *well* in hand."

"To show *Qe'andra* dea'Tolin a challenge is to see her rise to meet it. Truly, she is an inspiration to us all."

"Not only has she risen to meet it, she is bearing Dyoli and Mar Tyn with her."

"As it should be. Now, Daughter, I am wanted very soon in sick bay for the rest of those tests. Have you told Dyoli that your Sorting shows a significant Talent for Healing?"

"Truly, sir, I have had no opportunity. I do expect to see her at nuncheon."

"Do, then, inform her. She may be able to give you some advice, or—forgive me!—exercises, so that you do not inadvertently use your Gift. Understand, this has to do with the action of Colemeno's ambient, rather than any doubt of your control."

"I do understand," Padi told him. "I'll speak with Dyoli."

"Splendid. I look forward to our next scheduled hour. Be well, Padi."

"Be well, Father."

. . . .

"THIS SESSION OF THE COUNCIL OF THE WHOLE IS NOW OPEN," Chair gorminAstir stated. "Our first order of business is to interview the Oracle for Civilization."

She looked down the table, at each of the eleven councilors dutifully in their places, and at the Warden of Civilization, who sat at his desk beside the council table.

"The Warden of Civilization is asked to bring the Oracle before us."

The Warden stood, robes rustling, and bowed to the Council entire. Straightening, he met Chair gorminAstir's eye.

"Asta vesterGranz sends her regrets to the Council of the Civilized. She has retired from her position as Oracle for Civilization, and has established her own household."

He sat down.

There was complete silence in the Council chamber for the count of twelve.

Majel ziaGorn raised his hand.

"The Chair sees Councilor ziaGorn," gorminAstir said, with great calm.

"Is the Council, as the representative of Civilization, required to sign off on any legal documents, or otherwise perform actions that will release Luzant vesterGranz's retirement benefits to her?"

"That is not *Luzant* vesterGranz, Councilor," snarled tryaBent, "it is *Haosa* vesterGranz."

Majel turned toward the councilor and bowed.

"I am corrected." He turned back to the head of the table.

"The former oracle was employed by this Council, which represents Civilization. She served selflessly, and for many years.

401

It behooves us to be certain that any benefits she has earned by her long service be released to her in a timely manner."

He sat down.

azieEm raised her hand.

"The Chair sees Councilor azieEm."

"I agree with Councilor ziaGorn in principle," she said. "It is our duty to provide the former oracle everything that is owed to her, under contract, and by tradition. However—and perhaps the Warden may enlighten me, since I believe that the Oracle's upkeep comes under his office—I do not recall seeing a budget line dedicated to the Oracle's retirement benefits."

"The Warden of Civilization may answer Councilor azieEm's question."

Bentamin rose.

"The Oracle is by tradition a ward of Civilization," he said. "Civilization provides lodging, food, servants—all the necessities and no few of the luxuries of a comfortable life. Because Oracles reside within the Wardian, these expenses are met by the Warden's Office."

azieEm raised her hand. He paused.

"I wish to be clear. This is also the case for the Oracle's salary? It is paid from the Wardian's budget?"

Bentamin spread his hands.

"The Oracles do not draw a salary, as their every need is met. This continues to be the case upon the occasion of an Oracle's retirement. Their upkeep is guaranteed for the rest of their lives."

Majel ziaGorn raised his hand. Chair gorminAstir merely inclined her head.

"As Asta vesterGranz has chosen not to avail herself of the Wardian's continued care," he said, "I suggest that the Council offer a one-time compensation equal to cost of that care."

"Are you mad?" tryaBent demanded. "This woman has deserted her post—one of the most sensitive and critical in all of Civilization! And instead of formulating a plan to return her as soon as possible to duty, with an appropriate chastisement, you wish to reward her act of treachery with a sizable payout!"

Majel drew a breath. "The Oracle has retired," he said, calmly.

"The Oracle *cannot* retire!" tryaBent shouted. "Until and unless a new Oracle arises, the existing Oracle must serve!"

"Coracta, calm yourself," Chair gorminAstir said. "Councilor ziaGorn, your suggestion has merit, but other business precedes it. Warden, has a new Oracle arisen?"

"As far as I am aware; as far as the former Oracle was aware—no. A new Oracle has not arisen. It is the belief of the former Oracle that Civilization no longer has need."

"Self-serving claptrap," tryaBent snapped. "Aside anything else, to speak of compensating Haosa vesterGranz, as if her pockets are flat, is past absurd. The vesterGranz are *quite* able to care for her, as the Warden well knows, theirs being the cadet Line of his own house."

"That is quite aside the point," Majel ziaGorn said. "The point is what she is herself owed, for the service she has give—"

"The matter of compensating the former Oracle on her retirement is tabled for the present," Chair gorminAstir stated firmly.

Majel inclined his head. "Your pardon, Chair."

tryaBent said nothing.

gorminAstir was seen to take a deep breath.

"The Council will adjourn for one hour. Please clear the chamber. Warden, stay with me, if you please."

gorminAstir stood in the window until the room was cleared, looking down at the street below. Bentamin drew two cups of tea, and offered her one.

She took it without looking aside, and without a word, which was not much like her, though Bentamin could hardly blame her for being abstracted. He would not, in fact, have wondered if she had been angry, but the wonder was instead that she was not.

"I suppose you had a good and compelling reason for allowing the former Oracle to escape the Wardian," she said, after she had taken a sip of tea. She was still staring down at the street; her face in profile was tight, and showing lines at the corner of mouth and eye. It struck Bentamin that she was not so very much younger than Aunt Asta.

"In fact, your use of the word *escape* illuminates my decision," he said.

"I had wondered if that was it," she said, and raised her cup to her lips.

Bentamin sipped his tea, and looked down. The street was abuzz with morning traffic. At the far end of the block, he could see the cart that sold cut flowers, a dazzle of indolent color among the bustling busyness.

"Shall I tender my resignation?" he asked.

"No, why should you? The Warden's mandate is to preserve the integrity of Civilization. I believe that you acted within that mandate, as you have done for years, unfailingly. Civilization could only be made less by refusing to allow its faithful servant to rest.

"I do ask—had the former Oracle *Seen* that Civilization no longer needs any Oracle?"

"She did not say so specifically. My impression was that she considered the fact of there being no replacement Oracle as its own proof."

He paused, sipped tea, made a decision.

"She *did* say that she had Seen the end of Civilization and the Haosa, too."

gorminAstir turned her head to stare at him, face expressionless.

"Did she, indeed? If that is the case, then I agree—we no longer need an Oracle."

"Long Sight is notoriously unreliable," Bentamin murmured.

"No one knows that better than an Oracle, I would think," gorminAstir answered. "The fact that she chose to mention it to you makes me think that she felt that particular insight was... more possible than others she might have had."

Bentamin said nothing.

"I wonder if you know where the former Oracle has retired to, and if you will tell me," gorminAstir said after a moment.

"She retired to Ribbon Dance Village. As you know, she and the Speaker for the Haosa are kin."

"As you are." gorminAstir sighed, and turned to face him fully.

"Do you think it might be possible for me to visit the former Oracle in her retirement?" she said. "Myself alone, with your escort, if you will grant it. The Speaker for the Haosa will of course wish to be present, as well."

"I'll ask if she will permit such a visit."

"Thank you. Tell her, please, that I honor her decision, and wish to discuss what compensation she would find appropriate, upon leaving Civilization's service."

"I'll tell her," Bentamin promised.

gorminAstir smiled, and drank off what was left of her tea.

"And, now, I suggest we open the door, and try if we can't attend to the rest of our business today."

Off-Grid
The Tree House

. . . .

RIBBON-LIGHT DANCED WITH THE SHADOWY TREES, AND THE wind blew chilly, damp from the river.

Tekelia was leaning, elbows on the rail, looking out at the night.

Padi had her arms around Tekelia's waist, her cheek against Tekelia's shoulder. It seemed to her that she could feel the Ribbons sliding over her skin, warm and cool all at once, with an occasional spark, too brief to be painful, that excited the center of her Gift.

"I spoke to my father," she said, lazily.

"How does he go on?" asked Tekelia.

"Well enough. The ship's Healer pronounces him well. The ship's medic, who is not a woman to trifle with, is insisting on an entire suite of tests before she ventures to have an opinion."

"And Captain Mendoza?"

"He only said that she was being tested, as well, having given herself over to the Healer so that he could make our call."

She sighed slightly, and nestled her cheek closer against Tekelia's shoulder.

"He is trying to quantify our bond," she murmured, and felt Tekelia stiffen slightly, even as she felt the flicker of a question inside her head.

"No, he does not dislike it—though I own he may not perfectly *like* it. Only, he wishes to *understand* it, so that he may know what is—what is due and what is owed, that proper honor is given, whether you will come into our Line, or, indeed, under the Dragon's wing at all—"

"What if you came into my Line?" Tekelia asked, and Padi tasted a certain sharpness to that query along their link.

405

"Then you and I will need to talk about what that means, and what we may do to make it possible, pleasurable, and profitable for all."

Tekelia laughed.

"Too reasonable, Padi yos'Galan!"

"But why would I want to be unreasonable?" she asked. "We dance together. I want us both to be happy with that circumstance. Don't you?"

"More than I have wanted anything in...a very long time."

Tekelia straightened, and turned inside the circle of Padi's arms.

"Shall I speak with your father? I don't know that I can relieve his concern, but I'll try."

"We ought both to speak with Father, when he is returned to us."

"And if the medic decrees that he ought to stay with the ship? I am willing," Tekelia said, "to go to him, if that's allowed."

Padi lifted her eyes to meet one blue eye and one green.

"Can you?" she asked.

"Can I what?"

"Go onto the *Passage*. The ambient is—not so apparent."

"I'm not wholly dependent on the ambient," Tekelia said. "After all, I can manage perfectly well under the Grid."

"Yes, but there is still an ambient under the Grid," Padi said. "There may not be any ambient at all, on-ship."

Tekelia's eyebrows drew in a frown, then lifted in a laugh.

"Now, you've made me curious! I insist on being allowed to go aboard your ship!"

Padi laughed.

"I will let my father know that you take his concern seriously and are eager to speak with him when he returns to Colemeno, or to travel to him aboard the *Passage*."

"I leave it all to you," Tekelia said. "Speaking of travels, I'll be away for a day or possibly two."

"Oh? Where will you go?"

"To Visalee, first. Blays has something she would like my help with. After that, to Encharo."

Padi tipped her head. "These are other Haosa villages?"

"They are, yes. Further out from the Grid. You might, in fact, call them isolated. Since I am Speaker for the Haosa..."

"Certainly. You must speak *to* them in order to speak *for* them. Do let me know when you are returned."

"I will," Tekelia promised, putting hands on Padi's shoulders.

"Will you be sleeping here tonight?"

She looked around at the Ribbon-washed forest.

"Do you know," she said, smiling into Tekelia's face, "I think I will."

On-Grid
Cardfall Casino

. . . .

"HE'S HERE," ELZA SAID, WHEN MAJEL ARRIVED AT THE SHELTERED corner of the bar that had become their place to meet, at mid-night.

"I saw him in the main room, playing at the wheel."

Majel sighed. He had begun to wonder, when several nights had passed and no particular Luzant identified that perhaps Elza was toying with him—or that the Luzant, realizing his danger, had simply found another place to gamble.

"Have you told Seylin?" he asked now.

"Yes; she sent Veerin, and I pointed the Luzant out to him. He will watch and if necessary follow, until Seylin arrives." She glanced over her shoulder toward the main floor.

"I should go back," she said.

"Let us both go back," Majel said, offering his arm. "I have an interest in meeting this Luzant."

Elza smiled, sharp and feral. She took his arm, and they went out onto the floor, together.

Veerin had been floor security at the Cardfall for years. He was solid, calm, careful; and he blended seamlessly into the regular main room crowd. As he and Elza approached the wheel, Majel saw Veerin moving off at an angle, face intent, as if he were following a possible chizler.

"Your Luzant is on the move," he murmured to Elza, altering course to follow Veerin.

Elza tugged his arm, pulling him back toward the wheel.

"No, he's still there," she said. "Standing on the red side, wearing a puce half-jacket, and his hair braided close."

Majel looked and found him. A portly man, crowding the betting board, dark blond hair in tight, skull-hugging braids.

"You are certain that this is the man?" he said to Elza, glancing over her shoulder to find Veerin moving toward the card room.

"Yes!" Elza said sharply. "I don't know why—*now* he's moving! We can't lose him—"

She dropped his arm and went forward, on an intercept course with the man in the puce half-jacket. Majel glanced around, and spied Seylin in her uniform, walking with purpose across the floor. He raised his hand, caught her answering wave, and turned to follow Elza.

"You." The man in puce had stopped, and turned to face Elza, quite as if they were alone, and not at the side of a room busy with play. "Clever, are you, Deaf?"

"Not particularly," Elza said, stopping outside the range of the man's long reach.

"That's too bad. You're going to need to be clever to explain why you were shooting into the players."

A hand moved beneath the jacket. Majel caught the gleam of a weapon, and leapt, meaning to wrest the thing away, even as Elza shouted.

"Everybody down!"

Majel had the man's wrist. He twisted, saw the gun spin away—and stumbled as the Luzant shoved him back. There was a roaring in his ears, and an impact against the side of his head that sent him crashing into the wall.

He felt his knees start to give; straightened them in an act of sheer will as Seylin arrived, her face grim. The Luzant tried to turn, but his own feet tripped him, and he went down to the floor, hard.

Seylin grabbed his arms, jerked them back and twisted the wire around them.

"I've done nothing wrong!" the man on the floor said, his voice peculiarly calm, and for a heartbeat, Majel believed him—and then disbelieved, as Seylin knelt and slapped hush-tape over his mouth.

Majel felt an arm come around his waist, and carefully turned his head to look at Elza.

"Are you all right, sir?" she asked. "That was past foolish! Did he hurt you?"

His felt as if someone had brought a hammer against his skull; the headache was making him queasy.

"I'm...not...quite certain," he told Elza, who tightened her grip 'round his waist, and thrust her shoulder under his arm, taking some of the support his knees were unwilling to provide.

On the floor, those patrons who had heeded Elza's shout were rising, some moving toward the door, others watching Seylin finish trussing her prisoner, yet others going back to their play.

In the midst, Veerin arrived, looking chastened.

"Chief atBuro! I—he was heading for the card room. I had him in sight. How—"

"A suggestion slipped in when you were distracted," Seylin said grimly. "Get your shields rehabbed, but first Call Beni and Ikat here. Also, Principal ziaGorn will have the medic."

Majel took a breath, but did not argue the point. His head felt as if it would break in two; and he feared his stomach was about to betray him.

Seylin turned her head to meet his eyes, and snapped.

"Principal ziaGorn will have the Healer *at once.*"

Dutiful Passage
Colemeno Orbit

. . . .

KERIANA HAD AT LAST RUN OUT OF TESTS. ALL THAT REMAINED was collecting the results.

Shan and Priscilla retired to the master trader's office, there to work companionably, each at their own screen, with occasional murmured questions, or observations.

It was, truth said, peaceful, comfortable, and very nearly indolent.

Shan sighed with real contentment as he finished his letter to Denobli, and sent it into the outgoing mail queue.

He then spun his chair and addressed himself to his lifemate.

"I had no idea how oppressive it was to always be needing to eat something," he said. "Really, I feel quite liberated. Here we have been sitting for hours, and nary a slice of cake in sight!"

Priscilla looked up from her screen with a smile.

"Will I spoil the mood, if I ask you to bring me a glass of cold tea?"

"In fact, it will be my pleasure."

"May I ask what keeps you at your keyboard?" he said, arriving beside her with two glasses of tea.

She received one with a smile.

"I have the first questionnaire from Scholar rodaMildin—I told you about her, remember?"

"I do indeed! The first Colemeno sociologist to have access to barbarians since the Dust came in."

Priscilla laughed.

"She doesn't put it quite like that."

"I expect not, if she wants answers to her questions. What *are* her questions?"

411

"She wonders if we had access to any primary source material from Colemeno before we arrived in orbit."

"Are we, in fact, tainted with preconception?"

"I suppose she has to ask," Priscilla said, turning back to the keyboard. "I will mention Wu and Fabricant's Guide."

"You might even send her a copy, in case—"

The comm sounded.

Shan crossed to his desk and touched the button.

"yos'Galan."

"Master Trader, it's Keriana. I have the results of the tests, and I would like to discuss them with you and Captain Mendoza. Is now convenient?"

"One moment, please."

Shan looked to Priscilla, who had already closed her screen.

"Now is convenient," she said.

On-Grid
Cardfall Casino

. . . .

"MAJEL?"

Seylin's voice was soft, but firm enough to catch his wandering attention. He opened his eyes, beheld her sitting on the chair next the cot, and sighed.

"Well, old friend. How are you?" he asked.

"Unsettled, but that will wait for a moment. How does your head feel?"

He considered that seriously.

"The headache is gone, and my stomach is no longer offended. I believe I could stand, if you insist. Do you insist?"

She smiled, which called his attention to how tight her face was, how stern her eyes.

"Tell me," he said softly.

She sighed.

"The Luzant—who refuses to give a name, and is strong-willed enough to resist a Command to relinquish it—is in the high-risk room at Riverside Security Office. I have filed a complaint on your behalf, and we are warned that we will likely be called to witness within the next few hours.

"That said, we have a problem."

"Well, yes, we do!" Majel said sharply. "That person worked deliberately to ruin the casino. He pulled a gun and threatened to shoot into the crowd of those at game. I don't doubt he was manipulating the wheel—"

"He was," Seylin said. "Not only did he threaten patrons at play, he struck you with enough force that he might have inflicted real and lasting damage. Happily, you employ a Healer of superior skill, whose specialty is mind-burn."

413

Majel eyed her.

"Mind-burn?" he repeated.

"Mind-burn. And, yes, it's every bit as dire as it sounds. Dire enough that the law understands it as deadly force."

Majel blew out a breath.

"Well then, it seems that our Luzant has made an error. Employing killing force is rather more than mere mischief."

"Yes, but there's more. You recall the signature found at Pacazahno, that had imprinted on the smashed readers?"

"Yes..."

"Yes. I Saw that signature, at Pacazahno, and again tonight, before he locked his shields."

Majel stared.

"The one who *hates* Deaf."

"That one, yes." Seylin sighed, suddenly looking very tired, indeed.

"Seylin, take the rest of the shift off," he said. "You—"

"I'm exhausted. Terror does that, and I was certain I'd lost you. Majel—"

"I was foolish beyond permission. Even Elza said so. My excuse is that he was going to start shooting into the room—"

"Yes, yes." She extended a hand and patted his shoulder. "I would have done the same. But *I* have shields—and a much longer reach."

Majel smiled.

"Will you forgive me for having frightened you, Seylin?"

"Oh, easily!" She patted him once more and withdrew her hand, her face locking down into grimness again.

"I have one more thing to report, then I'll go off duty and take some rest before we're called to witness. You recall that our Luzant will not give his name?"

"I do."

"As miserly as he is with his own, he is very free with his patron's name, and has demanded that she be called to his defense."

"This sounds like good luck at last. Who is his patron?"

Seylin's shoulders drooped.

"Betya seelyFaire."

Dutiful Passage
Colemeno Orbit

. . . .

"ALL THE RESULTS AGREE—THE TWO OF YOU ARE AS NEAR TO perfectly healthy as it's possible to get. Colemeno agrees with you."

"It must," Shan murmured, "be the cake."

"Or the ambient," Priscilla said, and looked to Keriana. "We were frequently tired, on-planet."

"Showing no signs of clinical exhaustion," Keriana said. "I think you said that the mission at Colemeno was ambitious and also shorthanded." She raised her hands. "People get tired."

"Very true. We will do better, when we return. Which will be—"

"Ah," said Keriana.

Shan looked at her.

"Ah?"

"Yes, sir. You're cleared to go—now, if you want. However, the tests also show that Captain Mendoza is close to delivery—early, but nothing to worry about. Now that she's come up to us, I'd like her to stay."

On-Grid
Riverside Security Office

. . . .

"REALLY," THE LADY SNAPPED AS SHE CAME INTO THE INQUIRY
room, "could this not have waited until sometime after dawn?"

"My apologies, Councilor," said the security officer, standing
up from behind the table. "The law is clear. Should a suspect
call for support, as of an employer, a patron, a commander, or a
lawyer, that support must be registered to the case no later than
three hours after the demand is made."

seelyFaire stared at him.

"How if I had been away from home?"

"Then an extension would have been filed, ma'am, which is
extra expense for all, and more time before a proper resolution
is made. So, it's fortunate that you were home."

"And asleep," seelyFaire said pointedly. She sat in the chair
opposite the officer. "Since I'm here, let's get this over with. Who
has called me to their defense?"

"As I said when we spoke on the comm," Security said, seating
himself with care, "the suspect does not care to give his name—
only yours."

"May I mention that this is open to abuse? Anyone might decide
to call upon a Council member at any hour of the day or night."

"We did have a Truthseer verify the information, Councilor.
The suspect believes that you are his patron."

seelyFaire sighed sharply.

"Now, because this is a case of material harm, there are remote
observers monitoring this proceeding, to ensure that all is done
properly. In addition, this session is being recorded. When we
begin, the suspect will be brought in, with his guard, and the
Truthseer. I must warn you that the suspect is under restraint.

416

This is standard for all suspects of violent acts. You will be asked to verify your relationship with the suspect."

"I understand. May we proceed?"

"Yes, Councilor. As this is a case of material harm, there are witnesses. They will be escorted in after verification has been made. The witnesses will present their evidence under the scrutiny of the Truthseer. The suspect will then be allowed to give his evidence, also scrutinized by the Truthseer. Do you understand the procedure, Councilor?"

"I do, but I wonder why I am here at all. If material harm has been done, I certainly did not—"

"In the case, the suspect has named you as his patron," Security repeated. "We will be seeking to discover if his actions were performed under your patronage."

seelyFaire drew a deep breath.

"If it is found that material harm was done as a result of the suspect's relationship with you, then you will share the penalty."

She closed her eyes.

"Have you any questions, Councilor?"

"I have not," she said. "Let's get this farce over with."

"As you say." He raised his voice slightly. "Please bring in the suspect."

The door opened. A portly man in a torn puce jacket, hair braided tightly against his head, entered, escorted by a woman in the uniform of City Security. The man's hands were bound before him, and there was tape over his mouth, which argued that he was a Persuader. There was a steely shimmer outlining his person, which would be the restraint provided by his guard.

Following them both was a robed Truthseer, hood pulled up.

The suspect was stopped at the foot of the table. The Truthseer took up position in the corner, where they would have access to the entire room.

"Councilor seelyFaire," said the Security officer. "Please give your name and position, so that the Truthseer may Hear you."

She did so. The Truthseer inclined slightly.

"I have my range, Officer bilVenta."

"Good."

He turned to address the Councilor.

"Since a complaint has been filed, and we do have witnesses, the Truthseer will only speak out if a lie or an ambiguity is detected. At the end of witnessed testimony, she will make a statement, which is for the benefit of the observers, and those who will review the recording.

"Have you any questions, Councilor?"

"I do not."

"Then we begin. Councilor seelyFaire, do you know who this person is?"

seelyFaire frowned, her eyes sweeping the suspect from braids to boots, then turned to Officer bilVenta.

"I believe him to be Jewlyus firnPeltir," she said, slowly.

"And are you his patron?"

Her frown grew more decided.

"I am a sponsor of the organization of which he is the second officer," she said. "One among a dozen, perhaps more."

"What is the name of this organization?"

"The Protectors of Civilization," seelyFaire said.

"And what is your relationship with this organization?"

"My name is on their letterhead," she said, still frowning. "I attend various of their functions, when my schedule permits, and occasionally give talks or presentations."

She turned sharply to look into bilVenta's face.

"I am not a *patron*," she said, "not of the organization, and certainly not of Luzant firnPeltir."

"That," said the Truthseer, "is ambiguous."

seelyFaire threw up her hands.

"I acknowledge it," she said, and looked to the officer. "How do we proceed?"

"As the suspect believes you to be his patron, and your own truth is ambiguous, prudence dictates that we proceed as if you are the suspect's patron."

seelyFaire sighed.

"May I know what he has done?"

"Yes." He turned to those standing at the end of the table. "The suspect will be seated."

This was done. Officer bilVenta rose, and poured four glasses of water from the pitcher at the end of the table. He put one at his place, one by seelyFaire's hand, and the other two at the empty chairs next to her.

Reseating himself, he sipped water, sighed and raised his voice slightly.

"Please admit the witnesses."

The door opened, and Majel ziaGorn entered, slowly, paced by a stern-faced woman in livery, who immediately stepped forward and pulled a chair out.

"Principal ziaGorn," she murmured. "Please sit, sir. You're not yet fully recovered from your wound."

"Wound?" seelyFaire repeated. "What has happened, Councilor?"

He glanced at her, his face pale and drawn.

"That," he said, "is what I am about to relate."

Majel came to an end of his story, and groped for his glass of water. His head had started to hurt again, though nothing like previously. He rather wished he could lie down.

"Surda ziaGorn has given a true accounting," the Truthseer said, that being for the record, and the witnesses.

seelyFaire had long since replaced irritation and even puzzlement with the cool expression of a councilor hearing testimony.

"Luzant Seylin atBuro, chief of security at Cardfall Casino, may now give her testimony," declared Officer bilVenta.

She did so, wonderfully succinct, stating that she had Seen the suspect's signature when she had apprehended him at the casino. She added that the signature had previously been found in the casino, with regard to an expensive piece of equipment, repeatedly Intending its failure.

She paused for a sip of water, and added, "I Saw the suspect's signature a third time at another scene of mischief."

The security officer frowned.

"What was the nature of that mischief, and how did you happen to See the suspect's signature?"

"The school at Pacazahno Village was vandalized," Seylin answered calmly. "Many pieces of student art were destroyed, and the library also. Several of the readers had apparently been selected for particular abuse. The Village Administrator had called in aid from Ribbon Dance Village, and one of those who answered was a psychometric. She was able to isolate the signature, and share it with the rest of us assisting."

The security officer frowned.

"A Haosa psychometric?"

"That is correct. Very skilled and careful."

The security officer pressed his lips together, and drew a breath, but seelyFaire was before him.

"A school?" she demanded. "Were— There were no injuries?"

Seylin faced her. "No injuries, Councilor. The mischief was carried out in the early hours, before school began." She glanced to Officer bilVenta.

"Have you more information, Luzant atBuro?" he asked.

"Sadly, it is hearsay, sir. I was not able to detect the alleged emotion, so cannot confirm that the pertinent signature bore a freight of hatred."

"That," said the Truthseer, "is a manipulation."

Seylin smiled and inclined her head.

"It is, yes," she admitted, folding her hands.

"The manipulative statement will be removed from the record," Officer bilVenta stated. "Luzant atBuro, have you any more to say that is pertinent to this event?"

"No, Officer. I am through."

He reached for his glass and drank water, then looked to the foot of the table.

"The suspect will now answer," he said.

The guard stepped forward, and pulled the tape from the suspect's mouth.

"You will state your name," Officer bilVenta said.

"Jewlyus firnPeltir, Telekinetic and Psychokinetic."

There was a pause.

Officer bilVenta looked to the corner where the Truthseer stood.

"That is," she said finally, "the Truth."

"You are called to answer the complaint made against you," Officer bilVenta said to firnPeltir.

"My patron, Councilor seelyFaire, will speak for me."

"I am not," seelyFaire said, in her Council-table voice, "your patron. I am a sponsor of the Protectors of Civilization. You are the second officer of that organization. I do not materially support you, nor do I give you orders."

"Oh, but you *gave* us our orders, didn't you?" firnPeltir said, with a knowing smile. "You spoke at meetings, and at our rallies. You told us—all of us!—how important it was to Civilization that the Deaf accept the guidance of their betters! That we couldn't go forward until there were no more factions—the Deaf brought under the protection of the Civilized and the Haosa Healed!"

seelyFaire made a small sound, rather like a whimper, and drew breath as if she would speak.

Before she could do so, however, the Truthseer stirred.

"This is True, in that Luzant firnPeltir believes what he says."

Officer bilVenta turned to seelyFaire.

"Has Luzant firnPeltir told the truth, Councilor?"

She raised a face that was ravaged.

"It is not—it is...*almost* true," she said, stringently. "He heard far more than I said, and certainly far more than I intended. What is factually true is that, yes, I did speak at meetings and rallies of the Protectors of Civilization on the topic of reinstating the patronage system, as the fairest and best way of ensuring that all living under the aegis of Civilization would be treated equally. I have never advocated targeting our Deaf citizens with violence."

"That," said the Truthseer, "is true."

On-Grid
The Sakuriji
Council Chambers

. . . .

THERE WAS ABSOLUTE SILENCE IN THE COUNCIL CHAMBER WHEN
the tape ended.

Eventually, ivenAlyatta said that she hoped Councilor ziaGorn
would experience a quick and complete recovery.

"I spoke to Councilor ziaGorn prior to calling this special
session," said Chair gorminAstir. "He assures me that he is well
on the way to recovery, only the Healer insists that he not only
rest, but sleep. He hopes to return to his chair no later than the
next meeting of the Council of the Whole."

"And seelyFaire?" tryaBent asked, rather subdued.

"Councilor seelyFaire offered her resignation when I spoke to
her," gorminAstir said. "On behalf of the Council, I accepted."

"Quite right," said tryaBent.

"One wonders what will now befall Luzant seelyFaire," said
azieEm. "If she is to share the penalty for a deadly attack—"

"I took the liberty of calling the investigating officer at Riverside Security. He allowed me to know that the Truthseer raised
reasonable doubt. Luzant firnPeltir does believe his statements to
be true. However, he may be of a disposition that allows him to
recast certain facts in his own mind, which he then believes to
be true. Luzant seelyFaire's testimony, that she did not advocate
violence as a method to return to the patronage system rang true
as steel, so said the Investigating Officer.

"Since the two true accounts conflict, Forensic Healers have
been called to do an evaluation. Security officers will be talking
with other members of the Protectors of Civilization. Luzant
firnPeltir will continue be held in custody, as he is deemed a
high risk. Luzant seelyFaire has been remanded to house arrest."

"If it's not out of order," ivenAlyatta said, "I volunteer to head the search committee to fill our vacant chair."

"Timely, rather," said gorminAstir. "Who are your seconds?"

"tryaBent and azieEm, if they are willing."

"I am inexperienced," azieEm said.

ivenAlyatta looked amused. "The cure for inexperience is experience. Serve and you will learn."

azieEm was actually seen to smile before she inclined her head.

"In that wise, I will serve, willingly."

"Thank you. Coracta?"

"Yes, of course."

"Thank you." ivenAlyatta glanced to the head of the table. "Chair gorminAstir, may the search committee begin its work?"

"At once. The committee will report its progress at every meeting of the Whole."

ivenAlyatta inclined her head and turned to her two committee members.

"After we are done here, let us meet for tea and cake in the lunchroom. We can go over the search procedures as outlined in the manual, discuss how we will share the mandated tasks, and if it will be wise to expand the membership of the committee."

The meeting ended not too long after that. Bentamin waited until the room had cleared before he approached gorminAstir.

"Warden?"

"I spoke to the former oracle last evening. She is willing to meet with you in her new home tomorrow midday, if that is not too soon for you. I cleared that time with the Speaker for the Haosa, and also with the Village Administrator, who will also be present."

"Tomorrow, midday," she repeated, and for a moment Bentamin thought that she would declare it ineligible.

Then, her shoulders softened, and she turned to look at him fully.

"I look forward to cordial discussion with the former Oracle, the Speaker for the Haosa, and the Village Administrator tomorrow at midday in Ribbon Dance Village. Advise me—shall I bring cake?"

"Cake is always welcome," Bentamin said with a smile.

"Then that is what I shall do. Will you call for me at my office?"

"It will be my pleasure," Bentamin assured her.

Colemenoport
Offices of the
Tree-and-Dragon Trade Mission

. . . .

"TRADER, MAY I SPEAK WITH YOU?"

Padi looked up from her screen. She had scarcely been needed over the last couple of days, and as a result had been able to make good progress with her reading for the route audit certification. In fact, she had just been about to take the half-course self-test when Jes had arrived at her desk.

She marked her place and smiled.

"I am at your disposal. Please sit. Will you like tea? Cake?"

Jes smiled, looking...somewhat less energetic than was her wont, and sat in the chair next to Padi's desk.

"No tea, I thank you, and I believe I have had a sufficiency of cake."

"I am familiar with the feeling," Padi assured her. She leaned back in her chair and spun slightly so that Jes had her whole face.

"Service?" she murmured.

Jes sighed.

"We," she said, "have a problem."

"Ah." Padi tipped her head. "It is, you know, running very close to schedule."

Jes laughed lightly.

"I suppose it is. And really, what savor is there in unchallenged success?"

"Exactly. What *is* our problem?"

"You will recall that we had good interest from a number of city-based accounting firms, and I had made appointments to speak with several."

Jes paused. Padi waited.

"The case is that none of those appointments have been kept. No one contacted me to cancel or to reschedule, mind you; they simply did not arrive. While one overwhelmed or rude person might exist in any particular set of persons, to have chosen all the unmannered accountants in the city at one go..." She took a breath. "I called those who had not kept their appointments, to find if we had perhaps sinned against custom..." She faltered.

"And no one will speak with you," Padi said. "I have seen this."

"Yes, of course, and so have I, only I had not hoped to see it *now*."

"The question is, why are we seeing it?" Padi said. "In the past, the reason had been undue influence from those who wished us ill. Have we made an enemy among the city firms? Someone perhaps who—"

She stopped.

"Trader?" Jes murmured.

"Yes, your pardon. I was only reminded that I had taken a meeting with one Zandir kezlBlythe, who had been quite put out that she was not to speak with the master trader, and who was quite clear that the trade mission will need contacts in the city, which she was uniquely positioned to provide."

She took a breath, and met Jes's eyes.

"She felt it necessary to relieve her feelings by—I will say, *throwing something*—at my shields."

Jes frowned.

"Were you injured, Trader?"

"A headache only. I am assured that my shields are prodigious. Had it been otherwise, I might, indeed, have been injured. As it was, her effort left a mark—and now I am doubting the wisdom of having repaired it."

"This, I apprehend, is why the master trader desired me to ask after kezlBlythe at the business associations," Jes said. "They have a syndicate in the city, and a friend in the chair of the business association, who assured me that they were our best option, and would make my work light."

Padi sighed.

"So we *have* sinned against custom," she said. "Is it a leap to think that the kezlBlythe Syndicate has put pressure on the independents with whom you made contact?"

"It seems a reasonable assumption. The question that remains

is, what shall we do? The master trader's instructions were clear."
Jes paused. "Do you think Dyoli might be able to See the repair
you made to your shields—understand, I am speaking from an
excess of ignorance!—and judge from that how much force was
brought against you?"

"I will ask her," Padi said. "In the meanwhile, let me call our
liaison and lay the kezlBlythe before him."

"Excellent." Jes stood. "I'll send Dyoli down to see you, shall I?"

"Yes, thank you, Jes."

Majel ziaGorn was not immediately available to answer the
comm. Padi left a message, asking that he call the trade mission
at his earliest convenience, and turned to find Dyoli leaning
against the table.

"Jes said you had taken a strike on your shields. When was this?"

"The morning of the day after Jes and Dil Nem joined us,"
Padi said. "I had taken the master trader's meetings—"

"And came back to us worn and full of information about
how the environment on Colemeno operates on Gifted individu-
als. I remember."

"I found, somewhat later, that my shields had been hit—it
Looked rather like someone had thrown a stone with an appreciable amount of force."

Dyoli's eyebrows rose.

"You were able to See that?"

"Yes. I made a mirror—though I hope you will not ask me
to show you how it was done, because I swear to you that I
don't know!"

Dyoli laughed. "No, I won't do anything so cruel. Though I
will, if you like, show you how *I* do it."

"That might be illuminating, thank you. You should be aware
that there is a large scar on my shields, from a previous strike.
My thought was that it would serve as a warn-away, and yet—"

"Some people simply will not take a hint," said Dyoli. "I'm
to understand that you repaired this second strike?"

"One does not," Padi said modestly, "like to boast."

"That would be bad form, I agree," Dyoli said, standing up
out of her lean. "If you please, sit down, close your eyes, and
visualize a white wall, by which I mean, try not to think about
anything."

"A challenge!" Padi murmured. Still, she did as Dyoli asked, bringing a blank wall before her mind's eye, and focused her attention on her breath.

"Just the thing," Dyoli said, and then did not say anything for a heartbeat or two.

"I See the previous strike, and I tell you frankly that it would warn *me* away. Otherwise, I—no. There *is* a newly polished area just to the left."

"That's it," Padi said.

"Allow me a moment..." Dyoli said.

Padi raised the white wall again, and brought her attention back to her breath.

Colored ribbons had begun to paint the surface of the wall before Dyoli spoke again.

"Open your eyes, please, Padi."

She did. Dyoli was sitting on the edge of the table, pale brows pulled, and a definite air of weariness about her.

Padi rose immediately.

"I will get cake," she said, "and tea."

Dyoli looked up at her.

"Thank you," she said. "Cake and tea would be most welcome."

"You did an excellent job of repair," Dyoli said, after she had dispatched a slice of cake and washed it down with tea.

Padi considered her.

"Why do I think that means you were not able to identify the original damage?"

"Possibly because that is what I had meant to say." Dyoli reached for the pot and refreshed her cup, and Padi's, too.

"What I may offer at this point is an opinion based on experience. Your shields are, indeed, formidable. The scar you have chosen not to erase is from a blow so powerful, it must have been intended to kill or unmind you on the spot. Does this understanding reflect what you know of your attacker?"

Padi drew a hard breath, remembering.

"She had other prey in her eye," she said slowly. "And I was interfering."

"So." Dyoli sipped tea. "Extrapolating from that, I judge that the smaller strike may have been an attempt to influence you to perform some action that you might not otherwise attempt—or possibly to ensure that you would without fail act upon a suggestion that had been made."

Padi put her teacup down with a sharp click.

"Have I hit near the mark?"

"You have struck the very center. A moment—"

She closed her eyes, and sent herself back to that moment in memory, the woman sitting at the table, the thoughtful glance, the question of her own *melant'i*—

"She said, 'You will tell the master trader that it will be very much to his advantage to come to my office in the city, so that we may reach an agreement regarding a mutually beneficial business arrangement.'"

She opened her eyes, and met Dyoli's pale gaze.

"At that moment, I heard—something—a ping, as of a stone thrown at a wall and bouncing away... And my head hurt until—until I *did* tell the master trader, precisely that, as part of my report."

She frowned.

"Which I would have done in any case."

Dyoli said nothing.

"Well, it's perfectly nonsensical!" Padi said, hotly. "There was not the least need to *compel* me to do my duty to the master trader."

"I have observed," Dyoli said, "that those without honor tend to assume that it means as little to others as it does to them."

Padi blew out a breath, and glared for a moment, over Dyoli's shoulder, at the blameless buffet.

When she had her temper in hand, she picked up her teacup and met Dyoli's eyes.

"It's all of a piece. Even had the master trader's policy allowed, we would not at all wish to do business with the kezlBlythe interests. That much is plain."

She drank off what was left of her tea, and put the cup down, more gently this time.

"One does wonder after local custom. The kezlBlythe have been allowed to flourish. Why have they not been brought to book? Are threats and compulsion the usual way of business being done in Haven City?" She sighed sharply. "We need advice."

"We do. Also—you ask excellent questions that bear on the trade mission and the master trader's long-term plans," Dyoli said. "However, I feel that I should point out that—we have no proof that threats and compulsion are in play."

Padi stared at her.

"Because I repaired my shields?"

"That is one factor. The other is that Jes does not have proof that intimidation is at work, or, if it is, that it is the kezlBlythe Syndicate which has brought pressure to bear. It seems to her—and to me, and, I gather, to you!—that the reason for these sudden cancellations and refusals to take calls is intimidation. What we are seeing matches a pattern familiar to you and to Jes. There is no doubt that *something* has put itself against the mission's best interest.

"Suspicion is not enough. We need to *know*."

"Which means that we need to meet with the kezlBlythe," Padi said, and suddenly smiled. "Well, it is what she had wanted, after all! Why should we not give it to her?"

On-Grid
Haven City

. . . .

AUNT ZANDIR HAD MET WITH A HEALER.

Jorey knew this because he kept a very close watch on clever Aunt Zandir now that she was threatening him.

Aunt Zandir was a great one for *plans*. And her plans had been put significantly forward when Jorey had broken through the wall the Healer had built between himself and his soul, killing Grandmother in the doing of it.

He had been, a little, sorry about that. Grandmother had spoken against having the Healer come in to do the work. It had been *Mother* who had insisted that Jorey be made Deaf, inept, and stupid, in order to keep him close to her.

Much good that had done her. Mother had fallen straight off the roof. Why she had been on the roof so late in the evening was never explained. It was not the best time to view the roof garden, and in any case, she had not been an admirer of flowers or any other sort of plant.

Yet, fallen from the roof she had, and that was Mother out of Aunt Zandir's way.

Jorey had for a long time thought that Aunt Avryal had been the reason for the fall. She and Mother had been at odds for as long as Jorey could remember. More lately, he had come to think that the genius behind the fall had been Aunt Zandir, even if it had been Aunt Avryal's hand on Mother's back.

In any case, Grandmother's death had suited Aunt Zandir right down to the ground. She became head of the family and the syndicate, which gathered even more influence and wealth under her guidance, and with Jorey as the enforcer of her will. She had praised him, then, for his strength and his daring. When he had learned how to siphon and copy signatures from the ambient, she had declared him her clever boy.

Aunt Zandir had not seen any reason, *then*, to have the Healers build a stronger wall, or cast him out into savagery. No, Aunt Zandir had seen that Jorey would be *useful* to her *plans*.

But the nature of Aunt Zandir's plans had changed as the family, and she as its head, had come more fully forward. Too many deaths, even unproved deaths, around the kezlBlythe Syndicate, would adversely affect their momentum. It was Aunt Zandir's ambition to be the leader of business and of policy in Haven City, and therefore, she refined her methods.

She had sought influence over well-connected Pel chastaMeir, thinking to reach the Warden though his kinsman. But Pel was deeper than Aunt Zandir had understood. Jorey had watched him shake off her control again and again, even as her influence corroded his shields.

Jorey's Sight wasn't best suited to such things, but he had come to believe that Pel had *two* sets of shields, one inside the other—the first meager and permeable; the inner as seamless and as slippery as glass.

Jorey watched Pel, clever Pel, kin to the Warden, willing to toy with Aunt Zandir—waiting for her to make a mistake. And if Pel brought down Aunt Zandir, he would also net Aunt Avryal—and Jorey.

He would be Healed again, cut in two, half-remembering what he had been, and all of what he'd lost.

Jorey had acted. Pel, clever, clever Pel, had stumbled when Jorey hit him in the back, falling beneath the wheels of the incoming train.

Zatorvia had been another of Aunt Zandir's *plans*. But Zatorvia had been no more in thrall than Pel had been. Maybe Pel had taught her how to double-shield, too.

She had been better at pretending, Zatorvia, and maybe Aunt Zandir *had* held some part of her. After all, she had never gone to the Warden, or called a Healer, or even a security officer. But she *had* gone to the port. Jorey had seen her, coming away from the Isfelm Trade Office, where Zatorvia had no business to be.

He had told Aunt Zandir that Zatorvia was going to try to run off-world. She had laughed and told him that Zatorvia was well under control.

The risk had been too much.

Jorey had acted again.

And now Aunt Zandir was threatening *him*, meeting with the Healer. Aunt Zandir would have to be dealt with, soon.

But there was something else that had to be done first. A new development.

There had been an eyewitness to Zatorvia's death. Right now, it was only a whisper on the streets, but it would be on the news services soon enough, and Aunt Zandir would hear it.

One of the brats must have seen him.

The lucky thing was that not only were the brats not of age, they were savages, living among the savage.

Jorey had no clear understanding of what sort of legal work might need to be done in order to allow the brats to testify against him. He thought it might take some time. On the other hand, it had *been* some time since Zatorvia's death, and the news only now being released. That spoke of confidence.

The legal work might already be done.

The Warden's office might be closing in on him—right now.

But they weren't here yet, Jorey thought.

And it didn't matter how legal the witness was, if the witness was dead.

Jorey took a hard breath, bringing a signature forward in his mind.

Mist swirled.

The room was empty.

Off-Grid
The Lilac Cottage
. . . .

"I HOPE YOU DON'T MIND BEING OUT IN THE FRESH AIR," AUNT Asta was saying to Chair gorminAstir. "I've come to find that the pavilion is more private than my parlor—and it's such a *fine* day."

gorminAstir smiled and inclined her head slightly.

"Truthfully, it's been far too long since I sat outdoors," she said, and with a small bow presented the tin she carried.

"I brought cake," she said simply.

Asta received the tin with a laugh.

"How thoughtful! Come, let me make you known to Arbour poginGeist, our village administrator. Arbour, here is Zeni gormin-Astir, who chairs the Council of the Civilized. I believe you know Bentamin chastaMeir, my nephew, and Warden of Civilization."

Bows were exchanged. Arbour poginGeist professed herself pleased to meet Chair gorminAstir, and to renew her acquaintance with Warden chastaMeir.

"Let me just put the tin with the tea things," Asta said, turning toward the pavilion. "Shall I pour? I know you must be very busy, and as soon as Tekelia arrives—"

"But I'm here, Aunt Asta," a familiar voice said, sounding faintly amused. Bentamin turned his head to see Tekelia strolling toward them from the house, dressed in city business attire, hair neat in one long braid, tied off with a lavender ribbon.

Arriving at the pavilion, Tekelia bowed.

"Chair gorminAstir," said Aunt Asta, bestowing a fond smile upon Tekelia, "here is Tekelia vesterGranz, Speaker for the Haosa. Tekelia, my love, here is Zeni gorminAstir, who chairs the Council of the Civilized. Of course you know Bentamin."

Tekelia bowed.

"Chair gorminAstir, I'm honored."

Straightening, Tekelia flicked a glance and a grin to one side.

"Good day, Bentamin."

"Good day, Tekelia," Bentamin said, matching the tone of light amusement.

"I am pleased to make the acquaintance of the Speaker for the Haosa," gorminAstir said, moving slightly closer to Tekelia. "I wonder if you and I might make time to speak together on the topic of collaboration."

Tekelia's eyebrows rose.

"Collaboration, ma'am?"

"Indeed. The Civilized, the Deaf, and the Haosa share a planet. Why shouldn't we collaborate? While there is a Deaf Councilor seated at our table who speaks for and represents the concerns and goals of that community, there is no like member of the Haosa." She moved a hand suddenly.

"That's for later. My business now is with Oracle vesterGranz. But, let us not forget, Speaker vesterGranz. We should and ought to speak."

"I won't forget," Tekelia promised, with another sidewise glance at Bentamin, who was pleased to be able to show empty palms in answer.

"Excellent!" Aunt Asta said. "All of you, come to the table. I'll pour the tea."

Colemenoport
Offices of the
Tree-and-Dragon Trade Mission

. . . .

NEITHER MAJEL ZIAGORN NOR PORTMASTER KROGERSLYTE HAD returned her calls. Padi frowned and went to the *qe'andra's* office.

"Nothing," she said, sitting on the edge of the conference table. "Dare I hope that you have had a better result?"

Mar Tyn lifted his hands, palms up and empty.

"I called all of the possibles yesterday afternoon, begging that they contact *Qe'andra* dea'Tolin at their earliest convenience, and stating that the completion of the whole port inventory was essential in determining Colemeno's future as a Tree-and-Dragon hub."

"Did you actually speak to anyone?" Padi asked.

"I did speak to three, and left messages for the rest," Mar Tyn said. "My lack of notoriety served me. It was interesting that the three I spoke to pled an unexpected influx of work, which prevented them from participating in the inventory."

"Interesting in what way?" Padi wondered.

Mar Tyn moved his shoulders, and met her eyes.

"They all said *exactly* the same thing, using the same words, and the same inflection, as if it were a poem they had by heart."

"In the interests of completeness," Jes said, "I note that no one with whom Mar Tyn left a message has—thus far!—contacted me."

"And we don't expect them to," Padi said. "Do the Guild guidelines give us any leeway? Might we, for instance, employ more port-based accountants to perform the secondary tasks?"

Jes sighed.

"We might attempt it, citing a lack of competent professionals divorced from port business. Such things have been done, in the past, but it is a variation which must pass beneath additional scrutiny by the Guild. As this trade mission already encompasses several irregularities, none of them individually fatal to the master trader's hopes—"

"But if we keep adding to the pile, it will eventually fall over. I understand."

Padi frowned.

"I suppose there's nothing for it but to confront Zandir kezlBlythe."

"Is that the advice from our liaison?" asked Dyoli.

"Our liaison remains out of touch," Padi said. "Nor could I reach the portmaster. I suppose we might seek advice from the market manager, but he is a man who likes to share his news widely, and I believe we ought to favor discretion."

"I agree," Jes said.

"I do not like the idea of confronting this person," Dyoli said. "While I didn't See the violence she did to Padi's shields, violence was certainly done, and her subsequent actions strongly suggest that she intended to influence Padi to do her will. This is not how ethical persons conduct themselves."

She looked at Padi, eyebrows up.

"To state the obvious: A confrontation will only give her an opportunity to do more violence."

"But we are forewarned," Padi pointed out.

Dyoli flicked her fingers.

"If you know that there is a sniper on a roof somewhere along your route, does that knowledge give you protection?"

Padi blinked at her.

"No," she admitted, "it does not."

She sighed.

"My next call with the master trader is in six hours," Padi said. "I will put the problem before him. Jes, please give me a document, listing out what has happened with those who were initially interested in working with us, and also outlining any alternatives we may have, under the Guild's guidelines."

"Yes," Jes said.

Padi nodded.

"Now. Is there anything we can do while we are in this wait-state to— No!"

Rage swept through her, red edged in gold, and Tekelia— Tekelia—

Padi threw herself into the ambient.

Off-Grid
The Lilac Cottage

. . . .

"SINCE YOU HAVE ELECTED TO REMOVE YOURSELF FROM THE Wardian rather than continue under Civilization's care in your retirement, it has been suggested that you be awarded a lump-sum equal to the cost of that care. I worked with the budget office and have come up with a figure that seems equitable. There are, of course, unknowns. We averaged the retirement time of former oracles to arrive at twenty-four years. We also averaged upkeep."

gorminAstir paused, and reached into her pocket, for a piece of paper.

"The result of all this averaging is this figure."

She extended the paper.

Aunt Asta took it, blinked, and handed it to Arbour, who handed it to Tekelia.

"This seems very generous," Tekelia said, after a moment. "I wonder if I may share it with Aunt Asta's nephew on-Grid, who has a more intimate knowledge of costs and compensations."

"Certainly, she will wish to take advice," gorminAstir said, folding her hands on her knee.

"I should have said that this is an offer; it is open to discussion and negotiation. The Council wishes to reflect Civilization's care, and its gratitude for long years of service. I fully intended to leave this paper, and this key, as well—"

Another reach to the pocket, to extract a data-key, which she held out.

"Tekelia, dear, will you take care of that for me, as well?" Aunt Asta asked, and looked to gorminAstir. "I have lived retired and have very little sense of what money *means*, you know."

That was a hit, thought Bentamin, though gorminAstir took it with a sedate inclination of the head.

"I do know that, yes," she said, and reached for her teacup.

Everyone at the table took the opportunity to drink, and when the cups were replaced, gorminAstir spoke again.

"I wonder, Oracle vesterGranz, if you might illuminate for me your Seeing that Civilization and the Haosa will—end."

"Certainly," Aunt Asta said, leaning forward slightly. "You will wish to know that I have Seen this several times, and—"

Tekelia jolted upright with a cry. Bentamin leapt up as well, staring at a face gone suddenly feral, eyes flashing green and gold.

"The kezlBlythe, here!" Tekelia gasped, voice grinding. "The children!"

There was a *boom!* as air rushed to fill the void where Tekelia had been an instant before.

Bentamin whirled, finding gorminAstir already on her feet.

"We will both go," she said.

Bentamin snatched her arm; mist swirled, and they were gone.

Aunt Asta looked to Arbour, who was on her feet.

"We should go, too, I think," she said, extending a hand. "Help me up, dear."

Off-Grid
The Rose Cottage

. . . .

JOREY LEAPT FORWARD THE MOMENT THE GARDEN TOOK SHAPE around him, gun in hand, targets before him. He raised the weapon—and staggered as bright fire danced up and down his spine, sparking his Gift into pain.

His vision blurred—and cleared.

He heard one of the brats scream, "It's Cousin Jorey!" and raised the gun, sighting on two small fleeing figures. He squeezed the trigger—

Black lightning streaked between him and his targets. The gun spoke. The lightning screamed, fell away, and something hit him from the side, hands over his, trying to wrench the gun away.

Jorey *pushed*, and that distraction was gone. He found the brats under the tree, pressed against a table, their stupid furry pet standing on the girl's shoulder.

Easy targets.

Jorey raised the gun again, and fired three times.

There was a *zing* as something went past his ear, the brats improbably still standing at bay, and a sudden roar inside his head, teeth and claws rending.

Jorey screamed and raised the gun again.

A *boom!* rocked him back, and there was an obstacle between himself and the targets. An obstacle stitched with fire, eyes blazing green and gold.

Not an obstacle for long.

Jorey raised the gun.

The obstacle raised a hand and gripped Jorey's wrist.

· · · ✻ · · ·

439

"*Murderer!*" Geritsi screamed inside Tekelia's head, and there was a moment of disorientation in which Tekelia Saw the garden, the dark rumple of fur on the lawn, the twins at bay, and a man raising a gun. The scene snapped out in a flare of fury and pain.

Tekelia shouted a warning—"The kezlBlythe here! The children!"

...flung into the ambient...

...and arrived next to the downed *sokyum*, facing a man with wild eyes in a tight white face, rage and bloodlust spinning 'round him like a cyclone.

The man raised a gun.

Tekelia flung out a hand, grabbing his wrist, felt Chaos rising—and gripped harder.

The man—the murderer—spasmed, screaming, even as a *boom!* rocked the ambient, accompanied by a blinding flare of wild energies.

Tekelia felt strong fingers around one wrist, blinked away the afterimages of the flare, feeling Chaos stutter, ebb, and flow away.

It was Padi yos'Galan at the murderer's shoulder, holding Tekelia's wrist in a grip that would surely leave bruises, lavender eyes ablaze, and her voice frantic inside Tekelia's head.

No! Tekelia, do not!

I won't, Tekelia sent and shuddered to think what might have happened; what *would* have happened, had she—bright dancer that she was!—not intervened.

The man they held between them moaned. He no longer held the gun, and, indeed, his hand looked—odd.

"Let me go," he whispered, and Tekelia did.

Which was when Geritsi slentAlin hit him in the back of the head with a shovel.

Colemenoport
Offices of the
Tree-and-Dragon Trade Mission

. . . .

BOOM!

Ribbons of brilliant light filled the room, swirled, and faded.

Padi yos'Galan was gone.

Jes looked to Dyoli and Mar Tyn.

"Do either of you know where she has gone, and if she requires our aid?"

"I believe she may have been called to assist Tekelia vester-Granz," Dyoli said. "They share a . . . significant bond, as I have Seen. Whether our assistance is required, I cannot say. However—"

She pulled a portable comm out of her pocket.

Jes raised a hand.

"The trader's business is, of course, the trader's business. In the meanwhile, we have our own in hand.

"Dyoli, would you please check in with our contractors at the workroom? Mar Tyn, I will require your assistance in researching the Guild guidelines."

Dyoli had been gone for some time, and Mar Tyn was three screens into port audit exception clauses, when the door chime sounded and the light flashed twice.

Jes did not look up from her screen, where he expected she was pursuing an even more complex search through trade law. Mar Tyn therefore marked his place, rose, and crossed the room to answer the door.

The woman thus revealed was sharp-faced and arrogant, her hands glittering with gemstones.

Mar Tyn's feet moved, shifting him to the side of the door, just as the woman stepped forward.

"I," she said, her voice as hard as the shine of her rings, "am Zandir kezlBlythe. I will speak with *Qe'andra* dea'Tolin."

She crossed the threshold, and spared him one hard glance as she passed.

"Go away," she said.

He felt a jolt, as if a hard hand had struck him in the shoulder, but his feet were already moving, putting him on the far side of the door.

His feet kept moving. He made no effort to change their direction, but he did look over his shoulder.

The door to the *qe'andra's* office was closed, and the red light that meant "do not disturb" was lit.

Off-Grid
The Rose Cottage

. . . .

PADI STOOD AS IF FROZEN, LOOKING INTO TEKELIA'S EYES—BROWN, both of them brown.

"Padi?" Tekelia whispered.

With a gasp, she released the wrist she still held, and threw her arms around Tekelia's shoulders, pressing her face into the crook of their neck.

"I should not have—it is wrong to—" she whispered. "But I *could not* see you kill someone with your Gift. There is so much joy in you, my friend—and I would not see it blighted by—" She shivered and her arms grew tighter.

"I understand," Tekelia said, smoothing a hand down her back. "You did well, and I thank you with my whole heart."

She took a hard breath, and suddenly stepped aside, keeping a grip on Tekelia's hand as they looked about them.

Geritsi and Arbour, who had been introduced to Padi as the village administrator, were kneeling one on each side of Dosent.

"It will be well," Padi heard Arbour say. "So much fur served her well. I'll keep her stable. You fetch Maradel."

Geritsi flung to her feet and was gone, passing two persons in Civilized dress—one, Padi recognized as Tekelia's cousin Bentamin, the Warden of Civilization. The other—

"Chair gorminAstir," said Bentamin. "Do you witness?"

"I do witness, Warden," she said. "Will you bind that person?"

"I will."

"He may be—wounded," Tekelia said, going to one knee beside the downed man. "I needed him to drop the gun."

"Of course you did," Bentamin said calmly, kneeling in his turn. He raised the man's outflung hand. It was withered, the fingers wasted and bent. "Very effective."

443

He leaned back on his heels.

"This is Jorey kezlBlythe," he said. "He is Civilized. Councilor gorminAstir has witnessed his actions here, as I have. Justice will go forward." He paused as if he were concentrating, and Padi Saw an iron-grey field outline the man on the ground. "He is restrained. I will take him back to Civilization, as soon as the children—"

He stopped, and Tekelia leapt up.

"The children?" Padi repeated. "He came here to harm Torin and Vaiza?"

"He did, yes—there they are!"

Tekelia strode down the garden, Padi keeping pace, to the table under the tree, where Aunt Asta sat, the children cuddled against her comfortable sides, and Eet the norbear sitting on her knee.

"Torin, Vaiza—are you hurt?" Tekelia demanded.

"They're frightened—and angry, which is very appropriate," said Aunt Asta. "But they told me that they were not hurt."

"We made a shield," Torin said. "Eet helped."

"The pellets hit it and bounced back at Cousin Jorey!" Vaiza said excitedly.

"Is—" Torin said seriously. "Is Cousin Jorey—dead?"

"No," said Tekelia. "Warden Bentamin will take him back to Civilization. He witnessed what had happened, and so did the chair of the Council of the Civilized. Warden Bentamin says that justice will be served."

Vaiza and Torin exchanged a look not entirely free of worry.

"Cousin Jorey hurt Dosent," Torin said, "but Aunt Asta says she'll get better."

"And so she shall," Aunt Asta said, giving them each a squeeze. "Here comes Maradel, just as I told you she would."

"Yes!" said Vaiza and squirmed somewhat. "There's Geritsi, too. Cousin Jorey pushed her. We should see if she's all right."

"Off you go then," Aunt Asta said, releasing them.

Torin paused to take Eet into her arms, then the two of them ran for Geritsi, who dropped to her knees, and hugged them to her.

"Very good," Aunt Asta said comfortably. "And how lovely that there were Civilized witnesses." She turned her head. "Padi, my dear, you must allow me to thank you for your timely assistance. I was concerned that Tekelia might not be able to manage alone."

Padi felt the smile waver on her mouth.

"You're very kind, ma'am, and of course I had to come, just as soon as I knew—"

Ribbons fluttered in her vision, and she gripped Tekelia's hand, an orientation point in a world suddenly atilt.

"Padi?" Tekelia's arm came around her waist.

"I think," she said, taking very good care to speak clearly, "that I would like to have some cake."

Colemenoport
Offices of the
Tree-and-Dragon Trade Mission

. . . .

DYOLI LOOKED UP WHEN MAR TYN ENTERED THE WORKROOM, murmured something to the man she had been sitting next to, rose, and came forward to take his arm, and pull him to the side.

"What is it, my Mar Tyn?"

"Zandir kezlBlythe has come to speak with *Qe'andra* dea'Tolin," he said. "She tried, I think, to Influence me, but my Luck was before her. She also told me to go away."

"But you were already moving," Dyoli said, and took a hard breath, eyes widening. "We cannot leave Jes with that person."

She spun toward the door. Mar Tyn caught her arm.

"We need backup," he said.

Dyoli took a deep breath, deliberately quelling her panic.

"Very wise. Do you call the portmaster. If she is not available, then the market manager—"

She turned to the accountant she had been working with.

"Of your kindness, call Port Security. There is an emergency at the Tree-and-Dragon offices."

"Yes." He pulled a comm from his pocket.

Dyoli looked out over the room.

"We have learned that there is a person who has been targeting those who work, or who would work, for the Tree-and-Dragon mission, either threatening or otherwise convincing them that they ought not do so," she said. "We do not know if this person has accomplices. We do know that she previously tried to harm Trader yos'Galan. You are under no obligation to face personal danger. You may leave, without penalty. We will—"

Someone stood up from the back.

"Persuader can't do much with a crowd," she said. "It's a one-on-one talent. If all of us stay together, there's more danger for the Persuader than for us." She looked around the room.

"Who's for leaving?"

No one spoke.

Dyoli bowed slightly.

"Thank you."

"The portmaster is on her way to the *qe'andra's* office," Mar Tyn said.

Colemenoport
Offices of the
Tree-and-Dragon Trade Mission

. . . .

"THE MASTER TRADER'S ORDERS WERE PLAIN," JES SAID CALMLY to this hawk-faced woman with her bright, cold eyes. "More, we are constrained by the guidelines provided by the Guild. Even should we wish to do so, we cannot engage with your syndicate, Luzant."

"The master trader," said Luzant kezlBlythe, "is not in charge of the whole port inventory, *you* are. *You* are in a position to make whatever arrangements will produce data proving that Colemeno is worthy of becoming a Tree-and-Dragon hub. *You* will also be in a position to recommend to the master trader that he enter into a partnership agreement with the kezlBlythe Syndicate. Everyone will profit, and *you* will be rewarded with a fitting position in the new partnership."

Of course, that was delusion. Jes *knew* it was delusion, and at the same time, it sounded so *reasonable*. It was confusing.

Jes dea'Tolin was not accustomed to feeling confused.

She looked away from her visitor, to her screen where the guidelines for a whole port inventory were set forth. Her confusion faded as her eye followed the comforting, ordered list. Master Trader yos'Galan, partner with this woman who counted wealth in terms of personal influence? It was beyond delusional; in fact, it was absurd.

"Look at me!" snapped Zandir kezlBlythe, and Jes raised her eyes from the screen.

Off-Grid
The Rose Cottage

. . . .

DOSENT HAD BEEN MOVED INTO THE COTTAGE, TO HER SPECIAL pillow by the hearth. Tekelia had made part of that effort, and remained inside, lending support to Maradel's argument that Geritsi accept a Healing sleep. As Padi understood it, Jorey's *push* had not been gentle, and only her fury—and the ambient—had kept her upright so far.

In the meanwhile, the Warden had taken his trussed prisoner away to a more secure situation.

"I will come back for you as soon as I may," he had said to the woman who had been belatedly introduced to Padi as Zeni gorminAstir, the chair of the Council of the Civilized.

"Do not endanger yourself, Warden. I am in no hurry to return to my office, now that I have been sitting outside in the free air. Additionally, I wish to speak more fully with Oracle vesterGranz."

So it was that Padi joined Aunt Asta and the council chair at the table under the tree. Padi had disposed of several pieces of cake, and a cup of yeast drink provided by Maradel, and was feeling rather more the thing.

And before her sat—an opportunity.

"I wonder if you might advise me, ma'am," she said, interjecting herself into a pause in the conversation between the two elder ladies.

Zeni gorminAstir turned to her and inclined her head.

"I will do my best, Trader. How may I assist you?"

"You will, I think, have been informed that Master Trader yos'Galan has called for a whole port inventory. This step reflects his strong belief that Colemeno may be fit to serve, if not as a trade hub, then at least an important terminal for multiple Loops."

"I have heard this news, yes. Portmaster krogerSlyte keeps me informed, as of course does Councilor ziaGorn."

"We have good friends in the portmaster and Councilor ziaGorn," Padi said. "Indeed, I thought to seek their advice with the trade mission's difficulty, but neither was available to me."

Zeni gorminAstir smiled.

"And the ambient has provided you with another friend."

"I'm glad to hear that you are our friend, ma'am. The person just apprehended—his name was *kezlBlythe*?"

"That is correct, Trader."

"As it happens the trade mission's difficulty seems to arise from another person named kezlBlythe—one Zandir, who we are told is the principal of a business syndicate operating in the city."

"So it is, but—*seems*, Trader? Are you not certain?"

"For my part, *I* am certain, ma'am, but I have been strongly cautioned by Trader ven'Deelin of our team that, while someone may have attempted to put me under their influence, it does not follow that they are actively working to prevent the trade mission from accomplishing its inventory."

"Enlighten me, Trader. *Were* you attacked by Zandir kezlBlythe?"

"Ma'am, I was," Padi said, and felt Tekelia's presence in her head sharpen. "She dented my shields, and I foolishly repaired the damage, so that our team Healer was not able to assess the severity. That, however, is not the most concerning matter."

"That being this possible interference in the trade team's work," said Zeni gorminAstir. "What do you suspect the kezlBlythe Syndicate of doing?"

"Briefly, ma'am, I—and our *qe'andra*, also—suspect that the kezlBlythe Syndicate has intimidated the city professionals with whom our *qe'andra* made appointments into failing to keep those appointments, and refusing further contact."

Padi paused. Aunt Asta hefted the pot, poured tea into a cup, and handed it to her. Padi sat back and took a sip, feeling a warm hand land on her shoulder.

"The kezlBlythe again?" Tekelia said. "They are remarkably busy."

"Well," Padi said, craning her head backward to see Tekelia's face. Mismatched eyes looked down into hers. "At our first interview, it did seem that Zandir kezlBlythe was determined to increase her holdings by being the trade mission's...*friend*, as she had it, in the city."

"The kezlBlythe Syndicate has recently come to the attention of the Council of the Civilized," Zeni gorminAstir said. "If I understand you, Trader, you suspect the syndicate of restraining the trade mission's work."

"Yes, ma'am," said Padi, "but I am obliged to say that it is more than the trade mission that stands in peril from these tactics. There are protocols outlined by our Guild, which the master trader is bound to follow. If he cannot proceed in a correct manner, he will have no choice but to withdraw from Colemeno."

"Which means that we will not become a Tree-and-Dragon hub," Zeni gorminAstir said.

"Yes, ma'am. Understand, that might be the outcome in any case, depending on the results of the whole port inventory. And, indeed, now that the Dust has danced away, other traders will find you—"

Her pocket vibrated, and she snatched her comm out. A quick glance showed a familiar code. She looked up.

"Your pardon, ma'am—Aunt Asta. I left my office...rather suddenly—they must wonder where I am."

"Take your call, Trader," Zeni gorminAstir said, turning toward Aunt Asta.

Padi raised the comm.

"yos'Galan. Service?"

"Padi, it is Dyoli. Zandir kezlBlythe is alone with Jes in the *qe'andra's* office, and the door is locked against us. The portmaster and Port Security are on their way, also building Security, with the override code."

"Jes is alone with Zandir kezlBlythe," Padi repeated aloud. "How long?"

"Half an hour."

"I'm on my way," Padi said.

She closed the comm, to find three faces turned to her expectantly.

"Is there a problem, Trader?" asked Zeni gorminAstir.

"Zandir kezlBlythe has been alone with Jes—with our *qe'andra*— for half an hour. Jes is Deaf. I don't know—"

gorminAstir rose with alacrity.

"Oracle vesterGranz, I look forward to our next meeting. Trader, I will come with you."

Padi raised her hands.

"I'm not certain I can carry you, ma'am."

"We can both carry her," Tekelia said. "You hold the councilor's hand, and I will hold yours. You will lead—by which I mean, you will show the ambient where you wish to arrive, and make the leap. I will contrive to keep us all together."

"Done," said Padi, and showed the *qe'andra's* office to the ambient.

Colemenoport
Offices of the
Tree-and-Dragon Trade Mission

. . . .

MIST SWIRLED BRIEFLY BY THE DOOR, MELTING AROUND THE
figures of three persons.

This sudden advent did nothing to disturb the pair at the
desk, one intent on the other, and that one intent on her screen.

"Under terms of partnership," the one in the chair said,
"Tree-and-Dragon will be junior to the kezlBlythe Syndicate, and
will pass all its business and financials through the syndicate."

"The master trader will not sign that," said the one at the
screen, even as her fingers moved over the keyboard.

"The master trader doesn't have to sign it," said the woman
in the chair. "It will be enough that the trader signs it, and you
may be certain that she will."

Padi twitched forward, was restrained by Zeni gorminAstir's
hand on her shoulder.

"Have you finished that yet?" demanded Zandir kezlBlythe.

"It must be in the proper form, or it will be rejected by the
Guild," Jes said, her eyes on the screen.

Her fingers moved for another minute, and stopped.

"Percentages," kezlBlythe said. "kezlBlythe will award Tree-
and-Dragon thirty-five percent of gross. Tree-and-Dragon will
be invoiced for the services of the kezlBlythe Syndicate at a
discounted rate."

"The master trader will not sign that," Jes said, her fingers
beginning to move again on the keyboard.

"And nor will I!" Padi snapped, unable to tolerate anything
further.

Zandir kezlBlythe leapt to her feet and spun to face her.

453

"You will acknowledge me your master!" she stated.

Padi felt the ambient shudder, and Saw a dark wave rising up in that space just behind her eyes where she heard Tekelia and Lady Selph.

She slammed her shields shut, but the wave continued, hot, sticky—

And gone, melting away in a swirl of dancing ribbons.

"I don't think so," Tekelia said, and Padi saw the self-same iron-grey field form around Zandir kezlBlythe as the Warden had placed around Jorey kezlBlythe.

"Well done," said Zeni gorminAstir.

Zandir kezlBlythe made a sound of fury, but Padi darted past her to Jes, who was still typing.

"Jes," she said, grasping the other woman's wrists. "You can stop."

"No," Jes said, her fingers continuing to move, despite Padi's grip. "I cannot. Not until I've put what she's told me into proper form." She took a shuddering breath, and Padi saw the tears running her cheeks. "The recorder is on."

"Good," Padi said, releasing her. "You've done well."

She turned to look at Zeni gorminAstir, still at the back of the room.

"If you please, open the door. I believe that there are security officers on the other side, and also Dyoli. I very much want Dyoli. And the security officers have my leave to take that person away!"

Colemenoport
Wayfarer

. . . .

"AND HOW FARES QE'ANDRA DEA'TOLIN?" ASKED THE MASTER
trader.

"Better, though still unsettled, as anyone would be. She hopes
to be at her desk tomorrow. Dyoli was able to remove the compulsion, and release the horror. Lady Selph has been temporarily moved to Jes's room. Also, Dyoli has put Jes into a Healing
sleep, and says that when she wakens, it will be as if the entire
incident had happened some while ago. That, she said, will serve
Jes far better than simply forgetting it entirely."

"Very true. I would have applied a similar therapy, had I
been there to assist. I will call her tomorrow, to assure myself
of her good recovery."

Padi had a sip of wine, and closed her eyes briefly.

"And yourself, Daughter?"

"I am—tired, and extremely pleased that this day's work fell
to our favor. If you will have it, my admiration for Jes has only
increased. How clever of her to have turned on the recorder!"

"Very clever, indeed, though I would have rather she not had
that particular opportunity to exercise her ingenuity."

"Yes, sir."

"You have had an exciting day," Father said. "I will not keep
you much longer. I did wish to tell you that Priscilla and I have
spoken at length. She will remain aboard the *Passage*, and I with
her until such time as I may be of use on-planet. I depend upon
you to tell me when that time arrives."

"Yes, sir. I think you may rest easy for the next while. I
provided a list of those whom we contacted and who seemed to
have been . . . tampered with, to the security officers. They will be

gathering evidence. Also, Healers will be on hand to remove any compulsions, or inappropriate fears, that have been laid. Once that is complete, I think that we will be able to move forward with the inventory at good speed."

"You will keep me informed."

"Yes, sir."

"I wonder if I may be impertinent, Daughter, and ask what you have learned from these adventures."

Padi smiled.

"I have learned that you were correct—I do not fly alone."

"A valuable lesson, I agree. Have you other questions for the master trader or myself?"

"Not at the moment, I think. Please give my love to Priscilla."

"Certainly I will do so."

"Thank you. *Chiat'a bei kruzon*, Father."

"Dream sweetly, my child."

They ended the call there, and Padi sat back in her chair, her attention turned inward, to the bold red ribbon that was so much a part of her now.

The Ribbons have risen and the trees are afire, Tekelia's voice murmured. *Will you come and dance with me?*

Padi smiled, and rose.

Yes, she answered. *I will.*

Mist swirled and the room was empty.